Cut

Marc Raabe

MANILLA

First published in Germany in 2012 by Ullstein Buchverlage GmbH, Berlin

This paperback edition published in Great Britain in 2016 by Manilla
Publishing, 80–81 Wimpole St, London, W1G 9RE
www.manillabooks.com

A CIP catalogue record for this book is available from the British Library.

Paperback ISBN: 978-1-7865-8007-8
Trade paperback ISBN: 978-1-7865-8018-4
Ebook ISBN: 978-1-7865-8006-1

3 5 7 9 10 8 6 4 2

Printed and bound by Clays Ltd, St Ives Plc

Manilla Publishing is an imprint of Bonnier Zaffre,
a Bonnier Publishing company
www.bonnierpublishing.co.uk

APR 1 3 2017

*'We are each our own devil, and we make
this world our hell.'*

OSCAR WILDE

Prologue

West Berlin – 13 October, 11.09 p.m.

Gabriel stood in the doorway and stared. The light from the hall fell down the cellar stairs and was swallowed by the brick walls.

He hated the cellar, particularly at night. Not that it would've made any difference whether it was light or dark outside. It was always night in the cellar. Then again, during the day, you could always run out into the garden, out into the light. At night, on the other hand, it was dark *everywhere*, even outside, and ghosts lurked in every corner. Ghosts that no grown-up could see. Ghosts that were just waiting to sink their claws into the neck of an eleven-year-old boy.

Still, he just couldn't help but stare, entranced, down into the far end of the cellar where the light faded away.

The door!

It was open!

There was a gaping black opening between the dark green wall and the door. And behind it was the lab, dark like Darth Vader's Death Star.

His heart beat in his throat. Gabriel wiped his clammy, trembling hands on his pyjamas – his favourite pyjamas with Luke Skywalker on the front.

The long, dark crack of the door drew him in as if by magic. He slowly placed his bare foot on the first step. The wood of the cellar stairs felt rough and creaked as if it were trying to give him away. But he knew that they wouldn't hear him. Not as long as they were fighting behind the closed kitchen door. It was a bad one. Worse than normal. And it frightened him. Good that David wasn't there, he thought. Good that he'd taken him out of harm's way. His little brother would've cried.

Then again, it would've been nice not to be alone right now in this cellar with the ghosts. Gabriel swallowed. The opening stared back at him like the gates of hell.

Go look! That's what Luke would do.

Dad would be furious if he could see him now. The lab was Dad's secret and it was secured like a fortress with a metal door and a shiny black peephole. No one else had ever seen the lab. Not even Mum.

Gabriel's feet touched the bare concrete floor of the cellar and he shuddered. First the warm wooden steps and now the cold stone.

Now or never!

Suddenly, a rumbling came through the cellar ceiling. Gabriel flinched. The noise came from the kitchen above him. It sounded like the table had been scraped across the tiles. For a moment, he considered whether he should go upstairs. Mum was up there all alone with *him* and Gabriel knew how angry he could get.

His eyes darted back to the door, glimmering in the dark. Such an opportunity might never come again.

He had stood there once before, about two years ago. That time, Dad had forgotten to lock the upper cellar door. Gabriel was nine. He had stood in the hall for a while and peered down.

In the end, curiosity triumphed. That time, he had also crept down into the cellar, entirely afraid of the ghosts, but still in complete darkness because he didn't dare turn on the light.

The peephole had glowed red like the eye of a monster.

In a mad rush, he had fled back up the stairs, back to David in their room, and crawled into his bed.

Now he was eleven. Now he stood there downstairs again and the monster eye wasn't glowing. Still, the peephole stared at him, cold and black like a dead eye. The only things reflecting in it were the dim light on the cellar stairs and him. The closer he got, the larger his face grew.

And why did it smell so disgusting?

He groped out in front of him with his bare feet and stepped in something wet and mushy. *Puke. It was puke!* That's why it smelled so disgusting. But why was there puke *here* in the first place?

He choked down his disgust and rubbed his foot clean on a dry area of the concrete floor. Some was still stuck between his toes. He would've liked a towel or a wet cloth right about now, but the lab was more important. He reached out his hand, placed it on the knob, pulled the heavy metal door open a bit more, and pressed on into the darkness. An unnatural silence enveloped him.

A deathly silence.

A sharp chemical smell crept into his nose like at the film lab where his father had once taken him after one of his days of shooting.

His heart was pounding. Much too fast, much too loud. He wished he were somewhere else, maybe with David, under the covers.

Luke Skywalker would never hide under the covers.

The trembling fingers on his left hand searched for the light switch, always expecting to find something else entirely. What if the ghosts were here? If they grabbed his arm? If he accidently reached into one's mouth and it snapped its teeth shut?

There! Cool plastic.

He flipped the switch. Three red lights lit up and bathed the room in front of him in a strange red glow. Red, like in the belly of a monster.

A chill ran up his spine all the way to the roots of his hair. He stopped at the threshold to the lab; somehow, there was a sort of invisible border that he didn't want to cross. He squinted and tried to make out the details.

The lab was larger than he had thought, a narrow space about three metres wide and seven metres deep. A heavy black curtain hung directly beside him. Someone had hastily pushed it aside.

Clothes lines were strung under the concrete ceiling with photos hanging from them. Some had been torn down and lay on the floor.

On the left stood a photo enlarger. On the right, a shelf spanned the entire wall, crammed with pieces of equipment. Gabriel's eyes widened. He recognised most of them immediately: Arri, Beaulieu, Leicina, with other, smaller cameras in between. The trade magazines that were piled up in Dad's study on the first floor were full of them. Whenever one of those magazines wound up in the bin, Gabriel fished it out, stuck it under his pillow, and read it under the covers by torchlight until his eyelids were too heavy to keep open.

Beside the cameras lay a dozen lenses, some as long as gun barrels; next to them, small cameras, cases to absorb camera operating sounds, 8- and 16-mm film cartridges, a stack of three VCRs with four monitors, and finally, two brand-new camcorders. Dad always scoffed at the things. In one of the magazines, he had read that you could film for almost two hours with the new video technology without having to change the cassette – absolutely unbelievable! On top of that, the plastic bombers didn't rattle like film cameras, but ran silently.

Gabriel's shining eyes wandered over the treasures. He wished he could show all of this to David. He immediately felt guilty. After all, this was dangerous, so it was best that he didn't get David involved. Besides, his brother had already fallen asleep. He was right to have locked the door to their room.

Suddenly, there was a loud crash. He spun around. There was no one there. No parents, no ghost. His parents were probably still quarrelling up in the kitchen.

He looked back into the lab at all of the treasures. *Come closer*, they seemed to whisper. But he was still standing on the threshold next to the curtain. Fear rose in him. He could still turn back. He had now seen the lab; he didn't have to go all the way in.

Eleven! You're eleven! Come on, don't be a chicken!

How old was Luke?

Gabriel reluctantly took two steps into the room.

What were those photos? He bent down, picked one up from the floor, and stared at the faded grainy image. A sudden feeling of disgust and a strange excitement spread through his stomach. He looked up at the photos on the clothes line. The photo directly above him attracted his eyes like a magnet. His face was hot and red, like everything else around him. He also felt a bit sick. It looked so real, so . . . or were they actors? It looked like in the movie! The columns, the walls, like in the Middle Ages, and the black clothes . . .

He tore himself away and his eyes jumped over the jumbled storage and the shelf, and finally rested on the modern VCRs with their glittering little JVC logos. The lowest one was switched on. Numbers and characters were illuminated in its shining display. Like in *Star Wars* in the cockpit of a spaceship, he thought.

As if of its own accord, Gabriel's index finger approached the buttons and pushed one. A loud click inside the device made him jump. Twice, three times, then the hum of a motor. *A cassette!* There was a cassette in the VCR! His cheeks burned. He feverishly pushed another button. The JVC responded with a rattle. Interference lines flashed across the monitor beside the VCRs. The image wobbled for a moment, and then it was there. Diffuse with flickering colour, unreal, like a window to another world.

Gabriel had been leaning forward without knowing it – and now he jerked back. His mouth went totally dry. It was the same image as in the photo! The same place, the same columns, the same people, only now they were moving. He wanted to look away, but it was impossible. He sucked the stifling air in through his gaping mouth, and then held his breath without realising it.

The images pummelled him like the popping of flashbulbs; he couldn't help but watch, mesmerised.

The cut through the black fabric of the dress.

The pale triangle on the still paler skin.

The long, tangled blond hair.

The chaos.

And then another cut – a sharp, angry motion that spread into Gabriel's guts. He suddenly felt sick and everything was spinning. The television stared at him viciously. Trembling, he found the button and switched it off.

The image collapsed with a dull thud, as if there were a black hole inside the monitor, just like in outer space. The noise was awful, but reassuring at the same time. He stared at the dark screen and the reflection of his own bright red face. A ghost stared back, eyes wide with fear.

Don't think about it! Just don't think about it . . . He stared at the photos, at the whole mess, anything but the monitor.

What you can't see isn't there!

But it was there. Somewhere in the monitor, deep inside the black hole. The VCR made a soft grinding noise. He wanted to squeeze his eyes shut and wake up somewhere else. Anywhere. Anywhere but here. He was still crouched in front of his ghostly reflection in the monitors.

Suddenly, Gabriel was overcome by the desperate desire to see something pleasant, or even just something different. As if it had a will of its own, his finger drifted towards the other monitors.

Thud. Thud. The two upper monitors flashed on. Two washed-out images crystallised, casting their steel-blue glimmer into the red light of the lab. One image showed the hall and the open cellar door; the stairs were swallowed up by darkness. The second image showed the kitchen. The kitchen – and his parents. His father's voice rasped from the speaker.

Gabriel's eyes widened.

No! Please, no!

His father shoved the kitchen table. The table legs scraped loudly across the floor. The noise carried through the ceiling, and Gabriel winced. His father threw open a drawer, reached inside and his hand re-emerged.

Gabriel stared at the monitor in horror. Blinking, he wished he were blind. Blind and deaf.

But he wasn't.

His eyes flooded with tears. The chemical smell of the lab combined with the vomit outside the door made him gag. He wished someone would come and hug him and talk it all away.

But no one would come. He was alone.

The realisation hit him with a crushing blow. *Someone had to do something.* And now *he* was the only one who could do anything.

What would Luke do?

Quietly, he crept up the cellar stairs, his bare feet no longer able to feel the cold floor. The red room behind him glowed like hell.

If only he had a lightsabre! And then, very suddenly, he thought of something much, much better than a sabre.

Chapter 1

The photo hovers like a threat in the windowless cellar. Outside, the rain is raging. The old roof of the mansion groans beneath the mass of water, and there is a dim red light rotating above the front door on the half-timbered facade, lighting up the house at brief intervals.

The torch beam darts about the dark cellar hall, revealing the slashed black fabric of a sparkling dress, which dangles from a hanger. The photo pinned onto the dress looks like a piece of wallpaper from a distance; a pale, rough scrap that has absorbed the ink from the printer, leaving the colours dull, fading away.

The dress and the photo are still swaying back and forth, as if only just hung up, and the swinging makes them seem like a decorative mobile; moving but lifeless.

The photo shows a young, very thin, heartbreakingly beautiful woman. She is slender, almost boyish, her breasts are small and flat, her face frozen, expressionless.

Her very long and very blond hair is like a crumpled yellow sheet beneath her head. She is wearing the dress to which this photo is now pinned. It seems tailor-made for her; it resembles her: flowing, extravagant, useless and costly. And the front is slashed open all the way down, as if it had an open zipper.

Beneath the dress, her skin is also slashed open – with one sharp incision starting between her legs, over her pubis and up to her chest. The abdominal wall is agape, the fleshy red of the innards veiled in merciful darkness. The black dress engulfs the body like death itself. A perfect symbol, just like the place where the dress is now hanging, waiting for him to find it: Kadettenweg 107.

The torchlight is again pointed at the bulky grey box on the wall and the tarnished lock. The key fit, but was difficult to turn, as if it couldn't remember what it was supposed to do at first. Inside, there is a row of little red light bulbs. Three are broken, and they glow at irregular intervals. The tungsten filaments have corroded over the years. But that doesn't matter. The necessary bulb is glowing.

The torchlight hastily gropes its way back to the cellar stairs and up the steps. There are footprints in the beam of light, and that's a good thing. When he returns, they will guide him down the cellar stairs to the black dress. And to the photo.

All at once, he will remember. The hairs on the back of his neck will rise, and he will say to himself: this is impossible.

And yet: it is true. He will know it. Because of the cellar alone – even if it wasn't *this* cellar or *this* woman. And of course, it will be a different woman. *His* woman.

And on her birthday, too. A lovely detail!

But the best part is the way it all comes full circle. Everything started in a cellar, and it would end in a cellar.

Cellars are the vestibules of hell. And who should know that better than someone who has been burning in hell for an eternity.

Chapter 2

Berlin – 1 September, 11.11 p.m.

The alarm has already been going off for nine minutes. Anyone else would have reached for his weapon on the way to the car – at least for a moment, to feel if it was where it was supposed to be, just in case: in its holster, right on his hip.

Gabriel doesn't reach for it; he doesn't carry a weapon. For as long as he can remember, guns have made him profoundly uneasy. Quite apart from the fact that the German authorities would probably never issue him a gun licence.

By the time he reaches the car, rain is already trickling down his collar. Gabriel presses the button for the power locks, and the lights flare orange in the darkness. He throws himself into the driver's seat and slams the door. Water splashes in his face from the rubber seal on the door. It's pouring as if the heavens were putting out a wildfire. Gabriel stares into the rear-view mirror, where his eyes hover in front of the windscreen.

He knows he should start the engine right away, but something stops him; a warning tingle flows beneath his skin like an electric current. Something is wrong here. And today of all days. Now of all times.

Fuck it, Luke. What are you waiting for? It's not because of her, is it? an urgent voice whispers in his head.

I promised her I'd be back just after twelve, Gabriel thinks.

You didn't promise her. That's just how she took it. It's not your problem if she's going to get so stroppy about it.

Shit, he mumbles.

Shit? Why? Don't you see what she's doing to you? The moment you let someone in, you turn into a weakling. As if you don't know how dangerous that is! Better to worry about the alarm.

Gabriel grits his teeth. Damn alarm. He's been working at Python for twenty years and spent most of his time with alarm systems or personal security. Up until a few months ago, he even lived on the fenced-in grounds of the security company in two sparsely furnished rooms right by the gate to the street. His boss Yuri had taken him under his wing and given him some stability. Martial arts training in the mornings, night school from 6 p.m. and Python every other free minute of the day. The problem was the weekends. When there wasn't much to do, his memories would tear him apart. That is, until he discovered the wrecked car in Yuri's garage – an old Mercedes SL. Yuri gave him the run-down cabriolet, and Gabriel, who had never so much as changed his own oil, dove into the repairs as if he were restoring his soul.

When the Mercedes was finished, Yuri gave him a Jaguar E-Type and then followed it with other classics from the seventies, so the garage was never empty.

All Yuri asked in return was that Gabriel do his job. And Gabriel really didn't need asking, since work was the closest thing he had to a home.

Motionless, Gabriel stares into the rear-view mirror. The rain beats down on the bonnet of the car in the light of the yard. His eyes shine colourlessly in the darkness, and the three short, vertical wrinkles between his brows form deep trenches.

Gabriel turns the key in the ignition. The drumming of the rain on the car roof drowns out the sound of the motor starting. He turns on the windscreen wipers and steps on the accelerator, and the dark grey VW Golf with its yellow Python Security logo tears across the yard, past the other cars in the car park, through the open gate and out on to the street, where it blends into the darkness of the rainy night.

Kadettenweg 107.

Up until a few minutes ago, they hadn't even known that this address was in Python's database. The alert had practically come out of nowhere. With his perpetually red eyes, Bert Cogan stared at the monitor in the office as if a haunted house had just materialised on the spot. Cogan had been working for Python for over nine years and the monitors were his own personal parallel universe; in the affluent residential district of Lichterfelde, he knew every pixel and every house that Python protected. 'Hey, have a look at this,' he muttered in consternation.

'What is it?' asked Gabriel.

'This here, what else!' Cogan snapped. His pale, chapped index finger pointed at a red, blinking dot on the screen. 'Can you explain what this house is doing there?'

Gabriel shrugged. 'Not a clue. If you don't know, I sure don't.'

'I just thought. . .' said Cogan, fiddling with the stubble that covered his receding chin.

'What did you think?'

'Well,' he mumbled, 'you have been working here forever . . .'

'I may have been working for Yuri forever.' Gabriel pointed at the monitors. 'But that there is something else entirely. Did you look in the directory?'

Cogan grunted. 'I don't need to. I know the Lichterfelde directory. There's nothing there. Absolutely nothing.'

Gabriel furrowed his brow and stared at the silently pulsing red dot with the number 107 next to the thin white line labelled Kadettenweg. A shiver crept down his spine.

What's wrong, Luke? the voice in his head whispered. *It's just a red dot, like all the others. You've seen that a thousand times. Don't make such a big deal out of it!*

'All, right. All right,' he mumbled quietly, without realising it.

'What did you say?' Cogan asked.

'Huh? Oh, nothing,' Gabriel replied quickly. He then silently fished his mobile phone from the inside pocket of his black leather jacket and dialled Yuri Sarkov.

It rang for a while before Yuri picked up. 'Hello, Gabriel,' he rasped. His voice sounded wide-awake, even though it was already well past 1 a.m. in Moscow. 'What's up?'

'Hello,' Gabriel mumbled, wondering whether Yuri ever slept or turned off his phone. 'We've got something strange here. A silent alarm in Lichterfelde West. It's in the middle of the residential area, but the house doesn't belong to one of our customers.'

'Hm. What's the address?'

'Kadettenweg 107,' said Gabriel, holding the mobile so that Cogan could listen in.

Silence. Nothing but quiet static on the line. 'Yuri? Still there?'

'107? Kadettenweg? Are you sure?' Yuri asked.

'That's what it says on the monitor,' Gabriel growled. 'Does that mean anything to you?'

'*Blyad*,' Yuri murmured so softly that Gabriel could hardly understand him. Yuri was half-Russian, and whenever there was something to curse about he automatically switched to Russian.

'Is that one of our customers?'

'Essentially, yes.'

Essentially? Gabriel raised his eyebrows. Either someone was a customer or they weren't. 'Who's the owner? If you have the phone number, I can take care of it.'

'The house isn't occupied,' replied Yuri.

Gabriel paused for a long moment. 'So what now?'

Silence. Gabriel could practically see Yuri Sarkov somewhere in Moscow on an obligatory visit to relatives. He could see him thinking: the phone pressed to his ear; the narrow, expressionless lips that were always slightly blue; the thinning hair; the rimless accountant's glasses in front of his grey eyes; the unnaturally smooth skin for a sixty-year-old.

Finally, Yuri sighed. 'Send someone over. Who's there now?'

'Just Cogan and me. Should we report it to the police?'

'No, no. It's our issue. Doesn't sound like anything big. Send Cogan, that'll be fine.'

Cogan shook his head vehemently and pointed to his legs. Gabriel motioned him to keep quiet. 'Why Cogan? He doesn't usually do field work.'

'I said: send Cogan,' Yuri growled irritably. 'Otherwise he'll get stuck to his monitor. He doesn't even know what it's like out there any more.'

'OK. Cogan will go,' said Gabriel. 'And who's the owner? Don't I have to call before one of us shows up?'

'Let me take care of that,' said Yuri. 'You take over the office while Cogan is out.'

Cogan rolled his eyes, spread his arms in despair and pointed to his legs again.

'And the keys?' Gabriel asked.

'Just put Cogan on, OK?'

Without a word, Gabriel handed the phone to his colleague. With a tortured expression, Cogan pressed it to his ear.

'Boss?'

'Listen,' Sarkov's voice rasped, 'I want *you* to check it out, but don't do anything on your own, OK? Just the usual routine, that's all. First, I just want to know what's actually going on there.'

'Boss, couldn't . . . I mean . . . I don't actually do field work and –'

'Just shut up and do as I say,' Sarkov's voice barked from the phone.

'OK, boss,' Cogan said hastily. Red blotches formed on his cheeks.

'The keys are in the small key safe in my office. They're labelled K107. The combination is 3722. Report back when you find out what's going on there, OK?'

'OK,' Cogan responded apprehensively, but Sarkov had already hung up. Cogan lowered the phone and looked at Gabriel. 'Shit, man,' he groaned softly, rubbing his brow. 'He suspects something.'

Gabriel frowned. Cogan was a diabetic and his sugar levels had been bad for years. At this point, he regularly had cramps in his calves and pain in his legs, and it was getting harder and harder for him to walk, but he still made a great effort to hide it from Sarkov. He knew that he had virtually no chance of staying on at Python with a disability. He stared down blankly at the blinking red dot on his monitor. 'I can't go. Not with this pain.'

Gabriel bit his lip. He knew Cogan wasn't capable of driving to Lichterfelde. On the other hand, Liz was waiting for him, and if he took over the office, he could hand it over to Jegorow at twelve and get out of there on time.

'Shit,' Cogan groaned. 'What do I do if there is actually someone there? I can't even run away.'

'You're not supposed to run away. You've got a gun, after all.'

Cogan made a face. It was supposed to look angry, but it was really sheer desperation.

'All right,' said Gabriel. 'I'll go. I'm the one who does the field work, after all.'

Cogan breathed a sigh of relief. 'You sure?'

Gabriel nodded half-heartedly. He thought about how he wouldn't be back for at least two hours and wondered how to break it to Liz.

'And Sarkov?' asked Cogan. 'What do we tell him?'

'Yuri doesn't have to find out. I'll call you and tell you what's going on. Then you can phone him.'

'OK.' There was a faint gleam in Cogan's dull eyes. 'Thanks for saving my arse, man.'

Gabriel smiled crookedly. 'And you're sure there's nothing about the client in the directory?'

Cogan shrugged. 'My legs might not work properly, but up here,' he tapped his forehead, 'everything's still in top shape.'

Gabriel nodded and took a quick look at the clock. 'Shit,' he muttered. Just half an hour later and his shift would have been over. He stood up, dialled Liz's number and hurried up the stairs to Yuri's office to get the key.

When she picked up, he had to strain to filter her voice out of the pub noise in the background.

'Liz? It's me.'

'Hey,' she sounded cheerful. 'I'm still at the Linus. I was just chatting with Vanessa but now she's gone home. Are you coming? We're finishing our drinks and taking a midnight stroll in the park.'

The Linus. Ugh, what else? Suddenly, he was happy to have an excuse. Wild horses couldn't drag him to the Linus. 'To be honest,' Gabriel mumbled, walking into Sarkov's office, 'I have a problem here. I have to go back out.'

'Oh no. Please don't,' Liz said. 'Not today.'

Gabriel entered the combination on the key safe's number pad and the door unlocked. Three dozen keys from Python's VIP customers hung in front of him.

'Is it because of the pub?' Liz asked. 'If you don't want to see all the media people, you really don't have to come in. Just pick me up.'

'It's not about that.'

'Is it about David? Come on, you can't run away from him forever. Besides, he's not even here.'

'Liz, it's not about that. Like I said, I have to go back out.'

She was silent for a moment. 'Is there no one else who can do it?'

'Not a chance,' Gabriel said. 'Unfortunately.' He preferred to stay quiet about the thing with Cogan. She would just take it the wrong way anyway.

'You have a real shit job,' Liz said.

'So do you,' Gabriel shot back. Gingerly, he took two rusty security keys that had a pale-red plastic key chain labelled

K107 from the hook. 'And you never had a problem with my job before.'

She sighed, but said nothing. She seemed to be waiting for something. The noisy pub sounded like it was echoing inside a metal bucket.

'OK,' she said, sighing again. 'Then, the same as always, I guess.'

'Liz, look, I –'

'Spare me, OK? Anyway, I have to go to the loo.' She hung up and the sounds of the pub abruptly went silent.

Gabriel swore softly, closed the safe and hurried down the stairs. *Then, the same as always, I guess.* At some point that night, he would climb into bed with her, Liz would toss and turn once or twice and then the same thing as always would happen again, which he could still never believe.

He would fall asleep.

No staring at the ceiling, no loose fragments of memory keeping him awake like camera flashes. Only his dreams hadn't disappeared, even if they did stay in their dark cave more often, lying in wait, just to attack him again at some point – with dead eyes, with electric shocks, or with the sensation of being burned alive. But, unlike before, there was now something to calm him when he jolted awake with his heart racing from a chaotic dream that was so real that reality felt like a hallucination instead.

Barely two minutes later, Gabriel was driving the Golf through the courtyard, past his old flat and the garage with his two motor-cycles, through the open gate, and onto the street, where he turned left and followed the GPS towards Kadettenweg.

He didn't miss his old flat. On the contrary, he felt as if he had been freed of a burden, like an old dried-up part of his soul. When he had gone to Yuri a year ago, his guilt had weighed him down. Yuri had given him a new life. But still, Gabriel knew that he couldn't live at Python any longer. He had done so for twenty years, and it was only thanks to Liz that he had recognised that something had to change if he didn't want to become a part of the furniture at Python Security.

Yuri raised his thin brown eyebrows and took a long look at him. His grey eyes searched for the real reason. 'What's the problem? Is the flat not big enough for you any more?'

Gabriel shook his head. 'My new flat isn't any bigger. That's not it. But . . . I have to get out of here. The new flat is on the top floor and it's got a small terrace.'

'Terrace,' Yuri snorted. 'The entire courtyard is your terrace. And what are you going to do with your workshop?'

'I'd like to keep on using the garage.'

Sarkov nodded slowly, but it was clear that he was not pleased.

'Yuri,' Gabriel said. 'I'm forty. Sometimes I want to go out the door and find a pub or a café nearby. Nothing wild, just some little place right outside where I know the waitress and she brings me a decent coffee without my having to say much, where I can pick up a few rolls at the bakery. This here,' he drew a circle in the air with his finger, 'is an industrial area.'

'An industrial area with nice brothel around the corner,' Sarkov added. 'Or have you met someone?'

Gabriel shook his head. 'There's one where I'm moving, too, and the girls are pretty.' Gabriel looked Sarkov straight in the eyes and lied. Strictly speaking, Yuri was right. He had met someone. In fact, Liz had been the actual reason for his moving out, but Yuri wasn't to know about that under any circumstances.

'You can fuck as often as you want. Just not with the same girl,' Yuri had always stressed. 'It makes you weak and dependent.'

Gabriel had taken this advice, in that he hardly ever fucked anyone, and when he did, it was always in other cities where he was booked with a Python team as personal security. There were always women in celebrity entourages who operated just like him. Sex? Yes please. Intimacy, no thank you.

Until Liz called him about two months after their chance meeting at the Berlinale film festival.

Since then, everything was different.

Gabriel's eyes drift over to the navigation device. The small arrow is pointing to the right on Kadettenweg.

Gabriel turns the steering wheel. The windscreen wipers scrape across the glass. The rain has stopped, as if it were simply cut off. He turns off the wipers and leans forward a bit to better make out the numbers on the passing houses. There are trees at irregular intervals on both sides of the narrow street, many even older than the villas behind them. Lichterfelde is full of stately and often quirky houses: small palazzi, Swiss chalets, art nouveau villas and castle-like brick constructions with towers. A wrought-iron *31* shines above a curved entryway.

When his mobile suddenly shrieks at him, he flinches and the car swerves.

The thought of Liz immediately pops into his head.

Goddamn it, are you even able to think about anything else, Luke?

He already knows that it won't be her. Not after that phone call earlier. If not shut off entirely, then her mobile was at least set to silent and lost in one of her coat pockets.

He takes his foot off the accelerator and presses the green button. 'Hello?'

'It's me, Cogan. I checked again.'

'Checked? Checked what?'

'The address, Kadettenweg 107.'

'So it is in the directory?'

'In a manner of speaking. Not in the current one. I went down into the archives.'

Gabriel has to grin. Cogan hates the archives as much as fieldwork, but he hates it even more when there's something in his universe that he doesn't know. 'And?'

'Well, the file on the house isn't there anymore. It's strange, really.'

'So what now? Have you found something or not?' Gabriel asks, squinting, trying to determine whether it's a forty-five or forty-nine peeking out between two trees.

'Ashton,' Cogan says. 'The owner's name is Ashton. There's an old file with the name in it.'

'Ashton. Aha. Anything else?'

'Well, there's something. A little thing, but strange.'

'Don't make me drag it out of you, man. Just spit it out.'

'The name Ashton was registered on September 17th, 1975. It was probably when the system was first activated. But right after it is a second, handwritten date. And a small cross. And the name is crossed out.' Cogan takes a meaning-ful pause. 'It looks as if the owner died exactly two days after moving in.'

'Strange,' Gabriel mutters. On his right, a house with several imposing columns glides past. House number sixty-seven.

'We still haven't got to the part that's really strange,' Cogan whispers. 'Since then, the house seems to have stayed empty.'

'*What?*' Gabriel exclaims. 'Since 1975? That's almost thirty-five years ago!'

'You said it.'

'What kind of lunatic leaves a villa empty for thirty-three years in this neighbourhood? Is there no one to inherit it?'

'No idea. There's nothing written about it here.'

'And the alarm system? What alarm system still works after so many years?'

'No idea,' Cogan says. 'I don't know anything about it. I don't even know what brand. Up until today, it was never active in my system.'

'Once more, just so I understand correctly,' Gabriel says, deliberately drawing things out. 'The alarm system was dead for thirty-three years and then today it went active out of nowhere and spontaneously sent out an alarm?'

'I don't know exactly when the system was shut down. Judging by Sarkov's reaction, it or the owner still seems to be a client. But since *I've* been here, and that's around nine years, there has definitely been no activation. Let alone an alarm.'

'So who's that supposed to be now? A ghost?'

'Or maybe a malfunction . . .'

'Hmm,' Gabriel grumbles and cranes his neck. On the right, an open entrance gate emerges from the darkness. A weathered *107* is mounted to one of the brick posts. 'I'm here. Let me go for now and I'll be in touch later.'

'All right. My greetings to old Ashton if you find him haunting the place,' Cogan says and lets out a cackle.

Gabriel puts his phone away and rolls in between the brick posts of the opened gate. The gravel entryway has knee-high weeds.

A villa that's been uninhabited for nearly thirty-five years and the gate is wide open?

The gravel crunches under the tyres. Overgrown hedges alternate with dark fir trees. A large half-timbered mansion rises up from behind the treetops with its decorated bay windows and two towers pressed up against it. The villa looks like an oversized witch's house.

Moist air rises from the ground and evaporates. Above the entrance, the red light from the alarm system rotates like a fire detector and makes the misty air glow.

Goddamned haunted house, Gabriel thinks.

As always, when he stands in front of a building that he wants to enter, he has to think about the cellar, how the stairs leading down to it will probably look. The hair on the back of his neck stands up and he peers up at the roof.

This house is old, and in old houses the alarm systems are usually in the cellar.

Chapter 3

Berlin – 1 September, 11.22 p.m.

Liz fights her way through the packed pub towards the exit. Dr Robert Bug, the news director for TV2 is standing by the bar and doesn't move even a centimetre back, so that Liz has to brush up against him to get past. Bug grins and pushes his whole body up against her, grazing her breasts. 'Well, well, would you look at that – our very own Miss Top Journalist!' he exclaims, staring unabashedly down at her. 'Didn't you want to send me the synopsis for your new documentary?'

I'll only send you something if the other stations don't take it, Liz thinks. 'I'm still researching,' she says with an empty smile. That she had just heard about one of Bug's intrigues minutes before makes the whole thing even more disgusting.

She pushes the door open and steps outside. Mist rises from the wet street as rainwater flows from the gutters into the storm drains. The door closes behind her and the noise of the Linus subsides. The neon sign above the entrance bathes Liz in an orange glow, the yellow lamps on their posts beside the door do the rest. The fires of purgatory.

For a moment, Liz closes her eyes and sucks the damp air deep into her lungs. A gust of wind blows through her chin-length red hair. It's unruly and sticks out of her head in a sort of orderly chaos, as if she had sprayed a can of hairspray into it immediately after waking up. The cool wind does her some good. Inside, the air was hot and rancid, and downright stank. Lately, she smells things that she would've never noticed before: armpit sweat, cheap deodorants, lingering cigarette smoke or the sour note of coffee on the breath. The smell of strangers forces its way in and there is nothing she can do about it.

She finds herself thinking of Gabriel and how good his skin smells, even if he never wears the cologne that she gave him – or any cologne, for that matter. She feels the growing warmth between her legs and hurries to suppress the thought, especially to avoid renewing her disappointment from their telephone conversation.

Liz glances back at the pub. Through the high glass windows, she can see Bug's fleshy face at the bar and his thick brown hair. Mr News. She is immediately back in work mode. The most peculiar stories always take place where you least expect it, she thinks. For example, late at night in the men's toilet.

The men's lavatory stinks nauseatingly of urine but, unlike the overcrowded Ladies is empty. Disgust is relative. And her need is absolute – not least because of her current state. When she pushes open the door to the men's loo, one of those prim and proper girls glares at her from the women's queue as if she had scabies. Liz is familiar with the look and hates it. Her mother and younger, picture-perfect sister Charlotte had that same expression on their faces whenever they looked at her. For her mother, everything was wrong with Liz, just as everything was right with Charlotte. The situation had only been made worse by the fact that her sister had also married into the

British aristocracy and was now donning fascinators and showing off at Ascot.

Liz walks into the men's toilet and wishes that some unspeakable illness would strike Ms Prim and Proper, or at least a bladder as unbearably small as her own. It's unbelievable, but the space in her stomach seems to be shrinking already.

The door swings shut behind her, muffling the noise of the pub. She chooses the cleanest of the three cubicles and locks it behind her.

Just a moment later, a new wave of noise rushes in as someone else enters the dirty, yellow-tiled WC. She immediately recognises Bug by his voice, which floats atop the pub noise like the foamy crest of a wave. Apparently, he needs a quiet place to make a phone call.

'I don't understand,' Bug says, 'that's not what was agreed, Vico.'

Vico? Liz pricks up her ears and holds her breath. By Vico, he was probably referring to Victor von Braunsfeld, the owner of the BMC media group, including TV2.

'No, no. I don't mean to complain at all,' Bug hastens to say, 'of course this is a step forward, I can see that, but as director, I could promote the station in a completely different way.'

Liz's eyes widen. *Bug – director?*

'What kind of timeline are we looking at?' Bug asks.

It's quiet for a moment.

'I can live with that if you give me . . . what? No, it's just loud here. Get people talking?' Bug let out a raunchy-sounding laugh. 'You can count on it – I already have something in mind. It'll be the perfect storm. The newspaper boys will write their fingers to the bone, the hypocrites will moan and groan and everyone will be glued to their tellies.'

The perfect storm? Liz thinks. That could only mean a new television format, some kind of mediocre rubbish.

'What?' Bug asks. 'Oh, *her*. Yes, yes, I know. The documentary was great. I'm on it, she's already offered me the next one.'

A smug grin flashes across Liz's face. It seemed Bug was just talking about her. Roughly a year ago, she accomplished a small miracle: she made a three-part documentary about Victor von Braunsfeld. He was one of the richest men in the country and consequently had prevented any media coverage on himself for the last decade.

'No, on that I will have to disappoint you,' Bug said. 'A permanent position is not her thing, she just doesn't want that. She prefers to freelance.'

No surprise, you ass, Liz thinks. With a boss like that . . . 'Yes, yes. I know that she's good, don't worry, I'll try to get her another way.'

Liz raises her eyebrows.

'All right. I'll see you tomorrow for the formalities. Good night.' Bug hangs up and lets out an exasperated sigh. 'Damn bitch. Soon he'll be inviting her to *Carpe Noctem* . . . she probably sucked out the old man's brain while she was at it.'

Liz doesn't flinch. It was nothing new for Bug to hit below the belt. But what did he mean by *Carpe Noctem*?

When she hears the loud splashing in the urinal, she imagines the face Bug would make if she were to step out of the cubicle at that moment and give him a friendly 'hello'.

Even now, out on the street, she has to grin at the thought of it. Liz takes a deep breath and replays Bug's conversation in her head. She catches herself trying to construct a story out of it already. Not because she really believes that she'll be able to turn it into a TV report, but much more out of habit – and curiosity.

She had been driven by this curiosity since she was a small child, but in her mother's eyes, Liz had always focused on the wrong things. Liz was like her hair – red and unruly.

When Liz was nine, her father, Berlin's senior public prosecutor Dr Walter Anders, had caught her in his office rummaging through the files from his criminal cases out of curiosity.

At dinner, she had constantly had questions, but they were mostly just laughed off. Not only because she had been nine, but much more because she was a girl. Liz had hated being a girl. And if her father ever actually answered one of her questions, he usually looked at her brother Ralf, who was four years older, as if there were a spotlight always fixed on him.

As a gift for graduating high school, Ralf had been given a two-week trip to New York in addition to a brand-new VW Golf. He had managed to get a B average and had been duly celebrated.

Liz had graduated three years later with an A.

She had got a make-up kit and her mother insisted upon helping her pick out a dress for the graduation ball. Liz had felt out of place as soon as she'd entered the boutique. The strapless dress that her mother had bought her had cost 4,299 marks and looked like something an opera diva would have worn. Liz had hated it from the very first second. She had felt like a scarecrow wearing it and had fought against it tooth and nail, but her mother had still had them wrap it up.

The morning before the ball, she had woken up with a stomach ache. Her mother had come into her room, dress in hand.

'I am not putting that thing on,' Liz blurted out. 'You can forget it.'

'Oh yes, you are,' her mother responded, 'whether you like it or not. It makes no difference to me. You will wear this dress.'

'No!'

'That's enough,' her mother cried. 'Either you put on this dress, or you aren't going.'

'Then I just won't go,' Liz fired back like a pistol.

Her mother stared at her. 'Fine,' she said and then smiled. 'Then you will pay me for the dress. Every last mark.'

Liz's mouth hung open. You mean 4,299 marks? 'I didn't even want it. *You* gave it to me.'

'Think about it. Either you put it on or I'll get the money from your savings account.'

Liz had looked at her mother in disbelief. She had been squirreling away every mark she had into her savings account for years so that she could afford a trip or a car after graduation. She had suspected that her graduation gifts wouldn't be as opulent as Ralf's, but this was really unbelievable!

Furious, she had stormed out of the house and run aimlessly through the city until she had found herself standing in front of a dingy shop. The shop owner was a barrel of a man and stank of nicotine and sweat.

Four hours later, she was back home, peaky, but with a smile at the corners of her mouth. That evening she had willingly put on the dress she'd hated so much.

Her mother's first reaction had been a triumphant smile. That is, until her eyes had dropped to Liz's exposed neckline. Above the edge of the dress, she caught sight of a small freshly inked tattoo of a skull with two crossed swords beneath it and a knife between its grinning teeth.

Her mother had gasped. She had been livid and slapped her daughter across the face, spraining her hand in the process.

Liz had gone to the ball in a simple black dress with a high neckline.

The next morning, she had emptied her savings account and then piled some firewood on the freshly mown grass of her parents' garden. She had placed the dress on top of a pile of all the other skirts and dresses from her wardrobe. Everything had seemed so calm when she set the heap aflame. Black smoke and an acrid stench enveloped her.

With a leather jacket and a couple pairs of jeans and jumpers in her suitcase, she had moved out, got a job, enrolled at university to study journalism, scored an internship at the prestigious Von Braunsfeld Academy for Journalism and finished with top marks.

Her father reacted as he always had: he didn't. To top it all off, 'journalist' ranked very low on his scale of respectable professions.

A couple of years later, Liz had been at a bar at an editorial department party with her editor-in-chief and told him all about her father.

'Congratulations,' he laughed. 'You've essentially followed in his footsteps. Lawyer or journalist – it's all the same, just a different playing field. In either case, you have the same investigative streak as him and the same relentlessness when it comes to catching the bad boys.'

Liz had been astounded by the thought of it.

And when one of her documentaries had been nominated for a major journalism award three years ago – though the prize went to someone else – her mother quite unexpectedly got in touch. 'Well, Elisabeth?' she asked pointedly. 'Was it worth it?'

She still wishes she had won the prize back then. Then at least her mother wouldn't have called.

Liz sighs and tries to figure out whom she could ask about Bug's strange phone call. Usually, she's a walking address book, but her head is strangely empty at the moment.

Pregnancy Alzheimer's? Already?

'Oh, screw it,' she mumbles. 'Time to go home.' Her watch says it's 11.25. She had imagined this night differently. And, damn it, Gabriel had promised her that much.

She can feel how annoyed she is that Gabriel isn't there – and that's what annoys her the most. Not long ago, she would've simply shrugged and buried herself in her work.

She walks past the taxis and climbs the stairs up the train platform. She hates getting stuck in conversations with taxi drivers. She prefers the anonymity of public transport, where she can look silently out into the night or watch the people around her, as if she were on a distant island. Taking the train at night is one of the few quiet moments she has.

First she takes the metro one stop to Alexanderplatz, and then the U8 towards Wittenau. When she transfers at Gesundbrunnen to the S41 Ringbahn, Berlin's circular railway, a wave of fatigue crashes over her and she sinks into the plastic seat. 'Please stand back,' the train speakers rattle, as always. The lights over the doors flash bright red, then the train rumbles and jerks into motion.

Liz's eyes drift across the nearly empty coach. On a row of seats ahead on the opposite side, two young guys in dirty jeans are huddled together and looking at her. They got on at the same time as her. One of them looks like a real pizza face.

At Schönhauser Allee, a very young mother with a screaming baby in her arms boards the train. Pizza Face rolls his eyes. When the train jerks forward, the girl stumbles onto the seats directly beside Liz. The baby cries even louder and the girl starts anxiously rummaging through her shoulder bag.

'Shut that monster up, it's annoying,' Pizza Face says.

The girl nervously crouches down. Then she discreetly pulls up her T-shirt and presses the little bundle up to her chest. The crying is muffled to a dull scream when the little mouth is pushed against her breast.

Liz feels sympathetic towards the girl. The boys are repulsive.

The girl's face twists with pain as the baby bites down on her nipple. The two young men watch in disgust. 'Man, with *those* dried-up tits, I'd be screaming, too,' the second one proclaims and wipes a string of mucus from his nose with his sleeve. The spotty one grins.

Liz stares at the girl, then back at the two guys. What she really wants is to jump up and give the two of them a piece of her mind. Her heart starts pounding. Everything inside her screams: don't do it!

The train comes to a screeching halt at Prenzlauer Allee. Pizza Face leans forward and hisses at the girl: 'Get lost! Get your arse out the door.'

Liz stands up. Her green eyes sparkle. 'How about *you* get lost.' Her voice could be firmer and she tries to ignore the protests coming from her stomach. 'Or else shut up and leave her alone.'

Stunned, Pizza Face stares at her. He is twenty at most. The stench of alcohol wafts over from his mouth. The other guy looks away, out the window and through his reflection into the night. 'Well . . .' the spotty one says deliberately slowly, 'I guess you didn't mean that, bitch. But if you're just a bit nice to me, then maybe I'll let the slag keep on riding.' His eyes linger on Liz's breasts. Part of the skull tattoo peeks out of her top. The guy with the runny nose gives a dumb grin. There's an open schnapps bottle in his left hand, wrapped in a brown paper bag.

'If you shitheads touch anyone here, I'll make a huge scene.' She gestures up towards a security camera hanging under the beige-painted ceiling. 'And I can't wait to see what happens then. I bet you've already got into a lot of trouble with the police. Even done some time in your youth? Or maybe community service?'

The spotty one's grin fades. He opens his mouth to reply, but the other guy elbows him in the side. Pizza Face's mouth closes again.

Feels good, Liz thinks. Brilliant, actually. Except that her knees are still trembling. She catches a grateful look from the girl and smiles back. The baby is still sucking hungrily, and is quieter.

Without realising it, Liz lays her hand on her summer coat and her slightly curved stomach underneath. Despite all of the uncertainty, she has also warmed to the idea. At the beginning of her pregnancy, she felt as if she'd been thrust into deep black water. But now it feels good – like she's swimming up to the surface after years under water, her hands reaching out into the clear air.

When she gets off at Landsberger Allee near Friedrichshain Park, the two young men get off the train too. *Shit*. She walks faster and turns from Landsberger Allee onto Cotheniusstrasse. The footsteps behind her fall silent. The two boys seem to have gone off somewhere. Nonetheless, she quickens her pace until she is standing at the front door of her building.

She doesn't notice the large olive-coloured delivery van with black-tinted windows on the other side of the street. She also doesn't see the man behind the steering wheel, peering in her direction. Had she done so, a single look in his eyes would have warned her without a doubt: go inside. Lock the door. Get help!

The man remains in the dark to avoid just that. He knows that Liz is alone, and he knows that Gabriel is probably turning into a driveway at that very moment, and that the bright red gravel will soon be crunching under his feet.

Chapter 4

Berlin – 1 September, 11.41 p.m.

Liz puts the key into the lock, enters the building corridor and lets the door close behind her. On the first floor, a door is open. 'Everything all right?' a woman's voice calls out insincerely. 'Do you know how late it is?'

'Sorry, Mrs Jentschke, the front door is broken,' Liz answers and rolls her eyes. Not again, not now, she thinks and leans against the wall across from the letterboxes to wait until Jentschke disappears back into her flat. The wall's beautiful old art nouveau tiles cool her back and it helps some. Again, she strokes her abdomen. Twelve weeks! Or was it thirteen already? If Gabriel were there, she would walk another lap through the park now, but alone? She thought back to the walk when she told him about the small pale pink plus sign on the test.

Pregnant.

The gynaecologist had been telling her for years that she couldn't have children, at least not naturally, because her fallopian tubes were not intact. Her answer was always that she never wanted any. Why would she? Her job was her baby. And real babies, that was a job for women like Charlotte, her sister. The agonising menstrual pain was horror enough. She would've liked to end her period altogether – it wasn't good for anything anyway.

That is, until she was suddenly holding the positive test in her hands. The gynaecologist had managed to congratulate her on her pregnancy as if it were a matter of course. 'You see, the more relaxed you are, the more likely it is to work out. Or do you really not want the child?'

Not want it?

Liz had been in shock. She had given up on the prospect of children an eternity ago, but now, for some crazy reason, fate had dealt her a new hand.

And with someone like Gabriel, of all people. He was like a black knight, a silent Anakin Skywalker or Batman, trapped in his life, withdrawing when something seemed unfair to him. Then his anger would burst out of him, like that time when she first met him. Sometimes, with all of the injustices she faced every day and her accompanying powerlessness, she wanted nothing more than to be like him. But the only means she had to fight back were her documentaries and news reports.

When it came to her pregnancy, there was a silent competition between her and Gabriel as to whom it perturbed the most.

Now she knows that he is the clear winner of that contest. There is no place for children in his life. There isn't actually even a place for her in his life. The fact that she has one at all borders on a miracle.

The Berlinale. She had to smile when she thought about how she met Gabriel at the film festival a year and a half ago. Once again, her talent for unexpectedly finding trouble had shone through. First, her combative interview with TV creative David Naumann, followed by a washed-up heavyweight boxer,

Zabriski. He had been slowly letting himself go, since he didn't box any more and there were assault charges against him – he had beaten up a paparazzo a few days before. Nonetheless, he was still a celebrity and his fights had always guaranteed good ratings, so he was somehow involved in every third show on TV2. That he had recently been doing coke and his life was falling apart were so obvious it hurt.

Once again, she hadn't managed to hold her tongue. Once again, she had asked a question that lit a fuse. Zabriski snapped. When the first blow had hit her cheekbone, she was too stunned to run in time. When he had grabbed her by the collar and shook her, fear took over. The whole TV2 crew had been standing around, but no one had done anything. Even Neo, her cameraman who was directly behind her, did nothing. That is, he just kept the film rolling.

Then Gabriel was suddenly there. The cold blue eyes, the short black hair, black leather jacket, maybe half a head shorter than Zabriski and clearly thinner. 'Let go of her,' he said. Nothing more. To Liz, it sounded like the restrained growl of a jungle cat.

Zabriski had actually let go. But only so that he could pounce on Gabriel. What happened next was incredibly sudden. Afterwards, no one would have been able to describe exactly what happened, not even Liz, if they hadn't had the tape from Neo's camera. She had watched the tape over and over again – forwards, backwards, in slow motion.

When Zabriski's right fist was flying directly at Gabriel's face, he had deflected it away from his head with his right forearm. Then he grabbed his wrist and pushed his arm down, while his left arm shot up and slammed Zabriski's elbow upwards.

The elbow joint had fractured with a soft crunch and bent at a horrifyingly unnatural angle. At almost the same moment, Gabriel's right hand had let go of Zabriski's arm and shot out in a straight line, his open palm thrusting into the boxer's face. The blow had smashed Zabriski's nose and the boxer bellowed in pain and stumbled back. Gabriel kicked the side of his supporting leg and the heavyweight crashed onto the floor. Between Zabriski's first swing and his backside landing on the parquet of a posh pub, only a few seconds had gone by.

The Berlinale party had died down, as if someone had simply pressed the stop button.

It was strange that Gabriel hadn't cared about the boxer in the least. He had only been interested in the camera – it made him uncomfortable. Two quick steps and he was standing in front of Neo. He had pointed at the camera and held out his hand. 'The tape.'

Liz had struggled to focus and saw Neo press the eject button. The camera had spit out the cassette and Gabriel grabbed it, put it in his black leather jacket and had disappeared through the door with his lightning-fast victory over Zabriski – and Liz's interview with David Naumann – in his pocket.

Had he not taken the tape, she likely would've never seen him again.

But she had been forced to run out into the street after Gabriel. 'Hey! Excuse me,' she cried. 'Please wait.'

No response. He had just marched onward.

Out of breath, she had tried to keep up. 'I . . . I wanted to thank you. That was very kind.'

Again, no answer.

'Why did you do that?'

'I can't stand guys who hit women.'

'Neither can the others, but you're the only one that helped me.'

'Forget it.'

'Why should I? You've ...'

Gabriel stopped abruptly. 'What do you want?' he asked impatiently. His eyes were piercing. Three steep wrinkles formed between his eyebrows.

'I ... to thank you. You helped me.'

'I haven't.' He tilted his head, pushing his unshaven chin forward. 'I can't stand you either.'

Liz stared at him, dumbfounded. 'Then why did you do it?'

Gabriel shrugged. 'It was something like ... a reflex.'

'A *what*?'

Gabriel had suddenly looked tired; the energy in his features gave way to something else. It had seemed like confusion, perhaps even helplessness. He turned away and went to cross the street.

'Wait. The tape ... can I have it?'

'No.' Without turning around, he stepped into the street.

'Please. It's important.'

'Not my problem.'

'No! That –' She wanted to go after him, but a bus shot right past her nose, so that she immediately jumped back. 'Hello? Hey ... That won't work – I need the interview.'

Gabriel had reached the other side of the street. The cars rushed past them in a blur. He seemed to not be listening any more and had continued on at a punishing pace.

'Hey!' Liz yelled across the street, 'what do you want with the tape?'

No answer.

'Are you worried about the fight? Zabriski won't report you . . .'

No reaction.

'Do you want the interview with David Naumann? Are you a journalist? Maybe I can help you there. I know him.'

Gabriel had stopped as if he had hit a wall and stared over at her.

Success. Liz crossed the street and hurried over to Gabriel. His blue eyes swept across her body and followed her every movement.

'Are you really a journalist?' she asked, out of breath.

'I can't stand journalists.'

Liz raised her eyebrows. 'What about female journalists?'

'Not them either.'

'Maybe you should meet one.' Then she smiled. 'If you want to know something about David Naumann . . . come with me. I'll get you one last drink for the road.'

'Coffee,' Gabriel said.

'That's good too. Then maybe you'll be able to speak in full sentences.'

Full sentences had remained a problem, but she had still called Gabriel two months later, because the way he had taken down Zabriski had made an impression on her.

'Where the hell did you get my number?' he asked when he recognised Liz's voice.

'I'm a journalist. Remember?'

'And?'

She hesitated a moment and wondered if it had been a mistake to ring him. 'I might have a job for you.'

'I already have a job,' Gabriel said brusquely.

She was about to hang up, but something stopped her. 'You could take a holiday.'

'Holiday?' Gabriel asked. He sounded as if the word didn't exist in his vocabulary. 'Why would I do that?'

Liz cleared her throat. 'Honestly, I need someone who could save my arse in case something happens. And I thought of you.'

There was a brief silence on the line. 'What did you have in mind?' Gabriel asked.

'I have to go to Zurich for an interview with an accountant.'

'A bookkeeper? And why do you need a security guard for that?'

'His former boss threatened me,' Liz said. 'He'll stop at nothing to avoid a scandal.'

Nine days later, Liz and Gabriel had checked into two adjacent rooms with a connecting door at the Hotel Zurich. Liz had slept terribly on the night before the interview. She'd had a dream that her mother testified against her as a witness in a trial. The courtroom was as tall as a church and deserted. Her father stood at the bench, slammed a giant book against it, charged her with heresy and condemned her to death at the stake. Bathed in sweat and woken by the nightmare, Liz had stumbled to the bathroom and collapsed. Before she could get up, Gabriel was beside her, a black figure in a dark room.

'Everything OK?' he asked.

No, Liz would have preferred to shout. Kill them, both of them! Her lips trembled.

'Shhh,' Gabriel said softly. His voice was rough and deep. She felt a heavy weight in the pit of her stomach. Gabriel stroked her face and felt how wet it was. She grabbed his hand. She could not bear him leaving at that moment. The dream lingered in the air.

With her free hand, she held Gabriel's neck and pulled herself up to him. Her face was less than a hand's width away from his. She could feel his breath; feel how he suddenly stopped breathing and tensed when it was all too close for him. The moment stretched on infinitely, her heart opened up. Earlier, it had pounded with fear. Now it was beating with the fear that he could feel everything that she had just felt and would pull away. It was a single, drawn-out moment in which they both had to make a decision. And everything, everything screamed that he would just walk away. His hesitation, his held breath, his stiff neck, his fingers in her hand, which were ice cold, as if he had suddenly been seized by fear.

Did her eyes deceive her, or were his lips trembling more than hers?

She moaned and pulled herself in a bit closer to him. She couldn't help but move towards his face in the dark. At the same time, her mind rebelled. It was all wrong. The nightmare, the man in front of her, his hesitation – just everything. And despite all that, she pulled him closer to her, until her mouth was very close to his lips. It was not a kiss, it was breathing onto each other. It was the moment before a kiss. And it was so charged, as if Gabriel were already inside her, like a preview of something that would inevitably follow, something that was unavoidable and would last forever, a promise, no, the fulfilment of a promise, which neither of them would have ever dared to make. All of her despair, as well as her longing to heal, were in that moment. If she had been able to see inside Gabriel's head, she would have broken down in tears, seeing his defences so desperately at work. If she had been able to hear inside his head, she would have heard the voice: *Luke, run away. Don't lay a finger on her, she will burn you, you hear? You will burn!*

She would have felt his longing, the longing of an eleven-year-old in the body of a forty-year-old. It was as if the years between eleven and forty had suddenly been erased. He was standing on the edge of a diving board at a dizzying height, and simultaneously wanted to jump in and to run away, back down the steps, clinging to the safety rail.

She would've never thought that he would jump. She would've never even thought that she would jump.

But they had jumped. Both of them.

Liz sighs. The sound lands like an echo between the art nouveau tiles in the corridor. She is constantly annoyed by how often she misses him. She always considered herself to be independent. Her need for fresh air takes over. Directly around the corner is Friedrichshain Park and she considers again whether it is wise to go for a walk alone at this hour. It occurs to her how often she makes her decisions based on him, whether he is there or not.

She resolutely opens the front door, looks left and right down the street. Once again, she overlooks the olive-coloured delivery van and steps out onto the street. What the hell, she thinks. She's gone this way a thousand times, with or without Gabriel. And there are streetlights everywhere along the path. She ignores the red sign telling her not to walk and crosses Danziger Strasse, passing over the tram tracks in the middle. The badminton hall at the edge of the park has been long closed at this hour, but the sign is still lit. She trudges through the low trees casting their shadows on the path in the park.

It smells of dog faeces and wet earth. The quiet rustling of the leaves is calming. Small stones crunch under her feet and she zigzags to avoid the puddles. The breeze feels light and lively in her hair.

She doesn't notice the figure in the dark between the trees. The light wind blows away his smell, as it does his quiet footsteps following behind her. She doesn't notice that he is catching up steadily until he is close enough to reach out his arm and touch her jacket. He is close enough to smell the pub in her jacket and the perfume on her neck with his wide-open nostrils.

Until a thin, dry twig breaks under the sole of his shoes.

Liz stops automatically and her instincts take over at lightning speed. The hair on her neck stands on end, she wants to turn around, but is also afraid of what she'll see. Time expands – and tears brim. A man's arm wraps around her throat like a steel cuff. She is thrown back, a body presses against her. She can feel hot breath on her cheek, something leathery and scarred rubs against her ear. She wants to scream, but the arm is constricting her breathing.

'Hello, Liz . . .' a hoarse voice whispers.

Oh god, no! Liz frantically tries to draw air into her lungs.

'Let yourself go, little one,' the voice says and squeezes mercilessly. 'I'm taking you with me. We're going to celebrate – us and someone else. On the thirteenth.' He laughs and it sounds as hard and sharp as glass. 'Will that work for you?'

'Hrrr,' Liz tries to scream and throws her elbows back.

'How strong you are,' the voice says. 'I know so many who are so pitifully weak.'

Oh, please! Doesn't anyone see me? Liz's eyes bulge out like table tennis balls. The arm pushes against her voice box, her body weight pulls her down, and her neck is stretched out more and more, as if she were hanging on a gallows. The sky, bathed in the orange light of the city, becomes as black as the trees. Stars dance before her eyes.

All of a sudden, the arm lets go and she falls like a defence-less rag doll onto the ground. She blinks feebly. There, wherever the man with the steel arm and leathery skin was before, there is now – nothing.

Gone. He's gone! Liz thinks in disbelief. *But why?* She gasps. Her lungs almost burst with their longing for air. They almost burst from the oxygen that is flowing into her chest and spreading relief. She tries to stand up, but collapses back down. She looks around nervously. *Where has he gone?*

The fear immediately returns.

What if he is still here?

Her eyes run across the bushes on the right and left in front of her, and then down the path until she sees why the man left her. A street lamp is on less than ten metres away. Two male figures sway in its light.

Thank god! Liz wants to call for help, but instead she has to cough.

The two men stay standing directly in the lamplight.

'Well, look a' that.' One of them grimaces as he attempts to speak clearly. He squints and his lips form a grin amidst the countless spots. 'If tha' in't the slut from the train . . .'

His drinking mate sways and wipes a whitish string of mucus from his nose. 'An' no video camera for miles, bitch.' His voice sounds like the drone of a circular saw.

'Just this shit light,' Pizza Face growls and rams his foot against the lamppost, but the thing refuses to go out.

Chapter 5

Berlin – 1 September, 11.46 p.m.

Gabriel slowly gets out of the car, his eyes on the huge, dilapidated house. The gravel crunches under his shoes. The smell of resin, wet earth and pine needles lingers in the misty air. For a moment, Gabriel holds his breath and listens.

Nothing.

Only the silent, rotating red light of the alarm system over the entrance. It looks as if the villa is breathing.

Gabriel's eyes drift up the tall house. The ground floor is covered with a dirty, rough plaster that is overgrown with ivy like thick arms trying to pull the building down. Above that, the black skeleton of the timber framing begins. There are mullioned windows with peeling white paint along the facade. The red roof tiles on the towers are spotted with moss, and a bent metal rod pierces the clouds from the left spire. A pale hole is torn in the sky and, in front of the hazy three-quarter moon, a majestic black weathercock hangs from the bent rod with its head pointing down, as if it were dead. There is no one in sight. No other car, no light in the windows. Not even the beam of a torch.

Gabriel nervously glances at his mobile.

Are you still hoping she'll ring you, Luke? the voice in his head mocks.

Gabriel doesn't answer.

Forget it. She won't do it. And you know why? Because you're not important to her.

Shut up. She's just angry. That's all.

Angry? No! If she were angry, she'd ring and let you have it. But you're not even important enough for that.

Shut up, damn it!

I'm only looking out for you, Luke. Nothing more and nothing less. It's what you always wanted.

Gabriel bites his lip, sets his phone to vibrate and puts it away. As if Liz were going to call him now anyway. He turns on his Maglite and lets the beam of light dance across the house. The front door is made entirely of black wood in a herringbone pattern with a green tarnished angel head doorknocker. Beside the door is a tarnished nameplate with embossed italic letters: Jill Ashton.

Mr Ashton was apparently a she.

The cylinder lock in the door appears undamaged. Gabriel goes to feel the surface for scratches. When he touches the wet metal, the door swings open, creaking, and reveals a clear view into the entry hall.

Gabriel holds his breath and listens. Dead silence.

Behind him, a car drives past on Kadettenweg. The sound of the tyres on the wet street cuts through the silence.

Gabriel takes a deep breath and quietly steps inside. He is greeted by the scent of decaying beams. There is a massive wooden staircase in front of him that leads upstairs and gets lost in the darkness. To his left is the living room. Gabriel points his torch at the ground and his back tenses. In the thick layer of dust, he can see clear footprints – footprints that lead behind the stairs, where there is probably another staircase to the cellar, and footprints leading into the living room.

Gabriel's heart beats faster. He carefully walks parallel to the trail, putting one foot in front of the other, and enters the living room. There, the prevailing scent is of old house – of money, old books and old values. The furniture is draped with sheets, the outline of each piece alluding to a past life.

At the other end of the living room, where the footprints lead, is a wide Victorian fireplace, with a chimney breast covered with fine black marble to the ceiling. On the mantelpiece is a full row of silver picture frames. Gabriel follows the footprints until he is standing directly in front of the photos. He has goosebumps all over his body when he sees the faces in the pictures. They are instantly recognisable: a woman, around forty, with dark shadows under her eyes, but still beautiful with long black hair nestled around her neck; and a very young man, not even eighteen, with flaxen hair and the flawless and arrogant look of an Adonis.

Gabriel is frozen in front of the mantel. The woman's gaze pierces into his, as if there were a window to his soul that she'd just pushed open.

Suddenly, he thinks of Liz, even though the black-haired woman hasn't the slightest resemblance to her. He closes his eyes for an instant. When they open again, the moment has passed.

Gabriel stares at the ledge and the shiny glass on the photo. Strange, he thinks. No dust? Shiny glass? The dust on the mantelpiece is also smudged, as if someone had pushed the photos to the side. Gabriel leans forward and looks into the hearth. A large black marble slab stands in the middle of the fire grate, leaning against the black wall of the fireplace. Strange.

He straightens up and looks at the chimney breast. At eye level, just above the photos on the mantelpiece, hangs a picture covered with a sheet like the furniture. Gently, he takes it off the hook with his fingertips. Behind it is a recess where a smooth grey door to a metal safe reflects the light from his torch. It measures about forty by thirty centimetres, and has a key slot in the middle.

Gabriel taps on the safe with his fingertips. He hears a faint *thud* and the door moves, maybe one or two millimetres, no more.

He pushes the photos on the ledge aside, pulls open the metal door with a fingernail and looks inside the safe. Completely empty. Either it was always empty or the burglar found what he was looking for.

Gabriel closes the safe again, hangs the picture back in its place, and resists the temptation to get his mobile out of his jacket, conscious it must be after midnight.

He turns around, goes back into the hall, careful to avoid smudging the burglar's footprints, and goes around the massive old wooden staircase. He is now standing at the threshold of a long unadorned flight of wooden steps that lead into the cellar. Several red dots blink in the darkness of the cellar. For an instant, he is filled with the same fear that he always felt at the top of the cellar stairs in his parents' house. The irrational feeling that something is waiting there for him. He shines the torch down into the darkness and sees the central controls of the alarm system with their red lights.

OK. Go downstairs, reset the alarm, lock up the house and go home, Gabriel thinks. He can give a statement to the police tomorrow. From how everything appears, the burglar is already long gone.

He goes to take a step and his foot suddenly slips on the first stair. He stumbles, reaches for the railing and drops the torch, which tumbles down the wooden stairs with a deafening crash and a confused flurry of light.

Breathing heavily, Gabriel freezes.

With a metallic clatter, the Maglite rolls across the cellar floor and remains there, rocking back and forth.

The red dots on the alarm system blink in competition. It only just occurs to Gabriel how much the cellar stairs are actually like the ones in his parents' house. He is suddenly dizzy. The red dots glow like the peephole in his father's lab would sometimes glow whenever he was inside.

Luke! Wake up. This is not your cellar. Your cellar doesn't exist anymore.

And if he is down there? Gabriel thinks. If Dad is down there? He asks the question almost too earnestly, with the anxious voice of an eleven-year-old.

He is not. You know that, Luke. You know that!

Gabriel's hand clings to the railing and he closes his eyes.

Damned déjà vu. Damned lab. Damned father. Not once had he been allowed to see the lab. In his imagination, it had grown into something monstrous – a magical space with the fascinating yet repulsive power of a chamber of horrors, much like this house here. All of that would have gone up in smoke if he had been allowed to go into the lab just once. But he had never entered it. Not once. And in the end, it was too late. The lab didn't exist anymore.

Gabriel pulls his shoulders back, opens his eyes and pulls himself together.

Ridiculous.

After all, this is not the cellar at his parents' house. And the thing with red lights down there is nothing more than an antique alarm system.

Let's go.

With a few light steps, he goes down the stairs. He picks up the torch and his fingers are closing around the soothingly cool black steel when suddenly he feels something move. Something touches his head, falls over him like a heavy blanket. He flails about to break free. The beam of light twitches across the wall, a dark figure collapses beside him and something wooden rattles throughout the cellar.

Gabriel stumbles two steps to the side. Breathing heavily, he points the torch at where he had just been standing. On the bare cellar floor, there is a pile of fabric and a wooden hanger lying in a dark puddle. It's only at second glance that he realises it's not just any piece of fabric. It's a dress. Black, extravagant, expensive. A dress that you normally only see on television at fashion shows.

But what the hell is a dress like that doing here? He lifts the dress from the puddle. Water drips from the soaked fabric. Gabriel looks up at the cellar ceiling where a copper pipe is leaking.

The beam of light from the torch moves across the sparkling fabric.

The dress looks new, clean and not at all as if it could have spent decades in this cellar. And then there's a piece of paper.

Gabriel furrows his brow and stares at the soggy sheet before him. Where there probably used to be an image, the ink has mixed into an unrecognisable colour soup, as if a paint box had been leaking.

Whatever there was to see on the paper is now gone.

Chapter 6

Berlin – 1 September, 11.54 p.m.

'Well? Not such a big mouth any more, eh, bitch?'

Liz writhes on the ground and protectively holds a hand in front of her belly. 'I . . . I need help,' she stammers.

The spotty one blinks in surprise, then grins at her. 'Help. Well, all right . . .'

Confused, the one with the drippy nose looks at Liz's hand, which is still resting protectively on her stomach. 'Hey, Pit, is she . . .'

'Shut it, man,' the spotty one barks.

'There's a lunatic running around,' Liz groans, 'who wanted to kidnap me . . . almost killed me.'

'Look at that, the mummy's scared.'

'Pit . . .' the drippy-nosed one mumbles, unsure. 'And if there's really –'

'Shut it, Jonas!'

Liz tries to sit up again. 'What kind of cowards are you?' She drags her head up and is now kneeling on all fours.

'Cowards, eh?' Jonas stares at Liz and cocks his head. Liz glares at him; slowly, the life returns to her body.

'Guys like you just . . .' She doesn't get any further. The spotty one puts his foot against her shoulder and pushes her to the side like a sack of potatoes.

'Shit . . . cunt!' Jonas stammers. Then he kicks her in the chest and she rolls onto her back. Pit bends over her and stares at her. His eyes are hazy but there is a fuse smouldering somewhere deep inside. She sees the blow coming and, as she wonders how someone so drunk can throw such a good punch, she feels her nose breaking. A hundred pointed nails are driven into her face at the same time. The pain spreads like an explosion. She throws up her hands, moaning and rolling to the side. Blood sprays out in front of her on the path.

She hardly feels the kicks any more, as they hit her body like muffled explosions. She loses any sense of time.

Out of breath, Jonas finally stops. The sparse stubble around his mouth glistens with moisture. 'Ay, wait, man.' He looks down at the woman on the ground. 'Stop. She's had enough.'

'A bitch like this has never had enough,' Pit gasps.

'Man, it's done. Leave it. The slut got her thrashing.' Jonas grabs his friend's arm and tries to pull him away.

'Shit. Let go of me, fucking idiot.' With all of his strength, the spotty one pulls free. Then he grabs Liz's coat and rummages through her pockets. He takes her purse without comment, then reaches into the breast pocket on the inside, fishes out her mobile with two fingers and rejects it. 'Man, what rubbish,' he growls and drops the phone like a hot potato. With a soft clatter, it lands on the path right in front of Liz.

'Let's get out of here.'

'And if she talks?'

Liz groans.

'How? She doesn't know anything.'

'And if she does?'

Jonas contorts his face.

Liz groans again. The blood rushes into her skull. This has to stop. But no one stops the pain. The tiny bits of stone on the path sting like pins.

Pit looks down at Liz's head. Her red hair shines in the dull light of the lamp. He smiles viciously and doles out a powerful kick.

'Are you mad?' Jonas's voice cracks. He grabs Pit by the arm and tries to drag him away, their steps pounding against the ground in front of Liz's nose. Small stones spray like shrapnel into her face. The sole of his shoe buries the mobile beneath it with a miserable crunch.

'Shut up, man,' Pit snarls and breaks free from Jonas. '*Shut up already*, you pussy.'

Liz's head is spinning. Everything tastes metallic.

The pins feel strangely dull. Her eyelids weigh tons.

She blinks.

There's something lying there. *The mobile!* Directly in front of her, like a mirage.

What did they do to the mobile?

The two guys run off. Pit and Jonas. Their footsteps thunder like hooves. The phone's cracked case sticks out between the stones, the display is dimly lit. The time on the digital clock changes. Midnight.

It's September 2nd, Liz's thirty-fourth birthday.

Chapter 7

Gabriel points his torch at the grey switch box on the wall with its several red flashing lights. An old SKB 9600, a dinosaur of an alarm system, and way too large for a private home, even a mansion like this. On the bottom right, there's a faded sticker from Python with an emergency phone number. A thick cable leads out of the top cover. Two of the lines are freshly cut with a wire cutter, the copper strands shimmering in the torchlight.

Gabriel stares at the cut cables. One of them has to be the connection to the siren. But what is the other one for?

A gentle breeze, still damp from the rain, comes down the cellar stairs. Gabriel shudders and turns around, as if someone had breathed on his neck. Suddenly, he is no longer sure that he is alone in the house.

At that moment, his jacket pocket vibrates. Gabriel flinches. Damn it! His hand hurries into the pocket and fishes out the mobile, while also glancing nervously over at the stairs. No one in sight. Why does he feel like someone is there? The mobile purrs in his hand. The name Liz Anders comes up on the display.

Please, not now! he thinks.

He quickly presses the button to ignore Liz's call. The mobile is quiet again.

Tense, he listens in the dark. Nothing. Only the whisper of the wind on the stairs. He reminds himself that he never closed the front door. The loose cables lie there like bare nerves.

What the hell is going on here?

What burglar is interested in a house that's been empty forever? And how does he know the alarm system so well that he can deliberately disable the siren? Sure, there are plenty of burglars in the area who are able to manipulate alarm systems, but a model that's a good thirty-five years old? And if he really knows it so well, then why did he miss the silent alarm?

Suddenly, his hand is vibrating again. Liz! Again.

Now turn that thing off, Luke, the voice whispers.

And if it's urgent?

Urgent? Shit! What do you think we're doing now? What if the burglar is still here? And on top of that: what do you think it'll be about? It's her birthday, you aren't there, she's going to bitch and moan . . .

Gabriel doesn't answer, just stares at the shining telephone display and the little black letters.

Liz Anders.

Damn it! Put that thing away!

Gabriel presses the green button and puts the phone to his ear. 'Liz? I can't talk right now,' he whispers. 'I'll get back to you soon!'

'Help me . . . please. Help . .' a weak voice stammers.

Gabriel's body stiffens. 'Liz?'

'Pl . . . ease . . . help me . .' Liz stammers. Her voice is as thin as paper.

'Oh god. What happened?'

'I was attacked. I'm bleeding . . . there's blood everywhere . . . my head . . .'

Gabriel's heart stops. His chest tighters. The alarm system's red lights blink. 'Where are you?' he asks and presses the phone to his ear to hear her better.

'In the park. Friedrichshain. Near my flat, around the corner . . . please, I'm scared . . .' she sobs.

Gabriel opens his mouth, but no sound comes out.

'Gabriel . . . ?'

'I . . . I'm here. Liz? Listen. I'm sending you help. You hear?'

'Where . . . where are you?' Liz asks, distraught.

'I'm coming now. I'm coming, Liz. You hear?'

'I'm cold,' she whispers. 'So awfully . . . cold.'

'Liz?'

No answer. Red dots in front of his eyes.

'Liz!' he screams into the phone. His voice echoes through the cellar. His heart is racing. He hears a quiet noise from the telephone. A cold sweat forms on his forehead. 'Liz! Are you still there? Do you hear me?' Gabriel desperately presses the mobile to his ear. 'I'm getting help,' he says. 'Hang on. Please – hang on!'

Nothing. Just a soft crackle on the line.

Gabriel breathes in until he feels like his lungs are going to burst and then he ends the call. When the connection breaks, it is as if a rope has been cut and Liz is swept into the deep.

For a fraction of a second – or is it minutes? – he stands there motionless.

Then, with trembling fingers, he dials emergency services. Pick up, damn it! Pick up! With the mobile pressed against his ear, he sprints up the stairs and through the front door. The light on the alarm system bathes the garden in a red glow.

'Emergency call centre, Berlin,' a well-rehearsed voice squawks from the earpiece. 'What can I do for you?'

'Hello!' Gabriel says, throws open the driver's side door and jumps into the Golf. 'This an emergency, in the park . . .'

'Hello? Is anybody there?' says the voice from the headset.

Please, no! Gabriel thinks. Please don't be a dead zone! 'Hello?' he screams. 'Can you hear me?' He switches the mobile to his left hand and starts the car with his right, throws it into reverse and speeds out over the gravel road and into the street. 'Hello? Helloo!'

'Oh, yes, now I can hear you. What's the problem?'

The Golf shoots backwards out into the street. Gabriel frantically turns the steering wheel and hits the brakes. 'An emergency,' he shouts into the phone, 'at Friedrichshain Park.' He throws the lever of the automatic from 'R' to 'D' and slams on the accelerator.

'Listen, I can understand you better if you don't shout like that,' the man says, agonisingly calm.

'A woman was attacked in Friedrichshain Park. She is badly hurt and urgently needs help.'

'OK. Friedrichshain Park,' the voice repeats. 'And where exactly in the park?'

'No idea,' Gabriel replies. 'Well, wait. Probably near Cotheniusstrasse.'

'Near Cotheniusstrasse, got it. Do you know who the woman is?'

'Her name is Liz. Liz Anders.'

'Liz Anders. Good. Can you describe to me exactly what happened?'

'Goddamn it. She was attacked. Isn't that enough?'

'Of course. Attacked,' the voice answers stoically. 'Can you please tell me your name?'

'Shit! Damn it! Why all the stupid questions? I want you to send someone there. Straight away. She needs help.'

'Of course. Calm down. We are sending someone. Now please tell me . . .'

Enraged, Gabriel hangs up and throws the mobile on the passenger seat. Then he turns onto Drakestrasse. He presses down harder on the accelerator and speeds north. The speedometer needle trembles just above ninety kilometres per hour.

Slow down, damn it. Do you want to kill us?

She needs help! Don't you understand that?

Do you think you will help her by killing us?

Since when are you the white knight? I thought you didn't give a shit about her.

I don't, so pull yourself together.

'Fuck you!' Gabriel whispers, staring straight ahead through the windscreen.

Suddenly, his mobile rings. He looks at the display – it's Python. Cogan. He ignores the call and looks back at the road in front of him. From the corner of his eye, he sees a strip of light, followed by a dark shadow on his right. He reflexively hits the brakes and then there is a deafening bang as the other car rams him from the side and pushes him out of the way. The Golf swerves to the left, skids and the front left wheel jumps onto the kerb like a bucking horse with a heavy blow. He is thrown forward in the seatbelt and bounces back against the seat. There is a shooting pain in his shoulder. Then the Golf stops moving.

The sudden stillness is overwhelming. Gabriel gasps. His foot is still fully pressed on the brake pedal. The adrenalin makes him shake.

He turns around to the other car. His shoulder is screaming in pain. About fifteen metres behind him, a midnight blue Jaguar at the crossing looks like there was a bite taken out of the mudguard. The doors open up and the driver, a stout man in his mid-fifties, laboriously gets out of the sports car. The female passenger also gets out and points to Gabriel. She has smooth blond hair and is wearing black, tight-fitting trousers and a jacket with a leopard print pattern. Her heels clatter on the asphalt as she approaches, but the man grabs her arm and holds her back.

Furious, she stares at Gabriel's face.

Gabriel takes his foot off of the brake and steps on the accelerator. The Golf jolts into motion again. There is a crunch as the plastic part of the dented front end falls into the street and under the tyres. In the rear-view mirror, he sees the leopard woman, staring at him with her mouth agape.

I'm coming, Liz, he thinks.

You're making an idiot of yourself, Luke. Whenever it's about this woman, you lose control. And you know what happens when you lose control?

Chapter 8

Gabriel drives down the three-lane Danziger Strasse, staying on the edge of the park. The soft clatter of the damaged front of the car sounds like an irregular heartbeat. He can already see the blue lights flickering near Cotheniusstrasse from afar and his stomach ties in knots. At the densely overgrown park entrance near the badminton hall, there is a rescue van, an ambulance and two police cars.

Gabriel turns the steering wheel. As he drives over the kerb onto the pavement, the tyre is pressed into the crushed wing. It makes a pitiful crunching sound.

He gets out and starts running. As if powered by remote control, he runs down the curving path into the park. He knows most of the trees here. He looks at them when he walks here with Liz. They calm him and make him feel like taking a walk has purpose.

Around the next bend, the bend where Liz told him that she wanted to keep the baby, there is a long straight stretch of path where all he could do was stay silent. A baby. Him and a baby. All of it had completely thrown him off course. That night, he'd woken up several times, bathed in sweat from penetratingly intense dreams. In one, he was under a scorching sun in a desert with red sand, as his arms and legs grew and grew like vines. In front of him, there was a glass of water, a simple clean glass. And the water evaporated in the heat without him being able to reach it.

He shakes off his memories of the dream and hurries onward, deeper into the park. The path under his shoes gives way, softened by the heavy rain. About a hundred metres ahead, several strong torches dance in the hazy light beneath a lamppost. Uniformed figures are running around. A little off to the side, on the edge of the path, two paramedics and an emergency physician are all huddled together. One of them is smoking. In the middle of the path there is a shapeless grey mound. A body covered with a sheet.

Liz.

From one second to the next, he grows cold, as if he has fallen through ice. The shock paralyses him and he freezes, even though he wants to run. Run away or run straight to her. But he can't even tremble, he just stands there and stares at the sheet.

He doesn't even feel his feet start taking steps towards her. One after the other. Much too slowly. He sees nothing but the sheet and the body under it, not the police officers, who look at him suspiciously and call out to him, not the others. It was as if he were walking through a narrow tunnel, and this mound and the sheet were the only things at the end of it. Although he refuses to believe that it's Liz, the idea has already long settled into his brain and now cannot be removed. When he finally reaches the end of the tunnel, he falls to his knees beside her. Sharp stones pierce his skin, but he doesn't feel it. The wet ground instantly soaks his trousers all the way through.

She looks so big under the sheet! That is the first thing he thinks.

'Hey, you, get your hands away from there,' someone shouts. Gabriel doesn't even blink. His right hand reaches for the sheet. It feels damp. Dirty and sticky. Why didn't she at least get a clean sheet? he thinks, as he lifts the fabric and stares into the face of the corpse.

It is the face of a spotty young man with dead eyes and ashen skin. He is wearing a dirty denim jacket. His throat is slit with a deep cut. Sticky black blood shimmers on his neck and the collar of his jacket. Gabriel touches the young man's hands, which are sticky with blood. His body is ice cold, but the limbs are still moveable. A disgusting stench of urine and excrement surround the dead man like an aura. Presumably, his insides emptied when it lost its last bit of control.

Gabriel stares into this face. A narrow, off-putting and brutish face.

A face that is not Liz's face.

And that is all that matters right now. Regardless, the moment seems endless until another thought comes to mind.

If this isn't Liz, then where is she?

Somewhere nearby, a siren howls, high-pitched and piercing, approaching rapidly.

Chapter 9

Berlin – 2 September, 12.39 a.m.

Liz's closed eyelids bulge as her pupils move back and forth beneath. She feels that she is still alive, but her head and her body feel numb, much too numb to sense anything like joy or fear. It is exactly as if everything were embedded in a thick fog.

A constant humming sounds in her ears. *A motor, that must be a motor.* Then a siren so loud that it hurts in her head like pinpricks. She can't move her arms – it's like she is strapped down to a couch or something similar. She immediately tries to feel her stomach and check whether the straps are too tight for her baby. Straps. Why straps? Suddenly, a vague fear wells up in her. *Her spine. It's her spine.* Patients who have hurt their spines are always tied down in the ambulance.

The distorted image of an ambulance runs through her head, orange and creamy white, as it rushes through Berlin at night and oscillates in its own flickering blue light like a projection. But where is the siren? Why doesn't she hear the siren any more?

Then she hears a voice, a man's voice, muffled like it was coming through a wall. 'Hey, listen, I'm looking for the entrance to Vivantes Hospital. Where do I have to go?'

'It's right there, around the corner,' a second voice answers, quiet and younger than the first. 'Turn in there on the left and keep going straight.'

'Thanks.'

Now the motor noise is gone and a door slams. In her clouded thoughts, Liz already sees what's about to happen, sees what has happened millions of times in the past. Like all those other times, the stretcher will be lifted out of the ambulance by paramedics and then they will unfold the frame, so that its wheels can shake and rattle across the threshold of accident and emergency. She waits for the inevitable shaking and rattling, but strangely enough, it never comes. Nothing comes.

Except silence.

The vague feeling of anxiety has returned, which mixes with her indifference like a splash of blood in a bucket of white paint. And then suddenly Gabriel comes into her mind. She remembers that she called him, how she was lying there. She even has his voice in her ear: 'Liz, I'm sending you help.' If Gabriel gets help, everything will be fine, she had thought. But then why doesn't it feel like everything is fine?

For a moment, her thoughts float in the emptiness. Her unease is growing stronger. It is the same uneasiness that she had a few months ago.

Ding. She is amazed at how her memory just works, like a lift that goes up and down with her.

A few months ago. She had just found out that she was pregnant. Up until then, she had refrained from digging too deep into Gabriel's life. Don't ask, she thought. If he doesn't tell you himself, then leave it. And she'd done so. Despite her inherent curiosity and passion for research, she ignored her own questions because she instinctively knew that she could destroy everything between them. And then she was pregnant, and suddenly couldn't manage to ignore her questions any longer. Out of nowhere came the anxiety. The anxiety of having a child with a man who has no parents, no contact with his brother, no friends and a job to which he clings and hates with equal measure.

Since then, she has been carrying around this feeling whenever she thinks of Gabriel. This feeling that Gabriel is one big black spot, a spot she loves, with whom she is having a child, but whom she doesn't know. And that suddenly makes her afraid.

Ding. Again, the lift. Are those steps? She blinks and, to her own amazement, manages to open her eyes. Around her, everything is dark. When she moves her eyes, everything seems like it's swimming, even the darkness. Why is it dark in an ambulance? And why isn't anyone bringing me into the hospital?

There is a loud click and cool air blows into the vehicle. Finally. She squints, expecting that the lights will soon go on. Then the door crashes shut again and a figure is bent over her. A torch turns on and the light burns her eyes like fire. She wants to ask what is wrong with her spine, but nothing comes out. Suddenly, her body remembers all of the injuries and lashes out at her in pain. If she could smell, she would be taking in a strong scent, but her swollen nose makes that impossible. The only thing she can feel is a damp towel on her face.

Indifference suddenly dulls her senses again. Perhaps, she thinks, the hospital was full.

She doesn't hear that the motor has started up again. Had she heard it, she probably would have thought: so, now we are going to the next hospital. Please let there be a free bed there.

Chapter 10

Gabriel is still kneeling beside the body when he is grabbed by both arms and pulled to his feet. His shoulder protests with throbbing pain and he grimaces.

'For god's sake,' someone starts up. 'What's this about? What are you looking for here?'

Gabriel is dizzy and can feel nausea rising in him.

'Hey, you! I'm talking to you.'

'Where . . . where is she?' Gabriel asks.

'Where is who?' The policeman on Gabriel's right looks at him suspiciously. He is in his mid-thirties and has a goatee and giant hands.

Gabriel returns the look. In terms of deep-seated mistrust, for him, police officers come right after firearms. 'My girlfriend. Liz Anders. The injured woman. I called because of her.'

'All right, then,' the policeman growls. 'Then explain to us what this shit here is all about.'

'I don't know what you mean.'

'Well, this mess here,' the police officer says and gestures to the body of the spotty young man.

Gabriel looks at him blankly. He is still fighting back the nausea. The other policeman is still holding on to him and his hand is burning through Gabriel's arm. He hates to be touched and tries to shake him off. In vain. 'I have no idea what you mean. I am looking for my girlfriend. I called because of her. She was attacked here half an hour ago and I called.'

The policeman raises his eyebrows and scratches the back of his head. 'Listen, I . . .'

'What's going on here, Schuster?' a male voice rings out behind Gabriel.

The policeman with the goatee frowns and clumsily stands to attention.

Gabriel turns around and stares into a pair of piercing brown eyes in a weary, hairless face. Even the eyebrows are so thin that they are little more than a shadow above his eyes.

'Commissioner Grell, Criminal Investigation Department, Berlin,' the man says, already agitated. He has a short neck and is wearing an ill-fitting corduroy suit over his plump body. 'And you are?'

'Gabriel Naumann. I –'

'Jansen,' the commissioner rumbles without taking his eyes off Gabriel. 'Have you already done a background check?'

'N-no . . .' the other police officer stammers, still holding on to Gabriel's left arm.

'Then what are you waiting for?'

Jansen nods, steps aside and presses his mobile up to his ear.

'Headquarters? Hello. A background check. Naumann, Gabriel . . .'

Gabriel rubs his freed arm, as if to rub off the man's grip. Slowly, he is able to think clearly again and fear immediately takes hold of him. Where is Liz?

Commissioner Grell and Schuster, the officer with the goatee, are huddled together. Grell nods with his bald head and takes a lumbering step towards Gabriel. 'First: this is a crime scene. What makes you think you can just walk around here and mess around with my corpse?'

'I thought that my girlfriend was under the sheet.'

'I don't give a shit what you thought.' He gives Gabriel's compact stature a disapproving once-over. 'The main thing is that you stay out of my crime scene.'

'Like I said, I thought –'

'Spare yourself the thinking. It doesn't seem to be your strong suit.'

Schuster grins silently in the background.

'Where is your girlfriend now?' Grell asks.

'No idea,' Gabriel says, trying to remain calm. 'When she called me, she could hardly speak, she was badly hurt. That's why I called in the emergency.'

'Well, if she's not here any more, then it can't have been so bad. Is your girlfriend prone to exaggeration?'

Gabriel stares angrily at the bald man, but refrains from giving an answer.

Jansen, the other officer, walks up to the commissioner. 'Boss?' he whispers. 'I've got something.'

Grell nods and leads Jansen a few metres over to the side, beneath a large elm. The two huddle together and Jansen whispers something into his ear with a serious expression. The commissioner nods several times, raises his hairless eyebrows, and fixates on Gabriel. Then he pats Jansen on the shoulder and turns towards Gabriel with an ominous expression. The soft ground makes a smacking sound under his heavy shoes. 'I am going to ask you again,' he says slowly, 'and think carefully about how you want to reply: why are you here?'

Gabriel rolls his eyes. 'Damn it, how many times do I have to explain. My girlfriend was attacked. She called me because she was badly injured and needed help. So I drove here. I had no idea at all that a body was lying here. I don't care! I just want to know where my girlfriend is and if she's all right.'

'Well, Mr Naumann,' Grell smiles icily, '*I* am very interested in the body. And I am especially interested in what *you* have to do with it.'

Gabriel stares incredulously at the commissioner. 'What is that supposed to mean? You can't be serious.'

'Well, I look at this quite simply. First: you show up here as if it's totally normal to waltz in right after a murder. Second: you claim that you were called for help by someone who is not even here. Third: you are clearly, as Officer Jansen has just explained, a security guard and work for a company called Python. Interestingly, you are permitted to carry a weapon but, according to your police certificate, you do not. And fourth: you have blood on your hands and trousers.'

Gabriel's mouth hangs open. He looks down at his hands, which visibly have blood on them. 'You seriously want to insinuate that it was me? Why?'

Grell shrugs.

'Goddamn it,' Gabriel snarls. 'Go ask the other officers. They saw me kneel beside the body and touch the sheet. That's where the blood came from.'

'Maybe you had a good reason to come back and smear the blood on your hands.'

'What the hell kind of reason could that possibly be? That's sick.'

'That's exactly my point, Mr Naumann,' Grell says with a quiet, sharp voice. 'Or do you deny having been in the locked ward of the psychiatric clinic at Conradshöhe from 1983 to 1988?'

Gabriel was as white as a sheet. 'That ... that was twenty years ago,' he stammers hoarsely. 'That was removed from my record long ago, where ...'

The commissioner looks at him in anticipation as an ugly smirk forms across his lips. 'So, were you at Conradshöhe?'

'Yes,' Gabriel admits, 'but how the hell do you know that? It's ...'

'What? Illegal?' Grell raises an eyebrow. 'If I'm not mistaken, then you just told me yourself. I was just wondering if you would deny it ...' He grins smugly.

Gabriel stares at him furiously. 'Conradshöhe has nothing to do with this here. Absolutely nothing! I just want to find Liz Anders. That's all.'

'Certainly. Liz Anders.' Grell nods and his smile freezes. 'If it's true, all the better. But I think you'll understand if I need to take a bit of time to review everything under these circumstances.'

Gabriel feels Schuster's giant paw close around his right upper arm. Jansen steps up to him from the left and pulls a pair of handcuffs from his belt. A wave of panic and rage washes over Gabriel.

Here we go again, Luke, the voice whispers. *You see? I told you. Here we go again.*

Gabriel's eyelids twitch ever so slightly. Then his right forearm quickly swings up like a taut spring and his fist crashes into the middle of Schuster's face. The officer immediately lets go of him, staggers backwards and holds his nose. Blood wells up between his fingers.

Gabriel swings his left arm in a sudden windmill motion and twists out of Jansen's grip. At lightning speed, Gabriel closes in with a blow from the edge of his left hand and–

'Stop!' A sharp voice shouts.

Gabriel freezes. Grell is standing at a safe distance several metres away with his shiny black service weapon at the ready. 'Give me one reason to pull the trigger, you lunatic, just one!'

Gabriel slowly lowers his hands. A paralysing despair descends upon him. For a fraction of a second, he sees wide leather straps around his body.

Just don't lose control now, Luke. You know what happens then.

Haven't I already? he thinks desperately. I've already lost control.

The handcuffs that are put on him burn on his skin. Not being able to move his arms scares him. Nausea rises in him like a reflex and he tries to convince himself that no one here will stick electrodes to his head and flip a switch. But his body doesn't believe him; his body has its own memory.

All of a sudden, he thinks of David, of his little brother's firm hugs, and the feeling of having to cry and laugh at the same time. The longing comes over him like a fever, a longing for everything to finally be OK, for it not to happen this time, and for there to be only one reason that he can't remember this awful night: that it never existed and that everything is completely normal. That he can simply ring his brother, just like anyone else who has a brother. Please, please let that be the case.

But nothing is normal. For nearly thirty years, nothing has been normal. Since he can't just suddenly ring, out of the blue, and say: here I am again.

Even if there were no one else that would help.

Chapter 11

David Naumann brushes the chin-length blond hair from his face and reluctantly enters the outer office of Dr Robert Bug, the news director of TV2, as if it were the gateway to another world.

'You'll have to wait a moment. Von Braunsfeld is still in with him,' Karla Wiegand greets him. Her eyes drift across David's slender figure, his jeans, his dark blue sports jacket, the creased white shirt hanging casually over his trousers. 'Coffee?'

David nods. 'Victor von Braunsfeld? With Bug? What's he doing here? He usually only cares about the big deals.'

Karla Wiegand makes a serious face, but shrugs at the same time. The grinder in the coffee machine roars and the machine spits espresso and milk out into a cup. Wiegand is blonde and in her late forties, so a good ten years older than David. Her hair-line is already beginning to grey and her face, which is actually attractive, has clear wrinkles around the corners of her mouth like brackets, framing her latent discontent.

The recently relaunched station logo for TV2 is displayed above her like a sword of Damocles, in burgundy, the '2' in fresh, bright orange. David knows that she probably does a good job, otherwise Bug would have replaced her long ago with a younger model. 'Do you know what he wants from me?'

'No idea,' Klara Wiegand says. David can feel her avoiding his gaze. So, he has something to complain about, David thinks. Well, so what? It's nothing new for Bug to exceed his authority and move into the entertainment sector. Best case scenario, it's about a bit of cross-promotion for a new newscaster or presenter to be introduced before some show. It's just a question of why Bug didn't address David's boss, the head of entertainment, directly.

'Oh, by the way,' Wiegand says quietly and hands David the coffee, 'there was a call for you just now, a Mr Schirk from Commerce Bank . . .' David nods with deliberate indifference. *Crap. He's already calling me at the station.* He can feel the slight redness spreading across his face, which is probably even visible through his stubble.

At that moment, the door to Bug's office opens. 'Thanks again,' his dark voice purrs from somewhere inside. Only his hand is visible, as he eagerly shakes with Victor von Braunsfeld, a wiry man of over seventy with a snowy-white but full head of hair, wearing a tailored steel-grey suit.

'Very well,' von Braunsfeld mutters with light condescension. 'Oh,' he says, 'before I forget. There will be a new episode of *Carpe Noctem* on the first.'

'It's been noted,' Bug says.

Carpe Noctem? David thinks. During what time slot? Has he missed something?

Von Braunsfeld nods to Bug and energetically steps past Klara Wiegand's desk. In passing, his eyes land on David. Their eyes meet and von Braunsfeld stops short.

'Do we know each other?' von Braunsfeld asks, his light brown eyes fixed on him in a penetrating gaze.

'I don't think so,' David smiles uncertainly, as he always does when he is around people who exude so much power. He automatically switches the coffee cup to his left hand in order to shake von Braunsfeld's hand. 'I work for you. In the entertainment department at TV2. Development and production of shows and reality formats.'

'I see,' von Braunsfeld nods. He smiles. A peculiar straight smile in which the teeth are not visible and the eyes are not smiling either. His handshake is cool and firm, though his fingers seem thin and knotty. 'And your name is?'

'Naumann,' David replies quickly. 'David Naumann.'

Von Braunsfeld pulls his hand back quickly, a touch too quickly, David thinks, as if he had touched on a sore spot.

'Naumann? Ah, yes, the whole *Treasure Castle* story,' he says. 'Any relation to Wolf Naumann, the cameraman?'

David looks at him, stunned, then nods. 'I'm his son. Did you know him?'

Von Braunsfeld puts his hands up in a defensive gesture. His signet ring flashes for a moment. 'Not really. But it was indeed a bad story back then, it was all over the press.'

'Yes,' David says with reserve. He can feel Karla Wiegand's curious gaze on his back and prepares for the unavoidable questions. The questions that he hates so much and that are still asked over and over again, even today. There were times that he wished he just had 'I don't know either!' tattooed onto his forehead. After all, the whole nightmare happened while he was locked in his room.

'Well, then, keep at it,' von Braunsfeld says vacantly, nods to him and quickly walks out the door.

Relieved and surprised at the same time, David watches him go. Next to him, Karla Wiegand clears her throat and then gestures at the open double doors to Bug's office with her thumb. 'Mr News is waiting . . .'

David nods and his train of thought changes directions. He walks towards Bug's office, but hesitates. 'Oh, Karla, do you know what that was all about just then? A new episode of *Carpe Noctem*?'

Karla Wiegand shrugs. 'No idea. Some new format probably.'

'But not with us, right?'

'I don't think so, but von Braunsfeld does always seem to have his fingers in all the pies.'

'Well, then,' David mutters and enters the news director's office. A few drops of coffee spill over the edge of his cup and sink into the grey carpet.

Dr Robert Bug is standing at the window of his office and staring like a disgruntled grizzly out into the drizzling rain. He has the massive physique of a man in his fifties bursting at the seams, a square head with a powerful chin and thick brown hair. 'I didn't know that your father was a cameraman,' Bug says in place of a greeting.

'Were we talking that loudly?'

'In the news, you need good ears,' Bug replies without turning around.

'What was that "bad story" that Victor was just talking about?'

Not you, too, David thinks. 'Well, it was thirty years ago. Surely not something for the news.'

Bug turns around and looks at David. His dark, slightly bulging eyes sparkle. 'Seems mighty embarrassing for you and your family.'

I have no family, David thinks. He opens his mouth to give Bug a suitable answer, but his mobile vibrates at that very moment. *The bank!* is his first thought. He reaches into the inner pocket of his sports jacket and squints at the display on the off-chance that it's someone else. Some Berlin number, a landline. He hesitates because he thinks he recognises the first digits, but can't quite place them.

'Come on,' Bug says. 'I'll find out sooner or later anyway.'

David puts his mobile away again and looks over at Bug witheringly. 'Tell me, is it silly season or is there some other reason you're poking around in other people's private lives? Why did you actually ask me to come here?'

'Oh, screw it.' In mock despair, Bug throws up his paws and grins. 'It's an occupational disease. When I hear "bad story", I immediately think: good story. And the last good story was that Kristen thing that ran July.'

'Kristen? That model who went missing? Is there something new on that?'

Bug shakes his head. 'She is and remains missing without a trace. Along with all that haute couture la-di-da. No sign of life, no body, nothing.'

'Unbelievable,' David mutters.

'Yeah. That was a story. Something you could really grind out for six weeks across the media.' Bug sighs and envisions the headline. 'Supermodel Ciara Kristen missing from set without a trace. Along with a dozen haute couture dresses . . . actually, it's fortunate that she wasn't found, so we could speculate as to what happened to her. In a way, we should be grateful to the bastard.'

'You think someone kidnapped her?'

Bug snorts. 'My imagination occasionally runs wild, but I am much more of a realist. Kristen is dead and lying neatly buried somewhere in some forest. The woman earned one or two million a year – you don't just give that up to run off with a couple of unsellable haute couture dresses.'

'So, some kind of sex offender?'

'Sure,' says Bug. 'And I hope he doesn't let too much time pass before the next one.'

'Maybe you should try politics in the meantime,' David says drily.

'Politics!' Bug practically spits the word out on the desk. 'Yuck. We're a private station. Politics is for public broadcasters. No one wants that from us. Too complicated, too negative. We're more sensational. It's more personal! It's not about what a politician does. At most it's about how he does it, how often and with whom.'

David rolls his eyes. Bug's bad mood is obvious – it's just hard to figure out the reason for it. The mobile vibrates in the inner pocket of his jacket again. He automatically reaches for it. The same number as before. He tries to figure out how he recognises it. Some production company? The tax office? Some other government office? Suddenly, it occurs to him: *the police!* The first four digits are the number for the Berlin police. But why in the world would they want anything from him?

Bug uses the pause and takes a few steps through the open double doors into the waiting room of his office where he parks his wide bottom on his secretary's desk. 'Any calls, Karla?'

Karla Wiegand shakes her head. 'Just the usual . . .'

'What about Miss McNeal?'

'Nothing,' Wiegand replies.

David is still standing, mobile in hand, staring at the screen with a puzzled expression. The vibrating has stopped.

'Nothing? What is that supposed to mean, *nothing?*' Bug mimics his secretary. 'No time? No response?'

'No idea,' Karla Wiegand says. 'Maybe also *no interest.*'

Bug acknowledges the verbal jab with a shrug. 'And the Fire Alarm?'

'You mean Liz Anders, about the documentary? I still have no answer there. She has probably gone into seclusion doing research again.'

'Nonsense. I bumped into her at the Linus last night. She was still able to answer her phone then.' Bug rummages through his trouser pocket with his right hand and scratches his crotch. Deep wrinkles form on his forehead as he raises his eyebrows and turns back to David. 'What's happening with your Jaguar?'

David purses his lips and puts the phone away again. 'Can we get to the point? I'm sure my car isn't the reason you've summoned me here.'

'My goodness,' Bug grins. 'You're still not over the *Treasure Castle* settlement?'

'Spare me the gloating.'

'Boy, you're sensitive.' His eyes drift appraisingly across David's face, the narrow, slightly curved hook nose, the green-grey eyes. 'You stole the idea and were caught. Whatever. Put an end to it and –'

'I didn't steal anything, damn it!'

Bug shrugs. 'Well, then forget it. In entertainment, the ideas are all already out there. You just have to open you eyes and bam!' He snaps his fingers.

David doesn't respond.

'No ideas at the moment?'

'Nothing concrete,' David wavers. *And if I did, like hell would I discuss them with you.* He takes a sip of coffee and can feel his hand trembling with the cup. Goddamn it. He always lets Bug get to him.

The news director looks at him with narrowed eyes. 'Basically, I envy you,' Bug then sighs. 'If *I* want to have a good news story, then I have to kidnap a celebrity . . .' He stuffs his hands back into the already worn pockets of his expensive suit. 'Maybe that's it. "Mad news director kidnaps supermodel." Crime always has a draw. Look at Kristen. Why don't we just do something with crime in show business? The ratings would go through the roof. Guaranteed.'

'Because we know where the line is,' David replies. '*Crime* and *show* just don't go together.'

'You and your bullshit political correctness. I wonder how someone like you could even come up with an idea like *Treasure Castle.*'

'*Treasure Castle* dances around the line. Crime blows it up.' David tries to defend his recent TV show concept.

'Dancing around it. Blowing it up.' Bug shakes his head theatrically. 'You're just splitting hairs. As far as I'm concerned, your version stays behind the line when it works for you. But don't be so fussy.'

'What's that supposed to mean?'

'It means that I am asking you to think about a crime show.'

'Excuse me?' David's jaw drops. 'Have I understood correctly? *You* want to give *me* an assignment?'

'Think of it as an opportunity. You should be grateful.'

David turns on his heel and heads towards the door. 'If you need a sparring partner, then speak with our esteemed programme director. I am sure he will be thrilled . . . then he can pass the job on to me. Then at least it will have been assigned in the official way. Was that all?'

'I've already spoken with him,' Bug says impassively. His lips curl into a smirk.

David stops short. 'You *what*?'

'Since this morning, or to be more specific, since Vico von Braunsfeld was here, I am not only the news director, but also the *programme* director.'

David stiffens. He turns around in disbelief. He needs a moment for the full meaning of Bug's words to sink in.

'I see.' Bug grins widely. 'I've succeeded in surprising you. You are, in fact, the first to know. Please hold on to any congratulatory remarks until tomorrow when it's official. You know, he's old-fashioned that way.'

'Von Braunsfeld personally named you programme director?'

'He did so himself. And now I have his word and have to deliver.'

David opens his mouth, but no sound comes out. His stomach is in knots. Dr Robert Bug stands there like a nightmare in the flesh.

'So, if you want to keep your job, then you would be well advised to take my requests seriously.'

David looks at him, dumbfounded. He is incapable of responding.

Bug's BlackBerry shrieks and tears a hole in the silence. The grizzly pulls out his mobile. 'The editors,' he mutters. 'That's all, my dear. Let me know when you have something . . . and shut the door.' He waves his free hand as if to shoo a fly.

David flees out the door without closing it. The phone in his jacket begins vibrating a third time. Again, the same number. Again, the police.

Chapter 12

Gabriel stares blankly at the wall of holding cell 05 at the police station and presses the handset of the cordless phone to his ear. Pick up, damn it!

He won't pick up, Luke.

He will pick up. Maybe he wouldn't pick up if he knew it was me. But he doesn't.

And then? What will you say? Hi, it's me? The last time you heard from me was twenty years ago and everything was a bit ugly, but now I need help . . .

Rrriiinng . . . Rrriiinnng . . .

How many times do I have to tell you? He won't pick up . . . and he also won't help you.

He will! He is still my brother.

Oh yeah? I believe that you might still be his brother, but is he yours? I can't remember . . .

With every ring, the bare concrete walls of the cell move in closer. The small space depresses him and his worry about Liz makes him feel like he's choking.

He's been considering whether or not to call David for a long time. A while ago, he had seen his mobile number in Liz's contact list. And now he has the number memorised, having dialled it but not actually hit connect so many times.

Rrriinng . . . rrriinnng –

Then the sound abruptly stops. Ignored, Gabriel thinks and looks at the scratched display of the worn phone.

'What kind of a lawyer you got there?' A hoarse voice asks through the small window in the cell door. 'Never there when you need him, eh? Maybe it's time to look for a new one.' The face of a police officer appears in the window, with dark dead eyes and a drooping moustache, like a disappointed walrus. The officer demandingly waves his open hand in the window.

Gabriel hands him the telephone. 'I need to talk to Grell.'

'Right now you talk to me or no one at all,' the police officer replies coldly. A cleft lip is just visible under his moustache and thin pale blond hair sticks to his scalp. 'And besides, I would advise you to kindly address my superiors by the appropriate rank.' He slams the window shut and Gabriel sinks down on the saggy cot. The rough fabric of the brown blanket scrapes against his hands and stinks of old sweat.

His eyes drift, restlessly, across the cell walls and their waist-high lime green paint job, the drain in the middle of the cell, the sink and the steel toilet. Washable, unbreakable and unsuitable for suicide. Memories of Conradshöhe start crawling out of their caves.

Don't lose control, Luke. Think about something else. That's in the past – way, way in the past.

With painstaking effort, he pushes the images aside and then the agonising uncertainty suddenly returns: Where is Liz? What happened to her?

He stares at the green paint – there are hairline cracks, like veins under the skin. Green. Like Liz's eyes, only they're darker and wide-awake. And they can light up in such a way that the sharpness of her mind shines through.

Liz, the journalist. Back then, after the Berlinale, when she had run after him, he had assumed that it was only for the tape. The videotape that showed how he had humiliated a lumbering, coked-up boxing champion who had her by the throat. Nonetheless, he'd let himself be drawn in. At the time, the fact that she had mentioned David seemed to be reason enough to endure this woman for a few more minutes.

They had sat across from each other at the bar without saying a single word for the first ten minutes. Gabriel with a black coffee, Liz with a black tea. Neither of them took sugar. She'd looked at him with an expression that seemed like she was trying to see into his soul, sharp as a blade that splits everything apart.

Eventually, she looked down at her teacup. '*Treasure Castle* . . . does that mean anything to you?'

Gabriel furrowed his brow.

'The TV show . . .' Liz helped out.

'I don't watch any TV.'

'Never?'

'Never.'

'Why?'

'I can't stand watching television.'

Liz raised an eyebrow. 'There's a lot you can't stand.'

He shrugged.

'And David Naumann?' she asked. 'Can you not stand him either?'

Gabriel looked away.

Didn't I tell you, Luke? This was a shit idea! Why did you have to show up there?

I just wanted to see him. Just once, to see what David looks like, damn it.

Bollocks! Don't you understand where this is going?

Where?

Trouble! You're going to get yourself into trouble, obviously!

It had nothing to do with David. She needed help.

Help! Sure, of course. And you just had to jump in and save her arse.

All right, all right. I know.

You've got a real arse-saving problem. Now let's see how you get rid of her.

Gabriel looked up. Her green eyes dissected him. He knew it was better not to ask, but he couldn't help it. 'What's the story on David Naumann?'

'*Treasure Castle* – Naumann created it. The show is a real hit, a treasure hunt reality show. Pretty cleverly made. It currently only airs in Germany, but has been sold to fourteen other countries.'

Gabriel looked at her blankly.

'You really never watch TV, do you?' Liz laughed.

'I told you,' Gabriel replied. When she smiled, her face suddenly looked much softer.

Pull yourself together, Luke. She is a goddamned reporter. She wants the tape. Just the tape.

'Is that why you interviewed him?'

Liz nodded. 'More or less. For me it was more about the lawsuit.'

'What kind of lawsuit?'

'Well, the show is really a huge success, but the royalties, that is, the copyrights and intellectual property were claimed by someone else. Suddenly they were saying that Naumann copied it, stole the idea. It could get him into real trouble. It comes to several million.'

Several million? Gabriel struggled to keep his face as expressionless as possible. 'And how does it look for him?'

Liz shrugged. 'Why are you so interested in Naumann? How do you know him?'

'It's a long story,' Gabriel muttered.'

'Oh, come on,' Liz pressed, '*quid pro quo*.'

'Quid pro what?'

Liz smiled. 'This for that. I told you something, so now you have to tell me something.'

Gabriel grimaced.

'OK,' Liz said. 'As far as I'm concerned, we don't have to talk.'

Gabriel considered it a moment, and then reluctantly blurted something out. 'It's been a long time, we were just kids. I saved him from a burning house.'

Liz's eyes widened. 'Well, you seem to be ahead of the pack when it comes to rescues.'

Gabriel acknowledged her reply with a crooked smile.

Now, in retrospect, the sentence feels like a jab in the pit of his stomach. He remembers the helplessness and fear that were in Liz's voice last night.

He gets up, walks over to the heavy pale-grey metal door that has been painted over several times and pounds on it with his fists, but the pain in his right shoulder forces him to stop after the first few blows.

A moment later, the small window opens. The walrus is staring back at him with lifeless eyes.

'Commissioner Grell,' Gabriel says and strains to maintain the friendliest tone he can put on. 'I would like to speak with Commissioner Grell.'

An ugly smile flits across the face of the policeman. 'And why is that?'

'I'm begging you, we've been through all of this already. For the same reason as last night. I have to get out of here. I have nothing to do with the dead man in the park and I can prove it.'

'Listen, everyone wants to get out of here. And no one here has anything to do with anything. We're going in circles. But I'll say it again anyway: if you want to get out of here, then tell me what you know and then I will decide whether or not to tell Commissioner Grell.'

Always talk to the boss, never with the errand boy, that was one of Yuri Sarkov's golden rules. They usually worked. Just not here and now. 'All right,' Gabriel says, straining to remain in control. 'The main thing is that you let him know *quickly*.'

'We'll see about that,' the walrus replies. A greasy blond strand of hair falls in his face and he clumsily pushes it back. 'So, what now?'

'The dead man in the park,' Gabriel says. 'When he was killed, I was in Lichterfelde.'

The walrus raises his eyebrows. Wrinkles fold together on his blotchy forehead. 'Oh no. And when was the man murdered, in your opinion?'

'Between eleven thirty and twelve –'

'And how do you know that? Are you a doctor?' The walrus interrupts.

'No,' Gabriel growls, 'but it wasn't really that difficult to figure out.'

The officer snorts in disbelief. 'And where exactly were you between eleven thirty and twelve?'

'In Lichterfelde, like I said. At Kadettenweg 107. It's at least half an hour away from the park by car. There was an alarm at Python, the security company that I work for.'

'And did you see someone at the house on Kadettenweg?'

'No, not exactly. But I left the Python office at eleven thirty and arrived at the house at a quarter to twelve.'

'Did you shut off the alarm? Is there an electronic log or something?'

Gabriel hesitated. 'No. I didn't get to it. I went inside, there were footprints in the house, it looked like a break-in. Someone had been in the house. The gate to the street and the front door were both open. I went down to the cellar to the alarm system. Strangely, there was a dress hanging beside it, it looked new – a black, glittery, expensive fabric. Then my girlfriend called. She was in urgent need of help, she was badly hurt, someone had attacked her in Friedrichshain Park. Then I left right away.'

'And you didn't turn off the alarm?'

'No.'

The walrus sniffs air in through his nostrils. The drooping whiskers don't move in the slightest. 'And witnesses? Is there anyone who can attest to that?'

'Bert Cogan, my colleague at the office. And my boss, Yuri Sarkov. I called him at twenty past eleven when I was with Cogan in the office.'

'Anyone else?'

Gabriel thinks of the accident and hesitates a moment. Then he sighs. 'Two streets after the house on Kadettenweg, I had a little accident,' he mutters. 'A Jaguar, dark blue. A woman and a man. She had a leopard-print jacket. He was sitting at the wheel. He ignored my right of way and I rushed through.'

'Did you speak with them?'

'No,' Gabriel says and stares off to the side at the wall. 'It was just body damage. I drove on immediately. But I am sure that the woman saw me.'

The policeman looks at him, motionless. 'You know that's a hit-and-run?'

Gabriel nods, but doesn't say a word.

'Did you take down the number plate?'

Gabriel shakes his head.

The walrus snorts abruptly. 'All right. We'll look into this and I'll talk to Commissioner Grell. But even if it all checks out, you have a problem. The officer you knocked out is still in the hospital.' He turns and goes to close the small window in the door.

'Wait, my phone call,' Gabriel cries.

The officer stops and looks at him with hostility. He reluctantly hands him the phone. 'See to it that you reach the guy. But I'll tell you one thing: if your story doesn't check out, then you're going to need more than a lawyer to get you out of here.'

Gabriel takes the greasy receiver. If not David, then a lawyer. But a lawyer is not what he needs at the moment. He thinks of Liz again, he sees her face in front of him, her smooth red hair pointing in all directions.

You're a fucking idiot, Luke.

Why? Because I told the pigs about the hit and run?

Don't take me for stupid. You know exactly what I mean.

Shut up! Gabriel whispers.

I only want to help.

Chapter 13

Berlin – 2 September, 10.42 a.m.

David's stomach is in knots. Too much coffee. Too much Bug. In the WC, he examines his reflection. The creased white shirt, the pale face, the intense green eyes like Liz's and the deepening wrinkles around his mouth. He tries to smile, even though he doesn't feel up to it. Even that, he finds, is visible on his face.

He pushes his shirt and jacket sleeves up, turns on the cold water and lets it run over his throbbing veins. When a co-worker enters the toilet, he stops and acts as if he'd just rinsed the soap from his hands.

The shortest path to his desk leads past Bug's office, so he takes a detour through the station's post-production department, a long corridor with doors on both sides like a chicken coop; the editing suites.

Bits of interviews buzz through the air. In editing suite eight, a news report about Pope Benedict is being cut. Directly across the hall in suite fifteen, a pair of enlarged breasts flickers across the screens. And in seven, a prominent debt counsellor is debating with a banker. David smiles bitterly.

He pushes open the door between post-production and graphics and his pocket starts vibrating again. Without slowing his pace, he tries to fish out his mobile, but it's lodged sideways in his inner pocket. David squints down at it and tugs at the vibrating object, then hits his head against something – something hard. A dull, bony sound reverberates through his skull. He tumbles forward, knocks something over and trips over it. 'Shit! What . . .'

'Ouch!'

David rubs his aching skull. A pair of brown eyes glares at him angrily. Shona McNeal is sitting on the floor in the middle of the corridor. She is also rubbing her head. 'Shit! Do I have to paint a zebra crossing here to get safely to the other side?' She groans and feels around her scalp through her brown mane.

'I'm sorry. My phone . . .' He reaches back into his pocket, but the phone is silent. He looks at her, embarrassed.

Shona McNeal reaches her hand out without saying a word. David takes it and pulls her up. Standing in front of him, she shakes her head of unruly brown curls. A smile plays around her mouth. 'Is that your way of getting rid of unwanted colleagues?'

'Why unwanted?' David asks.

'I haven't heard from you since the last job, I thought –'

'Nonsense,' David says. 'It was fine. We took it without any corrections or changes. You saw the show.'

'Sure, I did.' Shona looks down at herself and adjusts her casual button-down shirt. Her bra flashes into sight. 'It just would've been nice to hear something ahead of time.'

'But you know that I liked the trailer.'

Shona rolls her eyes. 'Oh, man! You guys, you could really drive someone round the bend.'

'Honestly. I said that I liked it,' David insists and tries to focus on her face. Just no lower.

'*Said?* You mean this thing with words where one person talks to another? Like, for example "cool intro" or "good work"? She smiles teasingly and shakes her head. 'Sorry, but I don't remember that.'

David shrugs. He can't actually remember what had come out of his mouth on that day – or what hadn't. He had been far too busy watching Shona at work – her delicate hands designing the graphics for this show with ease and precision. He hadn't had to say much, just nod. The only real strain had been keeping his eyes from drifting back down to her cleavage, like now. He had been fascinated by how it seemed like she wasn't even trying to get attention. The loose shirt suited her perfectly, matching in style her Converse and the pilot's watch on her wrist. She seemed like she needed a lot of air on her skin in order to breathe, rather than to seduce. And that made it all the crazier that she had got involved with that egomaniacal arsehole.

When he realises where his eyes have landed again, he quickly looks up and blushes.

'Good. At least you're embarrassed in hindsight,' she remarks with a biting tone.

What exactly does she mean by that now? David hates blushing. Time to counter. 'Were you worried?'

'Worried? Why?'

'Because of the similarities with the *Mystix* design,' David says, denying himself a grin when he sees her reaction to his mention of their rival's TV show format.

'Shit,' Shona mutters. 'I thought no one noticed.'

'It's OK. Everyone here steals from everyone else.'

'So, happy then?'

David manages a nod with just the right amount of vagueness.

'Wow,' Shona tilts her head. 'What a great compliment! All that's left now is for you to buy me a whole cube of sugar for my coffee.

David is forced to laugh for the first time all day. 'I would do it in an instant, but I was just upstairs,' he nods in the direction of the executive offices, 'and I get the impression that Mr News is anxiously awaiting a meeting with you and I don't want to get on his bad side. You know how he can be.'

Shona's expression suddenly stiffens.

'Have I said something wrong?' David asks.

'It seems someone else was in his way,' Shona mutters with a strange inflection.

'What's that?'

'Oh,' Shona says, embarrassed. 'It probably hasn't got around yet. Funny. I somehow thought it wouldn't happen to me . . .'

David looks at her, perplexed. He needs a moment to process what he's just heard. 'Bug is like a stray dog,' he says slowly. 'He has to pee on every damned tree and doesn't understand that the most beautiful tree in the city is standing right outside his door.'

Shona frowns, but then she laughs. 'Well, that was the shittiest and the nicest compliment of the day. And all in one sentence. I would say that sugar cube is now well overdue.'

David can tell his cheeks are turning red and he feels like a schoolboy. Just then, his mobile vibrates again.

Chapter 14

Berlin – 2 September, 10:51 a.m.

'If it doesn't work out, then that's it with the lawyer, understood?' the police officer grumbles.

Gabriel sits there with the receiver pressed to his ear, stares at the bleak cell floor and imagines the walrus going moustache first into a shredder.

Suddenly, there's a click on the line and he holds his breath.

'Naumann,' a man's voice answers. David's voice was never particularly deep, but it sounds surprisingly grown up.

'Hello,' Gabriel says with a husky voice. 'It's me.'

There is silence on the other end of the line.

'David?' Don't hang up now, Gabriel thinks.

More silence. And then, after an eternity: '*Gabriel? Is that you?*'

'Yes.'

David's breath sounds like a wave breaking.

'Surprised?' Gabriel asks woodenly.

'I . . . no. Shocked is more like it.'

'Wrote me off long ago, right?'

Silence.

'Well, you know,' Gabriel mumbles, 'It's OK. I'm not complaining.'

'How . . . how are you?' David asks.

Gabriel opens his mouth and wonders what to say next when there's a pounding on the cell door. The walrus holds his wristwatch up to the window and impatiently taps against the tempered glass with a fingernail.

'Listen, David,' Gabriel says quickly. 'That's not relevant right now. I have to –'

'*Where the hell have you been?*' bursts out of David's mouth. 'I thought you were – I mean . . . it's like you fell off the edge of the earth. The last time we saw each other was in Conradshöhe. How long ago was that? Twenty years? And now you come out of the woodwork as if nothing happened?'

'David, it's important, listen! I have a problem, I –'

'You always have a problem,' David says dismissively.

Gabriel's lips narrow. 'It's not about me. It's my girlfriend. She was attacked in Friedrichshain Park and now she's missing.'

'That's usually a matter for the police.'

'You know my opinion of them.'

'That's the reason you're not there,' David says. 'The police. Otherwise you'd be there straightaway, right?'

Gabriel goes silent. His eyes wander to the window in the cell door, which is covered on the other side by the green of the uniform jacket.

'What do you want from me, Gabriel? I mean, if your girlfriend's disappeared, then why don't you look for her? What does this have to do with me?'

'You don't have to go looking for her, for heaven's sake. I just need someone to make a few calls to hospitals and other addresses. I'm worried.'

'Someone,' David repeats flatly. Gabriel could swear that he just shook his head. 'You need to call someone else.'

Gabriel bites his lip. 'No, of course not. I need *you!*'

'And why don't you ring them yourself?' David asks.

'Because I . . . I'm stuck.'

There is an uncomfortable pause. 'You're stuck?'

'Not what you think, don't worry. I just had a little disagreement with –'

'Oh no,' David groans. 'You're in jail, right?'

'No, not in jail,' Gabriel hastens to say. 'Just a holding cell at the police station. A misunderstanding, nothing more. I'll be out of here again soon.'

'Of course, a misunderstanding,' David sighs. 'What did you do?'

'That doesn't –'

'Matter?' David interrupts, irritated. 'Then what does matter to you? After spending twenty years getting used to the fact that you were dead or who knows what, you just call me up from jail and I'm supposed to go looking for your missing girlfriend? Goddamn it! Have you broken out of the nuthouse? Or are you stoned? Do you know how mad that is?'

Nuthouse. Gabriel purses his lips. 'You don't believe me,' he says bitterly.

He only hears David's breathing.

'OK,' David says. 'I'm sorry about the nuthouse thing. But to be honest, I don't know what to believe. Last time I saw you, they had to put you in a straitjacket. You weren't sane any more.'

'They pumped me full of drugs.'

'You pumped yourself full of drugs for years.'

'Oh, so that's what happened! Thanks for explaining it to me!' Gabriel's stomach burns with rage. 'And even if that were the case, could you blame me, considering what they did to me?'

'I don't think they had a choice . . .'

'*I* had no choice. *Me!*' Gabriel says. We're going in circles, he thinks. As soon as we begin talking to each other again, we're going in circles. 'David, listen. Forget what happened. I've been clean for almost nineteen years. You have to believe me. Please.'

David says nothing.

The silence roars like waves on a beach.

'Do you go to the grave sometimes?' David asks.

Gabriel cringes. The question came suddenly, like an attack in a dark alley. 'Sometimes,' he says. He actually hadn't been there a single time since the funeral. 'And you?'

'Every two or three months.'

For a fleeting moment, the old familiarity is back, their shared bedroom with its light-blue walls and the dormer and the rain pattering against it. They are both under their blankets. The poster of Luke hangs on the wall; the plastic lightsabres are on the shelf. Everything is so clear, so present, taking him back to a previous life. A life with posters, shelves and beds. And parents. He gets choked up and needs to clear his throat. 'Help me, David. Please.'

'OK,' David says. 'I'll try.'

Gabriel is dizzy with relief.

'Do you know,' David's words are drawn out, 'that this is the first time you've ever actually *asked* me for something?'

'What?'

'Seriously, I think that was the most reasonable thing I've ever heard come out of your mouth in my whole life.'

Stunned, Gabriel goes quiet.

'When was she attacked?'

'Last night, around midnight in Friedrichshain.'

'Hmm, Friedrichshain. Vivantes Hospital is right by the park there.'

Gabriel groans. 'Damn it. I should have thought of that much sooner.'

'Maybe she ended up there. It would certainly be the most obvious place. I will drop by. What's her name?'

'Liz Anders.'

'Liz Anders?' Deathly silence. 'Surely not *the* Liz Anders?'

Gabriel considers just saying yes, but it somehow seems unsuitable. He can hear his brother thinking on the other end of the line. The individual thoughts fall like dominoes. Click. Click. Click.

'Are you dating Liz Anders?' David repeats. 'The journalist? Does that mean you've been living here in Berlin for a while?'

'Yes.'

'How long?'

'How long I've been living in Berlin? Or –'

'My god, yes. It's like pulling teeth.

'I never left,' Gabriel says.

Another domino. Click. David is now probably considering how Gabriel managed to avoid running into him for twenty years.

'That's . . . crazy,' David mutters. 'I –'

'OK. Time's up,' the police officer interrupts the conversation from outside the cell. 'Time's up. That's enough.' His hand knocks on the narrow shelf in the window where plates and other things are usually placed.

'I have to go,' Gabriel says hastily. 'I'll be in touch as soon as –'

'Hey. I said that's it. Now.' The walrus pounds on the door with the flat of his hand several times.

'Yeah, yeah, OK,' Gabriel says and hands him the handset through the small opening.

David's voice is still audible through the speaker.

'Hello?' The walrus asks. 'Who's there?'

He listens for a moment and then snorts with contempt. 'Suspected murder,' he bleats into the handset and then hangs up.

Suspected murder. The sentence sends a chill down Gabriel's spine, even though he knows how absurd and unfounded it all is.

'And that there was supposed to be a lawyer?' The walrus asks.

'I don't need a fucking lawyer,' Gabriel says.

The officer shakes his head as if someone had just tried to explain that the sun goes around the earth. With a swift movement, he closes the window in the door.

Listen, listen, echoes in his head. *Sure, the pig is a fool. But against you, the porker is a real lightweight.*

Leave me alone.

That's what it's all about, Lucky Luke. Peace. I want it, too. Only, what you're doing is unfortunately best suited to wasting away in here. 'I don't need a lawyer!' What bullshit! Do you think that David is going to get us out of here? Now that the pig told him it's about a murder?

The main thing is that David look after Liz.

Liz! If I have to hear that name again! You're killing us, you know that?

Chapter 15

David stands in the middle of the corridor. He puts the mobile back in his jacket. *Suspected murder.*

He looks over to Shona, but she's gone. Snippets of an interview repeat over and over again from one of the cutting rooms.

Gabriel.

How often had he imagined him dead, dead of an overdose or locked away forever in an institution or prison? Yes, he had written him off. That is, at least as often as he had imagined what it would be like if his brother were still alive, if he were in his right mind and if he could talk with him, like before that horrible night – the night that destroyed their whole lives.

And now this!

Gabriel has been living in Berlin this whole time. And not only that, but he's with Liz Anders. He tries to imagine the two of them together, but he can't – just the thought of it ties his brain in knots.

Someone who hates television and a television journalist? The last documentary that David saw by Liz Anders was *The Von Braunsfeld Story*, three forty-five-minute episodes about the septuagenarian billionaire who had avoided any public appearances for years. The fact that she had been permitted to film in Victor von Braunsfeld's mansion on the exclusive island of Schwanenwerder was a sensation – no, it was an enigma. Not to mention the interview. Von Braunsfeld had quite success-fully avoided the press for a long time because, among other things, a large part of the media belonged to him. The surpris-ingly cosy relationship between Liz Anders and Victor von Braunsfeld had triggered a lot of speculation in the media. That being said, anyone who knew Liz knew that she not only had a knack for stepping on people's toes, but also for 'unlocking' people. The fact that Liz Anders had a relationship with von Braunsfeld seems absurd enough, David thinks, but it's even more absurd to imagine her with Gabriel.

'Everything all right?' Shona pokes her head out of her edit-ing room and looks at him, concerned. 'You look as if you've seen a ghost.'

Touché. David looks into her eyes and feels himself getting lost in them. Brown eyes with small, light flecks, like amber. 'I . . . I have to go. To the hospital.'

Shona's eyebrows move together ever so slightly. Then she nods and gets the bag with her MacBook from the editing room. 'Are there sugar cubes to eat at the hospital too? Then I'll take you there.'

'What?' David looks at her, confused. 'I'm still not entirely sure which hospital, I have to call first.'

'If the attack,' Shona says slowly, 'was in Friedrichshain, then she definitely was taken to Vivantes Hospital. It's right around the corner. When there's an emergency, they always take them to the closest hospital.'

David takes a long look at her.

Shona shrugs. 'You were pretty loud.'

'It's OK,' David mutters. 'I'll drive myself . . .'

'Do you have your Jaguar again?'

David can feel himself blushing again and Shona immediately holds her tongue.

Chapter 16

Berlin – 2 September, 11.38 a.m.

Gabriel paces next to the bed. The rock-hard cell floor under his feet is worn away and shiny – decades' worth of restlessness and doubt worn into its surface, like an image of his own thoughts, always pacing in front of the same wall.

Where is Liz? Pace back and forth and repeat: where is Liz? Back and forth, and so on. . .

When he punches the concrete wall in frustration, his shoulder responds with shooting pain. At least it's a distraction.

Then he hears something rattle in the lock in the door. With a metallic grinding, the outer latch is unlocked and the cell door swings open. The walrus adopts a wide stance in the doorway. Beside him is a burly bow-legged man with a few thin blond hairs on his head, a thick neck and a protruding jaw that gnaws away on a piece of chewing gum.

'Out,' the walrus says and gestures towards the hallway with his head. There are breadcrumbs in his moustache. 'The boss wants to see you.'

'Finally,' Gabriel groans. He steps out of the cell into the corridor where the bulky man grabs him by the upper arm. He winces from the searing pain in his shoulder.

The two officers lead him past several cells, through a security door and then a bare room with smoothly plastered blotchy grey walls and a brownish-yellow linoleum floor. In the middle of the room there is a table with a steel frame and a scratched wooden surface. On top, there is a microphone connected to a recording device with a long knotted cord. The hard plastic chairs look about as inviting as coarse sandpaper. There is a dented lamp hanging over the table that looks like it comes from before the Wall came down.

The burly man gestures with his chin at the first of the two chairs, shuts the door and sits down on a third chair beside it.

Gabriel sits at the table with the door behind him. The chair makes a crunching sound beneath him and is even more uncomfortable than it looks. Behind him, the officer noisily chews his gum. The sound puts Gabriel on edge.

Twenty minutes later, Grell waltzes into the room. A haze of nicotine, cheap aftershave and general irritation waft past Gabriel.

'Mr Naumann,' Grell says, letting all of his weight sink into the creaking chair and fixing his eyes on Gabriel. He is wearing the same corduroy suit as last night. The whites of his eyes are broken up by burst capillaries and beneath them are deep, dark red shadows. He turns on the recording device without taking his eyes off Gabriel and talks into the microphone without any transition. 'Document number 1443 27-1000/5, police department 5, section 51, interrogation for the case of the Pit Münchmaier murder.' Then he concluded with the date, time and his and Gabriel's names.

'Mr Naumann, where is your lawyer?'

'I don't need one,' Gabriel says, despite the sinking feeling in his stomach.

Grell looks at him as if his sanity were in question. 'Fine,' he finally says, sighs and shrugs. 'Makes things easier.' A joyless smile forms across his lips. 'Mr Naumann, last night a young man was murdered in Friedrichshain Park. Pit Münchmaier,' he pauses a moment and looks down into a small, tattered notebook. 'Twenty-four years old, unemployed, living in Berlin. Did you know the young man?'

'No.'

'Astonishingly, you were able to tell my colleague exactly when the murder happened. Where exactly were you between eleven-thirty and midnight?'

'At the house on Kadettenweg in Lichterfeld, or on my way there, rather. Around a quarter past eleven, there was an alarm at Python from Kadettenweg 107. I got in the company car and left straight away.'

'Are there witnesses?'

'As I already told your colleague: Burt Cogan, a co-worker at Python, and Yuri Sarkov, my boss,' Gabriel explains. It's clear to him that Grell already knows the answers, but he needs them again as part of the official interrogation.

Grell nods and doesn't break eye contact. 'Describe the conditions at the house when you found it?'

'The gate was open, the red warning light was on and the front door was open. The house is uninhabited. There were footprints inside and someone had presumably tampered with the safe over the fireplace.'

'A safe?'

'Yes. There was a picture hanging above the mantel and a safe behind it.'

'And what do you mean by "tampered with"?'

Gabriel shrugged. 'The safe was open and empty. I can't tell you anything more than that.'

'Hmm. Open and empty,' Grell says. 'And you mentioned an expensive, sparkly dress down in the cellar?'

'Yes, directly beside the alarm system.'

'Hmm. A strange location for a dress.' Grell scratches his bald head and then strokes it with the flat of his hand, as if he were petting a dog. 'You know what else is strange? We found no dress there. Can you explain that to me?'

Gabriel furrows his brow. 'No idea.'

'Hmm,' Grell repeats. 'Then where were you when you made the emergency call regarding Ms Anders?'

'Still at the house on Kadettenweg.'

'And then?'

'I dropped everything and want to the park. The police were already there. When I saw the body, I thought it was my girlfriend at first.'

'But it was not Ms Anders. Were you surprised?'

'Surprised? I was relieved. Listen, I'm worried as hell. Liz is somewhere out there and no one knows where. Something's happened to her. She is not the type to call and create a panic without good reason.'

Grell nods slowly, thinking. 'That might very well be, but –'

'Why don't you just drive past her place and check it out?' Gabriel asks heatedly. 'Or call her?'

'If it helps you to know,' Grell replies, 'we *were* there. Cotheniusstrasse, right? And we also called.'

Gabriel's heart starts pounding. 'And?'

'Well, she wasn't there.'

'So you believe me now?'

Grell scratches his neck. 'The problem is her voicemail. "This is Liz Anders. I am out on research and can't call back at present. Please leave a message."'

Gabriel groans and runs his hands across his face. 'She always has that message. Anyone who knows her knows that you just leave a message and she'll call back.'

'But you admit that Ms Anders likes to disappear for a few days or weeks at times?

Gabriel stares at Grell angrily. 'So you only react when bodies are washed ashore, right?'

'Like Mr Münchmaier, you mean?'

Gabriel holds his tongue. Under the table, he wraps his left hand around his right wrist, as if to hold himself down.

Grell smiles as if he has X-ray eyes and can see through the tabletop. 'When you left the house on Kadettenweg,' he says in a low voice, 'did you actually turn off the alarm system?'

'No.'

Grell looks him over without a word. Then he leans forward across the table and stares at Gabriel through narrowed eyes. The lamp above them burns brightly on his bald head, casting dark shadows across his face. The shadow from Grell's nose splits his fleshy lips into two halves. 'And how do you explain that the alarm system was turned off last night?'

'No idea.'

'A few too many "no ideas" for my taste,' Grell says softly. 'And the front door was also closed, *locked* even. Just like the gate.'

Gabriel looks at him, dumbfounded. He opens his mouth and wants to say something, but then closes it again quickly.

'And you know what your boss Mr Sarkov told me? He had expressly sent your colleague Cogan to the house on Kadettenweg and not you!' Grell leans heavily back into his chair. His face looks like a pale stony moon in the semi-darkness.

'I know,' Gabriel mutters. 'But I went anyway. Cogan has problems with his legs.'

'With his legs, aha,' Grell says. 'That wasn't mentioned at all. He only said that he went to the address on Kadettenweg, that there were no particular incidents, that he'd turned off the alarm system, closed the doors and then left.'

'Bullshit,' Gabriel says hoarsely. 'He's just scared that Sarkov will find out that he didn't go. If he were sitting here, he'd be telling you a different story.'

'Because then he would be scared of you?' Grell asks and stares at him with a piercing and calculating expression.

'No, damn it. Because that's what happened,' Gabriel says.

Motionless, Grell considers him from the semi-darkness. The soft rhythmic sound of chewing can be heard – the burly man and his gum.

'So, to summarise,' Grell whispers with feigned friendliness. 'We have witnesses who say Cogan went to Kadettenweg and not you. We have a bunch of details that you described completely differently to how we found them. And we have a black dress in the cellar that apparently only exists in your vivid imagination. But you continue to claim that your version is the truth and all others are wrong, right?'

Gabriel nods.

Grell's massive upper body springs forward. The light bulb in the lamp shakes from the sudden movement. 'Then please explain to me how you could name the time of death so precisely. Are you clairvoyant? Or did you happen to look at a clock when you were slitting Mr Münchmaier's throat?'

'No,' Gabriel says. His whole body cramps up. 'Neither of those things. But I touched your goddamned corpse! And a body is already cold after thirty minutes, but rigor mortis only sets in after an hour. Your body was cold, but not rigid. If you can also read a clock, then you don't need to be a genius to estimate the time of death. Happy?'

Grell purses his lips.

'Listen,' Gabriel says, struggling to maintain composure, 'your colleague probably also told you that I had an accident on the way. You just have to find the people with the Jaguar. That will take you five minutes, no more. Just go through all of the reports from yesterday from between eleven and twelve o'clock. The two of them will sure as hell recognise me.'

Grell nods thoughtfully and then smiles. 'Oh, right, the whole incident of the hit-and-run. I almost forgot.'

Gabriel leans back and exhales. He feels the tension leave his body. Better a hit-and-run than a murder.

'Indeed,' Grell says. 'It actually did take less than five minutes. But I have to disappoint you. No report to be found. No accident. Nothing.'

'*What?*' Gabriel stares at the commissioner in disbelief. 'And why do you think my wing looks like a piece of scrap?'

'That could've happened a long time ago.' Grell's smile congeals into a cynical grimace. 'An accident that does not exist. A fairytale dress that simply disappears. Doors that close themselves . . . to be quite honest, either you're having hallucinations or you're making fun of me, my friend.'

Gabriel's eyes flicker for a moment. 'I don't know what this is,' he finally says softly, but I can't shake the feeling that you want to pin it all on me.'

'Pin it on you? You came in here with your cock and bull story. Not to mention resisting authority . . . Just reading your file, there's no question about it. And quite frankly, with all this rubbish you're telling us here, I'm not even sure any more if you should be locked away in a normal cell.'

'What's that supposed to mean?' Gabriel asks flatly, although he knows very well what Grell is getting at.

'It was a bit of an effort finding someone who still remembers you. After all, it was twenty years ago. The only member of staff that I could find from back then who still practises is Dr Armin Dressler.'

Gabriel's whole body stiffens.

Grell's dark, lifeless eyes bore ruthlessly into his own. 'He was immediately willing to give up some of his time to take a look at you again. Tomorrow morning around seven, before going to work, he'll be here. Then we'll see.'

Instantly, like a Pavlovian reflex, Gabriel is dizzy and his hands begin to tremble.

Didn't I tell you, Luke, the voice howls. *Never lose control. Never.*

Chapter 17

Nowhere – 2 September

Liz is wrapped in cotton that must be a metre thick. It absorbs everything but a few faint sounds. Her nose is thick and swollen on her face. She is hooked up to wires and tubes.

Her senses are numb, frozen.

She knows that she has eyes. She has tried to open them, but it's like they're sewn shut. She can see images flit past like momentary flashes on the backs of her eyelids.

Like the steel arm that strangled her. She tries to reach for a shiny white phone, but always grabs at the nothingness that surrounds her. A heavy boot coming down on her face, getting closer, getting larger. She knows that it hurts when the boot reaches her face, but she feels nothing. She doesn't even feel her stomach where her child should be.

And suddenly she feels something.

Something warm, exactly over the area where her eyes should be. All of her senses, her entire body focuses on the source of the warmth, concentrates on this single point, like a lost diver being saved by the beam of light leading the way up and out of the darkness at the bottom of the lake.

Suddenly, she knows what it is: a hand. A hand on her forehead.

She can hear something beeping as quietly as a whisper. She can hear something rustling. She gets cold and feels metal around her body.

Her skin flinches and then the sheet rustles back over her.

Now. Liz summons all of her strength for this little bit of movement. Her eyelids flutter.

'Ssshhh,' she hears a woman's voice.

Liz pushes her lids apart. The light explodes in her eyes. She has to blink immediately. A shadowy figure is silhouetted against a light wall. Her light-coloured hospital gown and shoulder-length blond hair make her seem almost invisible in the white room. Her gaze rests on a video monitor with graphs and figures that is beeping right beside her bed.

Thank god! A hospital.

The nurse looks at her. 'Hello? Can you hear me?' Her voice sounds rough and strangely sad.

Liz nods. *Where am I?* she wants to ask, but the tube in her throat prevents her from speaking.

The nurse smiles. A joyless smile, but a smile. 'You had to be ventilated. That's why there's a tube in your throat.'

Liz nods again.

Her pupils slowly get accustomed to the light. Now the room looks darker to her. Her eyes scan the space and the walls. No windows, no flowers, no other bed. Still, at least they put her in a private room. She avoids hospitals like the plague, but she would hate it more if she had to be share her room with other people. The constant visitors, strange snoring, strange coughing . . . *thank you, Gabriel.*

But where is he? Where is Gabriel?

She tries to turn a little to the right – towards the door. A sharp pain at the top of her ribs stops her. Suddenly, she is frightened to the core. *The baby! What happened to the baby?*

She strains to lift her right hand and feel her stomach. The needle presses into her arm.

'I think the baby is all right,' the nurse says flatly. Her grey eyes rest on Liz's stomach.

Thank god! But why does her 'all right' sound like nothing is right?

'He will be here soon, he just has to make some calls,' the nurse whispers.

'Just don't move around, that would be best.'

Don't move around? Liz almost has to laugh. It's not like she could anyway. But why is the nurse whispering? And who is coming? Gabriel? The doctor?

Exhausted, she closes her eyes and slowly dozes off.

Chapter 18

Berlin – 2 September, 12.59 p.m.

'We can't park here, you have to go back. The visitor car park was full –'

Shona abruptly hits the brakes and spins the steering wheel to the left. 'That's why,' she says, steering the car over the high kerb and onto the landscaped lawn between two young trees, 'I have a jeep.'

The diesel engine of the ocean-blue Defender stops with a gurgle. 'You all right? Want to go in alone?'

David looks through the windscreen directly at the three-storey brick building. Vivantes Hospital Friedrichshain. It makes him anxious. Then he sighs and tenses his shoulders. 'If you'd like, you're welcome to come.'

He gets out and swings the passenger door to Shona's Land Rover shut. A cold gust of wind sweeps across the car roof, blowing dust in his face.

'So, tell me, have I understood correctly?' Shona asks and comes around the angular front bonnet of the car. 'It has to do with Liz Anders? *The* Liz Anders?'

David looks surprised. 'You know her?'

'Well, you can hardly avoid the name if you work in television. Ms Journalism. The Fire Alarm. What happened to her?'

'Apparently she was attacked,' David says, and speeds up his pace. The sky is grey above the hospital. The wide glass doors throw their reflection back at them and slide open with a soft hiss. The lobby is huge and white like a glacier. It smells of floor wax and sterility. He wishes he could turn around and leave. Hospitals and clinics of any kind still give him the same feeling as back then. Even though he had only been seven years old, every detail was seared into his brain, from the nurse's nametag to the burnt smell of his pyjamas that he never wanted to take off under any circumstances.

He blinks for a second and the smell leaves his head. There is a long beechwood counter with a mountain of a man sitting atop his throne behind it. David moves directly towards him.

'And what does all of this have to do with you?' Shona asks.

'With me, nothing. It's my brother. Apparently Liz Anders is my brother's girlfriend.'

'So you're a proper television family. Do your parents also work at the station?'

David's face darkens. 'My parents are dead.'

'Oh . . . I'm sorry,' Shona says. 'I had no idea.'

'It's OK.' He presses his lips together. *Nothing is OK*. Suddenly, everything is back. The images swirl around him, more vivid than they'd been in years. The fresh flowing blood, the two bodies, the smoke burning his eyes and the stench. He hears a muffled hammering echoing from the cellar. Gabriel becomes fixated by his hand. *I need to get out of here*. His short, thin fingers are ice cold and slippery, he's wearing his favourite pyjamas with Luke Skywalker on the front, the same ones that Gabriel had, too – just a few sizes smaller. Mum lies there, dark gaping craters in her head and chest, her bright eyes stare blankly at the ceiling, her limbs strangely twisted – like Father's, who is floating on a large, dark-red puddle. Everything is heavy and being pulled downwards as if there were quicksand below. Gabriel screams and pulls him closer, but he –

'Can I help you?' an exasperated voice asks. David shakes off the memories. The attendant sits in front of him and stares back, black pupils like pinpricks against his pale face.

'Uh, yes. Excuse me, we're looking for a Ms Liz Anders. Is she here?'

'The man squints. 'Anders? I've heard the name before, hang on.' He looks at his screen and types the word into a search box.

'She was attacked last night and was probably brought here.'

'Mhm,' the attendant grumbles and types something else in the search box.

'So where is she?'

'Well, not here in any case.'

'She *isn't* here? Are you sure?'

'If I say she isn't here, then she isn't here.'

'Any idea of where she could've been taken?'

'Nah. No idea at all.'

'Excuse me,' Shona says and leans just far enough over the counter so that her cleavage is right at the attendant's eye line. 'Tell me, the emergency call centre, wouldn't they know?'

The attendant looks at Shona, then his eyes shift back and forth to the edges of her loosely buttoned shirt. 'Uh, well, yes.'

'Do you think you could,' she makes the shape of a phone with her right hand, 'perhaps ring them up for us?'

'Listen, I . . . uh.' His pupils dart up and drift back down. 'Just a moment please.' As if he were being controlled by a remote somewhere, he reaches for the handset and presses one of the in-house speed dial buttons. He unsuccessfully tries to change his line of sight. 'Helmut? – yeah, it's me. Listen, have you heard anything about a Liz Anders? She was attacked last night in Friedrichshain . . . Yeah, I'm sure . . . I don't know either . . . *Nothing?* And no one from Friedrichshain either? . . . Are you absolutely sure?'

'She has red hair, is in her mid-thirties,' David says.

'Red hair, I'm being told, around thirty-five . . . No? . . . Strange . . . the police? Yeah, good idea, I'll try.' The attendant looks up at Shona, covering the mouthpiece and softly says: 'He's asking the police. It'll take a minute.'

Shona nods and drums her fingers on the counter. David sighs. His eyes wander through the lobby and he's annoyed that he came here. He probably could've accomplished the same with a telephone call. 'What?' the attendant blurts into the phone.

David and Shona stiffen.

'I see . . . just the man . . . Yes. Yes. It's OK. Thanks.' He hangs up and shrugs. 'I'm sorry. You heard it – no Liz Anders. Not yesterday and not today. And also no anonymous attack victim, or no woman at least. There was a call to the police about a woman being attacked last night in Friedrichshain . . . but all that was found was a male body.'

'A male body?' David asks. He immediately thinks of the police officer and Gabriel, who is currently in custody.

'Well, not a woman in any case. No trace of a woman.'

'Oh, OK,' David nods.

'Thanks anyway.' But of course, David thinks. How could it be any other way? Gabriel is just Gabriel.

'Maybe we can ask again in the emergency department,' Shona suggests.

David makes a face. 'Leave it. Maybe we don't need to do that at all.'

Shona looks at him, surprised.

David ignores her look. 'My stomach is doing backflips. All the coffee this morning ... let's just see if there's something edible in the canteen here.'

'Fine with me,' Shona says.

They walk towards the canteen without talking. Already in his first few steps, David suspects that he won't be able to get a single mouthful down, despite his hunger.

As soon as Gabriel turns up, everything starts falling apart. What's this all about? The sudden call from jail, the alleged attack, the dead man in the park?

'Hey! Hello!' a voice calls after them. 'Wait a minute!'

David turns around. The portly attendant waves to him with a brown envelope in his hand. 'I just found something.'

David goes back to the counter. The attendant waves the envelope. 'I knew I recognised the name from somewhere. Someone else at the hospital must have left this,' he says, handing David the envelope. 'Are you Gabriel Naumann?'

'No,' David says, confused. 'I'm his brother.'

'Well, that should do. The main thing is that I'm rid of it.'

David mechanically takes the brown envelope. It's padded, thick and about as big as a newspaper. In scrawled red handwriting on the outside it says:

Urgent! For Gabriel Naumann
From Liz Anders.

Confused, he turns the envelope over. Nothing. 'Will you give it to your brother?'

David nods. 'Yes, sure. Thank you.' Shaking his head, he goes back through the lobby to Shona.

'What is that?' she asks.

David shrugs. 'From Liz for Gabriel. No idea.'

'From Liz? I thought she'd been attacked? Or do you think she left that here before the attack?'

'That doesn't make much sense, does it?' David says. 'Why would she have assumed before the attack that Gabriel would march into this particular hospital to enquire after her?'

'Right. It sounds strange. Or else she wasn't attacked at all and just wanted Gabriel to come here and pick up the packet?'

David silently looks at the envelope in his hand.

'Are you going to open it?'

'I'm not sure.' He turns the envelope and looks at the back, but it's blank. 'Most things to do with Gabriel mean trouble.'

'Well, if you still have to think about it . . . then let's try out this great cafeteria in the meantime.'

The canteen is as soulless as the entrance hall. Shadowless light, potted plants that look anything but healthy and the people, who look even less so.

David mechanically sits on a thinly padded chair, puts the envelope on the Formica table in front of him and sinks into his thoughts while Shona pulls together a bit of unappetising salad, two sandwiches on baguettes and two Diet Cokes at the counter.

'Are you back in the land of the living?'

'Huh?'

'Never mind. Help yourself if you're hungry.' She puts the scuffed orange tray on the table and sits across from David.

'Sorry,' David says, 'it's all really . . .'

'Strange?' Shona adds, tilting her head to the side.

David tries to smile, but doesn't quite succeed.

'I don't mean to be nosy,' Shona says and pushes a huge forkful of lettuce into her mouth, 'but sometimes it helps to talk about it . . .'

'Are you offering me therapy?'

She shrugs and chews on her salad. 'Sure. It's my sideline.'

David smiles. 'Did it help Bug, too?'

Shona snorts. 'Oh god, no. For him, only something like broad-spectrum therapy could help.'

'What?'

'Broad-spectrum therapy. Just like broad-spectrum antibiotics. It covers everything.'

David grins sleepily.

'How do you know Liz, anyway?' Shona asks.

'She did a story on me a while ago. It was mainly about *Treasure Castle*. The way she asks questions, it got very personal. But we've hardly had anything to do with each other since.'

'And you didn't know that she was your brother's girlfriend? Is that right?'

David nods and looks at his baguette. Boiled ham and wilted lettuce stick out between the bread. 'To be more specific, I had no idea whether I still even *had* a brother at all until about three hours ago when he called.'

Shona raises her eyebrows. 'The phone call at the station when you ran me over?'

David nods again but doesn't look at her.

'When did you see each other last?'

'The winter of 1987.'

'*Twenty years* ago?'

'At the time, Gabriel was in a psychiatric hospital, in a closed ward. Drug problems, among other things. He couldn't kick the stuff on his own, it had gone on for years. He had absolutely no control. Either he'd go crazy, shouting at someone, or he was stoned in some corner.' He takes a deep breath and sighs. 'My brother is a psychopath – he was unpredictable and it just got worse. Everyone was afraid of him and so was I. I don't think he would've done anything to me. For him, I was always little brother David and he felt like he needed to protect me. But basically, if anyone needed protecting, it was him, from himself.'

'And I always thought you came from one of those perfect families . . .'

'Well, more or less. Until I was seven. Then . . . our parents were killed.'

'Oh god,' Shona exclaims. 'What happened? An accident?'

'It . . . well, they never found out exactly.'

Shona raises her eyebrows. She senses that David is avoiding the question, but doesn't push for any more information.

'Anyway, then we were put in a children's home – Elisabethstift in Hermsdorf, Berlin. All of it sent Gabriel entirely off the rails. Not that it would have been surprising if things went the same way for me, but with him it was different somehow . . .'

'You mean because of the drugs?'

'No, the drugs came later. He was violent, he lashed out. There were a half-dozen incidents where he'd put other children from the home into the hospital. In the end, he locked himself away with the director of the home and broke his nose and two of his ribs. After that, they took him to Falkenhorst, a home for troubled youths in one of those old Nazi villas along the Havel. But even they couldn't handle him – he fought against everything and everyone over the slightest thing.'

'And then?'

'The psychiatric clinic, the locked ward at Conradshöhe. The visits there were a nightmare. I felt like I was in a Stasi prison. Barred windows, doors without handles, the television behind security glass. In December of '87, just before Christmas, I visited him there. He was in rehab again.'

'Rehab? But I thought he was in the closed ward. They have psychiatric drugs, sure, but none of the illegal ones.'

David shrugs. 'In theory, yes. But there's probably always a source somewhere. In any case, the nurses found a suspicious package in his room. And on top of that, they had to give him Haldol or other psychotropic drugs to keep him calm. It was never quite clear to me how they separated the drugs from the medication.'

David pauses and looks down at his sandwich. 'When I was in his room, he was strapped to the bed. The second the nurse left us alone, Gabriel suddenly pulled his arms out of the cuffs. No idea how he managed it. But that's Gabriel, things like that were always happening with him. He felt persecuted; he was completely furious and wanted to get out of the hospital, to run away. He actually had this crazy plan that I would help him.'

'And how did he want to do that?' Shona asks.

'He had a kitchen knife.' David stares at the ham sandwich and the scratched tray with its countless grooves in all directions. 'He held it to my throat and wanted to get out with me as a hostage.'

Shona looks at him, speechless.

'He swore that nothing would happen to me. The crazy part is, somehow, I even believed him. He probably would have killed himself rather than let anything ever happen to me. Anyway . . . the whole situation was entirely out of control, it was pure madness. I was just afraid. Just the idea of what he would do when he got out . . .' David sighs. His eyes are blank, he's focusing on something inside himself. 'At the first security gate, I broke free and screamed for help. He hadn't expected it. They needed five men to put him in a straitjacket. He didn't make a sound, just fought back ferociously . . . If he'd at least screamed . . . When they finally forced him into the thing, they injected him with something . . .'

'Oh god,' Shona mutters.

David runs his finger along one of the grooves in the tray and goes silent. Gabriel's expression was burned into his memory. Blue eyes, like his father's. A lake with no land in sight, where no one knew what was hiding in its depths. In any case, there was no reproach or anger in his expression, not even sadness. Only goodbye. The shot worked within seconds and the lake filled suddenly with algae, dull and flat.

'Totally mad, your brother,' Shona says. David nods and grimaces in an attempt to smile.

'He'd always fancied himself a Luke.'

'A *who?*'

'Luke. Luke Skywalker.'

'From *Star Wars?*'

David nods. 'We loved the films, especially the first one. Our room was covered in posters.'

'Is he schizophrenic? Was he being treated for that?'

'The psychiatrist at Conradshöhe spoke of more or less severe schizoid phases and paranoia. If he was having an episode, they would treat him with Haldol, a strong antipsychotic drug. And then he seemed more like a robot. After that, things would be calm for a while.' He shrugs. 'Sometimes I got the impression that he would act like that just so they'd leave him alone.'

Shona's brown eyes take in David's sad expression. 'Well, at least your brother is in good company. Millions of children wanted to be Luke.'

'The problem with that is,' David says softly, 'he always acted more like Anakin Skywalker.'

Shona feels goosebumps form all over her body. She shudders and lowers her eyes. 'And today? Does he still have those episodes?'

David breathes audibly. 'If you ask me, I get the impression that he is currently having a particularly severe episode.' He stares at the tray. Somewhere nearby he hears the muffled ringing of a mobile phone.

'Is that yours?' he asks and looks at Shona.

She shakes her head. Her eyes drift across the table. 'I think,' she says softly, 'that it's coming from the envelope.' Puzzled, David looks down at the brown envelope with the scrawled red handwriting as it vibrates in time with the ringing.

Chapter 19

Nowhere – 2 September

First, Liz hears the sound as if it's coming from far away, as if someone were turning a key in a sky of cotton bandages. Suddenly, it's as if the walls, which she can't see, are moving in closer and capture the sound in her small room, her hospital room. I'm dreaming, she thinks, no one locks a hospital room. It clicks and someone comes in. She wants to open her eyes, but it is almost as difficult as last time. Just a moment, Liz thinks. Just a moment more to rest.

She senses someone approaching her bed. *Please, let it be Gabriel!* Her covers are lifted and set aside. Cool, moist air covers her body. The doctor, she thinks, disappointed.

She has no interest in opening her eyes, but she knows she has to do it. If the doctor could just see that she was conscious, they might take the tube out of her throat. If the doctor just knew she was fine, she would be released. And she wants to be released as quickly as possible.

She opens her eyes. Everything is bright again. The nurse has walked over to the wall. She looks subdued. To the right of the bed is a tall, slender figure wearing medical scrubs.

Liz looks up at his face – and is frightened to her core.

For a moment, she thinks she's in a nightmare and that her senses – or some kind of medication – are playing a trick on her. The doctor smiles at her. Although he must be around fifty years old, his face is almost flawless, the face of an angel, with very few wrinkles, and even they do not take away from his beauty and youthfulness. Before her is someone with the visage of a Greek demigod – were it not for the other half of his face.

This other half, the right side, looks as if someone had peeled off the skin and then crudely sewn it back on, unevenly, full of craters and scars. The eye droops a bit and has neither lashes nor a brow. It coldly and pitilessly stares down at her stomach.

Liz suddenly becomes aware that she is defenceless in front of him. She feels the urge to jump out of the bed and run away, but she hasn't the strength.

Pull yourself together, you fool. The man is your doctor and there's nothing he can do about the way he looks!

The doctor smiles again without taking his eyes off her stomach. With his right hand, he lifts Liz's thin hospital gown and pushes it up above her breasts, so that she is now naked before him.

When he lets go of the gown, there's a noise. Liz goes stiff. The hand isn't flesh and blood – it's a prosthesis. Horrified, she looks at the shiny plastic arm as it slides back into the sleeve of the white coat. And all of a sudden, the pieces of the jigsaw fall into place.

The steel arm!

This is the man from the park standing in front of her.

His grin turns the ugly half of his face into a terrifying mask. His left, fleshy hand wanders down between Liz's legs. The nurse stands against the wall with her eyes closed, as the man's index finger touches Liz, travels through her pubic hair and draws a straight line up over her stomach.

Liz begins to shake uncontrollably.

'Congratulations, Liz,' the man says coldly. His voice is neither high nor deep. 'We will celebrate later, on a very special day. But first I'll have to get in touch with our guest.' The grin turns into a distant smile. 'He just has to answer the phone. You really can't imagine how long I've waited – and how excited I am to see what he says.'

The man's chest rises and falls; he is visibly excited. His breath caresses her defenceless body. Liz wants to take a swing at him, but she has no control over her body. *Guest?* she thinks desperately. *What guest?*

'I also already have the perfect dress for you,' he whispers. 'Everything will work out when the time comes. It will be perfect. And he will suffer when he sees you. It will feel as if his skin . . .' He leans in further and breathes hot air across her breasts, 'as if his skin is burning.'

All numbness, exhaustion and fatigue have left Liz's body. Adrenalin drives her senses, everything is horribly clear. She wants to scream, but the tube in her throat is blocking her vocal chords. Suddenly, she wants nothing more than to lose consciousness. Her breath is completely out of rhythm, making her feel as if she is being choked. She wants to go somewhere else, where there is no fear and no despair.

Her wish is granted immediately.

The man in the white coat injects a clear fluid into her vein and then increases the rate of her intravenous drip.

'Let's hope,' the man whispers, 'that it doesn't take him too long to find the phone. Otherwise, I will have to send him something else from you.' His eyes drift across her arms and hands.

The trembling diminishes.

Gabriel! Where are you? I want to get out of here! she thinks before drifting off to the place where she no longer has to feel anything.

Chapter 20

Berlin – 3 September, 6.27 a.m.

Gabriel pulls on the handle with all his might, but the lightsabre is stuck. *Come on, Luke, don't be like that! She will die and it's all your fault.* But somehow his hands are too small. And the thing is glowing so damned red, as red as –

But why *red*?

His sabre is blue. Luke's sabre has always been blue.

He looks down at himself. His toes are small kid's toes and there is something nasty in between them that smells like vomit. He has a camera in his hands and looks through it at himself. In the viewfinder, everything looks strangely far away. Even the stench seems to disappear.

'We have to go,' David whispers in his ear. He looks up at him and wonders: why is David so big? He looks as if he were fully grown. He is wearing a blindingly white coat and wire-framed glasses. His hair is strangely blown out to the side. He smiles with dazzling white teeth and pulls out a syringe.

The camera starts beeping in the rhythm of a heart rate monitor. A small, blinking battery appears in the viewfinder. Battery empty. The viewfinder flickers, suddenly the picture is gone and everything is dark, and from all the blackness comes a voice like his father's, booming and godlike. 'Wake up, breakfast!' It repeats. 'Wake up, breakfast!' until he can no longer bear it and reaches for his gun. He can hardly grip the trigger with his little fingers. The shot sounds like a hand beating against metal. But Father dies and does not die, instead, he keeps calling: 'Wake up!' The next shot rings out so loudly that he opens his eyes in fright.

The dream shatters like a poisonous bubble.

'Hey, get up, man.' The walrus beats against the cell door with an open hand. 'Breakfast.'

Gabriel gets up in a cold sweat, shaking like a sick old man. 'All right, all right,' he mumbles, goes to the door and takes the metal plate and a thin plastic cup through the opening.

The coffee is hot and he burns his fingers. The bread tastes like cardboard with cheese and salami on top.

Half an hour later, the latch on the cell door creaks and the door swings open.

'Let's go,' the walrus says. 'The shrink is here.' Gabriel stands up much too quickly and is immediately dizzy. Last night, he barely slept a wink – but his nightmares lurk at the edge of sleep anyway.

The burly officer grabs him by the arm again and leads him to the interrogation room. Gabriel can smell peppermint. Even now, just before seven, he is chewing gum.

The interrogation room is as dull and dimly lit as the day before. Again, Gabriel sits on the same chair with the door at his back; the officer stands behind him and chews softly.

Five minutes later, the door flies open and the scent of an expensive cologne wafts into the room. Gabriel does not turn around; he has not forgotten how Dr Dressler smells and it still makes him queasy. Dressler's thin figure brushes past him, not in his white uniform like in the past, but in a well-tailored dark blue suit with a dark blue shirt underneath it.

Dr Dressler throws his keys on the table – there are about a dozen, in addition to the black electronic key to his Porsche. They clatter on the wooden surface. A pink tie is looped around his neck, tied with marked carelessness.

'Nice to see you again, Gabriel.' Dressler's watery blue eyes light up behind his black-framed glasses. His full head of hair is greying and carefully parted to the right as usual. 'Even if I would've preferred it be under other circumstances. May I take a seat?'

Gabriel looks at him silently. The palms of his hands are as smooth as leather rags, and damp.

Dressler sits down, places his manicured hands on the scratched tabletop and looks at Gabriel. 'How are you?'

Gabriel crosses his arms and remains silent.

'Gabriel, I know you are worried. But there's no need. I'm here to help you,' Dressler says paternally.

'I don't need any help.'

Dressler smiles endearingly. 'I would say you're in a difficult position. Or have I misunderstood something?'

Gabriel bites his lip. He feels like he's strapped down and unable to move his arms or legs. He hates that Dressler is still capable of triggering this feeling in him. 'I don't know how you would be able to help me. Or have you changed professions and are now working as a lawyer after failing as a psychiatrist?'

A shadow falls across Dressler's smile. 'Failed is not quite accurate. My treatments have had amazing success. It was simply not the right time for them back then at Conradshöhe. But this is twenty years later and that was just a fleeting moment. I've been a private lecturer and top specialist for sixteen years. And in this case, I was called in as an expert to determine your physical and, more to the point, your mental condition.'

'My condition is just fine,' Gabriel says.

'And good old Luke? How is he?' Dressler smiles. 'Does the voice still ask for him from time to time?'

Don't say anything wrong now, the voice whispers in Gabriel's head. *You know what he's like!*

'Luke is gone,' Gabriel says.

'And the voice?'

'What about the voice?'

'What do you say when it asks for Luke? I mean, you have to respond with something.'

'That he is gone,' Gabriel replies.

Dressler looks at him through narrowed eyes like a snake trying to crawl inside of him. 'Just the fact that you say that means that the voice is still floating around in your head, right? And wherever the voice is, Luke is not far behind.'

Just like before! The arsehole digs and digs!

Calm down!

What do you mean calm down? He twists your words and you want to calm down? Can't you see what's going on here? Beat the living daylights out of him!

In Gabriel's head, everything is a confused vortex of voices and thoughts. He feels like he's going to burst. 'Go back to the filthy hole you crawled out of,' he says, unable to conceal his anger.

Dressler's eyes light up. 'Pit Münchmaier – he came out of a hole too, didn't he? I wonder what Luke would've done with him?'

Gabriel feels affronted. The vortex stops. 'No idea,' he says slowly. 'When you see him, you should ask.'

For a fleeting moment, Gabriel thinks he can see disappointment in Dressler's eyes. A false sense of triumph comes over him. 'Is that good enough to convince you of my mental health?'

'Well,' Dressler says, 'just to give you an idea of the situation: your file describes you as mentally unstable, highly aggressive and paranoid, and attests to your having a personality disorder. All in all, the best recipe for a murder. So, if I were you, I would try to be a bit more cooperative. Otherwise you will only damage your reputation further.'

The feeling of triumph fades. Instead, he suddenly thinks of Liz. The fact that he is still stuck here and doesn't know what happened to her. He clears his throat. 'Listen, I don't know what's going on here. And I have no idea what happened to this Pit Münchmaier guy. I only know that my girlfriend is missing. In the park, she was –'

'– attacked,' Dressler adds softly. 'I know.'

'If you are really here to help me, then find Liz.'

'Well, the point is, there is no evidence of this attack at all.'

'She is missing, damn it. Call her, go to her flat at Cotheniusstrasse, ask her editors. After that, if you still think that –'

'The police have already done that, Gabriel. But your Liz Anders is a journalist and, as far as I've heard, she's known to disappear, often for days and weeks to conduct her research.'

'She's not conducting any fucking research. She was attacked!'

'Did you have a disagreement?' Dressler asks.

Gabriel stares at Dressler as if the psychiatrist had slapped him across the face and clenches his fists. 'You goddamned fucking arsehole.'

'Oh.' Dressler smiles. 'Is Luke actually still somewhere in there?'

Gabriel takes a deep breath and forces his fists to open up. Dressler leans forward across the table and drills into Gabriel with his watery eyes. 'You don't seem clear on the fact that I hold the keys. And I don't mean to the cell. I am here to decide whether you need to be transferred into the closed ward. It seems from this you haven't grown.'

Gabriel stares at Dressler. At the same time, his knees begin to tremble under the table. Anything but that! he thinks. The psychiatric hospital – never again. Never strapped to a stretcher again. Never given electroshock again. He nervously wipes his clammy palms on his trousers.

I say yes, Luke. I say yes. Beat the shit out of him! Or do something else. The main thing is that you do something!

Gabriel puts his hands back on the table, breathes in and out deeply several times, leans forward and makes eye contact with Dressler. The dented lamp pours light over their stony faces, which are now hardly even thirty centimetres apart. It is dead silent. Even the burly officer has stopped chewing on his gum.

With a sudden movement, Gabriel reaches for Dressler's keys with his right hand. His other hand grabs Dressler's very groomed grey hair and pulls his head down, so that Dressler moves awkwardly like a marionette, then groans and falls to the table on his back. In a flash, Gabriel presses one of the sharp, jagged keys against his outstretched throat.

The burly officer looks at him with his mouth agape as he gets up in slow motion.

'The gun,' Gabriel says, 'with two fingers, very slowly. If you fire, I will slit his jugular.'

Dressler groans. The police officer fishes his weapon out of the holster with two fingers. The chewing gum hangs in his open mouth, a shiny white lump.

'Now remove the magazine and put it in your trouser pocket.'

The brawny man stares at him blankly. 'Do it, goddamn it,' Gabriel insists.

Without taking his eyes off Gabriel, the officer removes the magazine from his gun with a quiet click and then puts it away in his pocket.

'Now put the gun on the floor and kick it over to me.' It makes a hollow scratching sound as it scrapes along the floor and stops in front of Gabriel's feet. It is a SIG Sauer 226 with fifteen rounds – when there's a magazine in the grip. Gabriel hesitates and stares indecisively at the weapon.

Are you insane, Luke? Do you really think you can get out of here without a gun?

I know what you want, but you can forget about it.

Take the damned thing! And have him give you the magazine. Do you think they hesitate to shoot for even a second out there?

I can't change it. That's just how it is.

You and your fucking fear, man. It could be so easy. But Lucky Luke is afraid of guns.

Gabriel grits his teeth, lets go of Dressler's neck, bends over quickly and picks up the matt black weapon. His trembling fingers close around the rough, hollow grip. It smells of gun oil and feels red-hot.

The policeman looks at Gabriel's shaking hands, then into his eyes. He slowly begins chewing again as his brain starts turning. It's clear that he is thinking about the magazine in his trouser pocket. His lips curl into a smirk and he dives at Gabriel with a heavy and clumsy movement. Gabriel doesn't have to do much. One hard and well-aimed blow to the officer's solar plexus does the job. The air escapes his throat and sounds like a can of beer being opened. Then the burly man slumps to the ground.

Dressler has crept away from the table. His now chalk-white face stares back at Gabriel and he falls back against the wall.

Gabriel takes two steps towards him and drags him back into the middle of the room, where he slams him on the table, the back of his head hitting the lamp, making it swing violently back and forth. The light beam wavers across the room, casting wild shadows over the walls. For a moment, Dressler seems as if he is about to topple over.

'Take off your jacket and lay it on the table.'

Dressler obeys, staggering.

Gabriel rolls the jacket into a bundle, picks up Dressler's keys again and then pulls back on Dressler's pink tie like it's a bridle and wraps it around his left hand.

Dressler groans as Gabriel pushes the hard metal into his back beneath his ribs.

'Now take your jacket from the table with both hands and hold it tight. If you let go of it, whether it be with one or two hands, you're done,' Gabriel says. 'Let's go.' His heart beats into his throat.

The walrus and another officer are standing in the hall. They both stare at them as if frozen.

'Help me,' Dressler groans. The tightly pulled tie is cutting off his airflow and the SIG Sauer seems to be piercing a hole in his back. 'He's bluffing! His gun isn't loaded.'

The officers' eyes are fixed on the black metal in Gabriel's hand, but neither of them dares move.

Gabriel can feel the sweat dripping down his chest and neck as they pass the policemen. Suddenly, Dressler slows down. Gabriel gives him a hard jab in the kidneys and Dressler howls like a kicked dog. 'Shut up and keep moving.' Gabriel pulls on Dressler's tie as a warning. 'Otherwise I'll break your neck.' With hurried steps, he pushes Dressler onward past a dozen doors, down a flight of stairs and then through the main entrance of the police station. Cool, damp air greets them.

'Where is your car?'

Dressler gestures to the far left corner of the car park. There is a black Porsche Cayenne roughly a hundred metres away. The SUV towers over the surrounding vehicles.

Three officers get out of a police car and look over at him suspiciously; they are not even ten metres away. One of them instinctively pulls his weapon. Gabriel pushes Dressler to move faster. The psychiatrist turns to the officers. 'Shoot,' he cries. 'The gun isn't loaded, there is no magazine inside.'

The officer holds his weapon at the ready with an uncertain expression and follows Gabriel with the barrel of the gun like a metal rabbit at a shooting range. More officers funnel out of the main entrance of the police station.

'Why won't anyone do anything?' Dressler cries. His voice cracks. 'Shoot, damn it! Do something! He has no ammo. I saw it myself. The guy is a lunatic!'

No one moves.

'Help,' Dressler screams again. 'Why won't anyone shoot him?'

Nobody responds. Gabriel and Dressler's steps crunch against the asphalt. Otherwise, it's dead quiet.

'Open it,' Gabriel says when they reach the Porsche Cayenne.

'How?' Dressler asks. 'You have the key.' Gabriel shoves Dressler against the SUV, lets go of the tie, gets the key from his trouser pocket and presses the button to open the electronic locks. Then he shoves Dressler into the passenger seat, ties the loose end of the pink tie tightly to the headrest of the seat and then gives Dressler a warning punch in the stomach. The psychiatrist is too tightly bound to writhe in pain so, tortured, rolls his eyes.

Gabriel climbs into the driver's seat and puts the weapon on the dashboard above the glove compartment, right in front of Dressler's nose. The psychiatrist stares at the object, paralysed. It was not a matt black gun labelled SIG Sauer in front of him – it was the microphone from the interrogation room.

The eight-cylinder engine of the Porsche starts with a controlled roar. Gabriel's heart is pounding. He steps on the accelerator and speeds past the police officers. They are finally stirred into action. In the rear-view mirror he sees the three officers jump into their patrol car and his tyres squeal as he rushes out of the car park. He heads east out of Berlin, only to immediately turn left at the next corner. Sirens howl nearby. His eyes dart over to the rear-view mirror.

Still no police car in sight.

The officers probably wasted too much time changing direction. At the next corner, Gabriel turns left again, manoeuvres around two more corners and drives west towards Mitte. He can no longer hear the siren. After looking back into the rear-view mirror once more, he feels just the slightest bit less tense.

Dressler sits beside him and doesn't say a word. His grey hair is a mess and he continues staring at the dashboard. The fact that he was kidnapped from a police station using an old microphone clearly bothers him. 'Where . . . where is the gun?' he finally croaks, almost fifteen minutes later.

Gabriel gestures to Dressler's jacket, which the psychiatrist is still clutching with both hands as if it were the last thing to hold on to in a world turned upside down. Dressler gropes around the dark blue bundle of fabric and groans when he feels the weapon. For the first time in his life, his fingers close around the handle of a gun. He longingly touches the slightly curved trigger and it's clear how much he wishes that the weapon were loaded.

Gabriel continues driving in silence. His heartbeat has calmed down a bit, but Dressler's presence is enough to keep him uneasy. For him, the time he spent in Conradshöhe is like a thick fog in front of an all-devouring black hole. Dressler awakens in Gabriel the unsettling feeling of being at his mercy, as if the psychiatrist could still now – and at any time – pull a straitjacket over his innermost self. In vain, he tries to concentrate on Liz, tries to plan his next steps, but as long as Dressler is sitting beside him, he won't succeed.

Without hesitating, he spins the steering wheel sharply to the right and turns into a courtyard. The centrifugal force throws Dressler to the left and the tie presses on his throat. Gabriel turns off the motor, gets out, opens the door for Dressler and loosens the tie from the seat.

Unsure, the psychiatrist stares at him and then climbs out of the Porsche. The courtyard is empty and there are garage doors on the left and right.

'Undress,' Gabriel says.

'I beg your pardon?'

'Undress. Everything.'

Dressler turns red under his tangled grey hair. 'What ... what's this about? What do you think you're doing?' he stammers angrily.

'Undress or I will break your neck,' Gabriel hisses. His anger is like thick, old oil that should have been discarded long ago. 'Or do you doubt that I'm capable of that?'

Dressler opens his mouth, but Gabriel cuts him off. 'What was still in my file? That I suffer from paranoia and am highly aggressive? If you really believe that, then you should be desperately doing as I say.'

Dressler's lips tremble with indignation. Slowly, like a child who wants to protest but knows it's useless, he begins to strip down to his underpants. His skin is pale and has pink spots.

'The underpants and glasses, too,' Gabriel says. Dressler stares at him. Desperation mixes with his indignation. His eyes are pleading, asking why Gabriel is doing all of this to him.

'You know exactly why,' Gabriel says.

Dressler's expression flickers. 'I . . . I was just doing my job. That's what everyone did at the time. I didn't invent the treatment, I –'

'Take off the glasses.'

'But . . . without . . . that is, without my glasses I can't see very well, I'm –'

'*Glasses and underpants!*'

Dressler tilts his chin forward. He reluctantly puts the glasses on the other articles of clothing and then, with his fiery red face, he pulls down his underpants and stands naked in front of Gabriel. He genitals are reminiscent of a thin branch with dead leaves. The cool September morning makes him shiver.

Gabriel fishes Dressler's wallet out of the jacket and takes the cash, which is about 350 euro. The he opens the back hatch of the Cayenne, throws in the clothing and rummages around in the boot for something that he can use to restrain Dressler. The only useful thing he finds is a thick roll of packing tape.

Gabriel closes the boot and throws the SIG Sauer to Dressler. 'Hold that tightly with both hands, index finger on the trigger.'

Dressler stands there like an old man escaped from a home. 'I . . . I have to . . .'

'What?'

'I have to . . . go to the toilet,' he groans.

Gabriel rolls his eyes. 'In a few minutes, not now. Hands around the gun and then hold it out.'

Dressler's last attempt at resisting is over and he obeys silently. Gabriel wraps the sticky masking tape around Dressler's hands and the black SIG Sauer several times, so that both of the psychiatrist's hands are bound in a shooting position around the weapon, as if he were brandishing it threateningly. Finally, Gabriel tapes Dressler's mouth shut, manoeuvres him onto the back seat, forces him to lie down and leaves the courtyard in the direction of the city centre. Dressler shuffles around anxiously with his naked body on the beige leather upholstery of the Cayenne.

There is busy morning traffic on Budapester Strasse and Gabriel keeps a lookout for police vehicles. There is probably a search out for him by now. When he reaches the station at Zoologischer Garten, he stops at the side of the road.

The black Cayenne attracts a few fleeting, mostly envious glances. When a stark-naked man steps out of the rear seat of the SUV with a gun in his hands at the ready and staggers across the station square, the unease spreads rapidly. Several passers-by photograph the man with their phones. Two girls scream loudly and run away. The people scatter, unsure of what is happening. There are the first signs of panic, which splash over the square in a circular wave with Dressler in the centre. The anger and shame over his immense humiliation that is visible in Dressler's eyes only make him seem more threatening. No one notices the tape around his hands or mouth.

And no one notices the Porsche, which joins the traffic only to be parked on the side of the road a few hundred metres further down with the motor running, the door open and the key on the leather driver's seat.

Chapter 21

Berlin – 3 September, 8.12 a.m.

Gabriel shivers. The gusts of moist wind encourage him to quicken his pace. His worry for Liz, the persistent lack of sleep and the events of the last thirty-three hours eat away at him.

When he reaches the building, he stops in front of the door for a moment. His hot breath rises in thin bright clouds.

D. Naumann is written in small black letters on the upper-most of the eleven brass nameplates beside the buzzers. Gabriel has stood in front of this buzzer a thousand times and never pressed it.

Gabriel presses the button with his thumb. The metal is cool. He waits a while and then rings a second time.

Open up, damn it!

He was always a late riser. Have you forgotten, Luke?

He'll hear the buzzer.

He probably shut it off just in case his brother stopped by.

Gabriel bites his lip.

Then he pushes the buzzer beneath David's. A moment later an old woman's voice creaks over the intercom. 'Hello? Who's there?'

'Good morning,' Gabriel says. 'Your neighbour ordered fresh bread, but now isn't answering. I'd like to leave it in front of his door. You know how it is, people take everything these days . . .'

Instead of an answer, the lock buzzes open and Gabriel enters the stairwell. It smells of cleaning products. He ignores the shiny door to the lift and sprints up the steps two at a time until he reaches the top. David's door is the only one on the fifth floor. He pushes the doorbell and can hear a low buzz in the flat.

So much for the buzzer being switched off. Still, no one answers. Where the hell is David?

Didn't I tell you? You are and remain alone. It is a fundamentally good thing, Luke.

All right, all right, leave me alone.

Gabriel turns on his heel and goes to the stairs. At that moment, there is a soft metal click behind him. He stops and turns around. The flat door is open just a crack. The man looking back at him is blond with groomed stubble, messy hair and green eyes. They are Gabriel's mother's eyes.

An image flashes through Gabriel's head for a second. His mother is lying on the floor, twitching. Her left eye is wide open and the iris is surrounded by white, like a dead green sea. Where the right eye once was is a dark bloody crater with rough edges. He can see inside of her head. It's all so real. The air seems to taste like blood, as if there were a fine red mist lingering in it. The shock makes him gasp. Then the flashback is over, just as abruptly as it began.

'*Gabriel?*' David's eyes widen.

Gabriel nods and tries to control his breath. He wants to say something, but nothing comes out. He can feel his hands trembling and clenches them into fists in his jacket pockets. It helps.

David stands in front of him and stares at him like a ghost. *Twenty years*, Gabriel thinks. He could've sworn that he would feel more in this moment.

'What are you doing here?' David finally asks. 'I thought you were in jail.'

'It's sorted,' Gabriel mutters. 'Where is Liz? Have you found anything?'

David looks at him and then opens the door the rest of the way. 'Come in.'

Gabriel nods. Suddenly, the exhaustion comes over him fully. Swaying, he follows David into a long bright hallway.

'How did you get out so quickly?' David asks, leading him into the kitchen.

For a brief moment, Gabriel considers whether he should tell him the truth.

What then, Luke? You want to listen to Mister Law-Abiding-Citizen's next sermon?

'My psychiatrist stepped in,' Gabriel mumbles. His eyes glide across the hallway's powder-blue painted walls with a series of three framed *Star Wars* movie posters. The middle one is of Luke Skywalker.

'Do you have any coffee?' Gabriel asks.

'I'll make it now,' David says.

The living room of the penthouse flat is large, but sparsely decorated. Beside the door is a cherrywood bureau. In the middle of the room there are two grey sofas that form a corner, one of which has a pillow and a crumpled blanket on it.

'Visitor?' Gabriel asks.

David seems strangely embarrassed. 'She's in the toilet and is leaving soon.' He clears two empty red wine bottles and two glasses from the coffee table, places them on the counter in the open kitchen and gestures to the free sofa. 'Sit.'

Gabriel shakes his head. 'Where is Liz?'

'Unfortunately, I have no idea . . .'

'What does that mean, you have no idea? I thought you were going to ask around?' Gabriel stares at David angrily. Two bottles of red wine, a woman in the toilet. David couldn't have gone to much trouble.

'I have. I asked around. But she's gone, disappeared off the face of the earth.'

'That can't be,' Gabriel says heatedly. 'She *must* be lying in some hospital. Where did you try?'

'First at Vivantes Hospital in Friedrichshain. Then at the emergency call centre, where they also knew nothing, and then finally the police. Again, nothing. No Liz Anders and also no attack on a woman Liz's age or anyone with red hair. No woman has been admitted anywhere that fits her description or anywhere near it, let alone a Liz Anders.'

'That can't be,' Gabriel insists. 'I mean, she was attacked . . .'

'Won't you just take a seat?'

'Enough with your fucking seat.'

'OK, OK. Fine.' David raises his hands calmingly. 'Are you sure you understood everything correctly? Maybe the connection was bad? It was also really late, maybe you – or she – was drunk?'

'She wasn't drunk, damn it,' bursts out of Gabriel's mouth. 'She's pregnant.'

David looks at him, dumbfounded. 'Pregnant? By whom?'

Gabriel turns around and looks out the window. The silver Berlin television tower pierces the sky.

'By you?' David asks. 'You and Liz Anders?'

Gabriel makes a sound that is somewhere between a growl and a groan. 'In any case, she wasn't drunk. I know what I heard.'

But he doesn't believe you, Luke! the voice whispers in Gabriel's head. *Your fine brother is letting you down once again.*

'Leave me alone!' Gabriel replies quietly.

'What was that?' David asks.

'Nothing, forget it,' Gabriel says and makes a dismissive gesture with his hand. Somewhere in the flat, a mobile phone is ringing very softly, as if it were in a drawer.

'Listen David, I'm –' Gabriel stops. The ringtone. He knows the melody. For a brief moment, he even thinks he hears Liz's steps on the parquet flooring in the Cotheniusstrasse flat and her voice as she picks up the phone, until it occurs to him that millions of people probably have the same ringtone.

He blinks and then continues. 'I am sure that something's happened to her. Liz was neither confused nor drunk. She was scared, scared to death. She begged me to help her, she said there was blood everywhere, she could hardly speak.'

David looks at him in silence for a while. The ring of the mobile stops. 'Could it possibly be,' he asks gently, 'that it has something to do with her pregnancy . . .'

Gabriel shakes his head angrily. 'You don't believe me,' he exclaims.

Ah! the voice in his head rejoices. *Why would he, anyway? It's David. David's never believed you. Have you already forgotten, Luke?*

Gabriel doesn't answer. He's turned around and is now staring at the wall across from the two sofas. There is a pale rectangle, clearly indicating where a picture once hung.

'I don't know what I should believe,' David says and goes into the kitchen. 'And you know what makes it particularly difficult to believe you?' He opens a drawer and pulls out a brown padded envelope. 'Something like this here,' he says and throws it to Gabriel.

Gabriel catches it and furrows his brow as he reads the scrawled red writing.

Urgent! For Gabriel Naumann
From Liz Anders.

'Where did you get this?' Gabriel asks, perplexed.

'From the attendant at Vivantes Hospital, it had been dropped off there.'

Gabriel turns the envelope over, looking at it from all sides. 'And? Did you open it?'

David shakes his head. 'It's not my name on it.'

'When it's something hard to deal with, it's *never* your name on it,' Gabriel says.

A doorknob turns in the hall and then a woman's voice calls out. 'Jesus, is my head pounding. I would've done better to stay away from the second bottle of wine.' An attractive woman wearing only underwear and a man's white shirt steps into the living room and rubs the back of her head as she turns into the kitchen. Her brown, curly mane bounces along with her. 'Is the coffee already – oh, uh.'

She stops short when she sees Gabriel and David.

'Shona – this is Gabriel, my brother. Gabriel – Shona,' David introduces them.

Gabriel looks her up and down icily.

'OK,' Shona says slowly. 'I'm off.'

'No need,' Gabriel says. 'I was just going to leave anyway.'

Shona and David exchange glances.

'But do at least *one* damned favour for me. If anyone stops by here and asks if you've seen me, just say no. And if you're not going to do it for me, then do it for yourself.'

'And what's that about?'

'Just in case,' Gabriel mutters. 'And don't believe anything they say.'

'Can you be more clear? Who's going to stop by? And why the hell would they come here?'

'You'll see,' Gabriel says, nods to David and runs down the hall.

'What in the world have you been up to?' David calls after him.

Gabriel slams the flat door shut behind him.

Five storeys down, he steps out the front door, looks around and hurries down the street to the right, and then turns onto a quiet side street. He stops in the shadows of a small courtyard entryway. He looks at the envelope in his hand, at the sloppy red letters. It's not Liz's handwriting. He rips open the side of the flat brown package and looks inside. No letter, no note; just a mobile phone.

He fishes the phone out of the envelope and stares at it. The casing is dull and scratched and the plastic is cracked in several places. Nonetheless, he recognises it immediately.

As if the device could feel his touch, it begins to ring. The broken casing buzzes nervously in Gabriel's hand.

He also recognises the ringtone immediately. It's the same ringtone he heard in David's flat.

This is Liz's mobile.

Chapter 22

'Wow,' Shona exclaimed, as the door fell shut behind Gabriel. 'He could really scare somebody.'

'My brother, as he lives and breathes,' David says. Resignation resonates in his voice.

'Has he always been like that?'

David shrugs. 'Actually, yes. At least since our parents' deaths anyway.'

'What actually happened back then with your parents?'

David sighs. He stands in the kitchen, turning an empty red wine glass in his hands. Then he opens the refrigerator and pours orange juice into the glass.

'Sorry,' Shona says. 'I don't mean to . . .'

David clears his throat. 'They were murdered. Shot, to be specific.'

Shona stares at him in shock. 'Oh god, how awful.'

David tries to smile, but fails entirely. 'The night was one big horrifying trip.'

'How old were you?'

'Seven. I was woken up by the commotion downstairs. It sounded like a hippo was storming through the house. I wanted to go down and look around, but the door was closed. Locked.'

'You were locked into your room? Is that what your parents always did?'

David shakes his head. 'Never. I panicked and rattled the handle, but then suddenly I heard a shot. And then three more shortly afterwards. Then it was dead silent. For an eternity. I crawled under the bed and didn't move.'

'Where was Gabriel?'

David goes silent for a moment and then quietly says, 'No idea. Not in our room, at least.'

Shona looks at him, dumbfounded. 'You mean you were locked in your room all alone and Gabriel was somewhere else in the house when your parents were shot? Did he see who it was?'

'I don't know.'

'Have you never spoken about it?'

'No. I mean, yes. The problem is that he can't remember that night.'

'You mean something like a memory lapse?'

'A trauma,' David says, nodding. He takes a sip from his glass and the juice is cool as it runs down his throat. The sour taste spreads in his mouth. 'A severe amnesia-causing trauma. As if he'd obliterated the night from his brain entirely.'

'Oh god,' Shona repeated, shaking her head. 'And who let you out of your room?'

'Gabriel.' David takes another big sip. 'After half an eternity. It suddenly smelled of burning and then I heard someone run up the steps and unlock the door. Then Gabriel was there, looking totally distraught and haunted. He just grabbed my hand and pulled me down the stairs. They were both in the living room . . .' David stops. 'The image still haunts me.' He puts down the glass and pours more orange juice. 'Anyway,

Gabriel pulled me out of the house and out to the street. At some point, the fire brigade came.

'The fire brigade?'

'The house burned down. All the way to the foundations. Nothing could be saved, literally nothing.'

'Oh – you . . . Shit,' Shona whispers.

David nods and stares out the window. Rain clouds are forming over the TV tower, heavy and impenetrable. Suddenly, the flat buzzer sounds.

David sighs and runs his hand through his hair. 'Damn it, he's back.'

He lumbers over to the door, to the intercom.

'David? Hang on,' Shona says. 'You don't have to open it for him – you know that, right?'

David nods, resigned, and then pushes the button on the intercom. 'Yes, hello?'

'Good morning,' a voice crackles on the speaker. 'My name is Grell. I'm from the Berlin Criminal Investigation Department. It's about your brother.'

David can feel his knees go weak.

'I have a few questions.'

'Could you tell me what this is about exactly?'

'That would be better discussed in person – can we come up?'

'I . . . can't we? –'

'Mr Naumann, please just open the door.'

David groans. 'My . . . what was your name?'

'Grell.'

'Mr Grell, I am no longer in contact with my brother. It's been twenty years since –'

'Listen, Mr Naumann, I know that your brother called you from prison. Your number was saved in the telephone. The point is, your brother escaped police custody this morning, armed and with a psychiatrist as a hostage. So, please open the door. Or do you want to share this with the whole street?'

David stares at the speaker in silence. It feels like time has been turned back twenty years and everything is starting up again exactly where it left off.

'Mr Naumann? Hello?' David buzzes them in.

Shona stares at him with her mouth agape. 'Hey,' she says. 'Don't worry about it. We'll just say that he wasn't here and you haven't seen him in a long time.'

'And the phone call?'

'Well, and so what? Then he just called you. But they don't know why. And you had no idea. The only thing that they can ask of you is to let them know if he shows up here again.'

There is a banging on the flat door and David flinches. 'I am fed up,' he says softly.

Chapter 23

Berlin – 3 September, 8.53 a.m.

Gabriel looks at the display on Liz's mobile, mesmerised. A hairline crack stretches across the middle of the digital characters. Unknown number. He hesitates briefly and then presses the button to pick up. 'Hello?'

Silence.

'Who's there?'

Soft laughter comes from Liz's mobile. 'It's taken you a long time, Gabriel, very long!' It's a man's voice, frosty, muffled and neither high nor deep.

'Who are you?'

'Oh, you'll find out who I am soon enough. What's much more important to you is who I have here with me.'

A shiver runs down Gabriel's spine. 'What's that supposed to mean?'

'What,' the man whispers, 'do you miss the most?'

The voice enters Gabriel's ear chillingly. A single word forms in his mind. *Liz!*

'Do you love her, Gabriel?' the voice whispers. 'Can you actually love anyone after everything that's happened? Isn't that much too dangerous?'

He has Liz! Gabriel thinks.

And he can see into your head. Be careful, Luke!

Gabriel's heart is racing. It really is as if someone far, far away can actually see his innermost thoughts.

'So, you love her,' the man whispers excitedly. 'I had hoped so, Gabriel. I had hoped so . . .'

'What have you done with her? Where is she?'

'Slowly. Everything in due time. Let's start with your last question: where is she?'

'If you hurt a single hair on Liz's head . . .'

'Shhh! *Slowly!* Let's stick with your question, Gabriel. Where – is – she? Since that is the only useful question if you want to save her.'

'All right. Where is she?'

'Bravo, now we're getting somewhere,' the voice says. 'She's with *me!*'

'And what do you want?'

'You really haven't got a clue?'

'I have no money. If you want money, you'll have to look for someone else.'

'Haven't you seen the photo? You just have to think of the photo and then you'll know.'

'Photo?' Gabriel asks, dumbfounded. 'What photo? The mobile was the only thing in the envelope.'

'The photo in the cellar,' the voice says indignantly, 'that was hanging on the black dress . . . isn't the similarity amazing? Doesn't she look almost exactly like in the video?'

The black dress. Did he mean the dress in the house on Kadett-enweg? 'I don't understand a word,' Gabriel says in a husky voice. 'There was no photo. And what video? What's this all about?'

Silence. Gabriel can hear the man on the other end of the line breathing.

'I'll say it again: if you want money, then you've called the wrong man.'

'It's not about money. It's about you! It's about what you did to me.'

A psychopath! The guy is a damned psychopath, Gabriel thinks. Maybe it's someone from Conradshöhe who was in the closed ward at the same time as him? 'Who the hell are you?'

'You still haven't guessed?'

'Is that supposed to mean we know each other?'

'Oh yes. We do indeed,' the voice says. 'Think of the video. Think of the night of October 13th . . .'

Gabriel freezes.

October 13th! The night his parents were killed. He immediately feels sick, as if someone has rammed a fist into his stomach. His hands begin to shake.

'A special night, Gabriel. A night that bound us to each other.' The man laughs coldly. 'And the thirteenth! Apt, don't you think? You'd know right away that it was not a good night. It was hell!'

Gabriel's throat closes up.

'Do you know who I am?'

'I . . . I have no idea,' Gabriel says with a trembling voice. 'I can't remember that night.'

'You *can't remember?*' The voice breathes in and out several times. 'Of course you remember. You're *lying.*'

'No, I –'

'You're LYING!' the man roars in a distorted voice. Gabriel automatically pulls the phone away from his face a bit, but the man is already silent. His hand trembling, Gabriel presses the phone back up to his ear. 'I have amnesia,' he says. 'I only know that my parents were shot and that the house burnt down. But I can't remember what happened that night for the life of me.'

The man's breath rushes into the telephone. 'But you should,' he finally whispers. 'You really should. This is your only chance! If you want to find her, then you'll have to find *me*.'

'What's this supposed to be?' Gabriel hisses. 'A game?'

'Call it what you will, but one thing is certain: on October 13th, she is dead. And I will give you a gift you'll never forget. I don't want you to ever forget me again. I want you to suffer as I've suffered. No. *More*. I want you to suffer more.'

Gabriel grits his teeth. Everything is spinning as cold sweat drips down his forehead. '*Who* the hell are you?'

'I can't believe you've forgotten,' the man says. 'But believe me, you will remember again. You simply must. Oh, and something else: not a word to anyone. You hear? Not to the police. Not to anyone else! I'm warning you – if you bring anyone else into this, you will sorely regret it. Otherwise I'll scatter your Liz around the park in pieces. First a breast, then a hand, then an eye . . . understood?'

Yes! Gabriel wants to say, but nothing comes out. Then there is a click in the earpiece and the line is dead.

Gabriel stands paralysed in the shadows. His hands are shaking so hard that he can barely manage to get the mobile into his right jacket pocket. He stuffs the envelope into the left.

Liz!

He wants to kill Liz to take revenge on me. But why? Guilt rushes over him. The world is spinning around him in all directions. Raindrops fall from the sky and burst on the street.

October 13th, 1979.

It's almost thirty years ago and he can't remember the night, not in the slightest. He thinks of the clinic at Conradshöhe and recalls the agonising therapy sessions with Dressler. Dressler, with his silver pen, writing down everything Gabriel said in his delirium. What he would've given back then to rip the pen out of his hand, so that he would finally stop writing, so that he would stop digging into his wounds.

But now he wants nothing more than to ask Dressler about his notes and to have his old medical records, so he can look for any clues. But since his escape, Dressler is probably now the last person he can ask for information on the past.

The file. If there were something that could help him remember, it was his file. Was it still at Conradshöhe? It must be; the police had access to it.

A paralysing pain immediately spreads through his head. Just the thought of returning to Conradshöhe is enough to fill him with panic.

Leave it! Just leave it alone, the voice whispers to him. *Believe me, it's better this way. There is no woman in the world who's worth descending back into this shit.*

How do you know? Can you remember?

Me?

Yes, for fuck's sake! You. What do you remember?

My memory is as good as yours.

What happened that night?

I've forgotten, like you. Do you still not understand? We're a team. We are one. Except you want to save everyone else's arse and I want to save ours.

Helpless, Gabriel clenches his hands into fists. He desperately tries to think of who would know anything about his file.

And then it suddenly occurs to him.

Chapter 24

Nowhere – 3 September

Liz feels like she's washed up on a beach. The saltwater burns in her lungs and passageways. She keeps swallowing again and again. Her hands claw at the wet sand, until she realises that the sand is made of fabric. A damp sheet in a bed.

She doesn't know how long she's been conscious. She still has no sense of time. And, although she immediately remembers the man with two halves of a face, it all seems unreal, like a bad dream.

It takes a while before she realises that there is nothing in her windpipe any more and that she is no longer being helped to breathe. Suddenly, she is overcome with a feeling of boundless relief and freedom.

She opens her eyes.

It's the same glaringly bright room as the last time she awoke. The longer her eyes are open, the darker it seems, until it finally looks dark and dirty like a barren utility room. Only, she still seems to see a bizarre blurred corona surrounding everything.

It takes a while before she is sure that she's alone. No woman placing her hand on her forehead, no man with two faces. It's as if her memory is out for a walk and individual parts must be picked up from the wayside. The attack in the park. The man's disfigured face. How he ran his finger across her body as if he were drawing the path of a blade. Strangely, she fears very little. Far too little. She suspects that this is because of the drugs she's been given. But despite her confusion, her mind is still constantly and unequivocally prompting her: *he will kill you!*

She realises that she needs to get out of there. Out of this bed, out of this room. Right away would be best.

Liz tries to sit up, but her body refuses. All right, her mind whispers, swing your legs out of the bed and then it will be easier to get up. She digs her hands into the sweaty sheets and drags her body to the right across the bed, to the edge. Every centimetre is a struggle, but giving up is not an option. She thinks of her mother, imagines her watching derisively, her face stiff from her last expensive facelift, her lips curled. 'Child,' she whispers condescendingly and shakes her head, 'you'll never make it.'

With all of her strength, Liz pulls herself further across the bed. She thinks about the child inside her, imagines how the embryo is floating in its warm cocoon with no idea of what's going on outside. 'I'll get you out of here,' she whispers. She thinks of Gabriel. She even remembers their last phone conversation. Right. It was her birthday and he couldn't come. When was that? And where is Gabriel now?

Centimetre by centimetre, she approaches the edge of the bed. She can feel the cool metal edge of the frame, feels her right leg land on it, then her right shoulder. Careful now, her mind warns her.

She tries to follow with her left leg. It shifts to the right and suddenly her right leg falls out of the bed. She can't stop it, it just falls and she can feel her whole body rolling to the right after it. It's like she's on a seesaw – no, a log. She's lying on a log and rolling to the right.

When her body hits the floor of the room, she is stunned at first. And then the wave of pain comes crashing down.

You have to stand up, her mind whispers.

No, her body says. I can't.

She is freezing. The floor is so much colder than the bed. The blanket is out of reach and she can't move. Tears fill her eyes. You shouldn't have moved, her body cries, now we're freezing.

At that moment, the door rattles. Not now, Liz thinks. I have to get back in bed. If he finds me like this, he'll kill me.

But it's too late.

He's entered the room.

His two-sided face is an angel and a devil in one. The surprise distorts his features. He comes closer, bends down and leans over her. She can see his teeth, yellow and pointy. She knows that he will hit her now – or something much worse. Fear and disgust overpower her.

'You shouldn't do that,' he whispers. 'You will hurt yourself. And I want you to be beautiful. Beautiful for me. And beautiful for him.'

Beautiful for him? The cold floor reaches inside her with icy claws. *Him?* Who's that? Suddenly, she's seized by a panicked fear that this man with the horrible face is just the beginning, that there is someone else controlling him, and that there is much more to fear and she can do nothing about it.

Almost tenderly, the man reaches beneath Liz's drooping arms and under her knees and lifts her up. No cover is protecting her from him and the hospital gown has slipped to the side. She lies naked in his arms. She sees his face, the beautiful half, and is suddenly thankful. Thankful that he is rescuing her. If she can't run away from there, then at least she won't die on the floor.

When she is lying back in her bed, covered up, connected to the tubes, bandaged and rubbed with ointment, when the key turns in the lock outside and she is alone again, she thinks: So this is it. So this is when the Stockholm syndrome begins.

The neuroleptic is already working again and her mind has begun to dissolve into soapsuds. Nonetheless, she still notices the dark square panel with a grill over it, located just below the ceiling in the corner of the room.

A camera, she thinks. There's a camera behind it! That's how he noticed that I fell out of the bed.

Next time, I'll wait until it's dark.

Chapter 25

The darkness envelops Gabriel like a coat. It smells like weeds, blackberries and rubbish have been thrown over the fence. The only thing missing is dog poo. The undergrowth is too dense. With difficulty, he makes his way along the towering fence that edges the rear of the Python property. Hawthorn and brambles tear his trousers and scratch his calves bloody. He would have just used the front door, but less than ten metres away from it is a dark blue Passat that stinks of undercover cops.

About twenty minutes ago, Yuri Sarkov drove up in a taxi, probably directly from Tegel Airport, where his flight from Moscow had landed. Gabriel watched from a safe distance as he heaved his hard-shell suitcase from the taxi – an old habit. Yuri never let anyone take his luggage. His iron-grey eyes lingered briefly on the dark blue Passat. Then he pulled the brim of his hat down deeper and hurried into the low, two-storey, flat-roofed Python Security building.

Finally, Gabriel thought, and stalked along the fence in the darkness. Yuri was probably his last hope.

After another ten minutes, Gabriel arrives at the old back entrance to the Python grounds, a two-and-a-half-metre high moss-green barred door. The hinges are rusted in place but, unlike the wire fence, it is perfectly suited for climbing.

Now, Gabriel waves into the infrared camera mounted above the door, then he stretches his face into the camera and puts his index finger in front of this lips. He knows that his pale face will light up on one of the monitors in the office like a full moon and Cogan will probably choke on his coffee with fright.

His right shoulder hurts as he climbs over the door and jumps into the courtyard. He hurries past his old flat. To the right is the entrance to the garage where the old SL has been sitting – Yuri hasn't driven it since Gabriel repaired it – as if there were some sort of curse on the black Mercedes or he were refusing to accept Gabriel's thanks.

With a few quick steps, he is at the door to the main building. He opens the lock with his electronic key card and rushes into the office.

Cogan is sitting behind his monitors as usual, slightly hunched over, receding chin and all. He looks at Gabriel suspiciously. 'What are you doing here?' he asks. His expression makes it clear that he's already heard everything about Gabriel's arrest and escape.

'Ask yourself how you could fucking betray me like that,' Gabriel says.

'What . . . what do you mean?' Cogan's face fades into an unhealthy looking blotchy white.

'Well, how nice. Just two days ago I saved your arse. I went out to Kadettenweg for you and now, when I need an alibi, you give me a big "fuck you" and act all smooth, as if you had been there yourself. Can you explain to me what that's all about?'

'I . . . I coordinated it with Yuri, you have to –'

'I don't give a shit who you coordinated with. Man, this is not about some little thing. They want to pin a murder on me.'

Cogan swallows and goes silent.

'From today, you don't just owe me one – it's at least two. Understood?'

Cogan nods automatically.

'Where's Yuri?' Gabriel asks.

The security officer gestures in the direction of the steps leading to the upper floor where Yuri's office is located.

Without so much as looking at Cogan again, Gabriel storms past him up the stairs, past the bare walls with their easy-to-clean fibreglass wallpaper. He pushes open the door to Yuri Sarkov's office, bursts in and stands in the middle of the room.

Yuri Sarkov is perched behind his desk. 'Come right in, my boy.' His voice sounds the same as always. Calm, a bit reproachful and ironic. His Russian origins make him roll the 'r'. The request sounds like a gloomy, droning melody. 'Please take a seat.'

Gabriel takes a deep breath and drops into a chrome-and-black leather chair across from Yuri. The office smells of cigars. He suddenly feels like a moody teenager: stupid and with a short fuse. 'Hello,' he mumbles.

Sarkov's grey eyes look him over coolly. 'The police called me several times.'

Gabriel nods.

'I hear that you were in custody for murder. And that you fled, knocking out a police officer and kidnapping a psychiatrist ... What the hell are you doing? Have you gone mad?'

'I know,' Gabriel tries to appease him. 'But –'

'How long is it now since we agreed to put a stop to this madness?'

Gabriel is silent.

'Twenty, my boy. It's been twenty years. And you have still not figured out that it reflects poorly on me when you misbehave?'

Gabriel grimaces. 'You aren't my guardian any more. Not for a long time.'

Sarkov looks at him piercingly. 'Perhaps it would be better if I still were.'

Gabriel avoids his eyes and looks at the huge yellowed map of Berlin, a relic from the time before the likes of Google.

'Explain it to me!' Sarkov demands. 'I take you out of Conradshöhe, take responsibility for you and you manage to keep things more or less calm for twenty years. And now *this*? You leave me hanging. Why, damn it?'

'You have no more responsibility for me, Yuri. This is my thing, you understand? You took over the guardianship for five years, that is long over.'

'Your thing? Right.' Sarkov growls. 'And yet when you fuck up, I still get caught up in it. Somehow, I'm still responsible.' He sighs. 'Your thing, right?' he repeats. His mouth turns into a narrow line. 'But if it's your thing, then why are the pigs in front of *my* door?'

Gabriel looks down. 'They'll be gone in a few days. I made sure that no one saw me.'

'I assumed so. Still, if someone works for my company and gets into this kind of shit, then it reflects on *me*, understood? It doesn't matter if you think it's your thing! Do you know how long it takes to get customers? And do you know how quickly they leave again when something like this gets around?'

Sarkov snaps his fingers with his pale right hand.

Gabriel holds his tongue.

Sarkov's eyes drill into his. 'You still haven't told me *why!*'

Gabriel looks away and feels like a child who doesn't want to get caught in a lie. His urge to tell Yuri the truth, to tell him about the kidnapping and ask him for help is almost overpowering. But the brutal and very clear warning from the kidnapper holds him back.

Not a word to anyone. You hear? Not to the police! Not to anyone else! . . . I'll scatter your Liz around the park in pieces . . .

'Fine,' Sarkov says with deliberate detachment. 'If you don't want to tell me anything, then maybe you can at least explain why you went to Kadettenweg instead of Cogan.'

'Cogan isn't doing well.'

'Like hell!' Sarkov roars. His flat hand crashes down on the desk so loudly that Gabriel flinches. 'I don't give a shit how anyone's doing. When I say you don't go, you don't go!' His grey eyes flash behind his glasses. 'Why did you go? What did you want there?'

'What did I want there?' Gabriel asks, taken aback by Sarkov's outburst. 'Well, what do you think? To look into an alarm. To be honest, I could've done without it.'

Sarkov's nostrils quiver; he leans back, crosses his arms again and looks at Gabriel suspiciously. '*Blyad*. And now? What should I do with you?'

'Help me.'

'Help?' Sarkov sighs. 'Haven't I already helped you often enough?'

'I just need –'

'I know,' Sarkov interrupts. 'Some money and a place to stay, to disappear for a while.' He sighs again. 'All right then. Old age is probably making me soft. OK, I'll help you, but only if you disappear immediately from the scene. You can go to Moscow. I could use someone like you there. The offices there need support and Oleg is a goddamned child.'

'Moscow?' Gabriel asks, surprised.

'What did you have in mind? Hawaii? Sorry. I can't offer you that.'

'I . . . I don't want to leave here. I just need –'

'Listen, boy,' Sarkov says, 'what you want doesn't matter here. I tell you to disappear and then you disappear. Because it's actually your only chance of avoiding jail, understood?'

Gabriel grits his teeth. 'I can't leave here. No way. Not now.'

Sarkov stares at him in disbelief. 'Have the pigs shit in your brain? What's this nonsense about? What do you want?'

'Back then,' Gabriel says softly, 'when you took over my guardianship, they let you look at my file, right? My patient records, that is.'

Sarkov's eyes narrow. 'I don't understand the question.'

'I . . . I need to know a few things. About the night my parents were killed. I thought that if you had read the file, maybe . . .'

Sarkov looks at him as if he has now finally lost his mind. 'So, let me just summarise this again, OK? You were arrested because you allegedly slit someone's throat. Then you take a psychiatrist hostage, break out of jail, all of the police in the city are looking for you, and now you have nothing better to do than to brood over your shitty past?'

'It's important,' Gabriel insists. 'Have you seen it?' Sarkov looks at him through narrowed eyes and then shakes his head. 'No,' he says brusquely.

'Do you know how I can get a hold of the file?'

Sarkov looks silently at his fingers.

'Is it still at Conradshöhe?'

'No.'

'How do you know?'

'Because they handed it over to me.'

Gabriel's heart skips a beat. Hope and fear rise in him at the same time. 'Everything? With all of the findings, transcripts, all that?'

'Why are you asking? It never interested you before.'

'But I'm interested now,' Gabriel says, trying to contain his agitation.

Sarkov leans forward onto his elbows and folds his hands. 'I can't give it to you. And I want you to disappear. Right now. To Moscow. That's my final offer.'

'OK,' Gabriel says slowly. Then give me my file and I'll disappear. Sarkov's face closes up as tight as a clam. 'There is no file.'

'What's that supposed to mean?'

'It means what I said. There's no file any more. I got rid of that rubbish.'

Thrown away. Gabriel needs a moment before he comprehends what Sarkov just said. Thrown away. Sarkov had the key to his memory in his hand and with it the key to saving Liz – and he threw it away? He stares at him in disbelief. 'You're lying,' he says softly.

Sarkov shakes his head. 'Why would I?'

Gabriel's eyes wander through the room and stop on a large matt silver safe to the left of Sarkov's desk, directly beside the small key safe. 'It's in there, isn't it?'

Sarkov shakes his head again.

'It's . . . *my* . . . file, damn it! It's *my* life!' Gabriel says heatedly.

'Your life?' Sarkov repeats mockingly. 'Without me you wouldn't have a life. And now you're whining here about a few dusty papers? Enough about your goddamned file, get your things and piss off to Moscow before you make everything worse.'

Gabriel claws at the arms of the chair in a helpless rage.

'Gabriel . .' Sarkov takes a long look at him and then sighs. 'Honestly, I don't have that crap anymore. Let me help you.'

Gabriel can't take his eyes from the safe. Something in the back of his mind tells him that it's a terrible mistake, but a mistake he has to make, because there is nothing he needs more than that damned file. When he stands up, he feels very heavy. He nods, just as he's always nodded when Yuri seriously demands something of him. He turns to the door and takes half a step and then he jumps.

Sarkov's reaction comes much too late.

Gabriel's hands grab his head and throat. It feels wrong, but also right at the same time. The vertebrae crack under Yuri's thin skin. A little more and. . .

'A little more and you're dead,' Gabriel whispers in Sarkov's ear. 'And now open the safe for me.'

'You're a fucking idiot,' Sarkov chokes out.

'OPEN IT!'

Gabriel pushes Sarkov up to the bulky, almost man-sized safe. He stares at the thin fingers, Yuri's fingers, which he trusts more than any other fingers, as they enter the combination on the keypad.

'Faster,' Gabriel hisses.

'This won't help you.'

He's lying! repeats in Gabriel's head.

Luke, what're you doing there?

Shut up, this doesn't concern you!

When the safe door swings open, he stares inside. A large stack of money laughs at him, several folders and a couple of envelopes. He skims over the writing. Nothing.

'Take that stuff out. Show me,' he snarls.

Sarkov groans under Gabriel's grip, flips open the folder, takes out the envelopes, one by one.

Nothing.

This can't be, booms in Gabriel's head. His hands cling firmly to Sarkov's throat. This can't be true!

He stares into the open safe like an empty black pit. A pit with matt silver edges in which something shadowy is reflected behind him. Something that looks like a man with a raised hand.

He tries to turn his head away, but at that very moment something slams down on his head, slips and crashes down on his right shoulder. The pain is like an explosion. He lets go of Sarkov, stumbles, falls to his knees and cannot believe that he is not unconscious.

'Fucking arsehole,' he hears Cogan's voice behind him. *Cogan*, Gabriel thinks, stunned. Cogan, who still owes me!

Sarkov gasps for air. 'Is this the thanks I get?' he asks, turning to Gabriel. 'And all this because of your fucking file?' His voice sounds strange and infinitely distant. 'Do you really think that I would fill my safe with that shit?'

Gabriel looks up, dazed. Yuri is a giant, he thinks, confused.

The giant bends down to him and hisses, 'I don't have it, understood?'

Gabriel opens his mouth, but nothing comes out. He is queasy, maybe with shame, because he thought that Yuri was lying to him and that the file was in the safe. Maybe also just because of the pain. For a moment he thinks about whether it would be good to ask for forgiveness, so that he doesn't lose Yuri as well. But he looks at Yuri, who doesn't seem ready to forgive. And Gabriel doesn't actually know how it works, asking for forgiveness.

Then he takes a second blow in his throat. And again from behind. Again from Cogan. Gabriel's blood pressure drops immediately. The world around him goes out like a light, his body switches to the emergency power supply for his most important organs. His muscles go slack and, even before his head hits the ground, everything is as black as a grave.

Chapter 26

Berlin – 4 September, 4.09 p.m.

Gabriel's eyes twitch under the closed lids. Directly in front of his bare toes, a free-floating staircase leads into an abyss. The steps are like folded paper without supports or railings and they disappear into the depths. This is only a dream, he thinks, to rein in his anxiety.

He knows that he has to go down the stairs, into the darkness to get it – but he doesn't know *where* it is.

Step by step he climbs downwards. His toes are cold because the steps are made of steel. The hands on his watch spin as he keeps going on and on to the bottom of the steps, where a thin red column grows endlessly. Passenger planes roar above his head like lorries. He would like to fly with them, but he can't. He has to get the book. The book where someone wrote down his dreams, including those he can no longer remember.

He stops at the foot of the stairs in front of a pair of sky-high black curtains that are attached to the ceiling and run down to his feet. Between the curtains, a slit of light. Red and seductive and sinful. The book must be somewhere here.

When he moves the curtains, he has to summon all of his strength. He braces himself against the heavy fabric, which swallows every sound, even his own loud breathing. Between the curtains, he thinks he's being crushed, a silent and agonising death as punishment for crossing over a forbidden threshold. Then he is suddenly through. The curtains swing behind him like a prison door – permanently closed for all time.

The walls down here are red and fibrous with veins as thick as arms. It's like the inside of a giant womb where someone is holding up a lamp that radiates an immense amount of light from the outside.

Suddenly, he is overcome with panic that he will always be stuck down here. He knows that he's found the book, but it has imprisoned him and he can't read it. He gropes along the wall for an exit, but there's only this red fleshy thing with glass balls grown into it as large as heads. There is something glowing in the balls that are each surrounded by a white halo. Black contours form and wriggle. There is his father and his mother; they are stuck in the balls and though he can see them, he doesn't understand what they're saying. He moves closer. His mother has green eyes, like Liz.

And then he sees that the woman beside his father looks exactly like Liz.

I have to get her out of this ball, he thinks, but the glass is too hard. Below the ball is a button and he extends his hand, a child's hand, and presses the button.

An unbearable noise swells then roars and the walls shake like a huge membrane that's threatening to burst because it can't echo thousands of voices at the same time. The acrid smell of burning flesh rises into his nostrils.

The button in his hands is suddenly a telephone handset, the coiled cable is transparent and blood flows inside it. There is a trigger stuck to the mouthpiece like a revolver. He has to pull the trigger to dial, but whenever he dials, no one picks up. The line is dead and the only sound is the nerve-racking cawing of birds . . . and the roaring.

Consciousness crawls up on him like a reptile. He tries to hold on to the nightmare, knowing how important it is, but the images drift away with the pull of a heavy tide.

His head is howling in pain. A hideous stench lingers over everything; it smells like he feels.

The birds are still cawing.

Dazed, Gabriel blinks in the light. Around him are mountains of garbage with crows hovering above them, coal-coloured spots under a sky of grey, heavy rain clouds that are so low they echo the roar of the lorries back into the landfill.

Then he sees the bin lorry.

It's several metres above him on the edge of a ramp. The hydraulics hiss and then the back of the vehicle tips, so that a wall of rubbish falls directly onto him.

The adrenalin rush wakes him suddenly. He tries to stand up, but it's already too late. A ton of rubbish avalanches over him and pulls him down with it. The pressure takes his breath away. Then the avalanche comes to a crackling halt.

Everything around him is black. His arms and legs are being held down.

You have to burrow, he thinks. Burrow your way to the top. But his hands can't manage it, the mountain of waste is too dense. Panicked, he tries to make space with his arms. The weight of the rubbish squeezes the last air out of his lungs and his head feels as if it's going to explode. A syrupy mass runs across his chest and then up his neck and cheeks.

Up?

He realises that he is upside down in the rubbish. The blood rushes to his head and he doesn't have much time until he is unconscious or, worse, the next bin lorry comes.

He desperately tries to kick his legs and rotate his hips back and forth. Around his foot, the refuse gives way a bit and apparently the layer above him isn't too thick.

Keep going!

He kicks until he can hardly breathe anymore. He eagerly tries to suck in what little air comes in through the narrow cracks between the rubbish bags. The stench of sour milk and rotten eggs makes his eyes water. A piece of cling film gets into his mouth. He has to gag and he is sure that he will soon suffocate on his own vomit, from the lack of air or the next load of rubbish. Somehow, he manages to cough up the cling film and pucker his lips so that he can breathe.

Keep going.

Keep breathing.

And keep kicking. That's his only chance. Centimetre by centimetre he manages to compress the rubbish around him and make some space. Gradually, the pressure is released from his ribcage. Then with a last mighty effort, he manages to push through the top. Rustling, the rubbish beneath him gives way and fills the hole he's left behind. He is now almost horizontal and can turn his head. There is now only a thin layer of waste above him and the light seeps through. Light and air!

He suddenly hears voices. *Two* voices, to be specific. He wants to call for help because something heavy is now pressing on his chest. At first he thinks it's a second load of rubbish, but then it occurs to him that he can't hear any bin lorries or hydraulics. Instead, it's just the voices directly above him.

'What a shit job, man!' someone complains.

The pressure on Gabriel's chest shifts and he gasps for air.

'Sarkov is slowly going soft in the head,' the second man growls.

Sarkov? Gabriel thinks, puzzled. All of a sudden he remembers what happened in Yuri's office before he lost consciousness.

'Watch what you say. Otherwise you'll wind up in the tip, too.'

'I'm just saying. First we're supposed to dump him here, and then Sarkov decides that we have to get him back again?'

Gabriel can't believe his ears.

'He'll have his reasons. Just because you're too stupid to understand that doesn't mean that it makes no sense.'

'And what the hell kind of sense is that, man?'

'In any case, he wants to have another go at him. Otherwise he wouldn't have made such a fuss. Cogan said that Sarkov was out of his office and then suddenly hollered that we should immediately get that son of a whore back.'

'Did he say son of a whore?' the man laughs like a horse.

'No idea. Cogan said it.'

'Fuck. But the arsehole isn't there any more. At least not where we left him. He's gone.'

'What if one of the bin lorries emptied its rubbish here? I mean onto him.'

For a moment, there is silence. Only the crunching of rubbish above Gabriel when one of the men shifts his weight. 'Don't know. I don't see any lorries.'

'Hang on,' the other says. Then there is suddenly a sharp sound directly beside Gabriel, as if someone had drilled into a pumpkin.

Tschrk!

And then again a few centimetres away. *Tschrk!*

Gabriel freezes.

'Hey, what's that supposed to be? Rubbish on a spit?'

Tschrk!

A long rod pierces through just below Gabriel's shoulder, only missing his chest by a few centimetres.

'I'm just checking if something's there.'

Tschrk!

This time, the rod pierces though the refuse right next to Gabriel's left eye. So close that he can feel the metal on his skin.

'You going to stab the whole tip or what?'

'Oh, fuck it.'

The metal rod pushes through the rubbish again, right near the top of Gabriel's head this time. He holds his breath, thinking feverishly. It's only a question of time before it hits him. Is it better to just give up?

'Maybe we shouldn't have thrown him in. Because of the bin lorries, I mean, if he's buried now. Shoulda just been a warning.'

'Well, I don't see any bin lorries,' the other repeats.

'Then did he run off?'

'Shit, what do I know? What's the difference? If he's under here, he's pretty much gone. And if he's gone, then he's gone.'

Silence.

'And Sarkov?'

'We'll just tell him. That he's gone. Run off. Gabriel was always a tough bastard.'

It's quiet again for a moment. Then the muffled sound of a squawking crow through the rubbish.

'Then let's get out of here. Let him look himself if he wants to have another go at the arsehole.'

The two men's steps rustle away. Gabriel's heart races and the only thing he can do is lie there.

A while later, all he can hear is the crows and he finally dares burrow up to the surface. As he squints into the heavy grey sky, he is dizzy with relief. He looks over to the ramp to make sure that there are no other bin lorries. The two men are gone.

Gabriel stares down at the desert of waste. Disposed of like a sack of rubbish, he thinks. Yuri's warning couldn't be clearer. It's just a question of why he sent the two men back to get him.

An overwhelming feeling of loneliness comes over him, spreading through every last fibre of his body. David didn't believe him, the police are on his tail and Liz is at the mercy of a psychopath who wants to take revenge on Gabriel, and he hasn't the slightest idea why. Everything seems to be slipping away from him.

Now don't start crying here, Luke. Please pull yourself together.

But he can't hold it in. It's like a break in the dam. Tears suddenly just run out of him as if he were still eleven and trapped in a nightmare. The stench of rubbish makes him nauseous again. The image of his bare toes and vomit on the cold stone floor flashes into his head. He trembles, then gags and pukes. As he wipes his mouth, a desperate rage flares up in him. How could Liz just happen to get pulled into his story? How sick does a person have to be to hurt her, even though it's about him?

October 13th.

He knows that he just needs to open this *one* door in his head – the door to this *one* night. Behind the door, Liz is waiting to be saved. It's that simple. And that complicated.

He thinks about the dream he had a few minutes earlier, about how he stood at the foot of the stairs. He tries to make his way backwards in his memory, to put the fragments together. His parents had argued that night. David had been asleep when he crawled out of his bed barefoot in his pyjamas and snuck past the kitchen to the cellar door. His memory doesn't go any further than that. In the dream, he had gone down into the cellar. And the red room with the fleshy walls that drew him in like magic must be the lab.

Father's lab.

Forget it, Luke, you can't remember.

It must have something to do with the lab. Only, what?

Listen, it was just a dream!

Gabriel presses his lips together. It's useless. The door is closed.

He stares into the sky and wonders what day it actually is. September 3rd? Or is it already the 4th? There are still just under six weeks until October 13th. A muscle under his eye twitches uncontrollably. He tries to get up. The rubbish beneath him gives way, he stumbles and falls back into the soft filth.

Pull yourself together, he thinks.

He puts his hands in his jacket pockets and rummages through them feverishly. Nothing. Entirely empty. No keys, no ID, no money. Even the money that he took from Dressler is gone. His pockets are empty except for the one on the inside of his jacket. His fingers feel for the object. The mobile, he thinks. *Liz's mobile.* He fishes it out with two fingers. The plastic casing is split, the display has turned green and blue and the electronic plate inside is broken. His heart skips a beat. The mobile is his only connection to Liz, or rather, her abductor.

With trembling fingers, he removes the battery and pulls out the heart of the mobile: the SIM card. He looks over the finger-nail-sized chip on both sides and breathes a sigh of relief. The card seems undamaged and it will work in a new phone. The abductor will ring him again. If that's what he had planned.

Suddenly, he wonders if it wouldn't be better to go to the police and tell them the entire story. Liz would have gone to the police. David, too. David has always believed in justice, like a child grabbing at straws.

Justice? Forget it, Luke. There's no such thing. What do you think the pigs will do with you if you go to them? Justice! Look around. God and the devil are both just rolling the dice. The only thing you can count on is yourself.

A raindrop bursts on his forehead. He looks up. The sky is a mountain of slate and individual raindrops fall like spears. The cries of the crows and the roaring of the bin lorries are swallowed up by the swelling patter of rain.

Gabriel grits his teeth, ignores the headache and gets up, stag-gers, stands.

And now?

A shower, a new mobile and a hiding place. And all of it will cost a pile of money.

Gabriel takes a deep breath and ignores the stench. His heart beats faster and the cold rain forces him awake. He stalks slowly through the mountain of refuse towards the sound of the lorries. The rubbish shines in the rain like it was freshly painted.

In vain he tries to remember where the landfill sites are in Berlin. No matter, he will have to wait for a bin lorry anyway. It takes over half an hour before he is standing beside an orange painted vehicle from the Berlin Sanitation Department that is about to unload its cargo of household rubbish. Drenched and shivering, he beats his open hand against the driver's side door.

A thin face with bushy eyebrows stares out at Gabriel. The man rolls down the window. 'Well look at that, the tramps are running around the tip now.'

'Can you take me along for a stretch?' Gabriel shouts over the noise of the lorry.

The driver looks at him blankly and then shrugs. 'Depends on where you need to go.'

'Chausseestrasse. To the Dorotheenstadt Cemetery.'

'Well, then get on in.'

Gabriel thanks him with a nod and climbs into the seat.

About an hour later, the brakes squeak in front of the main entrance to the Dorotheenstadt Cemetery.

The path across the cemetery had been burnt into his mind for almost thirty years. The dry, pale brown gravel crunched under his and David's feet in front of the two oak coffins as they walked up to the open grave that swallowed his parents like a hungry mouth.

Now the gravel shimmers, wet and dark. The ground is soaked wcuish into the softened path. The earth on the graves is dull and black, an all-equalising nothingness that swallows every ray of light.

Exhausted, Gabriel drops to his knees in front of the gravestones. The rain runs in crooked paths across the faded gold inscription on the red marble:

Clara and Wolf Naumann, 13 October 1979

He is suddenly overwhelmed by a feeling of infinite sadness.

Is that what you wanted? the words are whispered through his skull. *Shock therapy?*

You know exactly what I want here.

But don't you see how right I was? Where it all leads?

You just want to scare me.

No, Luke. You ARE afraid. And rightly so. Actually, you just want everything to stay the way it is, don't you?

YOU want that. I want to remember.

I only want what's best for you. I just advise you on what would be best.

You're a shitty advisor.

Gabriel slides on his knees to the right, beside the marble stone. Water runs down his collar, the ground squelches beneath his legs. His knees are several centimetres deep in the mud and he begins to dig a hole to the graves beneath the stone.

Aren't you afraid of going through it all over again?

Gabriel doesn't answer, stubbornly digging further, always deeper. Black borders form under his fingernails.

Be careful, Luke! If you dig too deep, then you'll be holding their brittle bones in your hand!

He has to give in, but his clammy fingers keep pulling the earth out beneath the stone.

Keep digging for all I care, I have nothing against it.

'Shut up!' Gabriel shouts. His voice cracks, lost between impassive stone angels, trees and countless graves.

Suddenly, his mind is silent.

All Gabriel can hear is the patter of rain and an unsteady wind tugs at him. He feverishly continues digging until his fingertips chafe, before he finally touches something soft. He carefully loosens a tied bundle the size of a packet of cigarettes. With trembling fingers, he pulls apart the tape and removes several layers of cling film.

The key is small, shiny silver and lacks engraving or any distinguishing features.

As he walks into open his safe-deposit box at the branch of Credit Suisse on Kurfürstendamm, a boulevard full of fine shops and restaurants, he has to smile at his appearance – stinking, dripping wet and dressed like a bum.

And he especially feels like smiling, because now a warm bed, dry clothes and a new mobile are within reach. He laboriously straightens himself up, wipes his hands on his trousers and puts the key into his pocket along with the SIM card from Liz's mobile.

Chapter 27

Liz's eyes wander sluggishly through the room. She keeps falling asleep and, since there is no natural light, she has no sense of how much time has passed – even if the lights are turned off and on at specific intervals, providing a fake rhythm of day and night.

The only sound she hears is her breath. At least it's her *own* breathing that she hears, and not the mechanical pumping of the artificial respirator; the tube has long since been removed from her throat, and breathing still burns against the wounds in her airways.

At this point, she knows every centimetre of her prison. The massive metal door with a slit that opens from the outside to look in; the barred fluorescent tubes; the painted white brick walls; the concrete floor with a drain in the middle of the room, as if her remains were going to flow into the pipes at some point; the two barred ventilation ducts – one in the ceiling for fumes, and one near the floor for the air supply; the small screws anchoring the bars; the nightstand beside her; the IV; the machines; the bag for her catheter.

Again and again, her gaze lands on the hanging IV bag and, for the thousandth time, she wonders what medications are flowing into her bloodstream.

Then she hears the key turning in the lock. Her body instantly stiffens, her mouth goes dry and the skin under her hospital gown is covered with a thin film of sweat. *Don't let it be him. Please not him!*

Her prayers are answered. The nurse enters the room silently, closes the door behind her and silently changes the IV. On the first day, she had at least said a few words. Since then, she has gone quiet. At the moment, Liz needs little more than the sound of a voice, just a few sentences or a few words.

Liz opens her mouth, wanting to say something. Her tongue is a furry, wagging thing. 'Wha ah'ou givin . . .' a strange voice pours from her mouth, 'what are you giving me?'

The nurse glances over at her but doesn't answer.

'Because of my baby,' Liz croaks.

Another glance. The hint of a smile flits across the nurse's face. She has a straight nose and – were she to actually smile – dimples. 'Your baby is OK.'

'Please, what's in there?' Liz insists.

The nurse looks at the door and then back at Liz. 'A neuroleptic. It calms you. Not so bad for the child.'

Not so bad. 'Who . . . is he?'

The nurse's grey eyes widen imperceptibly and she looks around quickly. 'Shhh,' she hisses softly and leans forward. 'You'd better shut up.'

'Please help me,' Liz pleads.

The nurse says nothing, just shakes her head.

Liz's eyes fill with tears that run out from the corners. A deep desperation takes the air out of her, making her feel like she's suffocating.

'Shhh,' the nurse hisses again. She pulls out a syringe and puts it in the vein access in Liz's arm.

Liz wants to fight back, but she is too weak. It's already hard enough to speak and breathe. 'Where . . . where am I . . . ?

The nurse's grey eyes seem to see through her. Then she shrugs.

Liz can feel her strength slowly fading, she doesn't have much time. 'He's going to kill me, isn't he?'

'I don't know,' the nurse says, but her eyes give her away.

'Please,' Liz pleads again.

The grey eyes withdraw to the nightstand.

You have to address her with her name. Ask for her name. 'What's your name?'

'Yvette,' the nurse mumbles.

'I'm Liz. Please – Yvette. Help me.'

'No,' Yvette whispers.

The 'no' grips Liz's heart like a cold hand. Fear threatens to cloud her mind. She can feel tears in her eyes again. *And this weakness.* 'Could you . . . maybe . . .' Liz gestures to the half-empty syringe with her eyes, '. . . is that also this stuff? Is it Haldol?'

Yvette nods.

'I'm scared,' Liz chokes out. 'Terrified.' Tears run down her cheeks. 'Can I . . . keep that?'

Yvette's grey eyes wander from Liz to the syringe in her hand.

'Maybe I would be . . . less scared . . . if . . .'

Yvette's eyes twitch, only a very short blink, and then she puts a plastic cap over the needle and quickly pushes the syringe under the blanket. 'Before it starts, just inject it into the vein access.'

'Before what starts?'

Yvette shakes her head in silence.

Liz's whole body is covered in goosebumps. Each individual hair is standing up in horror. Suddenly, it's dark, as dark as in the park. She thinks she can feel the leathery skin on her cheek; his voice is in her ear. *We're going to celebrate. On the thirteenth*, he whispered. On the thirteenth? Oh god! What day is today? It couldn't possibly be the thirteenth already.

Her left hand grabs the syringe and her fingers wrap around the plastic like a lifebelt. She hears the lock, the key inside. 'When is it time?' Liz mumbles.

'It's better if you sleep now,' Yvette says and then she shuts the door behind her.

Liz's eyelids are heavy as shutters. Her thoughts clump together like cotton wool. A tremendous need for quiet takes hold of her, even if she can't be sure that she will wake up again after falling asleep.

But if so, she decides – her fingers wrapped around the thin syringe – she will need a weapon.

Chapter 28

A pale morning has dawned behind the grey felt curtains at Caesar's Hotel. Through the tilted window, muffled street noise blows into room number thirty-seven.

Gabriel lies on the bed and tries in vain to rein in his impatience.

Finally!

Finally he has a trail.

Six days ago he emptied his bank safe-deposit box. Six days of research, of running himself ragged in search of a trail, trying to hide from the police and lying low the whole time. Six days of his heart racing every time the new mobile with Liz's SIM card rang.

'Hello? This is Karla Wiegand from TV2. I was hoping to reach Ms Anders. Isn't this her number? – I understand. Then please tell Ms Anders that she should contact Dr Bug as soon as possible.'

Then it rings again: 'Liz. It's me, Verena. You wanted to . . .' – 'Oh, OK. Can you ask her to call back? Vanessa Sattler. About the Fössler story, she knows already. I have some new information.'

And less than an hour later: 'Uh, could I please speak with Liz Anders? – Oh. Then when should I call back? – It's about von

Braunsfeld, she knows the old fellow quite well. I wanted to ask her to put us in touch.'

Other callers hung up immediately upon hearing Gabriel's voice, or apologised for having the wrong number.

The kidnapper remained silent.

Up until last night, Gabriel had the unbearable feeling of running in place.

Gabriel takes a deep breath. Dusty air swirls down into his lungs. Caesar's is neither clean nor reputable. The small hotel is unremarkable: a narrow, unimpressive building from the sixties that fell into one of the countless holes that World War II tore into Berlin. It's as if the hotel were ashamed of being such a hole and now has to go into hiding, just like its guests.

Gabriel's room is on the third floor at the end of a hallway where the walls are lined with stained, beige patterned carpeting. Three metres from room number thirty-seven there is a bright red box with an old fire extinguisher on the wall. The first thing Gabriel did when he got to the hotel was to open the red box, drill a small hole into the door and install an infrared barrier behind it.

'What in the word are you doing there?' Liz had asked him anxiously when he'd hidden the small plastic housing for the infrared barrier in the corridor of her building on Cotheniusstrasse.

'Precautionary measure,' he muttered. He'd slept at her place three times and, during the first two, he'd struggled to control himself.

Liz just rolled her eyes at first, but when he stuck the two electrodes on his forearm at bedtime, she looked at him like he was a nerd. 'Oh my god. Is that what I think it is?'

'I've no idea what you think,' Gabriel said. He hadn't the slightest bit of interest in discussing it. 'It's linked to the infrared detectors in the hallway. Like I said, just a precautionary measure.'

'And what exactly does your *precautionary measure* do?'

'Not much. It tingles.'

'It *tingles*? Are you really telling me that you've just installed an alarm system here that shocks you when someone comes too close to my door?'

'Just a little electrical current. It's enough to wake me up.'

'But . . . why not a *normal* alarm system, like one that beeps or something?'

'Much too loud. Everyone would hear that.'

Liz's green eyes wandered down to the electrodes and then back up. 'Shit! I'm sleeping with a guy with full-blown paranoia.'

'Now don't make a fuss. It's just –'

'If it were at least a sex toy, for stimulation or something,' she groaned, 'I could live with that. But *this* . . .'

Gabriel's expression was dismissive, and the light from the bedside lamp threw long shadows across his face.

This system had been following him for half an eternity. Since he'd left the psychiatric hospital, he'd always installed infrared detectors. The technique was simple, efficient and available in any large electronics store for very little money. This was his bedtime story. Just as he was calmed as a child by the stories that were so unbelievably exciting but still had a happy ending, he now knew that everything that could happen in real life also had the possibility of a good ending – as long as he could take care of it *himself*. And he could only take care of it if he were warned in time.

'Why are you so damned sensitive?' he asked. 'It's your safety, too.'

'To hell with my safety. The last thing I want is to share your paranoia.'

'How is this any of your business? It's my decision *how* I sleep.'

'And it's my decision *who* I sleep with!' Her eyes sparkled, her red hair looked like copper wire.

'Then that's that,' he said and reached for his bag.

Tell her, Luke. Tell the little journalist witch that she can fuck off, the voice in his head rejoiced.

Gabriel said nothing.

He just left the flat and slammed the door behind him. The fact that it was far too late for such a stunt was clear to him the moment the door crashed shut. But he needed a full six weeks before he spoke to her voicemail – although he couldn't stand the thing.

He didn't apologise. It wasn't him. He didn't even act like he was sorry. He just removed the infrared detector. Liz held back, contrary to her usual habits, because she realised that other men were afraid of things too: losing their job, falling from a ladder, women, being ridiculed. Gabriel was apparently afraid of something intangible, something that could descend from the darkness, as if the devil had just pulled his name out of a hat.

The following nights on Cotheniusstrasse were restless and brief. Without the electrodes on his skin, he was constantly scared awake and listening in the darkness. Usually, there was nothing to hear but Liz's breath, a regular up and down, like an ocean swell.

It took months before he finally admitted to himself that it was because of this sound that he slept better and deeper in that flat than anywhere else. He still woke up briefly, sometimes feeling like he was lying in his old, childhood room with the blue covers over his bare toes, together with David who would breathe in the darkness, just as Liz did beside him now.

Gabriel runs his hand across his face and wipes the memory away.

He looks at his new mobile with Liz's old SIM card. The display shows 9.18 a.m.

It's time to go.

In the metro, he stares through the window at the tunnel, where colourless pipes and ducts run above him, tightly packed and seemingly endless, as if they were tying the city together underground.

He thinks of Liz's call, of her voice, thin and breaking. Again and again he's replayed it in his mind.

'I was attacked. I'm bleeding . . . there's blood everywhere . . . my head . . .'

'Where are you?'

'In the park. Friedrichshain. Near my flat, around the corner . . . please, I'm scared . . .'

Liz had been brutally beaten; her broken voice left no doubt about it. But *why*? Kidnappers stun their victims, carry them off and sometimes kill them in the end. But what sense does it make to hurt the victim so badly right at the *beginning* of the kidnapping?

Even if the kidnapper is a vengeful psychopath – he clearly had a plan and it ends on October 13th. So, he would hardly want to risk Liz dying before then. So why such senseless brutality? And why had Liz been able to make a phone call *after* she'd been beaten? Where was the kidnapper then?

With all of these questions in his head, Gabriel searched Friedrichshain Park, ran from the area around Cotheniusstrasse to the point where he'd found Pit Münchmaier. The traces of chalk where the CID had drawn the outlines of the body were faded. Where the neck of the roughly outlined body had been drawn, the blood had left behind a dark shadow.

The longer he stood there, the stranger everything seemed. According to the *Berliner Zeitung*, the police autopsy had determined Pit Münchmaier's time of death as midnight, give or take ten minutes.

Liz had called Gabriel at 12.02 a.m.

A murder and a kidnapping – both at the *same* time in the *same* park very close to each other?

A coincidence?

Unlikely. There must have been some connection between the death of Pit Münchmaier and Liz's kidnapping.

So he began to do research on Pit Münchmaier. Münchmaier was only twenty-four years old. He was unemployed and had lived in Kreuzberg near the metro station at Kottbusser Tor in one of those ugly building complexes from the seventies that look like concrete multi-storey car parks for people. The knife used to slit his throat was exceptionally sharp and thin, not the classic weapon of a knifeman, but much more the tool of a surgeon. There were scratches on Pit's hands and bloodstains on his shoes.

On the next night, Gabriel took the metro to Kottbusser Tor. It was risky; he knew that the area was a popular spot for drugs, full of junkies and dealers – and for that very reason, also a place where the police always turned up. But he had no other choice.

The walls of the eight-storey building where Münchmaier's flat had been were covered in graffiti and there was a hypodermic needle by the front door that had been trampled. The flat was on the seventh floor and there was a police seal stuck to the door. It was about the size of rabbit hutch – and, when he got inside, smelled as bad.

The computer had an impressive range of violent video games, an Internet history with countless porn sites, and an inbox overflowing with spam from the associated providers. Amidst all the junk, Gabriel found an email address with the anonymous handle JHERO at Gmail. JHERO seemed to be the only person in regular contact with Pit. He took down the address and decided to look into it later.

Next, he asked around the neighbourhood if anyone knew Pit. First, he limited himself to bakeries, bars, sex shops and news stands. He had been going around in circles until he got lucky last night at a small, brown-painted news stand on a side street about five hundred metres from Kottbusser Tor.

'Pit? Yeah, sure. The poor devil.' The kiosk owner pulled a bottle of cola from the refrigerator and pushed his chunky, black horn-rimmed glasses back up his nose. His curved moustache bent into a sour grin. 'Was always hanging around with Jonas. Like Siamese twins, the two of them.'

JHERO. J for Jonas. Gabriel took the bottle and pushed a hundred-euro note across the counter. The moustache twitched with annoyance, he dug through his cumbersome metal box and counted out the change on the laminated counter.

'And what's their story, the two of them?' Gabriel asked and pushed the change back a few centimetres, towards the kiosk owner.

Mr Moustache threw Gabriel a quick glance over the rim of his glasses, his eyes narrowed. Then he looked at the money and pocketed it with a swift movement. 'Not great, I'd say. Pit's been takin' a beating from his stepmother for years. Even had to go to a hospital once. With Jonas, it was his father. Always showed up plastered.' He shakes his head. 'Drank himself to death. Been better since then, for Jonas, I mean.'

'And what's Jonas doing now?'

'Nothing. Just had bad luck. That's how it goes. Finished school, took forever until he got an apprenticeship and then the shop went bust. What can you do? If I were him, I'd be throwing one back now and then . . .' He lifts an imaginary bottle to his lips.

'Where do I find this Jonas?'

Mr Moustache scratched his head as if he had to consider whether he was going to tell Gabriel any more details.

Gabriel's expression, rather impassive up until that point, hardened for a brief moment. 'There isn't any more money. And don't breathe a word of it to Jonas.' He leans over the counter and his eyes drill into the kiosk owner's. 'Otherwise I'll burn your shitty stand to the ground, understood?'

Mr Moustache blinks in surprise. 'Understood,' he mumbles. 'His name is Schuster. Jonas Schuster. Lives with his mother.' He looks past Gabriel. 'Right above the Rex, it's a cinema, just round the corner.'

Just before ten, the doors to the metro hiss shut behind Gabriel. Ten a.m. is a good time to look for Jonas Schuster. Most of the neighbours will be working, and he's probably just got up.

Gabriel goes slowly up the stairs, step by step, even though he'd prefer to run. The blue sign that reads 'Kottbusser Tor' hangs heavy against the sky above the exit. The day sticks to the city like a film.

Three blocks further and Gabriel is standing in front of a beige five-storey building with cracked plaster and dirty windows. The first two floors belong to the cinema. Its entrance has glass doors set in brass. Above the doors is a programme board, and above that, 'Rex' in neon red lettering from the seventies. A few metres to the left is the building entrance to the floors above. Gabriel rings the top floor for Verena Schuster and waits a while.

Nothing moves.

He quickly rings the lowest bell.

'Yes, who's there?' a grumpy and nondescript voice snarls from the intercom.

'Post,' Gabriel says.

There is a buzz to unlock the door. It sounds broken.

'Thanks!' Gabriel calls. His voice echoes through the building hallway. He climbs the stairs to the top floor where there is only one door. A paper strip with 'Schuster' written in crooked letters is taped over a lacklustre nameplate. An unpleasant smell lingers in the air in front of the door.

Gabriel rattles the knob and then pushes a thin plastic strip between the door and the frame, pushes the catch into the lock and cautiously opens the door just a crack.

He holds his breath, listens, waits. Nothing.

He silently enters the flat's dark hallway. The textured wallpaper and ceiling are covered in a yellow layer of nicotine. On the right, there are three framed photos on the wall, two of a boy around seven years old who is straining to smile, the third of the same boy, only clearly older. At the top end of the hall, daylight is coming in through an open door that seems to lead to the kitchen. Gabriel can hear the angry buzzing of insects. The wooden planks creak under the matted carpet as he approaches the kitchen door. It smells like bad food and rotting meat, repulsive and cloying. Gabriel recognises the scent and knows how long it lingers. He's had it in his nose more than once.

He steps into the bright rectangle of light and then reluctantly through the doorway. The kitchen measures around three or four metres. Across from the door is a large window with an old-fashioned, formerly white curtain that blows in the breeze of the open window. The kitchen table stands in the middle of the room. On top of the table is a woman, maybe fifty years old, on her back. Her legs hang over the front edge of the table, her arms dangle to the right and left and her head is tilted back over the edge. Her neck is overstretched and her larynx is sticking out like a thorn that will soon pierce through the skin. It looks as if someone placed a very large animal on a very small dissecting table.

Her dress, like the rest of her clothes, is cut open and the pieces of fabric are draped to the side like flaps of skin. She is lying there naked with her legs spread in front of Gabriel.

He automatically puts his hand in front of his mouth and nose, feels the urge to run out of the room, but he can't look away from the pale, waxy body.

One cut – deep and sharp – starting from her vagina, drawn up through the skin, across the pubic bone. Through the abdomen. Through the abdominal wall. Up to the sternum.

A flame shoots through Gabriel's head, a blinding flash, so suddenly, as if a grenade were detonated inside his skull. There's a vortex of images racing around, but none of them stays long enough for him to really see it. For a disturbing moment, he feels like he's been here before, although not in a doorway, but a window. As if he has seen the body head first from outside the kitchen window. Then the moment is gone, as if someone had thrown a cloth over a glass sphere.

Gabriel stares at the body. The slit genitals, the open abdominal cavity, the viscera bulging out, the lake of blood on the chipped kitchen tiles – it looks as if someone had laid out a slaughtered animal to let it bleed out.

He wants to move his feet, go backwards, but it's like his soles have grown into the floor. The kitchen floor is dark with dried blood, a black cloud of flies buzzes over the bloated body of Verena Schuster.

It takes a while for Gabriel to get a hold of himself.

OK. Out of here, Luke.

He steps back automatically in retreat, through the dark hall, out into the corridor. On his way, he takes one of the three photos on the wall and puts it in his inside pocket.

Close the door. Cover the tracks.

Gabriel carefully shuts the door and then wipes down the doorknob with the lining of his jacket.

His steps echo softly in the stairwell. No one crosses his path. Even the street seems surreally empty and the cinema like a haunted house. It's only after he gets two blocks away that he sees the occasional person or car. At Kottbusser Tor, Gabriel is back to reality. The metro station spits a torrent of people out onto the surface.

A delivery van honks because a junkie and his dog have made themselves comfortable in a parking spot. A bus leaves the pungent smell of diesel in the air.

Gabriel sits on a bench, leans back and closes his eyes for a moment. What remains is the sound – he is there, and somehow also far away.

Calm down, Luke!

I am calm, enough with the clever shit.

Well then . . .

What?

Then can we get down to business?

You mean the body.

I would stay away from that.

You call that getting down to business? Giving me cowardly advice?

Cowardly? I'm not a coward. Just intelligent.

Goddamn it, who did this? Who does something like this?

A psychopath. A killer. I've warned you. Stay away from it. Your stubbornness and your obsession will get us killed.

Obsession?

Yes, obsession. Liz here, Liz there, Liz everywhere. Without considering what you have to lose.

And what exactly am I supposed to be considering? What have I lost?

No answer.

Why are you suddenly pulling your tail between your legs? You're usually always on the prowl.

But I just do what you want, Luke.

Oh. I thought it was more the other way around.

Can we drop this shit? I don't want to talk about it any more.

We can! But only if you answer a question for me. What do you think? Who did this? The same person who's got Liz?

You're making me sick with your Liz.

There must be some connection. Liz's kidnapping, then Pit Münchmaier's throat getting slit at the same time in the park, and then the mother of Pit's best friend Jonas is sliced open . . .

What would be the connection?

Maybe Pit and Jonas saw something? Something that they shouldn't have seen? Maybe that's why the kidnapper killed Pit.

But then why Verena Schuster?

Because maybe he was looking for Jonas Schuster, like I am. Maybe she should've told him where her son was hiding . . .

As far as I can tell, he pushed a knife into her cunt. She would have likely told him where her son was then. So, why did he still kill her?

Maybe she had no idea where Jonas was. And then he was angry . . .

That looks like more than anger. That looks like something else.

Yes . . . maybe. But what?

Gabriel squeezes his eyelids shut and thinks hard. The confusing flood of images from when he first saw Jonas's mother's body and the feeling of déjà vu rush back into his mind.

Can we drop this now?

Not if you won't help me.

But I am. You just don't understand. It's all for our own good.

For our own good? Ha! You egomaniacal arsehole!

Altruistic idiot! All I ever hear is 'Liz, Liz, Liz' and 'Save, save, save' . . .

Shut up. I need to think. I need to find Jonas.

Gabriel opens his eyes. He needs a moment for his eyes to grow accustomed to the light again. If Liz's kidnapper and Verena Schuster's murderer are actually the same person, and if the psychopath is now possibly after Jonas, then I will have to find Jonas before he does.

He takes the photo out of his jacket. It's framed lovingly and shows a young man who is most likely Jonas. He is in his early twenties and wearing jeans; behind him is the Eiffel Tower, cut and a bit crooked in the picture. Jonas has thin blond hair and his eyes are close together with a crooked nose in between. He is smiling into the camera insecurely.

With a little luck, Gabriel thinks, Jonas is the perfect decoy. If Jonas really knows something, then the killer is trying to track him down.

But then he has another thought. A thought that scares him, that eats at his brain like poison. If Verena Schuster's murderer and Liz's kidnapper are really the same man, then . . .

He tries not to think about Verena Schuster, about her spread legs, the blood, her open stomach . . . but all he can think about is a woman staring at a shiny knife in horror and at the fist guiding the knife, since the knife must have been pushed inside of her up to the handle. Suddenly, he remembers that Liz is pregnant.

Chapter 29

Nowhere – 15 September

Liz stares into the nothingness. About two hours ago, the lights went out and now she is surrounded by an impenetrable blackness, like the depths of hell. The devil put out the fire himself. Liz knows that he wants to show her that it's night and that she should sleep.

His face is lurking somewhere in the darkness, that face, like a mask of pure alluring beauty, a mask with one half torn off so that now the monster beneath is revealed.

He's not here. And he can't see you, it's dark, she tells herself.

The thirteenth of September. It was two days ago. She had lost her sense of time and asked Yvette nonchalantly.

'Is today the thirteenth?

'No,' Yvette answered automatically. 'Tomorrow.' And then she stopped short as if she'd said something she shouldn't have.

Liz could feel the fear deep in her core for the entire day. Then the door opened and he entered the room. If she were only a bit stronger, a bit more conscious, then she would have tried to do something, no matter how senseless it might have seemed. But it was as if she were nailed to her bed.

His eyes stared down at her, his nostrils flared; he could smell her fear and it excited him. 'Pull off the blanket, I want to see you.'

With trembling hands, she pushed the blanket aside.

'The gown.'

She hesitated, knowing it was useless. It was just a stupid instinct.

Before she could see it happening, he came over to her, rammed a needle into her calf and let go.

Liz cried out, more in shock than in pain. She stared at the needle stuck into her leg. She can see the syringe shaking with the rest of her body.

'You see the liquid in the syringe?' he whispered.

Liz couldn't even nod, but that probably didn't matter to him.

'If I inject this wonderful crystal-clear solution into your muscle, you will have excruciating pain in your leg. Pain like never before. You'll wish,' he whispered and brought his face close up to hers, 'that you could cut your leg off just to stop the pain. Do you want that?'

She pressed her lips together and shook her head. The syringe in her leg shook like a gauge for her fear.

'The gown,' he repeated. This time, she didn't hesitate.

His eyes fell onto her breasts and then lingered on her skull tattoo. 'I know that you're strong,' he whispered, 'and that at some point you swore not to put up with anything. But believe me, everything is different here. Here, you have to forget all of that.'

His eyes wandered down her body, over her slightly swollen abdomen down to the bladder catheter. 'It's about more than your life here.' Then he groped her body with his healthy left hand – the ribs, the bruises, the scrapes, all with the practised dexterity of a physician.

'What have those beasts done to you?' he whispered distantly. 'How much effort it takes for everything to heal again.'

With the thought that he could be a doctor and that *he* might have administered her catheter, she grew queasy.

'I should've helped you much sooner, really.' His index finger runs across the top of her stomach. 'It's his, isn't it?'

His? Liz looked at him uncomprehendingly.

'Is it *his?*' he hissed.

Gabriel. He knows Gabriel. Liz nodded. Speaking doesn't work.

'I knew it,' he chuckled mechanically.

Liz felt more vulnerable than ever. *What does he know? How long has he been following me?*

His eyes bored into her. Cold brown eyes with a yellow ring of fire in the iris.

'More than you suspect,' he whispers.

Liz shudders and looks quickly to the side, as if her eyes were giving away her innermost thoughts.

Suddenly, he straightens up, pulls the needle out of her lower leg and squirts the liquid into the air. 'Sodium chloride – better known as saline solution.' He smiled coldly, but at the same time, his expression was intense. 'I don't want to hurt you. You are prettiest unharmed. You have this fair and sensitive skin, so smooth and . . .' His two-sided face suddenly shines with excitement. He takes a step back, as if to cool down. 'One more month. Then we have our celebration. Now sleep! It's good for your complexion.'

Not a minute later, she was alone again. She pulled the cover over herself and trembled like a leaf. Then the light went out. *One more month. And then what?*

Ever since that moment, she's been counting. Light. Dark. Light. Dark. Now she knows what day it is and, even more so, what night: it's the night of the fifteenth going into the sixteenth of September.

When the fluorescent light had gone out about two hours earlier, she felt her way up the vein catheter to the roll closure of the IV, disconnected the medication intake and waited, just as she had done for the last five nights.

Now, around three hours later, the time has come. The effects of the medication have worn off.

She sits up and manages it on the first try. *Very good*. She carefully climbs out of the bed, sits down on the cold floor and feels around for the infusion. She sticks the syringe that she'd got from Yvette carefully into the rubber stopper of the infusion bag hanging above her head, sticks the needle through and sucks the liquid out into the empty syringe. Seconds later, her fingers find the drain in the concrete floor. *Out with the poison*. It's not a splash so much as a whisper as the liquid flows into the drain in a fine stream. Yvette won't notice that the infusion has ended up in the sewer instead of Liz's bloodstream.

She repeats the whole procedure several times until the infusion bag is three-quarters empty, always anxious that the needle couldn't possibly remain sterile with what she was doing. An infection was really just a matter of time.

Then she begins training. One step after another. Slowly, from cellar wall to cellar wall. She holds the IV with its rolling stand in one hand like an elderly person using a walker, and the catheter in her other hand.

Liz's legs are like jelly. She suspects that the infusion not only provides her with drugs and medications, but also with liquid nourishment. But if she has to choose between nourishment and a clear head, then the decision is easy.

She touches the wall in front of her, turns and goes in the other direction. Step by step. *Please don't let him ever think to come here at night.*

Another two steps to the wall.

Why doesn't he strap me to the bed? Why risk my running away?

Turn and go back again.

He is very sure of himself. Damn sure.

She forces herself to go more slowly to keep from falling.

Is he overestimating himself? Or am I overestimating myself?

The exertion makes her sweat.

What does he know about me? And what does he want from me? Why did he ask if the baby is Gabriel's?

Chapter 30

Berlin – 15 September, 11.37 p.m.

Gabriel peers across the street through the tinted rear windows of the Chrysler Voyager and sips on his cold coffee.

Nothing.

Five days have passed since he found Verena Schuster's body. Five days with no sign of life from Liz or word from the kidnapper. The only thing he's had to hold on to in this time is the search for Jonas.

He purchased the dark-blue Chrysler van on the very same day that he found Verena Schuster. He paid the used-car dealer in cash without negotiating. The van had only three months left on the MOT and a mileage of just over 130,000, but none of that mattered. He didn't need it for driving.

Everything is quiet in front of the kiosk on the other side of the street. In the bright, open shop window, Mr Moustache leans against his elbow on the counter, smokes and leafs through a magazine. Between puffs, he glances alternately at the television inside to his right and at his mobile, presumably to check the time. It is 11.38 p.m. In twenty-two minutes, he will roll down the exterior shutters and go home on time, like every night.

An elderly gentleman passes behind the Chrysler on the street and goes up to the kiosk. His dachshund sniffs at the street lamp in the very same spot as yesterday and the day before and lifts his leg.

Then the man buys a beer at the news stand and disappears.

Mr Moustache looks at his mobile again.

Five days of nothing . . . the wait is killing him, but he has no choice. This is his only and best lead so far.

On the other side of the street, someone approaches from the opposite direction with the dragging gait of an elderly man.

Just another pensioner.

As the man approaches, Gabriel tries to make out his face, but he has a hood pulled over his head that casts a shadow over his features. A sports bag hangs at waist-level.

Pensioner?

The man goes up to the kiosk counter and gets a surprised smile from the Mr Moustache. Gabriel reaches for his binoculars and tries to make out the man's face again, but he only sees the edge of the hood.

Mr Moustache hands him a bottle of spirits over the counter, takes his cash and rummages through the till.

The man with the hooded jumper turns around, first to the left, then to the right in Gabriel's direction. For a brief moment, the light from the street reveals the pale features of a twenty-something with a crooked nose.

Jonas.

Gabriel puts the binoculars aside and unlocks the van's sliding door. With a grinding metallic noise, the door opens.

Jonas turns his head in his direction and looks suspiciously over at the van. Mr Moustache puts the change on the counter.

Gabriel climbs out and walks casually towards the kiosk, as if he wants to buy one last beer for the evening. There are about thirty metres between him and Jonas. There is a light drizzle.

Jonas stands there, frozen, his eyes hidden by his hood. A fox in his hole.

Another twenty metres.

Jonas doesn't move, clutching his bottle of spirits.

There's something about Gabriel's appearance that Jonas doesn't like. All of a sudden, his body jolts into a run.

Gabriel sprints after him like a jungle cat. The drizzle lands on his face in a wet film. Jonas is clearly younger than him – and clearly in worse shape. He turns the next corner, looks around, spots Gabriel – who is rapidly catching up – and hurls the bottle at his feet. The momentum of the throw makes Jonas lose his balance and he stumbles, losing valuable time. With a loud crash, the bottle smashes on the asphalt. Gabriel jumps over the shards, reaches into Jonas's hood and pushes him against the building with all of his weight. The rough plaster scrapes Jonas's cheek.

'Ow. Shit, man. Let go!' Jonas squirms around like an animal trying to free himself. He is shaking; his chest is pounding with exertion. Gabriel wrings the fabric of the hood into his fist, constricts Jonas's airway and forces him to his knees.

'What's this about? What do you want?' Jonas pants. 'I didn't do nothing.'

'Sure, that's why you ran off.'

Gabriel guides him a few metres back into a dark doorway, shoving him into the corner. The pungent odour of the spilled spirits on the pavement rises in his nose.

'Ow! Man, shit,' Jonas howls. Whaddaya want?'

'Are you Jonas Schuster?'

Clearly afraid, Jonas squints up into Gabriel's eyes and tries to assess his pursuer. 'And if I am?'

'I have a few questions.'

'I ain't saying nothing, man.' Jonas pushes out his chin. 'You can forget it. Only with a lawyer.'

'Lawyer, right.'

'I won't let anything get pinned on me.'

'So you're some kind of smart arse, eh?'

Jonas looks at him, unsure.

'You can forget about a lawyer, it wouldn't help anyway. I'm not a cop, the cops always show up in pairs. Someone like you should know that.'

'Not a cop?' Jonas asks suspiciously. 'Really?'

A light turns on inside the building. They hear footsteps on the stairs.

Gabriel pulls the hood tighter. 'Listen,' he hisses, 'I know you're in trouble. I can help you. Or I can beat the shit out of you. Your choice.'

Jonas's expression flickers. The steps from inside grow louder. 'Help,' he mutters hoarsely.

Without a word, Gabriel grabs him by the armpits and pulls him up onto his feet. He puts his right arm around his shoulders and pushes him along the pavement. Shards of glass crunch under their feet, the street lamps glow like fog lights in the drizzle. On the other side of the street, the Chrysler peers out of the darkness. 'Over to the van.'

He manoeuvres Jonas into the passenger seat and starts the engine. In silence, he steers out of the side street and turns onto Kottbusser Strasse, the main road. The windscreen wipers squeal. Jonas droops in his seat, misery personified.

'If you're not some pig,' he asks feebly, 'then what?'

'Private investigator.'

'A snoop?'

'Private investigator,' Gabriel repeats flatly.

'And what are you investigating?'

'I'm looking for the person,' Gabriel says, 'who did that to your mother.'

Silence.

He isn't asking *what* had been done to her, Gabriel thinks.

Jonas bites his lip. His pupils dart restlessly from one point to the next. 'She – she's dead, isn't she?'

Gabriel nods.

'How do you know –'

'I saw her.'

Jonas's eyes glaze over. 'That fucking arsehole,' he says with a shaky voice and wipes his nose with his palm.

'It wasn't even about her at all. He was after you, wasn't he?' Gabriel asks.

Jonas looks to the side. His chin is trembling, but he clenches his teeth so that Gabriel doesn't notice and nods silently.

'What happened?'

'I . . . I got home in the afternoon –'

'When?'

'Last week, Friday. Eigh . . . eight days ago.'

Gabriel counts back. So, on September 7th, three days before he'd found Verena Schuster.

'So, around three, I heard . . . something, outside, at the door. I thought she had a visitor, some guy. It happened a lot.

So I quietly opened the door and went into my room. And then I heard it. I . . . I recognised the voice. And the door to the kitchen was open and I . . .,' he swallows and wipes away a whitish string of mucus from his nose, 'I saw the knife, as he . . .' He goes silent and stares out through the windscreen at the wet street.

'What did he say?'

'He kept repeating the same thing. Kept saying, "Where is your son? Tell me where he is." And then he . . . the knife was inside of her and he turned it,' Jonas sobs.

'And then?'

'I ran. I . . . I was scared shitless, I ran away. He didn't notice me.'

'And then?'

'What do you mean?

'Did you go back, or. . . ?

Jonas shakes his head. 'He's waiting there for me,' he whispers. 'He'll kill me. I can never go back.'

'Why haven't you called the police?'

'I . . . because –' He stops short and stares at the windscreen wipers as they swing from side to side and sniffles loudly. 'Don't know.'

'What does he want with you?'

'Don't know,' Jonas whispers like a broken record.

Gabriel turns slightly left from Kottbusser Damm onto Sonnenallee. The drizzle envelops everything in a hazy black soup with flecks of light floating on top.

'Listen,' Gabriel says gruffly, 'the man's a psychopath. He didn't just kill your mother, he literally slaughtered her. He slit her open from below and then pulled out her guts. She was probably still alive at the time and had to watch. What do you think he has planned for you if he catches you?'

Jonas's face is white as a sheet.

Silence spreads and surrounds them. The damp asphalt whooshes softly and the rubber from the windscreen wipers scrapes across the glass.

'So,' Gabriel starts, 'if I am to help you, then you have to talk to me. Understand?'

Jonas chews on his lip for almost a minute. Finally, he quietly says, 'I already . . . I already saw him.'

'Where?'

'In Friedrichshain. He . . . killed my friend Pit. But I got away. That's why he's looking for me.'

'Because you know what he looks like?'

Jonas nods. He wipes his nose with his hand again and then wraps his arms around himself, as if he needs to hold on tight. 'He was wearing some kinda mask or hat, but Pit ripped it off. He . . . his face is . . . one half looks like a zombie.'

'A zombie?'

'I don't know, like after an accident or something. The other half was totally normal.'

'Which half?'

Jonas shrugs. 'I think the . . . right?'

'And what else?'

'His hand was weird. It didn't look real, like plastic or something.'

'A prosthesis.'

'Yeah, maybe.'

'Which side?'

'. . . Also the right.'

'What else can you think of?'

'Don't know,' Jonas says with a hoarse voice. His eyes stray out the windscreen. 'He's blond. Maybe fifty. Roughly as tall as you.'

The headlights of an oncoming car illuminate the narrow strip of grass between the trees. 'Will you . . . catch him?'

Hopefully, since you can't seem to shake him! Gabriel thinks. And otherwise, I'll probably have to serve you up on a silver platter . . .

'Will you?'

Gabriel's hands clutch the steering wheel more tightly. He thinks about Liz and can feel his self-restraint turning to rage. 'Why didn't you call the police when you were in the park?'

'I . . . what?'

'What happened in the park? Why did he kill your friend?'

'I, I don't kn—'

'Don't lie to me.'

Jonas stares at him. A glaring beam of light from another car shines on his face and he blinks uncontrollably.

'Spit it out. What happened in the park? Something must've happened, or else you would've called the police. What are you afraid of?'

Jonas groans. 'There was . . .' he mumbles, 'there was also a woman.'

'And?'

'She had red hair. She was just lying there.'

Liz! Gabriel's stomach ties into knots. 'What does that mean, *she was just lying there?*'

'Don't know.'

Silence.

'She was just lying there on the ground. Something was wrong with her.'

'And then?'

'Well,' Jonas squirms around. 'She was giving us shit. Earlier, on the train. She was all worked up, tryna start something. She needed a real thrashing, so we gave it to 'er –'

Gabriel abruptly slams on the brakes and turns the steering wheel all the way to the right. The front wheels of the van slam against the kerb and the vehicle jumps and then comes to a screeching halt on the edge of the street, just before the crossing. Thirty metres further, a flyover hangs above the street like a concrete guillotine.

Smash his skull in – now, right now! the voice in Gabriel's head encourages.

Stay out of this, damn it. Just stay out of this.

Gabriel swallows and tries to get his seething emotions under control.

Just bloody do it. Then we'll finally have this behind us. You'll feel better.

'Thrashing?' Gabriel asks. His eyes bore into Jonas. 'Did you say *thrashing?*'

Jonas shifts away from him and leans against the door. 'Well,' he mumbles. 'So, she was, I mean . . . she really insulted us . . . anyone would have –'

He doesn't get any further.

Gabriel's fist lands square in the middle of Jonas's face. The back of his head slams against the window and his upper lip splits. Jonas howls and spits blood into his hand along with something white. 'Shit,' he whines, 'my teeth.'

'That was for the thrashing. Enough of this shit. Come clean. What exactly happened?'

Jonas is deathly pale. The pain drives tears into his eyes. 'I . . . I didn't want to,' he stammers. 'It . . . it was Pit's idea.'

'*What* was Pit's idea?'

'The girl really laid into us on the train earlier, like I said, threatened us and wanted to get the cops and everything. Pit thought she needed a beating.'

'She was lying there on the ground and you beat her up?'

Jonas swallowed. The tears run in dirty trails across his face. He sniffles. It sounds like a blunt saw.

'You . . . you're not really an investigator, are you?'

Gabriel's hand shoots out and grabs him by the throat.

Squeeze, Luke. Squeeze!

Jonas lets out a desperate gurgle, his eyes bulge out and he starts turning blue. Helpless, he grabs Gabriel's arm. A dark wet spot spreads across his trousers.

A twisted smile comes across Gabriel's face.

More, more! the voice whispers in his head.

I still need him – I can't.

An eye for an eye, Luke. Do it. If you don't do it, no one will.

I need him to find Liz, he's my decoy!

Stop thinking and just do it!

Gabriel closes his eyes – and lets go.

Jonas groans and gasps for air like an asthmatic. His whole body is shaking.

'And then?' Gabriel asks. '*What then?*'

'Then,' Jonas wheezes and his face changes back from blue to red, 'then this guy came out of the bushes. Wearin' a black hat with holes in it like in a horror film,' he pants. 'He came towards us and we thought, let's get out of here. Pit was already moving, but I wasn't as fast. He . . . he was after us and had me . . . and Pit saw and came back. He dived at the guy and pummelled him, and then pulled off his hat . . . but the man was stronger and . . . and had him,' Jonas sobs and stops, his chin trembling. 'He had a knife, such a little thing, not a real knife, and used it to slit his throat . . .'

Jonas's hands nervously grope around for something to hold on to, but he can't find anything to give him support.

'I . . . I didn't want to,' he stammers. 'I'm sorry, man. Really . . .'

Suddenly he hooks his right hand into the door handle and instinctively pulls on it until it clicks and the passenger-side door swings open. Jonas falls out of the Chrysler onto the pavement.

Gabriel reacts quickly and grabs him by his lower left leg. Panicked, Jonas tries to pull away and kicks with the other leg. His foot hits Gabriel's chin with a thud. Gabriel sees stars. Jonas sees his chance and immediately kicks again, hitting Gabriel's already injured shoulder. Gabriel growls in pain and lets go. Jonas flails his arms, squirms the rest of the way out of the Chrysler, falls and pulls himself together again right away.

Gabriel opens the driver's side door in a daze. The wind from a car speeding by nearly rips the door out of his hand, a horn blaring angrily in his ears. He looks at the crossroads, sees Jonas staggering away in the direction of the flyover. Gabriel takes off his seatbelt and jumps out of the van.

Jonas turns around in a panic and trips further in the direction of the train tacks. The opening to the underpass is gaping ominously. Eyes wide, he stares over at Gabriel, who is catching up and crossing the street when the blood-curdlingly loud sound of a horn approaches behind him.

Jonas snaps his head around. The forty-ton lorry bursts through the underpass like a monster and shoots into the crossing. The Mercedes star is as big as Jonas's head and directed right at his chest. Jonas's mouth hangs open with fright; it looks grotesque, almost as if he'd hoped to swallow the lorry at the last minute. It's too late to scream. The impact sounds like hitting plastic, like kicking a dustbin.

Gabriel stops mid-motion, freezes. From a few metres away, he sees Jonas hurled into the air like a weightless doll made of straw, only to immediately fall beneath the fully-loaded lorry one second later. The vehicle shakes briefly, but hardly more than a bulldozer driving over a rat.

The lorry only comes to a screeching halt after another hundred metres.

Chapter 31

David rinses the toothpaste down the sink and looks at himself in the mirror. Tired green eyes with dark circles underneath them. He rubs his hand on his chin to see if his intentional stubble still looks intentional.

He can hear the television through the open WC door – an advertisement for a women's razor. He thinks of Shona, whom he hasn't seen in two weeks and has plans to meet this evening. She was ambushed with a job that's monopolised her time. It wasn't a problem for David, since Gabriel's sudden appearance had thrown him into a deep depression. When the police were standing at his door while Shona was there and explained that there was a search warrant out on his brother because he was suspected of murder, and for fleeing from custody and armed hostage-taking, he felt the ground fall from under his feet.

He digs his electric razor out of the drawer. The device only offers him a tired buzz before stopping. Cursing under his breath, he opens the drawer in search of the power cord, as he squints at the time: 9.17 p.m.

At least Shona's call had given him a little breathing room. 'Sorry . . .' Her voice sounded annoyed. 'I'm still at work. The usual. Terrible meeting and now everything has to be different. Everything blue will be green and round will be square . . . I just can't make it before half past nine.'

'Are you sure you'll even make it by half past nine?'

'If not, then I'll pour a drink over the keyboard. Half past nine at the Santa Media.'

Somehow, time ran away from him. Applause comes from the television.

The doorbell buzzes. *Shona*? He glances back at the clock. Twenty past nine. David furrows his brow. They had plans for the Santa Media, one of the popular after-work drinking spots, but there was no talk of picking him up. The woman is *unpredictable*! He grins, slips on his shirt while walking and tries to button it quickly, but the lights are off in the hall. His finger automatically lands on the button for the intercom. 'Hi. Just come up, I'm almost ready.' He buzzes open the building door, opens the door to his flat in advance – and then jumps with fright.

In the doorway is a pale, slender man with thinning grey hair and accountant's glasses. 'Good evening, David,' the man says. His face is in partial darkness; the lighting of the corridor gives him a strange aura. For a moment, David thinks it's a police officer, maybe an inspector, in front of him. But don't they always identify themselves?

'Do we know each other?'

'No, but we have a shared acquaintance. Your brother. Is he here?'

'No. Sorry. We don't have the best relationship.' The man raises his almost hairless eyebrows.

David makes out the slender figure. He must be in his sixties. His hands are in the pockets of his short, light-grey trench coat and the right pocket bears the outline of an unmistakable shape: the barrel of a gun.

David's heart skips a beat. The man seems to be able to read his thoughts. He pulls his hand out of the coat pocket without the gun and shows it to David. 'Your brother is a dangerous man,' he says apologetically.

David takes a step back. 'What do you want?'

'May I come in?'

'I'm sorry. I'm in a hurry.'

'Don't you want to finally get answers to your questions?' the man smiles, joyless and calm.

'What questions?'

'Everyone has questions, but you have a few in particular, don't you? And your brother can't give you the answers. He says he can't remember that night. Or maybe he just doesn't want to.' The eyes behind the small glasses focus on David's face, waiting for a reaction. The thinning hair shines like wire against the light. David has a bad feeling; he wonders how he knows everything – and, more importantly, what he knows. Without saying anything, he opens the door and lets the man in.

The man acknowledges this with a smile, nods at him politely and enters. His pale, colourless eyes dart across the parquet floors, walls and furniture. In the living room, he sits on one of the two grey sofas and crosses his legs like it's his own home.

David watches him silently. With his smooth grey trench coat and his pale skin, he almost disappears on the sofa. An accountant, David thinks, were it not for the gun in his coat pocket.

'Nice flat you've got here. A bit empty, but nice.'

David grimaces. 'What do you know about my parents' death?'

The man ignores the question and gestures to the rectangular stain on the wall. 'Where has the lovely Dali study gone? I thought you had it right there on that wall.'

David stares at him, mouth hanging open – and then closes it again.

'Gone? Like everything else?'

'Who the hell are you?' David whispers.

'Your brother worked for me for a long time,' the man says. 'A very long time.'

David considers the man without saying a word.

'They screwed you, David. That settlement was a damned disgrace. *Treasure Castle* was your format. You should have let it go to trial. Your chances weren't bad at all.'

'What do *you* know?' David says.

The man shrugs. 'You don't like to fight, right?'

David's uneasy feeling grows stronger. 'What the hell do you know about the night my parents were murdered?' he asks in a husky voice.

'How deep in debt are you now, David? Two million? Three?'

'That's none of your business.'

'With the mortgage on the flat, the losses from the property fund, the legal fees and the remains of the settlement, it might actually be three million on the button, isn't that so?'

'Why do I have the feeling,' David asks, 'that you know more about my life than I do?'

The man leans forward. 'Listen, David. To be honest, I really don't understand why you aren't angry. You have every reason to be. They made a fool of you and stripped you naked . . .'

David's mouth is suddenly bone dry. He wants to say something, but nothing comes to mind. All of a sudden, he thinks of Shona. He looks at the stove in the kitchen: 9.23 p.m. *She will be furious.*

'I can help you, my boy. I can help you climb out of it.'

'*You?*' David looks at the man sceptically and then lets out a bitter laugh. 'How do you propose to do that? Give me the three million?'

The man chuckles and shakes his head. 'No, certainly not. I'll give you something much better. Something you need far more urgently.'

'I can't imagine what that could be.'

'I'll give you back your self-respect, my boy. Your *pride!*' Full of energy, the man's eyes flash from behind his glasses. 'I could give you back the rights to your format.'

David stares at him. His hands get clammy, his heart beats faster. 'I . . . I'm not sure I want to hear what I'll have to do for that.'

'You just have to tell me where I can find Gabriel.'

'Didn't you just say that he works for you? So why don't you know where he is?'

'I said he *worked* for me.'

'What does that mean?' David asks, even though he's already got an idea of what it means. 'You gave him the boot?'

'In a sense.'

'Just so I understand correctly – first you kicked him out and now you're looking for him?'

'Let's just say that a few things have changed. In any case, I need to find him.'

'Why?'

The man hesitates for a moment. 'He stole something, something very important. I need to get it back.'

David goes silent for a beat, then sighs, turns around and goes into the open kitchen, steps behind the counter, and leans heavily on it, as if he needs support.

'So,' the man says, 'you help me and I'll help you.'

David takes a deep breath. 'I'm afraid you'll have to find him yourself. I can't help you.'

The man's eyes widen in feigned astonishment. 'Are you serious?'

'He's my brother,' David says. 'Have you got a brother?'

The man looks at him. At first, he seems as if he's lost his train of thought. Then he sighs, 'I was afraid of this. You trust Gabriel.'

'He's my brother,' David insists.

'Then why did he lie to you?'

'He . . . he is . . .' David stops.

'Or maybe you don't consider silence a lie?'

David looks at the man, examines him. 'How do you know what happened back then?' he whispers.

'Tell me where to find your brother and you'll find out.'

'I don't believe a single word that's come out of your mouth.'

'It's very simple,' the man explains. His grey eyes are like pebbles – hard, smooth and lifeless. 'You give me a little information and I will answer the most pressing question of your life.'

'You're lying,' David says and swallows. 'There was no one there that could have seen anything, except Gabriel . . . and the one who shot . . .'

The man smiles and nods.

David suddenly feels like he's walking on an incline and is completely unbalanced.

'There is a lot of material,' the man says. 'Much more than you think. The files, psychiatric evaluations, records form therapy sessions. A real goldmine when it comes to Gabriel's dreams and nightmares – and his subconscious.'

David is dizzy and has to close his eyes for a moment. 'Even if I wanted to tell you,' he finally mutters, 'I don't know where he is.'

'Do you actually know who it is you're protecting?'

'What do you mean by that?'

'Do you believe your brother? I mean, do you trust him?'

David looks away from the man and runs his hand across his face.

'The one who shot your father . . .' the man says slowly, emphasising each individual syllable, '. . . that was your brother.'

David's heart stops.

Silence. No breath, no heartbeat, not even a thought.

Then his heart begins working again, pounding, hammering in his chest. 'That's . . . that can't be.'

'What can't be?' the man snorts. 'That an eleven-year-old would shoot his father?'

'I don't believe a word of it.'

'Look at your brother. What do you think? Why is he the way he is?'

'He lost his parents. Isn't that enough?'

'You also lost your parents . . .' The man's gaze bores into David. 'But you're still a normal person. You're calm, not violent . . . quite unlike Gabriel . . .'

David could feel the ground opening up beneath him. Gabriel's fights at the Elisabethstift home, the attack on the director at Falkenhorst, the drug abuse, the mental hospital – all the madness. Suddenly everything seems to make sense. 'Prove it,' David says softly.

'Tell me where to find your brother. Then you get the file – and your proof.'

David is chilled to the bone. He coughs, stomach acid rises in his oesophagus and a sour taste spreads through his mouth. The question comes out without his being able to stop it. 'And – did he also shoot my mother?'

'Have we got a deal?'

'I don't know,' David mutters weakly, 'if I can do that.'

'Oh, you can. You just have to want to. But don't tell him that I was here. Don't tell him what I've told you. He would deny it anyway. He trusts no one. But you know that better than anyone.'

'I . . . I have no idea if he'll actually contact me again. I think he has other things to worry about.'

'Because he broke out of custody? Believe me, that is exactly when one needs friends and relatives. He will call. Sooner or later.'

'What are you going to do,' David asks, 'when you know where he is?'

The man shrugs and looks at David with an impervious expression. 'I just want to find him. And I want to get back what he took from me. That's all.' The man gets up, surprisingly agile for his age, and leaves a business card on the grey sofa. On the thin white cardboard is a phone number and nothing else.

'Ask for Yuri,' he says. Without looking back, he disappears into the corridor. The blue walls cast a coloured glow on his drab coat.

Then the door slams shut and there is silence.

Chapter 32

Berlin – 18 September, 4.34 p.m.

Gabriel puts down the *Berliner Zeitung* and pours the remainder of his coffee into the sink. The boiled black concoction that the receptionist at Caesar's claimed was filter coffee tastes terribly bitter. Despite the caffeine, he is heavy with fatigue, as if the pull of gravity has tripled.

The persistent buzzing of a fly that got caught between the window and the curtain in his room is getting on his nerves. It reminds him of the swarm of flies over Verena Schuster and the cloying stench.

Yesterday, the police finally found her already highly decomposed body. Shortly before that, the body of a young man who had been run over by a forty-ton lorry was identified as Jonas Schuster. The officers wanted to inform his mother and found her body spread across the kitchen table in her flat. The *Berliner Zeitung* cites the police spokesman, who explains that this is 'one of the most heinous acts of crime in recent Berlin history.'

Gabriel places the empty mug on the scratched square table, rolls the paper up into a firm tube and quietly pushes the curtain aside. The orange and pink autumn sun shines softly into the room, as if the last few days never happened.

With a swift flick of the wrist, Gabriel swats at the fly with the newspaper. The buzzing ends instantly and a twisted black lump lands on the windowsill.

Gabriel lies back on the bed and sinks deep into the saggy mattress. His right shoulder has been hurting more since Jonas kicked it, his eyes burn from fatigue and the dusty air.

Ever since Jonas Schuster was run over by the massive lorry, time has been passing painfully slowly, but also far too quickly.

At least now he has a description of Liz's kidnapper: white, around fifty years old, blond hair, the right half of his face is disfigured and he has a prosthetic hand or arm – so, a man who would have a very difficult time hiding, at least, if you knew where to look for him.

But Jonas's death lost Gabriel his only chance to lure Liz's kidnapper out. Now all he has left is to dig back into his lost memories, into the farthest, darkest corners of his mind, in the hope of finding something that connects him to this man.

For three days, he's been racking his brain and sleeping very little or not at all. Even when he does manage to drift off, it's a restless, exhausting sleep that's full of nightmares that raise more questions than they answer.

Gabriel stares at the ceiling, but no matter how hard he tries, October 13th is and remains a blind spot.

Enough of this madness, Luke.

I can't stop. Not any more.

It's not worth it. Look at yourself. Do you know what you're up against?

Spare me.

What can I say? I'm attached to your madness. Free yourself at last. She is dragging you down. Nothing more.

You really are an arsehole.

You confuse cause and effect. She's hurting you, not me.

Better to hurt than to feel nothing at all, like you.

We know each other well, don't we?

Gabriel clenches his fists.

It's hopeless.

I'm not David.

No, certainly not. You're Luke.

You sound just like my psychiatrist.

Careful, you wouldn't want me getting angry!

And you, kindly stop constantly calling me –

The shrill ring of the mobile cuts through the silence. Gabriel tenses. *Unknown number* appears on the screen.

'Hello?'

'Hello, Gabriel.'

Gabriel inhales sharply. He knows immediately that it's him.

'I'm surprised that you took care of my work for me.' The voice sounds calm and cool.

'I don't know what you mean,' Gabriel replies. 'What work?'

'That useless boy,' the voice chuckles. 'Do you regret it already?'

Gabriel remains silent, although he would prefer to scream.

'I would have regretted it. Cheap revenge, a lack of self-control. It would torture me. So fast, so short, that's nothing to me. Revenge is worthless when it ends so quickly. And then the price. . .' He laughs again. 'How will you find me now? Me and your girl?'

'Who the hell are you?' Gabriel asks.

'You can call me Val.'

'Val,' Gabriel repeats. Finally, a name. 'Is that German or English?'

'Don't try to get me caught up in a conversation about my name. It's amusing, but pointless. You know, I had to think for a while about what to make of the fact that you don't know who I am any longer. And honestly, I think this is all much better than I'd hoped. A real scavenger hunt. A scavenger hunt in your mind. God, that must be exhausting. Do you have nightmares? A warm welcome to my world. You really don't remember anything, do you? And even after the boy told you what I look like . . . He told you, didn't he? One doesn't forget my face so quickly. Did he tell you what I did with the other boy?'

Gabriel can hear the blood rushing to his head. He clenches his jaw to keep from saying anything wrong – to avoid making a mistake that Liz would have to pay for.

'You don't want to say anything . . . You're *scared*, right? I can smell it now.'

Gabriel just listens to the noise.

'I know that you know what I did. Of course, he told you. But do you know *why* I did it?' He goes quiet for a provokingly long time. 'I did it for you,' Val finally whispers. 'It was revenge. Revenge for what they did to your girl. They hurt her. Your girl. And I wanted her to be perfect for me!'

'You had Liz already, right?' Gabriel asks. 'You had her already – and then those two suddenly showed up and got in the way.'

'Yes, it was ugly. The two were so brutal. And I was so stupid and a bit of a coward. I didn't want them to see me, so I hid in the bushes. I should have just stayed and not left her alone. I hated those boys for it, making me feel so stupid and cowardly . . .' Val groans as if the memory still haunts him. 'But now I feel better again.'

'Because you slit his throat . . .' Gabriel mutters.

'Oh no! No, no. That is not the most important thing. I saved *her* and punished *him*. But most of all, I got to see him die. Every moment of his pathetic, shitty, unworthy life flowing out of him. I looked in his eyes until the very last second. And he saw that I saw. The last thing he witnessed was my joy at his death. That, you see, *that* is revenge.'

'And Verena Schuster, the other boy's mother? Why her?'

Val is silent for a moment and then says, 'Ultimately, I did that for you, too.'

'For *me*?'

'Oh, yes. I wanted to help you.'

'That . . . that's mad,' Gabriel says, horrified.

'Mad? *I* see everything clearly. The mad ones aren't the problem, you know. It's the normal ones. You of all people should know that. And yet, still you act as if you're one of them, one of the *normal* ones.'

Gabriel's hand grips the telephone. Snapshots flicker in his worn-out brain. Straitjacket, straps, Dressler's face . . .

Val whispers, 'I'm the one showing you the way, so you can find your way back. At some point, we all have to go back to where we began.'

'What good is that?' Gabriel asks. 'What do you want from me?'

'I want you to *remember* and to understand what you've done. I want you to remember it every day and every night.'

'Then leave Liz out of it. She has nothing to do with this.'

'How touching!' Val snorts. His voice suddenly changes and becomes sharp and aggressive. 'Do you actually hear yourself talking? Do you really believe in this film hero shit?

Do you think that you're going to accomplish anything with someone like me that way? You must know that you're not getting through to me with this noble bullshit. It's a good thing that she has nothing to do with it. All the better for you to remember!'

'At the moment, I remember absolutely nothing. And if you want to insist that I remember, then just bloody *tell* me what happened that night and maybe I'll finally understand what you want from me.'

'Oh, no! I won't make it that easy for you. You will have to torture yourself even more if you want to see your girl again.'

'You know what?' Gabriel blurts out. 'You live in a sick world. And who knows, maybe you have no idea at all what *really* happened on that night. I don't understand what you want. You're holding me responsible for something that happened to you. Good. Understood! But as long as you come at me with all this vague hinting shit, nothing will make any sense . . .'

There is a heavy silence on the line.

'Don't you believe me?' Val asks.

Gabriel immediately regrets what he said. Maybe he went too far and put Liz in danger.

'All right,' Val finally says. His voice suddenly sounds deliberately calm. 'Do you remember your pyjamas? With Luke Skywalker on the chest?'

The pyjamas. He remembers the pyjamas.

So what? You wore the damned things often enough.

'On the hem of your pyjama top,' Val continues, 'you had a bloody handprint. You clung to it when you went into the cellar.'

That can't be. He can't know that.

Oh god. He was there.

'Who the hell are you?' Gabriel whispers breathlessly.

No answer.

'What do you know?' Gabriel's voice trembles. 'Hello?'

'Carpe Noctem,' Val says.

Then the connection breaks off.

Chapter 33

Val's call pushed Gabriel over the edge. He hadn't realised he was standing so close to the abyss. And now he was in a free fall.

The effect was shocking, like an overdose of cocaine. His heart raced as quickly as his thoughts. Again and again, violent trembling ran through him, as if he had a fever and his over-wrought body were crying out for sleep.

He marshalled his last reserves like a drug addict on the hunt for one more hit and bought a packet of sleeping pills.

Then he slept like the dead.

When he awoke, he was wearing the pyjamas. He wondered why they still fit him. Luke Skywalker hung loosely over his eleven-year-old chest, as flames climbed into the blood-red night sky. The house was ablaze, but he knew that it was no use to keep waiting. He had to go in. Barefoot, he ran across the scorching pavement, the fingers of his right hand clutching the hem of his pyjama top.

The front door was open, its frame entirely in flames, and just behind it was the cellar stairs. He climbed down, step by step, amidst the scorching heat. The walls whipped red tongues of fire at him and the stairs seemed endless, even after a thousand steps. He looked around and was shocked to see that the front door was still right behind him. Now there was a fireman standing in the doorway – or was it a police officer? – offering him a hand. He recognised the police officer's face, but he didn't want to take his hand and instead slapped it away, ran further down the never-ending stairs and fell with a crash. When he got up, he was suddenly in the lab and started to panic. No one was allowed to know about Dad's lab. Not even the police!

All of a sudden, the dream ends, like a rubber band that has been stretched too far and then snapped. Gabriel sits up, bathed in sweat.

It is 4.27 p.m. He has slept for almost sixteen hours. His legs are like jelly, but they carried him. He stares at the strange man in the mirror and tries his best to wash him away with cold water.

What was that last thing Val said? *Carpe noctem*? It didn't make the least bit of sense.

He tries to slowly organise the chaos in his head. The fact that Val had mentioned the Luke Skywalker pyjamas was terrifying. The pyjamas were the only things that he and David could save from their former life. The bloodstain on the hem was a mark left behind by the horror of that night. And even if Gabriel had no recollection at all about when and how it had got there, at least he knew that it had not been there before.

Val's voice echoed in his thoughts. *On the hem of your pyjama top, you had a bloody handprint. You clung to it when you went into the cellar.*

The cellar. So, he had not only dreamt it, but actually had gone down into the cellar that night. And the lab? Had he also been there? Was it about something in the lab? And what had

Val been looking for there? How had he even got into the house? And why did he – Gabriel – have blood on his hand? Was it even his own blood that had stained his pyjamas?

In the children's home, it took numerous washes to get the bloody handprint out of the fabric and, in turn, the image of Luke had faded. But, despite the washed-out colours and their connection to his terrible experience, the Luke Skywalker pyjamas were his only souvenir of his previous life and he clung to them like a treasure. And Gabriel knew that David, who had the same pyjamas, had done exactly the same.

Did David still have his pyjamas after all this time?

The thought of his brother stung. That night should have bound them together, but instead it tore them apart.

For the first time in his life, he'd wished that he hadn't locked David in his room. Maybe then his brother would have been able to tell him what happened on that night. Even today, he thinks, I still don't know what he heard up there and what he didn't.

Would it help to ask him?

Gabriel threw on his clothes, black jeans, a dark jumper and a plain black leather jacket, along with a cap to hide his face.

He had nothing left to lose, and David was his last hope of getting any information to jog his memory.

So, he left Caesar's and walked to David's flat. He'd left the Chrysler on a distant side street just after Jonas's death, just in case the kiosk owner remembered the van and saw them together.

Now that he's standing in front of David's door, Gabriel is no longer sure whether it is a good idea to ask his brother. He looks around in all directions and then presses the buzzer. This time, the button isn't cool metal, but warm from the midday sun.

He won't be there, Luke. He's never there when you need him.

Gabriel wants to disagree, but then he hears the crackling intercom. 'Hello?'

'Hey, it's me, Gabriel.'

Silence.

'David?'

'Are you insane? The police were here. They're looking for you.'

'I know,' Gabriel says. 'But they're gone now, right?'

Again, silence. Then the buzzer. 'Come up.'

Gabriel takes the lift. Once more, he finds the cleanliness of David's building striking. David is already standing in the doorway, thin, pale, green-eyed.

And now?

'Can I come in?'

David looks him over and then nods. Somehow, he seems uneasy.

'You look like shit,' David says.

'That's how I feel, too.'

'Are you on something?'

Gabriel shakes his head. 'No. Just a couple of sleeping pills.'

David says nothing.

'Listen,' Gabriel begins cautiously.

'I don't want to know anything,' David interrupts. 'I don't want to know anything about all your shit. Just leave me alone, OK?'

'OK,' Gabriel says. 'I don't mean to annoy you, or convince you of some story that you would never believe from me anyway. I don't want you getting involved in any way. Things are already complicated enough between us . . .'

Gabriel looks at David, whose green eyes are strangely indifferent. He is suspicious, guarded, but there is also something else, something he can't put his finger on.

'I need to know something. I . . .' Gabriel stops and tries to find the right words for something that has no right words. 'You know that I can't remember . . . that night.'

David nods coolly. 'Or at least you always blocked it.'

'I really don't know, David. I simply can't remember. But now I *need* to know, you understand?'

David looks at him, surprised. Apparently he'd thought of every possible scenario except for this. 'What do you mean? Why?'

'Don't ask. It is what it is. I need to know.'

David laughs bitterly. His cheeks go red with anger and he's visibly fighting to maintain composure. 'My god,' he finally exclaims. 'You're silent for thirty years. You answer nothing, not one of my questions and you leave me to think you're dead. And now, all of a sudden you want to know what happened?' David shakes his head. 'Honestly, I can't believe it! I was the one locked up in my room. I didn't hear anything. And now you're asking *me* what happened? Again, what about *my* bloody questions?'

'You never asked.'

'Like hell,' David replies, 'you always just shut down. I had a thousand questions!'

'Then why didn't you ever ask them?'

'I thought, I . . .' David stops and looks for the words. *'Oh, fuck it!'* he finally blurts out. 'Why do you think? I was scared. You were always so . . . I don't even know what to say. I was a child, damn it. And you were my big brother, you understand? I had no father, no mother and I was so scared of losing you, too. So, when you always shut down like that, I thought, just leave him alone . . . You always looked like you were about to fly into a fit of rage – or have some sort of permanent psychological trauma. Usually, I was just scared you'd have a breakdown.'

Gabriel stares at him in disbelief. David had tried to take care of *him?* 'You . . . you never told me that.'

'Of course not. How could I? You were completely gone, lost in some film that I couldn't watch. You couldn't be stopped on your trip . . .'

'I was protecting you, the whole time you –'

'*No*, damn it,' David says. Tears glisten in his eyes. 'You were preoccupied with yourself. It had nothing to do with me, it was always about you. With every fight you started, every time you jumped in for me . . . it was about you. I never asked for that . . . I hated it.'

Gabriel swallows the growing anger and the shame. His head is pounding. 'Nonsense. Maybe you were too little to remember . . . What about that time with the boys that messed with you at the Elisabethstift? Do you really want to say you could've managed that alone? Or the nun, who –'

'Oh, please!' David rolls his eyes. 'Why do you think they picked on me . . . it wasn't about me. They were just too chicken to go after you. Most of the trouble I had was because of *you* . . .'

Gabriel stares at him, dumbfounded. *Trouble, because of me?* The countless times he'd saved his little brother's skin because he didn't want to fight and . . .

It doesn't matter! Pull yourself together!

'OK,' Gabriel says, straining for calm. 'Anyway. Believe me, David. Even if you had asked me about that night, I really can't remember anything. I couldn't have told you anything, nothing at all, you understand? That night . . . there's nothing, it's like . . . a blind spot.'

David looks at him incredulously. 'And in the hospital? You were in a psychiatric hospital. There were professionals, doctors, psychologists. With everything they did to you, you couldn't remember anything?'

'They locked me up and pumped me full of psychotropic drugs. That is pretty much the only thing that I *can* remember.'

David looks at the floor in silence. His eyes are focused on some point on the other side of the floor. Finally, he sighs. 'I still don't know why you locked me in the bedroom that night. Damned if I know what happened.'

'What did you hear up there?'

'I heard noise, it woke me up. Dad screamed something and then there was a bang. At first, I didn't realise that it was a gunshot. I pressed my ear up to the door, but heard almost nothing.'

'Almost nothing?'

'Something clattered just after the shot. It was quiet for a moment, and then there was another and another, and I realised that they were gunshots. I was terrified and crawled under the bed. After a while, it smelled of smoke, so I pounded on the door and yelled. Then you came and opened the door. You looked as if you'd actually seen the devil. I shouted at you and wanted to know what happened. You didn't say a single word. You just grabbed me by the arm and pulled me down the stairs. And then I saw the two of them lying there. It was . . .'

'Describe for me what you saw,' Gabriel says quietly.

David's face is grey and the wrinkles around his mouth look like sharply drawn hooks. 'Dad was lying on his back, a bullet had hit him in the side of the stomach. Another shot had hit him in the chest, probably in his heart. There was fresh blood all around him.' David clears his throat, stands up, and turns his back to Gabriel. He goes to the window and looks out over the rooftops of Berlin. 'She . . . she took a bullet right . . . right in the head, in her right eye.'

'Can you remember anything else?'

David shakes his head.

Gabriel hangs on David's every word, absorbing every detail and waiting for a spark to ignite his memory. But nothing happens. 'How long were we standing there?'

'No time. You pulled me out of there right away. I saw them for maybe two or three seconds,' David says with a broken voice. 'Strange. Whenever I think about it, I see everything in front of me, like a photo where I can look at every detail, even the newspaper on the coffee table. I don't remember what was on it any more. I still couldn't read so well at the time, I guess maybe that's why.'

'And when did the fire start?'

'It was burning the whole time. As I said, I smelled smoke up in our room. It was worse downstairs. Smoke was billowing out of the cellar. I coughed like mad. I think that without you I would've stayed there and suffocated. I was so . . . I couldn't leave them. I was paralysed. It looked horrible, like a battlefield, but the whole time I had to –'

The mobile in Gabriel's jacket rings. 'Sorry.' He quickly pulls out the phone and his hotel key falls to the floor in the process.

Gabriel stares at the display. *Jens Florband*. One of Liz's acquaintances or work contacts. He quickly presses the red button, puts the mobile and the key back in his pocket and looks at David. 'Can you not remember anything else, like maybe the way from upstairs to the ground floor?'

David shakes his head. He is pale and agitated. Gabriel looks away at the floor. 'And – do you know if someone else was in the house?'

'*Someone else?*' David asks, bewildered. 'Why?'

Gabriel shrugs.

'No. There was no one,' David says.

'Did we go back down to the cellar, can you remember that?' Gabriel asks.

'To the cellar? No. Certainly not – but, wait a minute, there was something strange.'

Gabriel lifts his head and looks at David.

'When we went outside, we had to pass the cellar door. You pulled it shut – I think to keep more smoke from getting upstairs. For a moment I thought there was a sort of knocking and something that sounded like . . . like screaming.'

Goosebumps form across Gabriel's neck. That's it! There *was* someone else there.

'I almost forgot,' David says, 'it was just for a moment. I wasn't even sure it actually happened. And then the fire and . . . I was totally confused. Maybe someone outside had seen the fire and started screaming.'

'And what do you think now? Was it coming from the cellar or from outside?'

David takes a long look at him and then shrugs. 'I'm not sure.'

Gabriel nods. Slowly, as if he were carrying a heavy burden on his shoulders, he straightens up. 'Thanks,' he mumbles awkwardly.

David shakes his head. 'You really can't remember anything?'

Gabriel shrugs.

'And in the clinic?' David asks. 'They sure as hell tried to give you therapy. Is there no record or anything?'

Gabriel grimaces. 'The file is gone. Why do you ask?'

'Just because,' David evades giving an answer. 'I thought they had to save things like that.'

Gabriel's eyes look at him piercingly. David seems to regret having said anything. Maybe, Gabriel thinks, it would be worth asking at Conradshöhe. At that very moment, he feels his stomach cramp; he would do anything to avoid going to that place. Maybe the police would be waiting for him there anyway. 'No,' Gabriel says. 'Even if you don't believe it, I can't remember. I've had a lot of dreams about it lately. Nightmares. But I'm not sure what really happened and what didn't.'

'What exactly happens in your dreams?'

Gabriel shrugs. 'Messed-up stuff. No idea.' He goes over to the counter in the open-plan kitchen, picks up a pen that's sitting there and scribbles something on the edge of the newspaper.

David watches him and can feel his anger fade into a deep resignation, as so often has been the case.

Gabriel taps on the newspaper. 'If you think of anything else, this is Liz's number. You can reach me there.'

'OK. And what's going on with Liz? Has she resurfaced?'

Gabriel hesitates a moment.

Forget it, Luke, he won't believe it. He never believes you. Not even that you can't remember anything.

'Forget it,' Gabriel says. He opens David's refrigerator and looks inside. 'Do you have a beer? For the road?' It is entirely empty. 'Do you always eat out or don't you eat at all?'

'That's none of your business,' David replies icily. A hint of red appears in his cheeks.

'All right, I'll go,' Gabriel says.

David doesn't say a word.

When Gabriel has gone, David sinks down on the sofa and stares at the stain on the wall where the Dali used to hang. But instead of Dali, he's busy with another mental image – the image of Gabriel's hotel key that had fallen on the floor. The heavy key chain had looked like it was from the seventies and had a large '37' and the words 'CAESAR'S BERLIN' written on it in ancient-Roman-style letters.

Chapter 34

Nowhere – 21 September

Liz is lying on her back, semi-conscious. The light has been back on for quite a while now. It's the morning of September 21st, that is, if she's counted each time it switches from dark to light correctly. The fluid from the IV steadily drips into her veins. Now she is certain that the side effects are making her mouth feel dust dry.

There is also the urgent need to urinate. Ever since her catheter was removed, she has had to wait to go to the toilet, but at least now it is easier to train at night.

She impatiently squints towards the door. Yvette should have been there long ago to help her onto the toilet seat after breakfast, as she does every morning.

Breakfast.

It sounds good, so pleasantly normal. In reality, it's a bitter porridge with fruit and water. Healthy, but disgusting.

At least he's not letting me go hungry.

The key clicks in the lock and Yvette enters the room. As she has been doing for the past few days, she first makes sure that Liz is lying quietly in bed. Then she puts the commode next to the bed, places a bucket under the oval cut-out in the seat and closes the door from inside.

She looks over at the empty bowl of porridge and then she helps Liz up silently, as always, and heaves her onto the toilet seat.

Liz feels as heavy as lead. The effects of the drugs take away much of her muscle control and conceal her nightly training. For the past eleven nights, every time the drugs from the IV wear off, Liz struggles with every barefoot step, pacing in the absolute darkness of her cell from one wall to the other. In the beginning, she counted by step, then by wall lengths and last night, for the first time, in kilometres.

Yvette straightens up with a groan when Liz is finally sitting properly above the bucket. The nurse has strong arms, but her back clearly hurts when she has to lift Liz.

The cool surface of the toilet seat presses against Liz's naked skin. As before, she's wearing nothing more than a thin, open-backed hospital gown. Her thighs stick out from under the white edge of the fabric like stilts. For a brief moment, she is outside of herself, looking down from above, at how she's crouched there, naked, over a bucket, degraded and at the mercy of a psycho-path. She closes her eyes, feels the cool air between her legs and the pressure on her bladder. She immediately squeezes her legs together. *Not yet.*

Liz knows that this is one of the few moments she can control. For some reason, Yvette always waits until Liz is finished, maybe to keep her from falling from the seat and seriously hurting her-self. And she knows that she has to talk to Yvette. She went over the conversation the night before, just as she has always done with her interviews in the past. Now she is thankful that the drugs only impede her motor skills.

'Yvette?'

She shakes her head.

'Yvette, can you . . . I would like to be alone.'

She shakes her head.

Good. Liz has to make an effort not to smile.

'You're not allowed to leave me alone?'

A nod.

Very good! Liz turns slightly towards the dark panel and grill that she suspects has a camera behind it and then she turns back. 'Is he watching us?'

Yvette considers this for a moment and then she whispers: 'I don't think so. He doesn't like watching when . . .' Her eyes drift down to the bucket beneath Liz's seat.

'Then he also can't see if we talk now.'

Yvette doesn't nod or shake her head. 'Keep going,' she says flatly. 'I have to finish up.'

'I can't, like this.'

Silence.

'Why are you doing this, I mean . . . this here?' Liz asks.

Yvette remains silent and looks off to the side.

'Is he paying you?'

She shakes her head.

'Then why?'

She shakes her head again. 'Please keep going.'

'What has he promised you, Yvette?'

Yvette is silent, presses her lips together and peers at the bucket. The pressure on Liz's bladder is getting stronger. The seconds pass like minutes. *It's just an interview, Liz. Just an interview. Press on!* 'Do you think he will keep his promise? I mean, is he someone who keeps his promises?'

'Leave me alone.'

'He *has* promised you something, hasn't he?'

Tears fill Yvette's eyes.

'Yvette, what has he promised you?'

She looks around and turns her head so that her back is facing the dark panel. 'He ... he said,' she whispers, 'that he would let me go.'

For a moment there is a crushing silence. 'Are you done now, finally?' Yvette asks with a shaky voice and leans forward to get a better look in the bucket.

Liz shakes her head. Her bladder feels like a watermelon, but she continues to squeeze her legs together. 'He won't let you go,' Liz says slowly. Her mouth is dried out and her tongue sticks to her gums.

'Yes,' Yvette says softly. 'He will.'

'Yvette. Whatever he is up to, he *can't* let you go. You've seen everything, you know too much.'

'He will.'

Liz tries to moisten her cracked lips with no success. *Keep going. Stay with it.* 'How long have you been here?'

Yvette looks at the bucket.

'When –' Liz urges and then has to cough. Her bladder is burning. 'When did he kidnap you?'

Yvette winces. Her grey face is as hard as stone.

'He did kidnap you, didn't he? Just like me.'

No reaction.

This goddamned bladder!

'How long have you been here, Yvette? How long has he had you locked away?'

Yvette's chin trembles. 'October,' she says under her breath.

October? Liz gasps. It's already September! 'Does that mean . . . you've been here . . . almost a *year?*'

Yvette clenches her jaw and does not respond.

'Alone? For a year?'

'There . . . there were other women . . .'

'Other women? Where?'

Yvette's eyes drift over to the bed.

Liz's heart stops. *'Here?* In here?'

No response. The silence is like a vacuum, like someone was pumping the air out of the room and out of her lungs.

'How many?'

'Three,' Yvette whispers. 'A model and two others.'

'And you still think,' Liz asks, 'that he'll let you go?'

Yvette nods stiffly. 'I help him. He needs me.'

'My god. He doesn't need you, he's using you, wake up.'

She shakes her head like an angry child. 'You're the last, he said.'

The last. Liz can feel her fear crawling down her throat, into her guts and lodging itself there. Without the drugs, she would be panicked out of her mind. 'Yvette, he's a psychopath. He will kill you, just like he probably did with the other women who were in this room.'

The corners of Yvette's mouth twitch. *'Just finish up! Now!'*

Liz sits on the toilet seat as if it's burning into her backside. Easy, take it easy. Don't annoy her! 'Yvette?'

She shakes her head nervously.

'Why am I here?'

No reaction.

'Does it have something to do . . . with Gabriel?'

Yvette quickly glances at Liz from the corner of her eye and then looks away again.

'So, it *does* have something to do with Gabriel.'

Yvette looks like she is desperately trying to avoid saying something.

'Is it?'

'He says that someone is coming,' she whispers gruffly. 'Because of you.'

'Yvette, help me, please! We have to get out of here. Together.'

Yvette shakes her head. Her eyelids flutter. 'He said you would say that. He promised me . . .' She lowers her eyes.

Liz takes a deep breath to calm down. It's as if the dust in her mouth has fully absorbed any moisture in her lungs. 'He can't let you go,' she says as gently as she can with her raw, dry throat. 'You know what he is.'

'He certainly won't let *you* go,' Yvette hisses.

'Do you know his name?'

Yvette looks at her, almost hostile. 'If I knew, I would never tell *you*.'

'Yvette,' Liz continues, '*if* you know his name, then he'll never let you go. You know what he's capable of.'

Yvette's teeth are grinding audibly.

'What would you do in his place?'

Pink blotches form on her cheeks.

'Would *you* let you go? Would you –'

'Shut up!' Yvette shouts. 'His name is Val. Got it? Val!'

Liz winces in fear. For a moment, she loses control of her muscles and a stream shoots into the bucket. She quickly presses her legs back together.

Yvette suddenly leans forward, now red in the face, reaches between Liz's legs and forcefully pushes them apart. Liz lets out a startled scream. She immediately feels everything start to rush out of her without being able to stop it.

'So now you know,' Yvette says. With watery grey eyes, she looks at Liz. 'And now you know that he will also never let *you* go. Never! Since *you* know his name, too.'

Liz can hardly think any more, the sounds beneath her make her want to die of shame. She tries to ignore the smell, but it's impossible, even after she's finished.

Yvette grabs her roughly under her arms, pulls her up and over onto her bed without cleaning her up. Her grey eyes are full of rage. 'You filthy ginger witch. He's been warning me about you this whole time.' She takes the seat and the bucket to the door and unlocks it. 'I thought you were different.'

She leaves the room, slams the door shut and a second later Liz can hear the lock click into place.

Exhausted, Liz stares up at the ceiling.

Val.

Finally, a name. It's almost as if her tormenter is a bit less terrifying now that he has something as common as a name.

What makes her uneasy is the feeling that she's heard the name already.

Maybe I'm deluding myself, she thinks, and gives in to her exhaustion.

Chapter 35

Berlin – 23 September, 8.23 p.m.

David hangs up the phone and looks out into the rain, which is pelting against his office window in the gusts of wind. The section of the building across from where he sits is blurred behind a water-fall. As he puts the business card with the phone number back into his wallet, his hands tremble. He has a throbbing headache. He digs two aspirin out of the drawer of his desk and swallows them with a sip of cold coffee. Then he checks his phone for the time. It's 8.24 p.m., so he still has a good hour before it happens.

He would much prefer to lock the door to his office, curl up like a cat and go to sleep, deep and long for the rest of the year, but with the guarantee that he won't have any dreams. David rubs his eyes and sighs. As if he could sleep a wink now.

He looks outside at the storm again and shudders.

The sky is letting it all out.

If he could just get rid of the image. It follows him like a per-manent nightmare and appears again and again in his mind. His father's facial expression, lifeless and contorted. The grotesque bullet hole in his mother's head, the sticky red puddle on the oak floor . . . If someone were to scan his brain, this image would be there.

He tries to imagine Gabriel, Luke Skywalker on his chest and a gun in his hand, tries to understand why he would have shot them. He does not succeed.

If only the rain could wash it all away.

He thinks of Shona. He stood her up at Santa Media a few days ago and still hasn't apologised. His entire life has been set on fire, a fire that was lit by Gabriel's match.

He picks up his mobile, and is dialling Shona's number when the telephone on his desk suddenly starts ringing. He curses and hangs up his mobile as he picks up the landline. 'Naumann.'

'Bug,' trumpets in David's ear.

Of all people.

'Why haven't I heard anything from you?' Bug asks. 'We agreed that you were going to work on proposals for a crime show.'

'I'm still working on it,' David says lifelessly.

'Ah, and that probably means you have nothing.'

'Nothing that's finalised yet,' David lies.

Bug sighs, annoyed. 'Listen, David, while you're farting about, don't get any high hopes. I just had a very direct phone call.'

'What kind of phone call?'

'The old man called me about you.'

'Von Braunsfeld? Why would he call you about me?' David asks, taken aback.

'You met recently. Outside my office. You remember?'

How could I forget? David thinks. That was the day that Bug announced to him that he was now the entertainment director and, thus, his boss. 'Why do you ask?'

'Well. Von Braunsfeld places a huge amount of importance on integrity. He enquired about *Treasure Castle* again and now is rather irritated. He asked me why we're employing someone who's been convicted of copyright fraud.'

David gasps. 'Copyright fraud? Convicted? It was a bloody *settlement*. That is a very different thing to a conviction.'

'It's basically the same thing, David. You know how it is.'

David's palms are sweaty. 'And . . . what does that mean in plain language?'

'He wants to fire you.'

Fire. The word hangs in the air. David slumps back into his chair. Rain hits the window in a gust of wind. It sounds like nails hitting the glass.

'You can't be serious,' David says.

Bug is silent, which is worse than anything he could say under these circumstances.

'He . . . he can't do that.'

'He can, David. He owns the station.' Bug clears his throat. 'Listen, David, whether or not you believe it, I also don't particularly think this is right. You've got a creative mind – when you're not being a pussy or a moralist. And, quite frankly, *I* don't give a shit if you steal ideas. The main thing is that we get something out of it. The only problem is: we're getting nothing from it at the moment. So, I don't have anything to make a case for you to von Braunsfeld right now. You follow what I mean?'

'I . . . yes, understood.'

'So it's time you delivered.'

'When will it all be decided, the termination?'

'It's already decided,' Bug says. 'The letter will be in your mailbox tomorrow morning. You are relieved of the rest of your duties starting now.'

David closes his eyes. This can't be true.

'Now don't go making a big fuss,' Bug says, as if he can read David's thoughts. 'Use the time. If you come up with something good before it's too late, von Braunsfeld may rescind the dismissal.'

'Is that what he said?'

'No, *I'm* saying that.'

David is silent for a moment. '*You* would talk to him for *me*?'

Bug sighs theatrically. 'I would always stick my neck out for someone who brings me a few good ideas for show formats.'

'You fire me and I'm still supposed to deliver you more ideas?'

'Now don't be melodramatic. If you can't handle it, I'll have to find someone else. So, think about it. Good night.'

'What do you think?' David asks angrily. 'That I can just spit something out in three days?'

But Bug has already hung up.

Furious, David slams the handset down so hard that a piece of the plastic casing flies off into his face, directly under his right eye. He gets up slowly. It all feels strangely wrong; as if he should've jumped up instead, thrown open the window and screamed into the storm, the rain and wind blowing against his face. For a moment, he is so full of rage that he wants to smash everything in Bug's office to pieces with a baseball bat.

But he doesn't have a baseball bat and the window is shut. Instead, he is closed away in his office as if it were a glass storage box, looking at his own reflection in the thermal windowpanes. Annoyed, he sees the cut under his eye and touches it with his finger. Blood sticks to his fingertip.

He stares out into the darkness and it sucks him in. He's lost all sense of time. The space around him blurs, just like everything else. The reflection of the computer screen behind him is a bright island in an inky raging sea – his island. He wishes he could turn back. Simply sit at his desk and write. Essentially, everything is so simple here. Much, much simpler than in real life.

When he looks at the clock again, it's already almost half past nine.

With a jolt, he jumps up, throws on his Belstaff jacket and rushes out of the office. Two minutes later, he's in the car park and knows that he will be late one way or another. He starts the engine of the dark-green Saab 900, which a colleague has lent him for a week while he's away in England.

As the Saab shoots out of the car park, he's caught in a torrential downpour and takes his foot off the accelerator.

Four minutes later, he turns onto Kurfürstendamm without indicating and calls his voicemail at the same time. Shit, damn it. At least the Jaguar has a hands-free set. He pushes the Black-Berry up to his ear, lets go of the steering wheel and switches from second to third gear. And an automatic transmission, he thinks, that's another thing the Jaguar had.

Beep. *'Hi, it's me, Shona. Hmm. Voicemail. OK. Well, I can't do next week, I have to work. Let me know. It's your move.'*

Crap. She's still mad because he stood her up at the Santa Media. He knows that he has to call her to explain everything, and if not everything, then at least enough that it sounds like a viable excuse. His eyes drift to the windscreen wipers, which are groaning under the mass of water. The traffic light changes to red, brake lights shine in front of him. Brakes, clutch, idle.

The rain drums against the metal roof of the Saab and he presses the mobile up closer to his ear.

Beep. *'Good morning Mr Naumann. This is Mr Säckler from Deutsche Bank. Please call me back. It's urgent.'*

Bloody hyena! Just a few weeks and then the salary payments from TV2 will also stop coming.

Beep. *'You have no new messages.'*

A loud honk behind him makes him jump. The traffic light is green and the cars in front of him are already on the other side of the junction. David engages the clutch, the gears crunch and then he steps on the accelerator and continues down Kurfürstendamm until he finally reaches the bus stop across from a deli. He moves into the right lane and reverses hard to the end of the bus stop. When he stops, he checks the time on the dashboard – it's 9.43 p.m., he's almost fifteen minutes late.

The rain beats against the windscreen, the wiper blades useless against it. Where the hell is all of this water coming from? Suddenly, he has to laugh, though he couldn't feel more like doing the opposite. Endless rain and overburdened windscreen wipers – there couldn't be a better image for the current state of his life.

He turns off the engine and leans back in the scuffed beige leather seat. With a violent jerk, the passenger door opens. David recoils, startled.

Bottom first, a man wearing a dark hat lands in the seat behind him, pulls his legs into the vehicle and shuts the door.

'Good evening, David.' Water runs off the brim of Yuri Sarkov's hat. 'You're late.'

'I'm sory,' David mutters, 'the weather.'

Sarkov calmly removes his glasses and wipes the water off the lenses. 'How are you?'

'Do you have the file?' David asks bluntly.

'So, apparently, not good,' Sarkov responds.

'Well,' David mutters. 'The bank wants to auction off my flat, I've been fired and other people are collecting the royalties on a show format that I came up with . . . and on top of that, you tell me that my brother killed my parents. And then pull me into your feud with Gabriel and demand that I give him up . . .' David takes a deep breath. 'Yes, "not good" is probably an adequate description.'

Sarkov smiles, unmoved. 'Whether or not you get involved is your decision.'

David keeps his eyes on the steering wheel to avoid looking at Sarkov. 'So do you have the file?'

Sarkov narrows his eyes and considers David for a moment, then reaches into his wet coat.

David stares at the white A4 envelope. The coat protected it from the rain and it's mostly dry, other than a few stray drops. 'Nothing will happen to Gabriel?'

'I wouldn't have the heart for that,' Sarkov answers.

David takes the packet. It feels heavy. 'And?'

David hesitates. His pupils flit restlessly back and forth across the water cascading down the windscreen. Finally, he sighs. 'Caesar's Berlin, Room 37.'

'What street?'

'I don't know,' David says. 'Sorry.'

'Stop apologising. I can't stand people who are always apologising.

David goes quiet.

Sarkov starts getting out of the car. 'And . . . the rest?' David asks.

'The rest? You mean the rights to *Treasure Castle*?'

David nods.

'I didn't offer it as a package. They were alternative options.'

'I . . . I understood it differently.'

'What then?' Sarkov laughs mockingly. 'Where is your idealism? I thought you wouldn't rat on your brother for money.'

David just looks at him, unable to reply.

Sarkov shakes his head. '*Babushka*,' he says disdainfully.

'What's that?'

'Grandmother . . . you're such an old woman . . .' Sarkov opens the passenger-side door and steps out into the pouring rain.

David opens his mouth and then shuts it again.

'A miserable coward.' It sounds as if Sarkov were spitting the words out onto the street. He slams the door shut. The wet mark he leaves behind is like a ghost on the seat.

David watches Yuri's silhouette as it disappears into the distance.

David's eyes fall down to the envelope. He feels miserable. Everything inside him cries out for help. He wants to run after Sarkov and undo everything. The world is under water, he thinks, and I'm downing. His telephone is his lifeline, so he takes it out to call Shona. Although he doesn't know what to say, he hopes for nothing more than for her to pick up.

Even if she just listens as he says nothing.

Chapter 36

Berlin – 24 September, 12.58 a.m.

Gabriel looks through the bars that fence in the property.

Drop it, Luke. You'll only find trouble.

I've already got trouble.

They'll wind up sticking you in a cell and strapping you down.

He peers into the darkness. It's 1.00 a.m. The wind tugs at him and drives the heavy clouds across the sky. At least it stopped raining.

He knows that the hospital is there, hidden behind the tall black maple trees.

He musters up his courage and clutches the old, square metal rods of the railing.

His grip is good enough to pull himself up to the top of the three-metre high fence, which leans inward. He jumps down to the other side. The wet ground gives way and Gabriel sinks several centimetres upon landing. The right strap of his backpack pulls uncomfortably on his aching shoulder.

For a moment, Gabriel stays crouched down, waiting to see if he's set off any alarms. Nothing stirs. They don't expect people to break *into* the psychiatric hospital.

He cautiously approaches the first trees. The soil under the grass is saturated and it squishes under his feet. It smells of wet leaves and mildew. Out of the darkness, a four-storey, L-shaped pre-war building appears: the Psychiatric Clinic at Conradshöhe. Originally, the building had two wings, but the eastern wing was destroyed by an aerial bomb during World War II and was never rebuilt. Then and now, the west wing houses the administration.

Three days earlier, Gabriel had phoned, giving the name of another patient there at the same time as him.

'What did you say your name was?' the secretary asked.

'Bügler. Johannes Bügler. I was in Conradshöhe from 1984 until 1987.'

'Hmm. Hang on ... Oh! There you are. You were here until 1988, not '87.'

'Right, of course. Have you still got the file?'

'Do you know how long it's been? We're only required to hold on to medical records for –'

'Eleven years, yeah, I know. But could you maybe check if you still have the files?'

'You've got a nerve. I'm not even sure whether we're allowed to hand over your documents – I'll have to check.'

'So, the file is still there?'

'That's not what I said, but ... if it were, then I am surely not permitted to give it to you.'

'But it's my file.'

'I'm sure Professor Wagner sees it differently,' she said pointedly.

Professor Wagner. The blurry image of a bald stocky man with a goatee appeared in his mind. Wagner was Dr Dressler's successor and Gabriel had only encountered him three or four times back then.

'Would you check for me?' Gabriel asked.

'Listen, I have more important things to do than to rummage through boxes full of dusty files in the darkest corner of the cellar, just to get told off by the boss in the end.'

'I could come by and look for myself if you show me where.'

'That would be even better,' she replied. 'Dr Wagner would certainly be thrilled to find out that I gave a former patient a key to the old archive.'

'The old archive?' Gabriel asked. That was in the historic part of the cellar behind the delivery entrance.

Suddenly, the line was completely silent. Eventually, the woman groaned with exasperation. 'Listen, if you really want to do it, that is, rummage through the messed-up part of your life, then get a good lawyer. You'll need one if you want to see your files here, Mr . . . what was your name again?'

Gabriel had hung up without another word.

Suddenly, a blood-curdling cry comes from the middle building. Gabriel jumps. A light comes on in a window on the third floor; the dark bars stand out against the bright rectangle. Male voices, clattering, the scream fades into a loud pitiful whimper. For a fraction of a second, he wants to run out of there as fast as his legs will carry him. The open window slams shut. The whimpering is silenced, as if someone had severed the patient's vocal chords. The silence is only filled with the wind as it rustles through the leaves of the thirty-metre-tall trees.

Do you know what they'll do with you if they catch you, Luke?

Leave me alone, I don't want to know.

Can't you remember it any more?

Leave – me – alone!

Washday, Luke. Think about washday.

The bright rectangle disappears again. It merges with the dark wall, as if there had never been a window, let alone a window with someone living behind it.

Washday. Dr Armin Dressler had perfected the procedure to the nth degree. It was always the same: lying down, strapped in, electrodes on the temples. The electrical current robbed him of consciousness every time. Washday was brainwash day and it usually took place on Fridays, before the weekend, when there were always too few staff to control the problem patients. After washday, the patients all walked around in a daze with their heads wiped clean – and left the staff in peace.

The wash *cycle*, on the other hand, was individual therapy. Right at the start of his time in the closed ward, whenever Gabriel lost it, fantasised or somehow misbehaved, he would get washed. Later, a syringe was the answer to losing it. Washing was no longer enough. Or it did nothing. Whatever the reason.

Gabriel's eyes drift across the building to two windows that are lit up on the left side of the third floor. The nurses' station. Directly below them, there used to be two visitors' rooms. In the smaller of the two, a bare room with tables and chairs screwed into the floor, his second life had begun without any warning.

Two nurses on the day shift, Giuseppe and Martin, had come into his room. Gabriel's eyes were closed, but he could smell them, just as he still always smells or feels everything. His senses are so delicate, it's as if he has no skin and feels every single nuance of human vibration.

He smelled Giuseppe's aftershave, which he'd been putting on for the past four days, since Martin had been working at the station. Martin, on the other hand, smelled of woman. Mentally, he was an idiot, but he had the body of an Adonis. The scent of Dr Vanja's perfume always clung to him. She was the assistant doctor at the station and always leered at his demi-god arse.

Gabriel hated being aware of it all – the smells, the moods, all of it flooded in despite the medication and there was nothing he could do about it. He was trapped inside himself; all sensors were set to input, but he just couldn't get anything out – all valves were shut.

'Hey, Lucky Luke,' Giuseppe said cheerfully, even though he knew that he wasn't supposed to call him that. 'You have a visitor today.'

'Not interested,' Gabriel mumbled. The medication turned his tongue into a lame, fat hippo.

They had silently loosened the straps on his arms, unbuckled him from his bed, placed him in a wheelchair, bound his hands to the armrests and pushed him into the visitors' room.

And there he was. Plain and thin, like an accountant, with a light-grey trench coat and a dark trilby, which he'd placed on the table in front of him, leaving his already thinning hair visible.

Giuseppe and Martin had parked him in front of the table like an old man – although he was just eighteen at the time – and left him alone with the accountant.

The man considered him with disconcerting hard grey eyes. He'd smelled of tobacco, cunning and cruelty. *Not an accountant. Maybe a doctor, maybe even something worse.*

'Hello, Gabriel. How are you?' he asked. His voice rolled, his understated Russian accent resonating with a warning tremble.

'I don't know you,' Gabriel noted with indifference. His voice rumbled like a rusty bicycle chain. The sedative in his blood made him dull.

'Sarkov. My name is Yuri Sarkov, and –'

'I don't know you,' Gabriel repeated lethargically. 'Fuck off.'

Yuri Sarkov didn't so much as flinch. '– I know, knew your father, he –'

'My father was an arsehole. If you had something to do with him, then you're probably one, too.'

Yuri smiled. Not a forced smile or a putting-on-a-good-face smile.

Careful, Luke. He's a gambler! And he's confident that he'll win.

Yuri got up, took his hat from the table and looked down at Gabriel in his wheelchair. 'Ultimately, it's not about your father. That's over. Right now, it's really about whether you want to get out of here.'

And how! But I won't tell you that.

'Leave me alone.' Gabriel's head slumped forward, as he'd barely had the strength to hold it up. 'You think I don't know that this is a test? I'm not taking any more tests.' He pauses, takes a breath and then: 'Tell Dressler, no more tests.'

'I'm not a doctor. I know, Gabriel, doctors are the plague. They tell you what you are allowed to think and what you're not. They tell you what is right and what is not. But I think you don't belong here. I think you can take care of yourself just fine.'

Careful, Luke. He's in your head. No idea how he got in there, but he's there.

'I can get you out of here, Gabriel.'

He's lying. This is the closed ward. You can't just get out of here.

'You don't believe me?' Yuri asked.

You see? I'm telling you, he's in your head. He knows what you're thinking.

No, no, Gabriel thought. You're too loud, he can hear us.

He can't hear us! But he's very clever!

'Gabriel?'

Gabriel's chin drooped down to his chest, drool dripping out the corner of his mouth.

'I'll come back next week, on Friday,' Yuri said.

'Friday is washday,' Gabriel muttered.

'Then, Friday morning. Think about it.'

Gabriel hadn't had to think about it. Of course he wanted to get out, at any price. Early one morning in February of 1988, there was a fresh layer of snow on the ground when Yuri pulled him out of the clinic as if it were the most normal thing in the world.

Even now, Gabriel still sometimes wonders exactly how Yuri managed it. And above all, why? To begin with, Yuri was his official guardian and had vouched for him. The rest is history. After all, Gabriel knew that Yuri always had his reasons for whatever he did, but he always played his cards close to his chest. In the end, all that mattered was that he could leave Conradshöhe.

They had gone through the locked door of the closed ward, then outside through the main entrance of the middle building and over the semi-circular staircase in the park. Gabriel's heart beat into his throat, his medication had been greatly reduced and he feared that someone would rope him back in with a lasso at any second.

The thin layer of snow melted instantly beneath their feet. Gabriel hadn't turned around. He never looked back. Their footprints left a long black trail in the snow that led out through the barred gate and up to the kerb, where the trail broke off.

A cold gust of wind blows against Gabriel's neck. He hunches his shoulders and hurries to the left, to the part of the building where the administration is still located. The west wing isn't barred up and it has such turn-of-the-century charm that no one would suspect that they were in charge of burying people alive in there.

The old delivery entrance leading to the cellar is tucked away beside a withered rose bush. Gabriel crouches in front of the door, gets out his pick set and opens the lock with a tool similar to a screwdriver.

The door gives way with a soft click and he can hear quiet drumming. Gabriel stops, peers out into the darkness of the grounds and listens.

Nothing. Keep going.

He slowly pulls open the door and steps through the delivery area. It smells musty, and the entrance and the storage room behind it appear to have not been used in years. When he turns around in the doorway to close the door, he hears the muffled drumming again, but very close this time. A shadow gallops toward him and knocks him to the ground. At the last second, as Gabriel tries to put the door between himself and the animal, the dark bundle shoots through the air with concentrated force. He feels hot breath on his skin and the door flies out of his hand. He throws up his left arm protectively, as teeth pierce through his jacket and into his flesh. He staggers, tries desperately to maintain his balance and then falls backwards onto the hard floor. *Oh god, don't let it get your neck!*

The beast towers over him, a large muscular Rottweiler, its jaw like a vice around Gabriel's forearm. It's breath stinks of rotting food, as the teeth sink deep into his arm. Gabriel swings his right arm, ramming the pick into its throat once, then twice, but not deep enough. Warm blood sprays onto Gabriel's hand and his injured shoulder is screaming in pain.

The dog winces, briefly lets go and then bites down again. The pain burns like red-hot iron. A deep rumbling rises from the animal's throat, its dark eyes shining. Gabriel pulls the pick out its throat, turns it in his right hand and rams the metal rod into the Rottweiler's eye with all his strength until it's deep in its brain. Instantly, the dog's jaw unclenches. The animal twitches, as if it had bitten a power cable, and then collapses over him.

Breathing heavily, Gabriel frees his arm from the dog's grip and strains to stand up. Then he pulls the monster into the cellar and peers out the door.

Everything is calm.

He turns on his torch. He has an ND filter on over the bulb, dimming the beam of light in front of him. He quietly closes the door, leans against it from inside and sinks to the ground.

The tough material of his jacket sleeve is torn and blood is smeared on the arm beneath it. The fangs pierced deep into his flesh, but at least the jacket prevented it from being much worse. He quickly takes off his shirt and wraps it tightly around the wounds. His fingers shake and he closes his eyes for a moment, taking several deep breaths. His pulse calms down noticeably and he tries to concentrate.

The Rottweiler has to go.

In the event that anyone misses the dog and gets suspicious, the body should at least be somewhere that it wouldn't be so easy to stumble upon. Gabriel heaves the stinking monster onto his shoulder. His injury there and the bite wounds shoot searing pain through his nerves. He puts the Rottweiler in a bush beneath an imposing beech tree around 150 metres away from the building. The heavy clouds split in the sky and the wind revives him a bit. In order to avoid leaving any evidence of the break-in, he pulls the pick out of the carcass. Liquid oozes from the wound and shines in the moonlight.

Then he wipes away any trace of struggle in the cellar with the lining of his jacket and cleans the soles of his shoes.

Done.

Goddamn it, what are you doing here, Luke?

You know what all too well.

Me, sure. But not you. Look at you, you're shaking like a child.

Just shut up for once.

You're well on your way back into the closed ward, you know that?

Are you hard of hearing?

How many people do you think read their own treatment records? And more importantly: what do you think happens when a man digs back into his own madness? Do you think you'll like what you find?

Gabriel doesn't respond. He breaks out into a sweat, despite the cool, musty cellar air. He scans the walls in the hallway behind the storage room with the pale torchlight. Sixteen doors, eight on each side. He proceeds systematically. Picking the locks calms him.

In the ninth room, he comes across a brown wall of cardboard packing boxes. When he flips open the lid of the first carton, a cloud of dust blows into his face. His heart starts racing. There are thick folders in front of him, organised by name. Dankwart, Dellana, Demski . . .

I'm begging you, Luke, you have to stop!

Since when do you beg?

Seven boxes later, he's arrived at 'N'. His fingers run across the folders. Next name. No. Next name. No again. And then: Naumann, Gabriel.

The dust dances chaotically in the torchlight, a swarm of fireflies above a glowing island. His heart is pounding, as his shaking fingers pull out the folder.

I warned you. Don't say I didn't warn you, Luke!

Don't call me that. You're driving me crazy.

Me? You?

Gabriel flips open the folder and leafs through the documents. Diagnoses, reports, assessments, letters from Child Protection Services, more reports and countless transcripts of the tape recordings from the meetings with Dressler. The terminology flits by like a series of ghosts. Schizophrenia, sedation, convulsion therapy. He suddenly feels feverish. Haldol, Fluphenazine, Dormicum, Lormetazepam – the psychotropic drugs greet him like old acquaintances that he'd long forgotten and are now suddenly standing in front of him once again. No one ever told him or the other patients what medications or what dosages they were being given. It was injected and that was the end of it. Because he had so often opposed them, they would strap him down. When he wasn't restrained and tried to resist them, he had bruises from the injections. Once a needle broke in his upper arm and then they started using extra-thick needles on him.

He automatically rubs his arm at the thought of it. The Rottweiler bite burns. Undeterred, he continues flipping through.

Naumann, Gabriel. 07.05.1986, 03.20 a.m. Patient defiant, rebellious, having severe delusions once again. Psychological assessment has been tape-recorded. Subsequent restraint, initiated immediate convulsive therapy for neuronal restructuring. Patient appropriately calmed, slightly confused.

Gabriel stares at the yellowed sheet of paper. He feels as though the dust has jumped into his nose like sparks, penetrated his brain and then crashed into a wall.

Tape recording transcript from 07.05.86:
... she's lying there ... just like that. Next to her, right next to her ... I've never seen eyes like that ... like fire ... red monster's eyes ... Luke, I'm scared ... we all are ... no, you're a coward ... take her ... he will kill me ... he isn't worth it ... Luke ... that's my father ... he is a monster, a dangerous, dangerous monster ... who is the monster? ... Luke, you are also a monster ... do you want to be a monster? ... No, no, no ... no one can see if I don't do it ... if you do nothing, you are a monster, like him ...

The wall suddenly has a crack, narrow, small like a keyhole in a door. An old dream is raging behind the door. It's as if he can hear his own voice in there, but there is nothing to see through the keyhole and he feels nothing, even though his heart is racing.

> ... why is she just lying there like that ... I need to pick her up ... then do it and shut up ... all right ... nothing is all right ... hurry ...do I have to go in front here? ... it's so hard, why is it so ... you're shaking ... stop it! ... stop shaking ... aim ... I'm doing it, I'm doing ... don't you see, I am ... totally drunk, he's totally dunk ... is he really a monster?
>
> How do you know? Are you sure?
>
> ... but it's Dad ... Dad!
>
> ... stay out of this.
>
> ... I'm pulling the trigger. I'm pulling the trigger now.
>
> ... I ... now!
>
> ...Ow! My arm, my arm!
>
> ... he ... I hit him
>
> ... Luke, you hit him
>
> ... yes, yes ... I ... had to
>
> Will you help me now?

The realisation hits Gabriel like a swinging axe. The file slips out of his numb hand, the darkness closes in on him.

He feels nothing and everything at the same time. The pain in his arm and his shoulder have disappeared, not because it doesn't hurt any more, but because his whole body is screaming in agony.

I warned you, the voice wails.

Why didn't you tell me this before?

I didn't know.

And what were you warning me of?

I don't know.

You don't know? You know me better than anyone else and you can't remember that I shot my father?

I was scared, Luke. I didn't want to be punished.

Chapter 37

Berlin – 24 September, 5.28 p.m.

David slides uncomfortably on the dark brown leather uphol-stery of the wingback chair. It is already half past five and he has been waiting for over an hour and a half with little more to do than rustle the folded pages from the file, but Dr Irene Esser is as thorough as always.

David's eyes land on a piece by Uecker that's hanging on the wall behind her. Nails hammered into the shape of a spiral, as if fate were a magnet circling above them that had come to a halt. He thinks about Shona, about her silence, his silence and his awkward and taciturn apology. What more could he have said over the phone?

My brother shot my parents? The police are looking for him? I betrayed him?

The whole story is like the Uecker. Each nail is pointing in a different direction. The spiral is only clear when you see all the nails. David was relieved when Shona didn't ask any questions.

'You do realise,' Dr Esser says, 'that I should really be calling the police right now?' Her dark brown eyes are like polished marble beneath her sleepy eyelids.

David furrows his brow uncomfortably.

Dr Esser's gaze fixes on him over the edge of her red half-frame reading glasses and she places the thick packet of A4 copies on her desk. 'Where did you get this?'

David sighs. 'I told you already, it's all a bit delicate.'

Her eyes remain fixed on him across the antique desk, just like when he used to come to her years ago. Only, the chair was much larger then. And her hair was blond, and she got by without glasses. Or at least she didn't need any when it came to talking to people.

'Why have you come to me with this?'

'Because I can't work it out, I need your –'

'No, no,' she makes a dismissive gesture. 'I want to know why you came to *me*.'

'You're the only psychologist I know,' David says flatly. 'And I trust you.'

'The fact that you had a few sessions with me as a child does not mean that I am going to completely ignore your brother's rights.'

Her gaze is as hard as frozen ground. David looks off to the side. 'I thought you were the only one who could understand how important this is for me.'

Dr Esser stretches her small, wiry body up in her oversized chair. 'Did you steal this file?'

'No.' David's answer is the truth, but he still feels like the needle on an imaginary lie detector is going to jump at any moment and accuse him of lying. How is it possible to tell the truth and still feel so bad?

He hopes that she doesn't ask again.

'And your brother, does he know that you have this file?'

David shakes his head slightly.

'And what do you think I should do now? This is a clear-cut violent crime. I should really get the police.'

'This was all almost thirty years ago.'

'Murder has no statute of limitations.'

David lowers his eyes and lets them drift across the dark carved relief that runs along the edge of the table. Deer, wild boars, hares. The desk of a hunter. He regrets having come here. But he still can't resist asking. 'What do you think? Did Gabriel kill him? I mean, he was still a child.'

'I'm not sure I want to comment on that.'

'And if you . . . had to?'

Dr Esser sighs. 'David, quite frankly, I don't want to be part of your mess, regardless of what it's about or how important it is to you.'

'But?'

'Did you hear me say "but"?'

David looks at his hands intently. Irene Esser abruptly goes from massaging her right hand to crossing her arms. She blinks and stares at David, as if she were at the blackjack table awaiting her next card.

David remains silent and is glad that the balance of power has shifted, if only for a brief moment.

'Not to mention the fact that I have another problem on top of that,' Dr Esser says. 'After all, I know the doctor at Conradshöhe . . . not well, but . . . well enough.'

'You mean,' David asks reluctantly, 'that Dr Dressler may have administered the wrong . . .'

Dr Esser's head sways to the side. Her pale lips are more sharply contoured than usual, but she also suddenly seems very mousy. 'Why do you think that your brother killed your parents all of a sudden?'

David's eyes stop on the delicately carved antlers of a stag. 'Are you going to hand this over to the police? I mean, is there no patient confidentiality here?'

Dr Esser looks him over searchingly. 'Let's just call this a borderline case. If you're open, then I will be, too.'

'No police?'

'No police.'

David sighs with relief. 'There's a man named Sarkov. Yuri Sarkov. I got the file from him. He is – or was – Gabriel's boss. He seems to have known him for a very long time. A few days ago, Sarkov came to me and claimed that Gabriel had killed our father.'

'What *exactly* did he say?'

David tries to remember the wording. 'That Gabriel had shot our father, no more. I asked him how he knew. He said he'd read the file and that he knew Gabriel. That it was all there, there was no doubt.'

'But *you* have doubts after reading the file?'

David's eyes focus on the edge of the table and the carved stag, standing there, roaring. 'He was eleven. Just eleven years old.'

'And what would you prefer?' Dr Esser's eyes bore into him.

'What . . . what do you mean?' David asks, confused.

'That it was him or that it wasn't?'

'I just want clarity on the situation,' David mumbles uncomfortably.

Irene Esser sighs and leans forward onto her thin arms. 'Dr Dressler diagnosed your brother Gabriel with schizophrenia with paranoid and delusional traits. All of it as a consequence of a severe trauma, that is, the death of his parents.'

'I read that, too, but what does it mean?'

'I think that he was mistaken.'

David stares at her, dumbfounded.

'In the reports from the period before he was institutionalised, your brother was very introverted, but also very aggressive, almost explosive. At the Elisabethstift, he attacked the head of the home several times, went after other children, always with the motive that someone wanted to harm him or you, his little brother. At first glance, these are unequivocally signs of paranoid and delusional behaviour. To complicate matters further, he started talking to himself and calling himself Luke. It's no wonder that Dr Dressler naturally thought it was schizophrenia.'

'But then why do you think that the diagnosis is wrong?'

Dr Esser smiles faintly. 'From a more current perspective, I would say it's much more a case of post-traumatic stress disorder and a schizoid personality disorder.'

David stares at her blankly. 'Schizoid personality disorder and schizophrenia? That just sounds like two names for the same thing.'

'Therein lies the problem. First of all, Gabriel probably had a severe case of post-traumatic stress disorder, but the underlying cause of the trauma was wrongly assessed. Take, for example, the tape recording from May 7th, 1986. If you don't take Gabriel's delusions as paranoia or hallucinations, but see them as flashbacks, that is, actual memories of what really happened, then you're suddenly looking at a whole different picture.'

'What do you mean by that?'

'Well, imagine a patient was brought to you who was repeatedly aggressive. You know from him that he'd found his murdered parents a few years earlier and then burned his house to the ground. Now the patient is constantly talking to himself and thinks people are plotting against him and his brother at every turn. What could be more appropriate than to attribute this aggressive behaviour to his own powerlessness? Who would blame the patient for seeing hostility in everything around him? After all, someone killed his parents and burned down his entire world, right?'

'Yes. Undoubtedly.'

'You see? You've already confirmed the patient's paranoia. And everything that he says from now on will be classified within that rubric.'

David nods slowly.

'Now think back to the transcript of the tape recording from May 7th. You have a patient with paranoia in front of you and he's started having an incoherent and disconnected conversation with someone. It sounds very much like he was threatened. And then he talks about having a gun in his hand. He tells us that he pulled the trigger, that he hit someone, that his father is there and also some ominous monster. What would you think, considering his past history?'

'I would think,' David answers slowly, 'that he was mixing things up a bit.'

'Why would he do that?'

'Maybe he feels guilty that he couldn't help his parents. Maybe he wishes that he'd had a gun.'

'Guilt. Very good. Maybe you would even think, because he couldn't help, that he felt like he – in a manner of speaking – shot his father, even if he never actually aimed a gun at him.'

David looks at her in silence, hanging on her every word.

'In any case, that's probably what Dr Dressler thought. He thought that Gabriel was suffering from delusions and that he was schizophrenic. He also treated him with electroshock therapy at the beginning.

'Electroshock?' David asks, appalled.

'Convulsive therapy is noted in the file.'

'Oh my god.'

'Today, the effects would be much less pronounced – those therapies are better than their reputation. That being said, it's been very successful with manic-depressive patients, but seldom so with schizophrenia. Back then, people were less squeamish than now and would administer the shock therapy without even using anaesthesia.'

'What was this torture meant to accomplish?'

'Through the surges of electricity, certain stimuli are activated. The brain is essentially being shaken vigorously and then can reorganise itself, neural connections can be rebuilt. It also happens to have the side effect of calming the patients.'

'Dr Dressler treated my brother's delusions with electroshocks?'

'Gabriel's *alleged* delusions. No one thought that these delusions could be flashbacks. Flashes of memory from something that actually happened. From that perspective, Gabriel was *neither* paranoid *nor* delusional. He suffered a serious trauma that was so horrible he'd suppressed a large portion of that night. And a few years later, usually in situations with visual stimuli, the memories returned as flashbacks or intrusions.'

'Intrusions?' David furrows his brow.

'Something like a flashback, but during a flashback, the images run through your head like a chaotic film, while intrusions evoke the same emotions you experienced during the traumatic event. You suffer through everything again and again very directly.'

'That sounds awful,' David says.

'Oh, it is. It truly is. And now imagine that your brother was having such a flashback – or an intrusion – and then was treated with electroshock therapy.'

'What do you think it did?' David asks quietly.

'I would say that it's a prime example of negative conditioning. Gabriel has a flashback and then gets shocked. His brain saves it as: whenever I remember that time, I am punished with electric shocks. The mind reacts to that very pragmatically. It simply suppresses everything. In short: Gabriel doesn't have delusions, he has *memories*. He needed help – and all he got were messages like: "you're crazy", "you're dangerous", "you're wrong". That's a fail-safe way to drive someone insane. It probably cost him his last remaining memories of the events of that night.'

David stares at Irene Esser. 'What ... what does all of this mean?'

'Well,' Dr Esser says calmly, 'it means that your brother is much more normal than everyone thinks. He is very sensitive, very intelligent and often notices things that other people don't see, which might often seem strange to the people around him. If such a person behaves unusually and has difficulty with social contact – which is clearly the case with your brother – then it can easily seem like full-blown paranoia or, to be blunt, as if he were crazy.'

'So, they were entirely wrong to institutionalise him?'

'In the middle ages, women were burned at the stake as witches for much less. But, of course, it's all relative. They just didn't know what was happening with your brother. In any case, he was probably given the wrong treatment.' Her cold brown eyes stay on David. 'At least, if you look at the flashbacks as real memories.'

'So, you would say that he did shoot our father?' David asks, confused.

'He shot someone. That is the only possible explanation for all of this. It's just a question of whom he shot and why he did it.'

'Then is there a chance that he could remember at some point? Or are the memories completely erased?'

Dr Esser tilts her head from side to side. 'Yes and no. The brain functions sort of like a hard disk. The data is erased, but never overwritten; in a sense, it's just invisible. So, in theory, it could also be reactivated.'

'How?'

'That's precisely where the trouble begins.'

Chapter 38

Nowhere – 24 September

Val. The name floats through her brain like a pale ghost.

Don't look in the corner. He's staring at you.

Liz is lying on her back and trying to ignore the square panel just below the ceiling in the corner of her cell. *As long as the light is on, he can see you.*

Depending on how she turns her head, she can even see the faint shine of the lens on the surveillance camera behind the grille. Maybe he's even recording everything. Then he can always see you, every second. She imagines him pushing fast forward or rewind until he reaches something he finds interesting. She doesn't know what's worse – that he could walk through the door at any moment and do anything he wants with her; or that he owns and can watch every intimate second: when Yvette helps her wash, when she cries in desperation or when she strokes her stomach and wonders how it looks inside, how her baby is doing.

Please let it be dark! Please!

But it's not dark. Instead, the door opens. She can already tell by the way the door opens that it's not Yvette. She feels the draught on her skin like the hot breath of a predator. Everything closes in around her. Now she knows what's worse. It's worse when he walks through the door and can do anything he wants with her.

Liz's eyes look to the ceiling for support, clinging to the fluorescent tubes.

'Hello, Liz,' he says. 'Let's take a look at you.'

Liz does not move.

He slowly pulls away her covers. 'The gown.'

He doesn't need to say any more. Her hands move automatically and she even manages to make sure they are moving *slowly*, as if she were still too weak.

Val breathes loudly.

She can feel his breath on her naked body. She hates what happens next so much that everything contracts, her nipples, all of her pores, everything, right before his eyes.

Val's prosthetic hand reaches her between her legs, stroking upwards through the furrow of her vagina, through her pubic hair, in a terrifying straight line, purposefully continuing across her abdomen, over her baby, all the way up to the valley between her breasts.

'You're doing better,' Val mutters. 'Good. The skin must be unscathed, smooth and white and pink. Not full of bruises.'

The skin must be unscathed? *Why?* The frightening question permeates the farthest corners of Liz's consciousness.

'I've chosen a dress for you, for the thirteenth. It will be beautiful on you. You will look like a queen.' Val lets out a cackle. It sounds like icicles being smashed on the floor. 'Like a film star. I look forward to seeing his face.'

Whose face?

'You want to know what I have planned for you, right?'

Liz nods silently.

'I can hardly wait for it myself, if I'm being honest. But that's why I visit you so rarely, so that I'm not tempted. You know, it would be a shame to betray it all, the fear, the uncertainty in your eyes, the trembling. You're like a flame with no knowledge of how much candle wax remains beneath it. It's beautiful to behold.'

Tiny beads of sweat crystallise on Liz's face. Her mouth is a desert.

'I admit, I had to give him a bit of a leg up. A bit of knowledge. A bit of fear.'

'Who?' Liz asks, almost unable to breathe.

'*Him*, of course, your little Luke. *Your* Luke, Princess.'

Gabriel. He means Gabriel.

'You know, I'm unhappy. I can't see the fear in his eyes the way I see it in yours. He is still not here, I can only speak with him, hear him. But seeing fear is much more powerful than just hearing it. That's why I had to tell him something, so that I could at least *hear* his fear.'

Val leans forward over Liz. She sees his split face, the scarred grimace and the angelic smile, as his nose touches her shoulder and the tip of his tongue reaches into her armpit.

'I can even smell your fear,' he whispers. Liz feels like his hot breath is crawling under her skin. 'And taste it, too. If I could, I would put that flavour into an envelope and mail it to him.'

'Why . . . why are you doing this?'

'What he did to me,' Val's mouth is still on her shoulder, talking into it like an outer ear, 'was monstrous. I was free. For *one* night, I was free and could try, feel, smell, taste. It was phenomenal. It was the beginning of something big that should have gone on for ever. And then came along your little Luke.'

Val breathes hot air into her armpit. Liz winces as if she has been given an electric shock.

'Enough talk,' Val suddenly says, as if he has to tear himself away from the memory, and then stands upright. He quickly turns around. On his way out, he says: 'Think of me. I will think of you.'

The key grinds in the lock. Twenty minutes later, the light goes out and Liz is mercifully surrounded by darkness. The fact that Val will be blind for a few hours feels like a small victory in the midst of a long, losing battle.

Chapter 39

Liz knows that bright light will soon fill the room. She waits for it with her eyes closed. Her mind is clear and quick, except for the bottomless fatigue. She has not reconnected the drip.

Not today.

The tube from the IV hangs down from the frame and leads under the covers as usual. Only, this time, the end is lying loose beside her hand, along with the tube that is normally inserted into her vein, which she removed herself in the night.

The night before last, she took the seven steps from one wall to the other 1,400 times; last night, she saved her strength and only made the journey 800 times.

With her eyes closed, she goes over everything in her head again and again to distract herself and prevent herself from being paralysed by fear and doubt.

Bzzt.

With an electronic buzz, the fluorescent lights are on. The backs of her eyelids go from black to red. Still about five minutes until breakfast. She goes over everything again, repeats it like a mantra. He fingers close around the syringe in her hand. Every part of her is concentrated on the one moment. She knows that she has no more than three or four seconds and listens in the dead silence. Her eardrums are almost bursting in expectation. The blood is rushing so loudly through her head that she's afraid she could miss the crucial moment. She steps outside of herself, sees herself lying in the bed, like in a film, almost naked, the thin syringe in her fist, desperate, almost grotesque.

Then she hears the steps. Liz jumps up and throws the covers aside. Her feet touch the floor, the thin hospital gown flutters.

From the door, she hears the metallic staccato of each notch of the key sliding into the lock.

She leaps into the middle of the room, reaches out her arm with the syringe pointing upwards, focuses on the grating over the fluorescent ceiling light and jumps up. Luckily, the ceiling is low. The plastic syringe pokes through the grating and hits the delicate neon tube. The glass bursts and shards rain down. It is instantaneously dark.

The door swings open and Yvette stops in the doorway, bewildered. She is a black shadow and stands illuminated in a bright rectangle with a disgusting breakfast in hand. The key dangles from a link on her waistband. Liz's fingers close around the metal IV stand. Before Yvette can reorientate herself in the dark, Liz rams the metal rod into her stomach like a blunt lance.

Yvette groans and staggers back two steps. The bowl of porridge lands on the floor with a clatter. Instinctively, Yvette grabs the rod with both hands. Liz holds the other end firmly and braces herself, trying to push Yvette aside, as she is still blocking the door.

'Damn bitch,' Yvette gasps. Her strength is scary and Liz feels like she's losing ground. Centimetre by centimetre, Yvette pushes her back into the dark cell with the metal rod, over the shards of glass from the fluorescent bulb. Liz is overcome with panic. And at the same time, she has only one desperate thought.

I want to get out of here!

With all of her strength, she braces herself against the rod, and then she suddenly turns to the side and lets go. Yvette stumbles forward into the room, the metal pole crashes on the concrete floor and Yvette finally loses her balance. For a fraction of a second, Liz's impulse to flee takes over and she just wants to run out of there. But she knows she has to stay and render Yvette harmless.

She staggers towards the door and, just as Yvette pulls herself together against the opposite wall, Liz slams it shut. Suddenly, it's pitch black. As dark as all of the previous nights when she walked back and forth between the walls.

Welcome home.

Welcome to my turf, Yvette.

Liz knows exactly where Yvette is. Two steps, a hop over the shards of glass, then another two steps and she's on top of her, straddling her, frantically groping around for Yvette's hands. But there are no hands. An angry hiss behind her makes her neck hair stand on end. Wrong way. I'm sitting on Yvette the wrong way! In that very moment, a fist drives into Liz's side from behind. The pain makes it hard for Liz to breathe. At the same time, she feels a vast anger rise up in her like a flame. In one bound, half sliding, half jumping, she throws herself back. Her bottom lands in the middle of Yvette's face. Liz's hands feel something soft, narrow and round beneath her. Yvette's neck. Her fingers close around it like claws and she strangles Yvette with all her strength. Yvette rears up, writhes like a woman possessed, her hands thrashing about blindly, and then she pulls on Liz's arms and tries to loosen her grip. Liz makes herself as heavy as she can, squatting with the whole weight of her body on Yvette's face. She feels Yvette's open mouth beneath her pelvis struggling for air, desperately snapping her teeth like a dog and then actually biting her pubic area.

A burning pain fills Liz's body, she lets out a pained cry, lets go of Yvette's throat, brings her hands up above her head, squeezes them together and hammers down on Yvette's stomach like a wrecking ball.

Yvette's teeth immediately let go; she doubles over, writhing in pain.

Liz loses her balance and tilts to the side onto the floor. She feels an object directly beside her right hand and grabs the smooth cold metal. Yvette sits up, gasping for air, and then it is suddenly silent. Silent as the grave and pitch-black. Liz tries to hold her breath, but her lungs are screaming for oxygen. Without a sound, she kneels down and tries to estimate the distance between Yvette and herself. Two metres? Three metres? Or less? The metal pole in her hand rattles softly. If anything, it's about one and a half metres long. Liz strikes without knowing where she should be hitting.

Everything is still silent. That is, if you can call the rushing and pumping in her body silence.

Breathe, you bitch.

But Yvette doesn't oblige.

Liz continues holding her breath. The exertion drives sweat out of every pore. She stands there with the smooth rod in her sweaty hands as if she's holding a double-edged sword. To the left is the door, halfway to the left is the centre of the room, four steps straight ahead is the bed.

She wants to go to the door! shoots through her head.

At that very moment, she hears the crunching of broken glass. It's as if Liz can see through the dark. As if she can see Yvette standing in the middle of the room with her outstretched arms fumbling about, her head lowered and her back hunched forward.

Liz plunges the rod with all of her strength horizontally through the air. The impact on contact is so strong that it tears the pole from her hands and is accompanied by what sounds like a heavy copper pipe hitting a watermelon. Then the metal crashes across the floor. Wild triumph breaks out in Liz and she jumps in the direction she expects to find her opponent. She feels the warm body and throws herself at it to finish what she began. Her hands claw at Yvette's throat again. It's sticky and moist.

Blood!

Liz only just notices that Yvette is no longer moving. She lets go of her and waits to see if anything happens. Nothing. *Is she dead?*

With one blow, her triumph has turned into something disgusting and dirty.

The key. Pull yourself together, you need the key.

Liz feels around for the spring clip on Yvette's waistband, removes the key and rolls away from the warm body. Trembling like a leaf, she crawls to the door. She supports herself against the wall and stands up, and then she opens the door.

A broad strip of light falls into the dark room, shining directly on her opponent. Blood is gushing from under her hair, down her ear and across her neck. Her eyes are closed. *At least I don't have to look her in the eye!*

She takes several deep breaths to calm herself, but it doesn't work; she can't stop thinking about Val.

At some point, he will notice that something is wrong. A single glance at the security camera and he'll know.

So, keep moving!

Liz steps into the bright rectangle, places one foot in the doorway – and then two. Her heart is pounding wildly like it wants to betray her.

She closes the door, uses both hands to put Yvette's key in the lock and locks the door.

Then she turns around and squints. The corridor in front of her is roughly six metres long and ends in a ninety-degree turn. The brick walls are painted over in a dirty-looking grey. To the left and the right, there is one door on either side of the hallway. A bare light bulb hangs from a rusty socket in the ceiling.

Liz's feet tap on the stained concrete. She walks under the light bulb and her shadow overtakes her, growing on her path. She cautiously approaches the turn, peers around the corner with one eye – and gasps.

No. Please, no!

Ten steps ahead, a heavy barred door is blocking her way.

She looks down at Yvette's key. Hands shaking, she tries to fit the thin, silver key bit into the cylinder lock. No luck. It doesn't fit.

She turns around, scurries back to the two other doors and pushes on the left. A cell like her own, but larger and more comfortable. Blankets, pillows, a scuffed light-brown leather sofa, well-read books, an unmade bed, a sink and toilet, crude drawings of flowers on the walls, no windows, no exit. A cellar.

Yvette hadn't lied. Val had been holding her prisoner, too.

She turns around and pushes on the other door. The light is also on in here. Again, a cell; again, no exit. To the right, a simple kitchenette, a cabinet with medical products and drugs. On the left, a clothes dryer and an almost three-metre wide coat rail on wheels. About twenty strikingly elegant dresses are hanging from the crossbar, some of which are covered in plastic. All the way in front is something separate – a dress with a sweeping white-satin skirt, embroidered with hundreds of glittering roses. The front of the dress is almost as short as a mini skirt, but the back is long and billowy like a rococo gown. The inner lining of the skirt has a royal blue floral pattern. Liz can't help but reach out and touch the shimmering fabric. It's soft as silk, but also solid and bulky.

I've chosen a dress for you, for the thirteenth. You will look like a queen.

A shudder runs through Liz's body. She pulls her hand back, as if she's been burned.

Nonetheless, she can't take her eyes off of the luxurious dress. Such unique pieces often cost more than a hundred thousand euro and hang either on the thin shoulders of haute-couture models or in the walk-in wardrobes of the super-rich. With a jolt, she stares at the flowing blue floral pattern. Where the hell did he get dresses like these?

There is suddenly a noise out in the corridor. It sounds like the echo of a door being opened in the distance.

Val!

Liz spins around, thoughts running through her head in quick succession. Steps. She hears steps rushing down a staircase.

She looks up at the ceiling, the light bulb. She's under the light within a fraction of a second, reaching her arms out, stretching each finger. The heat burns her skin as she turns the bulb to the left. The light flickers and goes out. Only, it's too late for the light in the hall.

She can hear the metallic rattling of a key being put into a lock from outside. She can feel the blood pumping though her ears, her heart hammering against her ribs. The steps are getting closer. Liz has no choice. This is her only hiding place. She dives between the haute couture dresses on the clothes rail and squeezes all the way back against the cold brickwork. She wishes she could scratch a hole in the wall with her nails. She anxiously peers out between the expensive fabrics at the open door.

Please don't let him come in here.

Suddenly, a light goes on, a nerve-racking flicker for a fraction of a second.

Oh no! The bulb, she didn't unscrew the bulb far enough!

There is a growing shadow on the floor of the corridor. Val's figure appears in the doorway in the exact moment that the light bulb flickers again.

Val stops.

A smile flits across his tense face. 'Have I underestimated you, little Lizzy? Are you *this* strong?' he whispers.

Liz's knees go weak. Through the narrow gap, she can see him approaching. Unfaltering. Val's face flashes in rhythm with the flickering light.

'What were you thinking, Liz? That you could run away? Just like that? A small, weakened, naked woman in the middle of the mountains at these temperatures?'

Mountains. We're in the mountains! Liz crouches down, all of her muscles tense up.

'How far do you think you'll get, Liz, before I catch you? A hundred metres? Two hundred metres?'

The light crackles. Val passes under it and his face is suddenly pitch black; his silhouette is backlit, like an ominous aura.

'Shall we try it? I could let you go. But you'll have to run far, Liz, very far,' he says. His voice cracks with excitement to match the flickering light, as if an electric current were flowing through his body. His face grows to gigantic proportions, blocking the door, the bright bit of the corridor. Where there was just an exit is now only him. Gigantic. Black. Dominating everything.

'It would all be in vain,' Val whispers. 'And I don't want you to hurt yourself. I need you unscathed. Spotless.'

Liz desperately tightens her muscles until they ache. The light blinks tauntingly.

'Come out, little Lizzy. Come out, come out, wherever you are.' He is very close, towering in front of the dress rail.

Now!

Light as a feather, she hurries forward, pushing the crossbar of the rack from below. She wants to ram him under the chin, but the dresses weigh as much as a bookcase. The momentum pulls her down with the rack and the dresses as they tip onto Val. He flails his arms around, but he can't keep his balance and falls, his head hitting the concrete floor. Liz lands face down beside him. The dresses cushion her fall.

Suddenly, there is silence.

He's unconscious! she thinks and can hardly contain her excitement.

The bulb goes on again like lightning. Liz gropes around until she feels his body. The key! The key must be somewhere! Her fingers run across Val's trousers, his pockets.

There.

Her hand digs into his left trouser pocket. She grabs the key, which is caught in the pocket lining and touches his penis in the process.

Still, she manages to pull the key out. She struggles to her feet from amongst the tangled mountain of clothes. The light from the hall shines through the open door. She looks down at herself, at her thin hospital gown.

Val groans softly and deeply.

As if the room were on fire, Liz reaches into the pile of dresses, pulls one out and rushes to the door and down the hall. With her fingers shaking, she tries to put the key in the keyhole, but it slips and falls to the ground with a rattle.

Get it together.

She picks it up and tries again. Metal scratching against metal. The keyhole might as well be the eye of a needle.

Come on!

She tries with both hands, so she can control the shaking. Finally, she manages it.

The lock turns, the gate screeches open.

She hears a groan behind her, louder than before.

She pulls the key back out of the lock. The goddamn thing is refusing, clinging to its position. She finally slips through the door and pushes it shut from the other side.

Now lock it!

She tries again with the key. Her fingers shake uncontrollably. Violently.

Please!

She tries again with both hands. It's futile. Val's groans flow down the hall towards her.

Panicked, she leaves the key in the lock, grabs the dress and staggers onwards along the hall and around the corner. Her feet feel stairs. She feels for a handrail and climbs the steps, faster and faster – just get out of this hell.

The stairs end in the middle of a large room. The daylight burns her eyes like poison. Through the glare, she can make out a garden beyond. She manages to open the glass door and rush out.

The fresh air is almost shocking. She voraciously sucks it into her lungs. It smells of earth, resin and grass. She squints, trying to orientate herself. On her right is a garage door. She rattles it by the handle, but it's locked. There must be a car inside and there is surely a key in the house. But she can't go back. Not into this house.

In a daze, she hurries through a black wrought-iron gate in a stone wall. The sky is so vast she feels dizzy. The mountains around her are contoured so that it looks like they are suspended in the sky with their snow-capped ridges and peaks. Her legs remember the training. Always one step after another, faster and faster down the road.

She turns around, looks at the stone wall and the house behind it – his house, a cold dirty bungalow, alone, practically rammed into the mountain. The road ends at the entrance to his house, the double doors like a hungry mouth.

But you'll have to run far, Liz, very far.

Oh, I can run, you bastard!

The road in front of her winds through the mountains with woods on either side of the asphalt. Liz runs in the shelter of the trees, out of breath, always far enough from the road, but also always parallel to it. Several times, she bends around the steep slopes, branches hit her face and body, her bare feet in agony on the stony ground. Eventually, the freezing air begins to get to her. Birds squawk at her from the trees above. She stops, tears away the plastic, peels out the dress – and groans.

Haute couture.

There must be a scornful little devil out to get her somewhere.

Still, she thinks resolutely, it's better than nothing.

The dress is black and she wishes the sun would set, even though she knows that the day has only just begun.

Chapter 40

Berlin – 25 September, 6.42 p.m.

Gabriel closed his eyes, as if it could save him from the pain, as if he could just forget all of this insanity again.

Luke! Hey, Luke . . .

Gabriel doesn't react. Everything feels sore and numb.

And? Has getting back down into that damned cellar helped you?

Helped? It echoes in his head, although he can't find a suitable answer.

You see? We're a wreck because of you. And for what?

Silence.

Then, very quietly, the thought: maybe I should get rid of you . . .

Get rid of me? You don't really mean that.

And if I do?

Luke! We . . . we've always got along well . . . you know how many times I've saved you?

Maybe. Yes.

Maybe?

I don't know whether you've actually saved me.

What?

Maybe I would've been better off without you.

Goddamn it, you ungrateful arsehole. Who made sure you pulled yourself together? That you're not just blubbering all over the place? Who made sure you were strong? Who the hell made sure that the others didn't break you?

I know. Yes.

And still, you prefer HER?

It's not about that at all.

That's exactly what it's about. Ever since she came around, you've been . . . unpredictable. A danger to yourself . . .

I'm not sure.

You can still end it. Any time. You just have to decide to.

That's what you want? That I decide? That I turn against Liz? Do you understand what you're asking? Gabriel whispers. Listen! I killed my father! Me! I don't know why, I can't remember any more, but I know it was me. And now you want me to leave Liz to die? Her, of all people?

It will set you free.

Free?

That's what you've been longing for.

For freedom? *You've* been longing for freedom. I want . . . I don't know . . . salvation.

Salvation? My god, what kind of pathetic shit is that! There is no salvation. Salvation is jumping from a skyscraper. Freedom is the only thing.

Maybe I really am better off without you.

You should get some sleep.

I can't seep, damn it! Can you get that through your thick skull?

Our skull, Luke. Our skull! Incidentally, you've forgotten about the electrodes, Luke. The light barrier . . .

Gabriel opens his eyes. The electrodes, shit.

His fingers are trembling as he gropes around on the floor beside the bed. The dust swirls through the beam of light sneaking in between the closed curtains of his room at Caesar's. It shines onto his bed, casting a spotlight on the collection of loose papers from his medical records.

Somewhere between the pages, he finds the thin cable, places the electrodes on his forearm and closes his eyes again. From behind his eyelids, all he can see is a red glow – like the inside of a stomach. Suddenly, he is back in the cellar at Conradshöhe, sitting frozen in front of his own file. At some point, he had lost consciousness down there. When he came to, it was already late afternoon. The dog bite in his arm was burning and he felt feverish.

Normally, he would have waited for nightfall to break out of the psychiatric clinic in the cover of darkness. But there was no normal any more. Normal was over, for good.

He crept out of the archive room and was lucky to find an old grey uniform in an adjacent room, which he threw on immediately. Then he left the cellar the same way he got in: through the service entrance.

About an hour later, he was sitting in his doctor's waiting room. The arm was now very swollen, possibly infected from the bite. The doctor wanted to give him a rabies injection, but Gabriel refused. Instead, he requested antibiotics, had the wound cleaned and bandaged and flat out rejected being transferred to the hospital.

When he staggered out of the practice, exhaustion hit him like a freight train. He got the chills. His teeth chattering, he hailed a taxi, had it drop him off near Caesar's – just not up to the front door – and then dragged himself the rest of the way on foot.

In his room, he just fell into bed, peeled off the tattered jacket, shoved the mobile in his trouser pocket – just in case Val called again – and threw himself back on the mattress, feeling like his childhood was a malignant tumour that had metastasised and revealed its ugliest, truest form.

Although he was certain that he wouldn't be able to fall asleep, he dozed off. Memories drift around, and he runs back and forth between them, confused, like the silver ball in a pinball machine.

The blood. David, as small as a doll, but somehow heavy as a tank. He had to pull him away, away from the fire, away from the dead eyes that cut through him.

The cellar, the lab. An open door. His father shouting at him not to go down. But he couldn't help it. He felt something sticky between his toes, it smelled like chemicals. He walked through a forest of photos. Filmstrips hung from the ceiling, wriggling towards him like snakes. One of them coiled around his neck and choked him, his forearm burned like fire . . .

Like electricity . . .

He opens his eyes and the dream ends abruptly.

The electrodes on his arm have been activated. The infrared barrier. Someone is standing in front of his door.

Alert, Gabriel jumps up and presses his back against the wall between the door and the bed. He waits, his eyes fixed on the worn door handle.

Nothing. No movement. His heart is pounding.

Breathe! Be calm!

The setting sun behind the thick curtains bathes everything in dirty twilight.

At the doorway, there is a soft scraping at exactly the height of the lock. Someone is pushing a plastic card between the catch and the doorframe. Gabriel's muscles tighten. With a metallic click, the lock gives way and the door swings open, crashing against the wall beside the washbasin. A hulking figure storms into the room with a compact black pistol at the ready.

Gabriel's reactions are like a machine. His right arm speeds forward like the blade of a flick knife, the edge of his hand shoots to the side of the intruder's thick neck. The man groans, falls into the room and the gun slips away from him.

Two more men in black leather jackets follow behind him. Gabriel gives the first one a hard kick with his right foot. He stumbles back out into the hall against the second man. From the corner of his eye, Gabriel sees the hulking one reach for his gun on the floor.

Gabriel slams the door against the faces of the other two. He hears a thud and a cry in pain. Gabriel spins around and then strikes the hulk with another blow to the neck. The man's fingers go limp just a few centimetres away from the pistol. The gun, a Russian Baghira MR 444 made of carbon fibre, lies on the floor. Gabriel hears the two men outside fumbling with the door again. His thoughts are racing like a train so that everything from his side of it looks blurred.

Take the fucking gun, damn it.

No, no, no.

Fucking idiot, you and your hesitation.

No gun.

What do you think they'll do to us?

Gabriel doesn't answer. He doesn't know who 'they' are. He doesn't know what 'they' want. And he doesn't have any idea what he should do. He is stuck between the tracks – one step and the train will run him over.

And Liz? What about her? If you won't help yourself, then at least help her. You can't stop thinking about her. And now you're going to give up? Because of your idiotic fear of guns?

Suddenly, the train is gone, it has raced past and he is pulled onto the tracks in its wake.

His fingers dig into the gun's grip. It's light and compact, but still feels heavy in his hand. The trigger burns white hot against his right index finger. He is trembling; nonetheless, he throws open the door, Baghira at the ready. Surprised, the two men stare back at him with their guns drawn and pointed directly at him. One of them is holding his free hand in front of his nose, which is clearly broken. Blood seeps between his fingers and his wide-set eyes glisten with rage. Gabriel knows him from Python. His name is Koslowski, he's Polish.

'What do you want?' Gabriel asks.

'Take a guess,' Koslowski says between his fingers. His voice is shaking with anger and pain.

'I haven't the slightest idea.'

'The film,' the other man replies. 'Give us the film and we'll get out of here.'

'Film?' Gabriel looks at him, puzzled. 'What film?'

'Don't play dumb. We know you have it.'

'I don't have anything. Who sent you? Yuri?'

'You know who sent us. So, give us the tape and we're gone.'

'What tape?' Gabriel's eyes move from one to the other. 'I have no idea what this is about. If Yuri wants something from me, why doesn't he just say it? Instead, he throws me out and unloads me at the tip. And now you show up and claim that I've got some tape or a film . . . What fucking film would that be?'

Koslowski and the other man exchange looks.

'The video,' Koslowski says through his nose. He's clearly having trouble speaking. 'It was in the safe at the house on Kadettenweg.'

Gabriel furrows his brow. 'The safe was empty.'

'Sarkov said it was in there,' Koslowski mumbles and tilts his head back because of his bleeding nose, but doesn't lower his weapon. 'Sarkov says you pinched the thing.'

'Bullshit.'

'Sarkov didn't send us after bullshit, so let's go, hand it over.' He energetically brandishes his weapon. 'Give back the film. Your time is running out.'

Gabriel stares at the guns pointed at him. The Baghira in his hand weighs a ton. 'Have I understood this correctly? Yuri wants this film at all costs?'

'You said it.'

Gabriel smiles bitterly. 'Guns have one major disadvantage if you want something at all costs.'

Koslowski stares at him, confused.

'They're deadly,' Gabriel says.

Koslowski shifts his weight from his left to his right foot, as if to set his brain in motion.

'So, what do you think?' Gabriel says quietly. 'If I have the film and it's hidden in a secure place, how is Yuri supposed to find it if you shoot me now?'

Koslowski blinks. His forehead wrinkles and then he slowly and silently points his gun at Gabriel's knee and grins. Blood runs over his thick upper lip and reddens his teeth. The other man keeps his gun pointed squarely at Gabriel's head. 'So there you have it,' Koslowski declares.

'That is not the question,' Gabriel says. The exertion is making him sweat and he tries to focus on that so that they can't see how nervous he is. 'The question is more, how important is this film to you? After all, what do you think will happen if you shoot me in the knee?'

Koslowski stares at the Baghira pointed at him. The barrel of the gun is trembling in Gabriel's hand. 'You're afraid,' he mumbles and smiles meanly. The trembling gets worse.

'Yes,' Gabriel says. 'And that's exactly why I am going to shoot.' Koslowski's grin disintegrates.

Gabriel takes a half step forward. The two men don't move a centimetre.

'Your time is up,' Koslowski repeats. His breath smells like smoke. 'Give me the film.'

Gabriel takes a step towards Koslowski and presses the barrel of the Baghira against his left eye. Koslowski's finger trembles on the trigger, but he doesn't move. Gabriel puts more pressure on his eye. Despite himself, the Pole backs away, leaving the door free. Gabriel walks through the door and into the hall. With slow, focused steps, he goes backwards towards the stairwell with his gun still pointed at the men.

'Sooner or later,' Koslowski cries, 'I'll get you.'

'I'll recognise you by the bandages on your nose,' Gabriel says.

Koslowski furiously spits a mix of blood and saliva onto the hallway carpet. At that very moment, Gabriel storms down the stairs. Noisy steps charge down the hall. As he rushes out the back door of Caesar's, his movements are amazingly confident.

It won't be like this for long, he thinks, soon the adrenalin will subside.

He sprints to the nearest metro station. On the stairs, he releases the magazine from the Baghira and throws it into a bin. He discards the gun itself in another rubbish bin on the train platform and feels like he's removed the poison from a snake-bite. He boards the arriving train and sits on one of the colour-fully patterned seats. The square lights above the doors flash to indicate that the doors are closing. The wheels grind against the track and the train starts moving.

Shit!

How the hell did Yuri find him? And what film is he after?

Gabriel thinks of the night at the house on Kadettenweg, the living room with the heavy wooden ceiling beams and the aban-doned furniture, the photos on the mantel and the safe behind the picture. The safe was open and empty, so someone who had been there before him was in possession of its contents. But who could it be, and what did Yuri want with the film? And what did the house there have to do with anything? When it came to that address, Yuri had reacted as if the building were a part of his body.

Frustrated, Gabriel puts his hands in his trouser pockets. His cold fingers feel the mobile and he thinks of Liz.

The train brakes screech and a mother gets on with a buggy. The child inside has a bubblegum-pink dummy in her mouth and huge eyes.

Gabriel automatically wonders how old she is. He gets choked up at the sight of her. How many months along is Liz now? He clenches his fists in his pockets. Come on, think! What is your next step?

He can't go back to Caesar's, that's for sure. His hideout is blown and next time Yuri will send men who can't be so easily persuaded. The only problem is that everything he owns other than the mobile is at Caesar's, including the money.

Gabriel groans. He needs new clothes, since the ones he's wearing are covered in blood and filth, but without any money, he's in no position to find a place to stay, let alone get food and clothing. He closes his eyes. The rumbling of the train calms the chaos of his mind.

David, he thinks. I have to go to David.

You're incorrigible, Luke!

I just need some money.

He has never helped you. Why should he help you now?

He's my brother.

Family! the voice mocks. *You mean blood is thicker than water and all that?*

Gabriel doesn't answer.

And does it also count when that blood was shed by your own hand?

I want you to disappear!

Gabriel opens his eyes and stares at the flaming red horizon between the buildings. It looks as if someone has ignited the sky.

Chapter 41

Liz sits on the wooden bench at the local police station like a worn-out mannequin. She is wrapped in a scratchy Swiss army blanket and wants nothing more than a warm bed and to close her eyes, knowing that nothing else can be done for her. But the longer she listens to the muffled voices behind the glass, the more her desperation grows. Even if both of the local police officers behind the window think that she hears nothing – she actually understands every word. Now they're both laughing, they're talking about cars, as the shorter one compulsively turns his BMW key between his fingers.

She doesn't know where to look and just stares out in front of her. The sun has fallen like a stone behind the mountains and dusk hovers over Andermatt. Her feet are numb and every single muscle in her body burns.

She managed to fight her way through the trees for a full half an hour. The slope became increasingly steep and the sharp stones and branches hurt her feet so badly that she was in tears. So, she left the cover of the trees, made her way to the road and down the serpentine path. On the smooth asphalt, she progressed much faster. To calm herself, she began counting her steps. Every time a car drove by, she threw herself into the bushes and dropped to the ground. Each time, she prayed that the vehicle would keep moving and that he wasn't behind the wheel. She couldn't bear it if he saw a bit of her absurd black dress in the bushes, stopped and brought her back to her prison – or something even worse.

An eternity later, a white, onion-shaped steeple appeared behind a bend. Train tracks cut through the mountain landscape.

It was the village of Wassen.

Liz walked into town like a gothic bride. She had cut a slit in the voluminous, ill-fitting black haute-couture dress, so that her pregnant belly could fit in it. The black silk, which was sheer in some places, was dirty and had pulled threads from branches or thorns getting caught in the fabric. Her bare feet were covered in filth and her greasy red hair was sticking out in all directions. In the Middle Ages, she would have been burned at the stake as a witch. In the twenty-first century, she seemed like a lunatic, freshly escaped from the asylum.

As she walked past the first houses in the village, she could see from the corner of her eye that she was being stared at through the curtains. She kept going, step by step, as she had done in her cell. The soft tapping of her feet against the asphalt sounded like a metronome that guided her heart and mind to just keep going.

The first person that approached her was a woman holding the hand of a little girl around five years old. The child was the spitting image of her mother, with wide-set eyes and long blond hair, which was braided neatly down the back of her head.

Liz shook with relief. 'Please help me,' she begged. 'I need the police.'

The woman stayed planted at a safe distance and looked at Liz with her mouth hanging open. 'What . . . what happened to you?'

Liz swallowed, slowly shook her head and repeated: 'Please, I would just like to go to the police.'

The girl looked up at Liz from below and pulled hard on her mother's hand. The woman's eyes drifted down to Liz's round stomach. Then she nodded. 'Come on, I'll take you to the train station. You need to go one stop. The police station for the area is in Andermatt.'

'Thank you,' Liz nodded and followed behind the neatly dressed Swiss woman. She felt like a filthy vagrant in the eyes of the villagers. The daughter kept turning back to look at her. There was a mixture of disgust and confusion in her expression. Liz couldn't blame her. With difficulty, she smiled back at her. 'Nice fringe you've got there,' she said softly.

The girl looked up, her eyebrows raised in confusion.

'Your hair,' Liz said, gesturing to the top of the girl's forehead.

The girl pushed her hand away, as if Liz were some sort of leper, and turned away.

'We say bangs, not fringe,' the mother said.

Bangs. Liz didn't know whether to laugh or cry. The village train station was a simple building with six mullioned windows and a pointed roof with a single train platform behind it.

The woman, whose name she didn't even know, checked the timetable for her. 'The train will be here in ten minutes.' She looked at Liz, uncertain. The girl pulled on her hand again. 'Do you have any money?'

Liz shook her head. The woman gave her twenty Swiss francs, smiled a bit less stiffly this time and shot her daughter an angry look. 'Sorry,' she muttered. 'Will you manage it alone? I think my daughter . . .'

'I'll be fine,' Liz said. 'You've helped me a lot.'

The train entered the station, its brakes bringing the carriages to such a screeching halt that Liz had to cover her ears. Every sound seemed to pierce deep inside her, as if she no longer had any filter from the outside world.

She stepped on the train in a trance. It hadn't once even crossed her mind that he might think she was going to get away by train.

When the landscape started moving around her and the repetitive sound of the wheels turning crept into her conscious-ness, she began to cry again. Every fibre of her body ached and she was dizzy with hunger.

She absently stared out the window; the scenery sped past in long blurring strips. When the Swiss railway guard asked her for her ticket, she desperately looked for the twenty-franc note that the woman had given her. The money was gone. Apparently, she had lost it on the platform. 'I . . . I had it earlier,' she stam-mered, 'I just . . . excuse me.' She swallowed and tried to pull herself together. 'I'm sorry. Please help me. I was kidnapped. I . . . have to go to the police.'

In Andermatt, two police officers were already waiting for her. The guard gratefully handed her over to their custody – a confused pregnant woman without a valid ticket and incoherent delusions of being kidnapped.

Liz was relieved. At first.

At the station, she collapsed and then was given a Swiss army blanket. She finally had something to eat and drink and was permitted to wash up the best she could in the WC. When she saw her reflection in the mirror, she jumped. Not again, she thought. *Don't start wailing again, damn it!*

Then came the questions.

'Could you please tell us your name again?'

'Anders. Liz Anders, from Berlin. I'm a journalist.'

'And you were actually kidnapped in Berlin, and then someone brought you here to Switzerland?'

Liz nodded.

'Why did the kidnapper go to such trouble?'

'How should I know? Ask the man who did it.'

'You mean . . . this Val.'

'God, yes,' Liz snapped, nearly in tears. 'For the third time!'

'Are you sure that your description is accurate?'

'After giving you the exact same description three times, does it sound like I'm not sure?'

The two officers exchanged glances. The shorter of the two, who was one of the officers that had picked her up at the train station, cleared his throat. 'No, please don't misunderstand, but it all sounds a bit . . . well, yeah . . . a man with half his face disfigured and the other half . . . what did you say?'

'Beautiful, I said, exceptionally attractive,' Liz muttered weakly. 'Like a model for shaving cream or something.'

'You know, I believe you, that is, just . . . it all sounds a bit like Dr Jekyll and Mr Hyde . . . that is . . .'

'Well, I can't change it. It all sounds quite ludicrous, that may well be. But it is the truth. *It happened. Please!* Send a patrol car to the house if you don't believe me.'

Another exchanged glance. The taller of the two men sighed. 'Could you please give us the directions again?'

'The road past the church out of Wassen, continue along the stream the whole way, around 7,200 steps. Then bear right up the slope. I don't remember how many steps that was, I ran between the trees. But the house is at the end of the street. A bungalow, right on the rocks. Surrounded by a dry stone wall with a wrought-iron gate. The front entrance has double doors made of dark brown wood. There are no other houses there. You should probably be able to find that, right?'

'And you're sure you mean *that* house?'

Liz glared at him. 'How sure do you need me to be?'

The tall officer raised his eyebrows, placed the pen in his notebook and stood up. 'Well, then let's go.'

After a phone call and forty minutes of waiting, Liz looks at her feet. The phone rings in the office. The short officer puts down the car keys and picks up the phone. Liz's eyes are glued to the window. Suddenly, she recognises her own reflection in the glass and is shocked.

'Police, Canton of Uri, this is Schechtler,' the officer says.

He listens for a moment, then he nods, waves his colleague over and puts it on speaker.

'As you suspected,' the voice on the speakerphone crackles, 'this is the house. No doubt about it.'

Liz straightens up, blood charging through every last vein.

'And? What did you find?'

'Well, pretty abandoned upstairs. The housekeeper let us in, she's a bit eccentric, but no wonder when you don't see a single soul all day.'

The housekeeper?

Liz jumps up. Her entire body protests against the sudden movement. She stares through the window, flails about with her hands, gesturing as if she's hitting someone over the head.

The officer gestures for her to sit back down. 'What's the housekeeper's name?'

'Yvette Baerfuss, thirty-nine years old. She's been working for the family for fourteen years. Comes from Lucerne. The people in the area know her.'

For fourteen years? Liz's eyes widen. *Fourteen? This cannot be!* She opens the door and whispers breathlessly: 'What did she look like? Ask about a wound on her head.'

The officer angrily furrows his brow and gives Liz a withering look. 'How, uh, did she look?'

'How she *looked*? Well, a bit worse for the wear. Maybe if she was younger, I'd –'

'Man,' the short one says, 'I don't want to know if you'd sleep with her. I want to know what she looks like. Did you notice anything particular about her or . . .'

The tall officer snorts.

'Oh, uh . . . well, grey or blue eyes, shoulder-length blond hair, I think . . . she was wearing a headscarf . . . slim, medium height . . . her breasts were a bit more, in relation to, I mean . . .'

The tall one mimes huge tits with his hands and shakes with laughter.

The short one rolls his eyes. 'Did you notice anything else, you genius? Injuries or anything?'

'Injuries? Where?'

'No idea. Anywhere.'

For a moment, there is silence.

'Nope. There was nothing,' the voice says.

The short one covers the mouthpiece, looks grouchily at the tall one and gestures to Liz with his chin. 'If you're done laughing, then you can throw her out, in the hall.'

Liz stares at him in disbelief. 'You mean to tell me they found nothing?' She is suddenly a pale as a ghost. 'Please listen! He's there, I know it! You just have to go in. She's covering for him.'

The short one turns his back to her and gestures for her to go back out in the hall.

'Please,' Liz begs. 'Now they know I'm here. If you don't find him, then –' her voice suddenly fails her.

The tall officer gently pushes her out. 'Please, calm down. Don't worry, you're safe here.' Then he tries to close the door, but something is jammed and the door remains open a crack.

Liz sits on the bench. Her heart starts beating uncontrollably and her hands are shaking. *Control!* She thinks. *Stay in control.* She closes her eyes and tries to calculate. If it's 7,200 steps away, how long would that take by car? *How quickly will he get here?*

'Are you waiting inside now, in the house?' she hears the short one ask behind the glass window.

The voice on the speaker snorts. 'You know who owns the place, right?'

'I didn't ask who it belongs to, I asked if you were waiting inside, Christ.'

'All right, all right. Yes.'

'OK, so have you asked?'

'It was a bit of an effort, but I think I've set the right tone with her . . .'

The tall one grins and sways his hips rhythmically. The short one looks at him angrily until he stops.

'It's a pretty simple shack for such a moneybags. Really surprised me.'

'Did you see everything?'

'Every room. But there was nothing to do with a kidnapping or anything.'

Liz stares at the two policemen behind the glass, then her eyes anxiously drift over to the door of the station, as if it could spring open at any moment and Val would be standing there. His face appears in her mind, torn apart like raw flesh. With all of her strength, she tries to force him out of her thoughts, but he is everywhere. *Pull yourself together, damn it, and start thinking!*

'What about the cellar? Does it fit the description?'

'There is no cellar.'

'What?'

'I looked everywhere. I checked every door. I was surprised. But Yvette said it would be impossible to have a cellar here because the rock is too hard. Von Braunsfeld probably wanted one, but it wasn't possible.'

'Aha. So, did you find out anything about the kidnapping?' the short one asks and looks through the glass at Liz, who is sitting again and slumped over.

There is a crackling on the line.

'If you ask me, it's all nonsense. Didn't she say she was a journalist?'

The tall one drops into an old, worn-out swivel chair.

'Yes. Why?'

'Hm. Let me just look at something.' The tall one pulls over a dirty keyboard. 'L-i-z A-n-d-e-r-s,' he spells aloud while typing the name into the Google search bar and then presses enter. 'Seems to be true. She is actually a journalist, works for television.'

'Wait a minute,' the short one mutters into the handset, bends forward and studies the links. 'Look at that, she is,' he confirms. 'But if there was no kidnapping, then what is she doing here in this tattered get-up?'

'Look,' the tall one says with sudden excitement and taps his finger on a link on the screen. 'No way! She even made a documentary about von Braunsfeld.'

'You think she was chasing down celebrities and was looking for von Braunsfeld here?'

'Nonsense. He hasn't been to the chalet in years. That's what they say, anyway.'

'Hey,' the officer on the phone chimes in. 'Looks like it's probably a false alarm, right? Do you need me any more?'

'No idea,' the short one grumbles, displeased. 'Probably not, at least not out there. First we need to take care of this Anders woman.'

'Is she at least hot?'

'Oh, shut up and just come back. Bye.' He angrily slams the phone down. 'Christ!' he barks and stares at the screen full of links about Liz Anders.

The other officer makes a face like he's deep in thought. 'You know what I find strange?'

'No,' the short one says.

'If a super-rich guy like this Victor von Braunsfeld built himself an extra chalet here in the mountains, then why didn't he just have the rocks removed if he really wanted a cellar? The rich always just build whatever they want and don't give a shit about the cost.'

The short one shrugs. 'Eccentricity?'

'And why would he even have the chalet built in the first place if he's never there? Is that also eccentricity?'

'What do I know? Maybe some sort of love nest for secret meetings with this Yvette?'

'Von Braunsfeld is over seventy. And why be secretive anyway? His wife has been dead for years, what's there to hide?'

The short one contorts his face as if he's got a toothache.

'Never there, no cellar, it *is* kind of strange, isn't it?'

'Sort of. But then why would he need a cellar if he's never there?'

The tall one sighs and looks at the clock. 'All right, well, what are we going to do with her?'

'Maybe try to call her friend again, this . . .' the short one looks at a notepad beside the telephone, 'Gabriel Naumann.'

'And leave another message on the voicemail? How would that help? He'll get in touch at some point. Assuming she really is with the guy.'

'You think she's lying?'

'Who knows? I mean, look at her.'

'Hmm. Maybe we should call the clinic in Lucerne,' the short one says thoughtfully. 'They have experience with this type of thing, right?'

'And what type of thing is that?'

The tall one taps on the side of his head with his index finger.

'Well, she certainly looks it with that whole get-up and everything. And those directions with the *7,200* steps. Who counts like that? Maybe an autistic.'

'Autistic?'

'I've read about it. Autistics have cognitive disorders. There are a lot of things they don't properly understand, but instead they can count really well or can tell you how many grains of rice are in a jar.'

The tall one looks at him incredulously. 'Autistic and a television journalist?'

'You got a better idea?'

The tall one shakes his head.

'All right, I'll take care of her and you ring them. You can take over with her afterwards. I'll have to go then anyway, otherwise my wife will probably be annoyed. Tell them they should do it quickly.' His hand runs across the counter and reaches for the car keys that he'd put down earlier, but his hand grabs at nothing. 'Hey, do you have my car keys?'

The tall one stops dialling and looks at him blankly. 'What would I be doing with your car keys?'

The short one furrows his brow and looks through the window into the outer office. He turns white as a sheet. 'Shit,' he whispers. 'Shit, shit, shit.'

He throws open the door and stares at the empty bench where Liz had just been sitting a few moments ago.

Chapter 42

Berlin – 25 September, 9.17 p.m.

Someone erased the burning horizon. Low clouds reflect the street lighting and make the sky look like poisonous ash.

Gabriel rings the bell. At the same moment, a siren howls in the near vicinity and he jumps. His already agitated nerves make him very edgy. After a few seconds, he presses the bell again. This time, there's no siren. Instead, David's voice crackles in the intercom. 'Hello?'

'It's me,' Gabriel says.

Silence.

Gabriel thinks he can hear David breathing, hesitating.

'I . . . I have a visitor right now, can't we do this another time?'

'I won't take long.'

Silence again. 'OK, OK,' David finally answers, resigned.

The door unlocks with a buzz and Gabriel pushes it open. There's a draught in the stairwell that is heavy with the scent of cleaning products. The musty smell of Gabriel's clothes is about as discreet in here as dog mess at a dinner party. As he climbs the stairs, he fumbles around for the mobile phone in his trouser pocket and wonders when Val is going to call again.

The door to David's penthouse flat is already open and Gabriel steps inside. 'Hello?'

'I'm in the living room,' his brother calls. A moment later, he is standing across from David, who is leaning on the kitchen counter, his skin pale and his eyes sunken. The brown-haired woman that Gabriel saw the first time he was in David's flat is standing at the coffee maker behind him. She pours herself a coffee, nods to Gabriel and lets her eyes linger on his clothes.

'You already know Shona,' David mutters, obviously trying to avoid looking at him. Nonetheless, his eyes drift across the bandages on Gabriel's arm, the stained jumper, the tattered trousers and the shoes that are encrusted in dirt. His eyes widen. 'What happened to you?'

Gabriel makes a face. 'Can we talk in private? I'll be quick.'

David and Shona exchange a look. Gabriel immediately wonders what he's told her.

'How about you change into something else first?' David suggests and gestures to the open bedroom door. 'The size should be about right, just help yourself.'

'Suits aren't my thing and I don't want to stay long,' Gabriel answers. 'If you can lend me a bit of money, then I'll get myself some new clothes.'

'And how much is "some"?'

Shona glances warningly at David.

'Two or three thousand for now,' Gabriel proposes. 'You'll get it back, don't worry,' he quickly adds when he sees David's eyes widen. 'I was attacked and had to get away. The only thing I could take with me in a hurry was my mobile.'

David takes a deep breath and looks away. His cheeks are red beneath the blond stubble. You can see how much he hates that his every emotion is visible right on his face.

Shona looks first at David and then Gabriel. She noisily puts her coffee cup on the counter. 'Look, it's none of my business, but you are not the only one here who's having a hard time and –'

'Shona, please,' David says.

'What do you mean?' Gabriel asks suspiciously.

'Just look around you,' Shona says. 'Nothing in the refrigerator, missing pictures on the wall, the flat is half empty and to make matters worse, David now also –'

'Shona, that's enough!' David stops her.

'What?' Shona replies heatedly. 'He's bothering you with his problems. Why don't you just tell him that you were fired and you're also broke?'

Gabriel looks at David. 'Is that true?'

David chews on his lower lip and looks out the window.

'Well, yes,' David nods.

'Shit,' Gabriel groans and leans against the wall.

'Maybe I can help you some other way,' David says softly, 'but not with two or three thousand.'

Shona looks at David, stunned. 'Do you not understand what's going on here? Your wonderful brother hops from one catastrophe to the next and you want to keep helping him?'

'Shona, please,' David says.

'Bravo,' Gabriel says bitingly. 'Apparently she's your new babysitter.'

'And where is your psychiatrist?' Shona spits back. 'I'd really like to talk to him!'

Gabriel stares at her furiously. 'I don't think,' he says icily, 'that you are one to judge. So just shut up.'

'Oh yeah?' Shona hisses. 'And what if –'

'Shona,' David interrupts. 'He's right. You really have no idea. Please drop it.'

Shona looks at David, speechless. Her cheeks are burning, as if someone had slapped her across the face.

For a moment, everything freezes.

Then Shona turns on her heel, throws her bag over her shoulder and rushes out of the flat. The door crashes shut behind her.

'Great,' David mutters. 'Thanks for that.'

Gabriel shrugs. 'Ring her when I'm gone.' The dull pain in his arm makes sure its presence is known.

'So that you can scare her off again next time? No thank you! You're a real arsehole, you know that? No wonder people are always after you.'

'What do you mean by that?' Gabriel asks.

David's cheeks flush. A strange, indefinable expression shines in his green eyes.

'I asked what you meant by that.'

'Didn't you just say that you were attacked?' David says hastily.

Gabriel gives him a piercing look.

Did you hear that, Luke? the voice in his head prods. *You hear how high his voice is?*

He's hiding something. He's embarrassed about something.

Embarrassed? He's scared, Luke. He stinks of fear.

'Why are you looking at me like that?' David asks. The hand in his right pocket has been moving the whole time.

Guilty conscience, Gabriel thinks, and he's afraid. But why? Gabriel tries to shake off his rising queasiness and shrugs. The injured shoulder responds immediately with a sharp pain and he grimaces.

'What?' David snaps.

Gabriel huffs. 'I should be asking you. What's your problem?'

David nervously runs his hand through his blond hair. 'What do you think my problem is? It's the same as always,' David says. 'You're telling wild stories and I'm uncomfortable.'

'Nice try,' Gabriel says. 'You've always been a shitty liar.'

Awkward silence.

A pigeon flutters on the railing outside the window. The white bird shit reflects the light from the flat and shines in the darkness.

'They can smell your guilty conscience on the other side of town, little brother. So, what happened?' Gabriel asks. His blue eyes are as hard as metal.

'My god, what the hell to you think happened?' David's voice goes shrill. 'My brother appears like a ghost from the past and drags me into his mess, the bank wants to seize my home, my boss sacks me out of nowhere . . .'

'What mess? I haven't pulled you into anything. I only asked you to check and see which hospital Liz was in.'

'I . . .' David goes quiet.

'Now spit it out, man. I can tell there's something."

'I had . . . a visitor,' David says feebly.

Visitor? Gabriel stares at him. Suddenly, all the pieces fall into place. 'He was here,' he whispers. 'Yuri was here, wasn't he?'

David looks away.

'Yuri was here and you told him where to find me. That's why you have such a fucking guilty conscience.'

David's jawbone is visibly clenched. He looks as if he wants to bite down on a cyanide capsule but lacks the courage.

'How the hell did you know where I was?'

'The key,' David mumbles. 'The key fell out of your pocket.'

'You goddamned idiot,' Gabriel groans.

'I . . . he . . . he said that he'd known you a long time. And that you stole something from him.' Beads of sweat shine on David's forehead. 'He wanted it back, nothing more. He said nothing else would happen, he wouldn't do anything to you.'

'God, you're naive,' Gabriel says. 'What did you get in exchange?'

'Get?'

'Yes, damn it, *get*! Yuri only has two methods of getting what he wants from someone. He either threatens you or he buys you. So what was it?'

'David swallows. 'Your . . . file,' he says hoarsely.

'My *what*?'

'Your file, a copy of your file from the psychiatric clinic.'

'Shit,' Gabriel whispers and looks in David's eyes, their greenness dull like a stirred-up lake full of algae.

'I just needed to know,' David says so quietly it seems like he's only explaining it to himself. 'He said that you fired the gun . . . I asked you a thousand times. You only ever said that you couldn't remember . . .'

'And? Have you read the file?' Gabriel asks with a husky voice and knows how redundant the question is. Up until now, he was angry with David. And now? Now he's just waiting for David's wrath to descend upon *him*, for David to scream, to swing at him, for something to happen.

'I have,' David says and nods.

Why is he nodding? Why isn't he saying anything?

Their eyes meet. They are standing no more than two metres apart. Gabriel could take a step forward and reach out his hand, but it would always be the hand that fired the gun.

Since that night, something has been broken between them. One reason was that he had locked David in their room, but even though Gabriel had been there, had experienced or suffered through all of it, he still can't remember anything.

And no one could get over such a fragmented past.

'It would be easier if it all just came out now, wouldn't it?' David says.

Gabriel says nothing. Yes, it would, he thinks. Better to be blamed than to blame yourself.

'I'm just not sure,' David says 'if you really –' he suddenly cuts off. The metallic click of the lock is as quiet as the clink of a glass on a table, but it has the effect of a stick of dynamite.

Gabriel and David both go for the front door at the same time.

Out of the shadows of the corridor, a thin figure wearing a grey hat enters the flat with a gun in his hand. For an instant, Gabriel recognises David as the trembling mirror image of himself.

'Yuri,' Gabriel groans.

'*Dobri*, my boy. Good to see you.' Sarkov's smile is as sharp as a knife.

'How . . . how did you get in here?' David stammers and looks at the silencer screwed onto the pistol. All the colour drains from his face.

'I should've known,' Gabriel mutters.

Sarkov tilts his head to the side as if he can't decide between nodding and shaking his head. 'You seem to have a weakness for family members lately.'

'Whatever you want from me, Yuri,' Gabriel says with exhaustion, 'leave David out of it.'

Yuri Sarkov's cold grey eyes flash behind his glasses. 'Didn't you just say that I only have two methods of getting what I want from someone: to threaten him or buy him . . .' The corners of his mouth twitch mockingly and he points at the door behind him. 'Bad soundproofing for such an expensive flat . . . but in terms of the two methods, well, that's not entirely true – there's a third option.' He calmly steps up to David and presses the barrel of the gun directly into his ashen face. His eyes sparkle triumphantly. 'Where is the film?'

Gabriel stares at the round silencer that is pressed into David's cheek with such force, it makes the whole right half of his face look deformed. It feels as if Yuri is pushing a burning hot poker deep inside of him. *Where is the film?* The question echoes strangely in Gabriel's head, as if he's already heard it long ago.

'What film?' David asks with a shaky voice.

'I'd like to know the same thing,' Gabriel says. Down on the street, a lorry drives past. They can feel the vibration of the engine all the way up in the flat.

'If you'd like me to help you decide,' Sarkov hisses, 'I don't need to kill him right away.' He takes a step back and aims at David's genitals. 'I can also do it piece by piece.'

David stares at the weapon, frozen in place. The fear is practically written on his face. 'Just give him the bloody film,' he pleads.

'I don't have it,' Gabriel says softly. He would like to just run out of here, but his legs feel like brittle stilts and his eyes sink back into their sockets as if he were struck with a sudden fever. 'I don't even know what you're talking about, Yuri. The safe was empty.'

'You're wasting my time,' Sarkov says coolly. 'I know that it was in the safe. It had to have been there.'

Gabriel is paralysed. He wants to do something, anything, but all he can do is stare at Sarkov's index finger, a lean, old finger with strained tendons, curving around the trigger of the gun.

'Take a good look at that finger,' Sarkov whispers, noticing Gabriel's gaze. 'It's yours. Your finger on the trigger. *You* decide if I pull it or not.'

Gabriel's tongue is a dry sponge. It's as if his hands are bound and his eyes are locked on the gun. *Your finger on the trigger.* Like before. Blurry mental images flicker before his eyes. 'I don't know what you're talking about, Yuri,' he hears himself say. 'I don't have the slightest idea what film you're talking about.'

'Why are you such a fucking stubborn dog?' Sarkov growls. His index finger bends around the trigger, he aims from the wrist – and fires.

The muffled shot sounds like a knife being driven into a pillow.

David screams, falls back against the wall and slides to the ground. Horrified, he stares down at himself and presses his hand against the wound. Blood seeps out between his fingers on the inner side of his thigh. 'Shit! Fuck!' David shouts and looks up at Gabriel. 'Do you want him to kill me?'

Gabriel blinks. He can't look away from the wound; its feels like he shot him himself. A vortex grabs him and pulls him upwards, backwards in time, like leaves being blown back onto the branch.

The shot is still ringing in his ears.

'Is this still not enough for you?' David cries. 'First your parents and now your brother? Is this what you want?'

'It . . . I don't want this,' Gabriel stammers. There is a black hole in front of him. The stairs are beams that get progressively darker as they lead down into the cellar.

The next shot is like a hole in Gabriel's brain. A dot the size of a tiny pinhead. The dot at the end of a sentence as the letters are slowly combining to form words and make sense.

Where is the film? The film.

The words echo in his head. He's heard the question *Where is the film?* before. Previously. In another life. It's one of the last questions of his old life. The life that ended when he was eleven years old on October 13th.

The police officer had asked him that.

Where is the film?

And then he went down the stairs with him – into the lab . . .

'Gabriel, damn it!' David screams.

Gabriel looks through him. 'The lab,' he whispers. 'Of course! We went into the lab.'

Suddenly, there is silence.

'You were in the lab?' David says in disbelief. 'In *Dad's* lab?' His eyes drift over to Sarkov, who still has the weapon aimed at him, but is looking at Gabriel. The red blotches radiate on his grey cheeks.

'I . . . no, we! We went to Dad's lab *together*. He rummaged through everything!'

'He? Who is he?' David asks.

'There was a policeman, he wasn't wearing a uniform, but he was a police officer. He searched like crazy.'

'And he found it and took it with him, didn't he?' Sarkov says softly. 'He took it with him and hid it at the house on Kadettenweg in the safe. And then you found the film. Are there copies of it or only the original?'

David looks at Gabriel and then Sarkov and back again. 'What the hell is going on here? And why can you suddenly remember?'

'Copies?' Gabriel asks, confused.

'Yes. Copies of the film that he took,' Sarkov says.

Gabriel looks at him, puzzled. 'He didn't take anything.'

'What the hell is all of this?' David asks and looks at Sarkov. *Who are you?*

'He must have taken it,' Sarkov says, ignoring David.

'No, he didn't,' Gabriel insists. 'He couldn't, because I killed him.'

'You what?' David stares at Gabriel like he's a monster slowly stepping out of the shadows.

'I locked him in the lab,' Gabriel says. It's as if his forehead is going to burst from the strain of trying to remember the details. 'He used . . . some chemical to set the lab on fire. There was suddenly a huge burst of flame, like with alcohol or petrol. I don't think he was even expecting it. At that moment, I pushed him into the flames and ran out, closing and locking the door behind me . . .'

'You left him inside to burn?' David groans. 'A police officer?' His hand is still pressed against the wound. There is a growing bloodstain on his trousers.

'I . . . I think so,' Gabriel says softly, 'he must have burned in there. I heard him screaming, even upstairs, when I was back on the ground floor. You heard him, too, you know. You told me just recently. He beat against the door, again and again, and yelled and screamed like an animal.'

David sits there and stares into space. 'The pounding on the door,' he mutters, 'I remember it. I heard it, too. I didn't know where it was coming from.'

'Enough of this,' Sarkov growls and points the gun at David's uninjured leg. 'I've had enough. I'm only interested in one thing: where is the film now?'

Gabriel narrows his eyes and looks at Sarkov as if it were his first time seeing him. For a moment, Gabriel's thoughts shift inward. They float. Until they suddenly click into place on the image of his pyjamas. Luke Skywalker and the bloody handprint that Val mentioned on the bottom of the shirt. And suddenly everything is very clear. Val was there on the night of October 13th. He went into the cellar with Val. That's why Val knows about the bloody handprint.

Val was the one that had asked him: *Where is the film?* Val was the police officer. And he, Gabriel, had killed the police officer.

But Val is alive, he thinks. Why is he still alive if I killed him?

Gabriel looks at Sarkov, who is smiling. A mean, cold smile with something else behind it, a smile that was always hiding any number of things. And suddenly, Gabriel's heart begins to race. 'You know him, don't you?' he says quietly to Sarkov. 'The police officer. You saw him after he escaped the cellar. That's why you're so sure he took the film with him. Did *he* tell you?'

'It doesn't matter any more,' Sarkov smiles. 'It was all a long time ago.'

'Tell me his name,' Gabriel says.

'What name?'

'*Val's.* His real name.'

Sarkov looks at him and turns pale. 'Where did you get that name?'

'Val? Is that his actual name?'

'Where the hell did you get that fucking name?'

'Because the prick with that fucking name kidnapped Liz, my girlfriend,' Gabriel snaps. He immediately wishes he'd said nothing. *Not a word to anyone, you hear?* But it's too late for that.

Sarkov stares back at him with his mouth agape. He is paler than David and David is still as pale as chalk.

'Don't do that,' Sarkov says. 'Don't make fun of me.'

'I wish I were,' Gabriel replies. 'The prick is a psychopath. He mailed me her mobile three weeks ago. He's been calling me since then. He calls himself Val and he wants to kill her on October 13th.'

'Bullshit,' Sarkov rumbles. 'You're lying. And besides, what girlfriend?'

Gabriel goes silent.

'He's not lying,' David suddenly adds.

Gabriel thinks he misheard. '*You* believe me?'

David gives him a slight nod. 'The telephone. I just remembered the mobile in the envelope and the scrawed handwriting on the front: For Gabriel Naumann from Liz Anders.'

Sarkov looks past David at the wall. His grey eyes quickly move back and forth as if they were concentrating on a chessboard. 'When did this happen?' he finally asks quietly.

'On Liz's birthday, on September 2nd.'

Sarkov stares at him. 'Shit,' he mutters. '*Shit.*'

'Tell me his name, Yuri. You owe me that,' Gabriel demands.

Sarkov's lips form a straight line that not even air could pass through, let alone a name. He slowly starts moving backwards.

'Yuri! Tell me the name. Who *is* the bastard?'

The barrel of Sarkov's gun switches back and forth between Gabriel and David as he backs into the hallway and on until he disappears through the front door. The door closes with a soft click.

Chapter 43

Liz's hands tightly grip the leather steering wheel. *Control! Finally, back in control!* The accelerator feels cold against the sole of her bare foot as the motor of the BMW 3 Series Touring drives her frighteningly quickly down the street. The digital display of the speedometer says it's 9.46 p.m.

Victor von Braunsfeld. When she heard the name, a cold shiver went down her spine. The house where she'd been imprisoned for several weeks belonged to Victor von Braunsfeld! But what did Victor have to do with all of this? *Did* he even have something to do with it? Maybe it was all a coincidence, maybe Victor is totally clueless.

She stares through the windscreen past the bonnet at the section of road that the headlights are keeping brightly lit. The centre strip runs out in front of the car like tracer bullets.

Boulders on the side of the road flit past like grey ghosts in the headlights. Victor von Braunsfeld. She can still remember the day she'd got consent for the documentary. Three days with one of the richest and most powerful men in the country. She goes through his villa again in her mind, the exquisite furniture, the priceless paintings on the walls . . .

Suddenly, houses start to appear. The entrance to the town of Wassen has a tight curve right behind it. She slams on the brake to keep from drifting out of the turn. Her abdomen hurts as the seatbelt cuts into her stomach.

When she reaches the town centre, she takes the first exit to the left and then speeds down Sustenstrasse to get back out of there. The halogen headlights beam past the edge of the street. She catches a glimpse of an opening between the trees. Liz slams on the brakes and throws it into reverse. After about seventy metres, she reaches the turn-off, a bumpy forest path, and steers the car into the pitch-black woods. Her heart beats into her throat.

With the engine running, she stops, turns on the interior light and turns up the heating. Just don't turn out the lights, she thinks. The headlights make the undergrowth in front of the car glow. In front of her on the left and right, there is deep black darkness. A darkness where anything can hide. She tries to focus on the soothing purr of the engine, but it doesn't help. She feels her throat constrict very suddenly. The inside of the car is claustrophobic. She wants nothing more than to get out of this tight space, but she knows that she can't, not alone in this darkness.

Do something, she thinks. *Anything!* Her eyes land on the glove compartment and she opens it. She finds peppermint chewing gum, crumpled receipts, a few Swiss francs . . . and then she closes her fingers around something cool and heavy.

Her hand trembles as he pulls a silver pistol from the glove compartment and clumsily turns it back and forth. The grip is reddish brown and has SIG Sauer written on it with something sticking out of the bottom end. It takes a while until she manages to pull the magazine out. No cartridges! The weapon isn't loaded. Liz is disappointed, but also relieved. The heaviness of the pistol in her hand still gives her a sense of security, despite the lack of bullets.

She eyes the peppermint chewing gum. Ideally, she would stick them all in her mouth at once, but she knows that it would only make her hungrier. She takes a deep breath and thinks. She won't get far with the stolen car. In this horrible get-up, she won't get anywhere at all. In the torn black dress, beneath which she isn't even wearing underwear, she feels helpless and vulnerable. Underwear would be like a suit of armour.

Without a second thought, she puts the car in reverse. In the glow of the tail lights, she jolts back over the forest path to the street and steers the BMW back to the centre of Wassen. After five minutes, she finds what she is looking for: a small boutique on a deserted side street. She parks right on the pavement outside the door.

The anxiety makes her heart race as she opens the car door and gets out. She feels like a skydiver jumping out of a plane for the first time. The cold air burns on her skin.

And now?

She opens the hatchback of the BMW and her heart skips a beat. There's a toolbox there. Even though she understands very little about tools, the chisel and the hard rubber mallet look like exactly what she needs to break open a door.

When she puts the chisel between the door lock and frame, she breaks out into a sweat. The deserted street sends chills up her spine, as if Val could show up at any time.

The first swing of the hammer makes a muffled echo in the entrance. She quickly swings two more times and drives the chisel into the wood. She carefully places the hammer aside and then pushes with all her might against the chisel, trying to pry the door open. The wood around the lock sounds like a dry tree trunk bursting apart when it splits. Startled, she pauses and holds her breath for what feels like an eternity, but nothing happens. Then she swings open the door without a sound. When she enters the store, however, her black dress gets caught on the splintered door and the delicate fabric tears audibly.

Liz curses silently and pulls the fabric from the split wood.

She wastes no time inside the store. She grabs everything she can that's a dark colour: underwear, shirts, jumpers, jeans, shoes and socks – all of it in piles, because she doesn't want to take any time checking the sizes – and throws it all on the back seat of the BMW. Lastly, she takes a cap and dark-brown jacket with a Swiss emblem on the sleeve. Then her eyes catch sight of the telephone on the counter.

She quickly puts away the clothes and dials Gabriel's number. When she gets his voicemail, disappointment drives tears into her eyes. 'Hey, it's Liz. *Where are you, damn it.* I've got a . . .,' she sobs briefly, 'fucking horror trip behind me. I – I was kidnapped and . . . ran away. Please call me . . . oh, shit, my mobile . . . I have no phone. So please, leave your mobile on and set it to loud. I need to reach you, please! I will call again.'

She tries calling both Gabriel's and her own flat, but no one picks up. She hangs up, takes a deep breath and tries not to be overwhelmed by the feeling of bottomless loneliness.

She is about to go back to the car when her eyes land on the till. For a moment, she stops as if she were trapped and unable to decide. After all of the lines she's already crossed, should she cross this one, too?

Suddenly, it seems perfectly logical to her that it would be better to take the money to buy a train ticket than to keep the stolen car and use it to drive to Berlin.

Liz uses the chisel to break open the till. With both hands, she shoves the Swiss francs into the pockets of her new jacket, and then she hurries back through the door and gets into the car. In the very same moment that she turns the key in the ignition, there are headlights suddenly pointed at her, bright and head-on, like a slap across the face.

Val! is her first thought. He's found me. She sits behind the steering wheel as if she's nailed to her seat, blinking into the halogen glare. The shock renders her defenceless. Then she sees the blue lights on the top of the car.

Police! They are police officers, she thinks, relieved. Then she suddenly realises that she is sitting in a stolen car in front of a shop that she's just broken into and robbed. Just the thought that the police would lock her up here in Wassen or in Andermatt near Val makes her break out into an uncontrollable panic, like a thousand wasps in a glass ball.

The car doors open. Two officers get out and approach the BMW. They speak quietly to each other, one of them points to the number plate and the other laughs and points in her direction with his chin. Apparently, they are colleagues of the two officers from Andermatt.

As if her hand is acting of its own accord, Liz reaches into the glove compartment. The panic won't allow her to think of anything but the need to get away. The cold metal of the gun burns in her hot hand. Slowly, very slowly, she gets out of the car with her head lowered and the gun behind the door, hidden from the officers. She only raises the gun at the last second.

'Don't take a step closer,' she hears herself say. Her voice sounds firm. Only she can tell how much she is shaking inside.

The officers stop abruptly and stare at her like a ghost. The glare of the headlights makes Liz look like a fallen angel.

'Slowly take out your guns and lay them on the ground,' Liz says. The SIG Sauer trembles in her hand, just like her voice. She wonders if the two local police will try to use it to their advantage, or if they are all the more scared because of it. Scared of an unpredictable lunatic in a black evening gown with a trembling finger on the trigger.

Both obey in silence. One of them, who has a moustache and thick dark hair that lies flat around his face like a bathing cap, looks around for help. But the windows in the buildings all remain dark.

'Now the car keys, too.'

The plastic keys rattle on the asphalt.

She stares at the keys and feverishly tries to think of what to do now.

The police officers are standing in front of her, frozen in place. *Now think, girl. Think!*

Then she suddenly remembers how trapped she felt in the car just a few minutes ago, as if the interior were a cell. Liz slowly backs towards the BMW, opens the back door, takes out the chisel and lays it on the asphalt. 'You – with the moustache. Break off the handle on the inside of your door and the button for the central locking system.'

'You want me to do . . . *what?*'

'Passenger and driver door . . .' Liz says and suddenly winces. She feels a violent shooting pain in her abdomen. '. . . the handle on the inside and the button for the central locks. Quickly!'

The officer takes the chisel and gets to work on the police car. With a plastic crunching sound, the handles on the interior are destroyed.

'And get back in the car,' Liz groans and holds her stomach. 'Both of you put your hands on the steering wheel . . . and handcuff them to it.'

The two officers exchange a look. The one with the bathing-cap hair shrugs and gives in to his fate. The other sits in the car deliberately slowly without letting Liz out of his sight and bumps his head on the car roof.

While they are cuffing themselves to the steering wheel, Liz kicks the guns under the car and closes the doors. When she presses the button on the key to lock the doors, she almost has to laugh, even though her entire body is trembling. Once again, she feels like she's in a free fall. It's like a rush, and the adrenalin and the pain in her stomach make it hard for her to breathe.

The policeman with the moustache stares angrily through the windscreen. He has just realised that his police car has been turned into a first-class prison cell – any possibility of opening the central locks from inside is destroyed.

The officers' faces are lit up once more as the BMW veers off of the kerb and drives down the street. Then it is dark in front of the boutique.

Liz can barely manage to keep her bare foot still on the accelerator. The pain in her abdomen is now coming at regular intervals. *Shit, are these contractions? I'm not even in the fifth month!* Tears well up in her eyes. Gabriel shoots into her mind. She'd give anything for him to be here now.

She instinctively steers the car out of Wassen, back in the direction of Andermatt. There, at least she'll be expecting the police. And, with a bit of luck and a new outfit, she'll be able to go to the Andermatt station and get on a Gotthard Railway train unrecognised.

Just before Andermatt, she takes a narrow forest path that ends at a rocky slope. She parks the car in the darkness between the trees. It doesn't occur to her to be afraid for even a second. She feels like she's in a drunken stupor. When she gets out of the BMW, her legs give out. She lies there with one ear on the cool ground, which is covered in moss and grass, and she sucks in the earthy smell, holding her heavy stomach.

'I don't know if you can hear me,' she whispers, 'or how old you are now . . . but please don't leave me alone!'

Tears run down her nose to her lips. The salty taste distracts her a bit and she sits up. She slowly peels off the black dress, crawls naked to the car and rummages in the piles of clothes on the back seat. The interior lighting is dreadful and the tears in her eyes make it almost impossible for Liz to see the sizes. When she is finally dressed, she crawls into the driver's seat, locks the door and puts the electronic seat in a comfortable reclining position.

Then she turns off the light.

The darkness is a shock. For a moment, she thinks she's back in her cell until her eyes adjust and the trees stand out against the night-blue sky. She can tell from the slight movements that there's a light wind outside and opens the window a crack. The rustling of the trees fulfils her every need. There is a push and pull in her abdomen, as if the child wanted to protest against all of this madness.

'Stay with me,' she mutters and strokes her stomach. 'Please.'

The trees around her are like in the park where Braunsfeld's villa is located. In her mind, she enters the building again.

She never would have thought that it was so lonely here. A lonely castle with lonely furniture and pictures. The only living sound is the scratching of dog paws on the blackish-brown oak floors and the roaring fire in the fireplace.

The fireplace.

Her hand freezes in the middle of the gentle stroking motion. Her heart begins to beat wildly. At first she is absolutely sure. Then come the doubts.

It's been a while. Maybe you're wrong . . .

Chapter 44

Gabriel stands at the open window, his hands resting on the cool railing and he stares in the still-dark sky over Berlin. The TV tower hovers above everything. He can hear the soft beating of the blades as a helicopter buzzes past him like a hornet on a very direct trajectory.

He still can't believe what just happened a few hours ago. His eyes wander into the kitchen, where the green digits above the stove seem to be floating independent of their surroundings. 5.19 a.m.

Gabriel feels like everything is hanging in a vacuum, the memories are like images on glass shards with so much space between them that more than an entire life can fit inside.

'Have you had any sleep at all?' David's voice comes from the hall. He stands in the bedroom door, his face still grey, his blond hair rumpled. There is a thick makeshift bandage wrapped around the flesh wound in his thigh.

'An hour, maybe two,' Gabriel says. Actually, he hasn't slept a wink.

'You look like a corpse.

'Spare me your pity.'

'All right, all right,' David says.

After Sarkov left the flat, they were both so exhausted that there was nothing left to do but rest.

'What will you do now?'

'I have no idea,' Gabriel says, irritably.

David is awkwardly quiet for a moment. 'Will you look for him?' he finally asks. 'I mean Sarkov.'

'Look for him?' Gabriel snorts. 'That won't be enough. Not with Yuri. You can't find a man who doesn't want to be found.'

'But you know him, you know what makes him tick and where he could hide, don't you? How long have you worked for him?'

'Almost twenty years. He got me out of the clinic. And taught me a lot. An unbelievable amount. But, despite all that, I actually know almost nothing about him. He doesn't let anyone in, not even me. And I think I was closer to him than anyone else.'

David limps into the living room and plops down on the grey sofa. 'In any case, the bastard is your only chance.'

Gabriel nods, deep in thought. 'Probably, yes.' His eyes linger on the spot where the bullet went through David's leg and into the wall.

'What film does Sarkov want from you?'

'I don't know,' Gabriel mutters. 'And I have no idea where that fucking tape is.'

'Yeah, I could've guessed. After all, that's why this lunatic nearly killed me.'

Gabriel grimaces. 'The only thing I can remember is that Val also wanted the film – at any price. But I have no idea what's even on it.'

David looks at Gabriel for a long time. His green eyes seem ghostly in his pale face.

Gabriel sees him and smiles slightly. The silent agreement to ignore the dangerous questions between them is a balloon that could burst at any moment.

'So, why does Sarkov think you have the film?' David asks.

Gabriel shrugs and rubs his red, sleep-deprived yes. 'I don't understand that. It apparently has something to do with that mansion break-in at the house on Kadettenweg. It was on the same night that Liz was kidnapped. That's when everything started.'

'What mansion?'

'An old timber-framed house in Lichterfelde. It's been empty for decades, like a fucking ghost house, and suddenly the alarm goes off. Yuri didn't want me to go there and ordered Cogan, my office mate, to go instead. But he never goes out in the field, and couldn't really manage it, so I went anyway.'

'Who owns the villa?'

'I think the name was Ashton or something similar. A woman. I just can't think of her first name.'

David raises his eyebrows. 'Hmm, doesn't mean anything to me.'

'Well, in any case, it looked like someone had broken in. There was a safe mounted into the chimney that was open and empty.'

'And Sarkov thinks that the film was in the safe and that you took it?'

Gabriel nods, lost in thought. 'At least that's what he thought until last night.'

'What do you mean?'

'When I mentioned Val and that Liz had been kidnapped, the film suddenly didn't matter at all. Did you see his face?'

'He was properly shocked. It's just a question of why.'

Gabriel nods. The throbbing in his head feels like there is a crack in his skull. 'Yeah. What got him so spooked?'

'The kidnapping? Or that Val had threatened to kill Liz?'

'Hardly,' he says hoarsely. 'Yuri's sense of compassion has its limits, especially when it comes to women. It has something to do with that name. Val is apparently his real name or some sort of nickname. And Yuri doesn't want me to know who's behind it. He would rather bite off his own tongue than tell me who Val is.'

'So, we have to find Sarkov and convince him to tell us the real name,' David asserts.

'Convincing him won't be enough,' Gabriel says. Despite the pain and exhaustion, he manages a crooked smile.

'Why are you grinning like that?'

'You said *we*,' Gabriel answers.

'Did I?'

Gabriel nods silently.

'But I don't know if I meant it. I don't actually want to go looking for anyone who walks around with a gun in his coat pocket.'

Gabriel smiles weakly. Suddenly, the world is spinning around him. Just a short rest, he thinks. Exhausted, he sinks to the floor and leans against the wall near Sarkov's bullet hole.

Then he vomits.

Chapter 45

Liz curses and hangs up the payphone. The street lamps switch on, as the daylight is long past. Rain whips at her legs from the side under the half-open plastic shelter of the call box. Her trousers feel heavy and wet.

She stares at the scratched Plexiglas on the vast facade of Berlin Hauptbahnhof, which is lit up in a toxic yellow, where she just arrived by train fifteen minutes ago.

Gabriel, where are you?

She dials his mobile again for the third time in a row.

Again, voicemail.

That's impossible.

Eventually, she dials the landline at her own flat. 'Liz Anders,' she hears her own voice in the earpiece followed by the familiar *beep*.

'Hey, Gabriel. Are you there? It's me. Please pick up if you can hear me . . . *Gabriel?*'

Nothing.

She is still not even sure that the answering machine isn't set to silent.

Hang up again. Curse again.

Then she suddenly remembers Python Security, the firm where Gabriel works.

She calls information and is connected to Python.

'Python Security, this is Cogan,' a male voice says. *Cogan.* The name sounds familiar. Gabriel has mentioned him before. 'Good evening, this is Liz Anders, I'm looking for Gabriel Naumann, is he there?'

'Uh, good evening. What did you say your name was?'

'Anders. Liz Anders.'

'Uh, just a minute please.'

Liz hears a loud rustling. It sounds like the man is holding his hand over the phone. Her heart beats faster. Maybe Gabriel is nearby.

'Ms Anders? Excuse me. Mr Naumann is indeed here, but he can't come to the phone at the moment. Could you maybe come by the office?'

He's there. Sudden joy flows through her body. 'Please get him on the phone. I need to speak with him urgently. It's an emergency.'

The voice hesitates a moment. 'Well, I . . . I'm sorry, but that just isn't possible. Maybe you could tell me where you are and then he can come right to you.'

'That's fine, but please, I need to speak with him *right now* anyway.'

'He'll come to you,' the man says. 'Just tell me where to find you and we'll come to you.'

Liz pauses. *We?* Why *we?* 'Listen, Mr Cogan – or whatever your name is – why can't he tell me that himself? Or do you live in the Dark Ages and have no mobiles?'

Silence.

Then: 'Mr Naumann has an appointment and I am not to disturb him.'

'An appointment?' Liz asks. Suddenly, all of the alarm bells go off. 'With a customer?'

'Uh, yes. With an important customer, you know, a lot depends on this meeting. I am not to disturb him. Just tell me where you are.'

The phone in Liz's hand begins to tremble. Gabriel hadn't told her much about his work, but she knew one thing for sure: Gabriel *never* had appointments with Python clients. He drove out *to* the clients – for example, when there was trouble or an alarm – but he never had meetings with them. Talking to important clients was always a matter for his boss.

'Hello? Ms Anders, are you still there?'

'Yes.'

'We'll come and get you, if you'd like.'

Liz closes her eyes for a moment and then says: 'You have no idea where he is, do you?'

Silence.

Her heart is pounding as she hangs up the phone. Her knuckles have turned white from gripping her fingers so tightly around the black plastic. Her mind races. *He's in trouble,* she thinks, stunned. But why? And why does this Cogan guy want her to come to Python so badly? What is going on here?

She lets go of the phone and tries to breathe.

Focus. Stay calm. Who else can you call?

Gabriel had no one he could call in an emergency, no friends, just a few colleagues. Colleagues with whom he now clearly had problems.

Suddenly, she thinks of Gabriel's brother, David Naumann. Even if Gabriel had never tried contacting him before, maybe the situation had changed since she disappeared.

There's just the tiniest of chances, but still, there's a chance. Only, she doesn't have David Naumann's telephone number.

She quickly dials one of the few numbers that she has memorised.

'Pierra Jacobi, Jetset Editorial.'

Finally, a familiar voice. 'Pierra, it's me, Liz!'

'Liz! My god, where have you been? I haven't heard from you in weeks. Why haven't you called?'

'I'm sorry, I've been . . . out and about. Pierra, can you please do me a favour?'

'Anything, dear.'

'I need a phone number for David Naumann.'

'Um, does he even matter any more? I thought he was on his way out.'

'Petra, please!'

'All right. Which do you need? Mobile, office?'

'Definitely his mobile, but just give me everything you have in your special file.'

Pierra Jacobi rattles off two numbers and Liz writes them down in one of the damp phone books in front of her.

'Was that all?'

'No, wait. I need one more – for Victor von Braunsfeld.'

Pierra whistles through her teeth. 'Sweetie, what is going on there? Have you stumbled onto something that I don't know about?'

Liz rolls her eyes. The train station looks wavy behind the rivulets of rain.

'Pierra! Please just give me the number.'

'Am I the directory?' In the background, Liz can hear Pierra typing something at her computer. 'OK, I have the number for his office . . .'

'You don't have anything else?'

'That urgent?'

'Really,' Liz mutters. 'I just have to see him and I'm sure I won't reach anyone at the office. Are you sure that you don't have any other number?'

'Ha, you're funny . . . you know, the man's not some pizza delivery guy. Do you want that number or not?'

'OK,' Liz sighs and quickly notes down the series of digits beside the two numbers for David Naumann. 'You're the best. Cheers.'

'Liz?'

'Hmm.'

'Listen, if some story comes out of this, promise me that you'll think of me and my little magazine?'

Liz smiles, despite her situation. 'Promise.'

She hangs up and closes her eyes for a moment. It feels good to be in Berlin. It is almost as if the cellar in Switzerland were another world entirely, another universe in some faraway dream, and now she is back in her old life where she is a hard-hitting journalist with everything under control.

She knows that she can't go to the police, at least not yet anyway. First she needs evidence for her theory and she wants to find it before Val gets wind of what she's up to. Before he realises that he might know who he really is.

She rests her writing hand on the phone book. She throws a few coins into the phone and dials David's office. After the first ring, it crackles softly and the call is forwarded. Three more rings and she gets his voicemail.

Crap.

Liz slams the receiver down and decides to try again later. A gust of wind tugs on the side of the phone book and makes the scribbled digits of the third telephone number flutter as raindrops sprinkle on the top page.

It would be idiotic to call Braunsfeld's office. Her only chance of seeing the old man would be to surprise him at home when the last of his staff had left the villa and, if she remembers correctly, that happens around 11 p.m. Victor had always insisted upon having the villa to himself at night and since he, like many old people, sleeps very little, she has a real chance of getting him between 12 and 1 a.m. The only catch is that von Braunsfeld turns off his doorbell at ten o'clock.

With a swift motion, Liz tears the page with the numbers out of the phone book and puts it in her trouser pocket. Her sore leg muscles are killing her as she tries to hurry through the rain to the taxi stand.

Almost as soon as she sits in the taxi, it stops raining. The drive through the centre of Berlin is short and, although she's already slept on the train ride from Andermatt to Berlin, she nods off again now.

In her dream, she is racing down a steep, snow-covered mountainside, but she never sees her destination – she's just following Gabriel while Val follows close behind her. His skis make a crunching sound as they plough through the harsh snow.

'So, KaDeWe, we're here.' the driver says loudly.

Liz jerks awake. The illuminated facade of the Kaufhaus des Westens, the biggest department store in Berlin, beams at Liz through the side window like an old acquaintance. Liz pays the driver and opens the taxi door. The gutter is brimming with dirt and water, and shines in the lights of Tauentzienstrasse.

As she enters the store, she suddenly feels compelled to look around. Her heart rate accelerates at the thought of Val. Her eyes scan the cameras just below the ceiling as if he can see her through them, see all the way into the back of her brain. She secretly wishes it were dark. Pitch black. But the department store lighting is bright and merciless.

About forty-five minutes later, Liz leaves KaDeWe again, dressed in dry black jeans, lace-up boots with rubber soles, a polo-neck jumper and the dark jacket from the boutique in Wassen. In her right hand, she has a sports bag with all of her old clothing, in the left, a sturdy leather holdall full of dog bones and a pair of rubberised gloves. After that, she goes to a small hardware shop and gets six screw clamps. The wad of cash in her pocket has become noticeably thinner.

She glances at her new watch, a cheap black Seiko with an alarm. It is seven minutes to eight. She still has another three hours.

She doesn't dare go to Cotheniusstrasse. Both Val and the Swiss police know where she lives all too well. On top of that, she doesn't have a key any more – the key chain is in her grey summer jacket, which Val now has.

She holes up in the Quartier Friedolin, a small dusty guest-house with dingy beds and worn floorboards. She sets the alarm on her new watch to a quarter past eleven and falls asleep on the bed in her clothes.

When the alarm wakes her, she can hardly manage to get up. Her muscles are even sorer than before and her body is screaming for a coffee. She grabs the leather holdall and staggers out of the Quartier Friedolin across Bayreuther Strasse. At the metro station, she buys two extra-strong coffees in paper cups, sits on a bench and drinks them. Then, still tired, she takes the first available taxi. The city speeds past in an endless pattern of dark and light strips of colour like loose threads.

The black pavement of the Wannseebadweg shines under the deep clouds. Liz stares at the scattered raindrops as they drift through the beams of the headlights. Countless times she's driven along this road to go swimming. In front of her, the street bears gently left until a small nondescript bridge – the only access to the island of Schwanenwerder.

'Thanks. You can let me out here,' Liz says.

The taxi driver pulls over to the edge of the road and stops.

'That'll be twenty-seven fifty.'

Liz hands him three tenners and gets out. A cold gust of wind blows over the cab and into her face and through the knit of her jumper. Liz zips her jacket up to her chin and pulls the dark hat down to her eyebrows. Her fingers tightly clutch the handle of the bag.

The taxi turns and its tail lights vanish around the bend. It's silent except for the whisper of the light rain and the soft sound of Liz's steps.

She follows the streetlights, which have been there since the thirties, and guide her to the bridge.

The island of Schwanenwerder is just twenty-five hectares large, located in the Havel River at the outlet of the Greater Wannsee on the edge of Berlin. Since the time of the German Empire, it has been the domicile of Berlin industrialists and bankers. In the thirties, Nazi bigwigs like Joseph Goebbels and

Albert Speer were drawn to Schwanenwerder, and after the war they were followed by the publishing tycoon Axel Springer – as well as Victor von Braunsfeld.

Liz had called the island 'Alcatraz for the rich' in her documentary on von Braunsfeld, alluding to the high walls, thick hedges and sensor-controlled cameras that surrounded the villas with no names on the doorbells.

As Liz crosses the bridge, the wind whips against her face, cold and sharp. Then she suddenly feels small hard stones fly at her skin and hears them pattering all around her. Hail, she thinks, disconcerted. It's hail. But just a moment later, the raining ice subsides. Arriving on the island she hides behind the protective hedges. Old treetops creak above her. She can't help but think about the impenetrable blackness of the forest in Switzerland and it gives her goosebumps.

Needless fear is not permitted.

At the turn-off from the Inselstrasse, she decides to take the longer route and follows the one-way street, which circles the island like a hangman's noose. She walks in the direction of the traffic; if someone else drives down the road, she wants to have the headlights at her back instead of in her face.

But she's lucky. The street is deserted.

About ten minutes later, she reaches Braunsfeld's property. A three-and-a-half-metre-high wrought-iron fence runs parallel to the street. Behind it a dense evergreen hedge shields the villa from prying eyes. Liz stops. The entrance is located about twenty metres down the road, blocked by a massive double-winged gate, which is flanked by two ornate brown brick columns. From nearly four metres up, two surveillance cameras are pointed down at the gate. The glowing red LEDs on them dispel any doubt about whether the cameras are on and functioning.

Liz knows that it makes no sense to ring the bell. Victor von Braunsfeld can't stand late visitors, especially when they come unannounced. The bell has probably been turned off anyway.

She puts down her bag and looks up at the fence. Comprising tall rods topped with a series of long metal spikes, it towers above her in the night air like spears.

Liz grits her teeth. She reaches through the bars, rustles the hedge and then waits. *Where the hell are the dogs?*

Liz opens the holdall and throws one of the bones over the fence. She takes out one of the clamps. Her physical condition is far from good. Even if she were as fit as she had been before being kidnapped, it still would've been hard, but now? And with her baby belly on top of it?

Hurry up, damn it. A car could come at any moment.

She takes a deep breath and then she sets the first screw clamp about seventy centimetres high on one of the bars of the fence and tightens it with all of her strength. She tries shaking it to make sure it's not going to move and then she peers through the thick foliage of the hedges to try to catch a glimpse of the villa. Behind the dark green foliage, she thinks she can make out a few bright spots.

Still no dogs. Strange.

She attaches the second clamp at chest level, a bit off to the side from the first one, then the third at head height and the fourth and fifth side by side, as far as her arms can reach.

Her heart is pounding and she can feel the exertion in every one of her overworked muscles. She grabs the holdall and puts her arms forward through the handles, so that the bag hangs protectively over her stomach like an airbag. She shoves the last clamp into her mouth and bites down on the cold metal.

And go.

Liz puts one foot on the lowest clamp, grabs the bars of the fence with both hands and carefully pulls herself up. The clamp holds. But she is trying to hold as much of her weight as possible with her arms to keep from putting too much weight on the clamps. Then she puts her left foot on the step at chest-height. The metal of the clamp in her mouth tastes repulsively of oil. She puts her head back, sees the metal spikes at the top of the fence and her whole body seizes up. She steps out of herself, looks down at herself from above, how she's hanging on the fence. Snapshots of the last few days flash in her mind: her escape, Yvette's head smeared with blood, the stolen BMW, breaking into the boutique, the two local police whom she threatened with a gun. And now this.

Breathe. Keep going.

A quick glance down at Inselstrasse. She stops short. Past the bend, there is a faint light flickering on the street. Please, not now.

She hurries to get her right foot on the next clamp, pulling herself upwards.

Now she can hear the engine – the muffled, powerful rumbling of a sports car. The headlights appear and raindrops sparkle in their light. Left foot up, right foot follows. She is standing on the last two clamps about two metres above the ground, but it's not far enough to reach the top of the fence. She hooks her left arm into the fence, uses her right to take the last clamp out of her mouth and affixes it to the square rod at around waist height. The sound of the motor approaches like a growling dog.

She gasps from the strain, as she simultaneously tries to hold on and close the clamp as tightly as possible.

Now.

Her foot steps on the clamp and she pulls herself up with the fence posts. The pointed tips of the fence are now at waist height. Just as she lies on her stomach with the protective reinforced leather bag between her and the spikes, the clamp under her foot gives way. With an ugly noise, the metal clamp scrapes its way down the iron fence. Panicked, Liz grabs the metal rods and flails her legs around. The way she is lying there, the tops of the spikes are a knife edge. Her head and chest are projecting out over von Braunsfeld's property, her legs and bottom over the side of the street. The bag is the only thing protecting her from being impaled. All of a sudden she is terrified of dying there and then, on a fence with iron spikes during a clumsy and bumbling attempt to break into her boss's house, having made the rash decision to risk her life just because she thinks she needs to search for evidence, which should actually be a job for the police. She feels like the free fall is finite, that the ground is getting dangerously close, that she will burst open against it, just because she isn't willing to give in to her fear.

In slow motion, she tips back in the direction of the street. Her head hovers just above the spikes; if she were to slip now, they would pierce her voice box and then her brain. In a desperate last effort to clear the top, her arms burn like fire as she tries to pull her upper body over, shifting her centre of gravity. Her stomach is in pain and tears well up in her eyes.

The sports car's headlights approach the fence mercilessly. Like a row of spearheads, the tips of the fence bore into the thick leather of the bag. Bright halogen lights hit the wall of the neighbouring property and the sports car's growl is dangerously close. Liz can feel the blunt pressure of the fence spikes against her chest. *A bit further, just a little bit further, damn it.* Finally, she tilts forward over the fence, head first into Victor von Braunsfeld's property.

The hedge slows her plummet to the ground; a few sharp broken branches scratch her face. At that moment, the sports car roars past, a yellow Ferrari, low and flat.

Breathing heavily, Liz picks herself up. Her muscles are trembling uncontrollably. The ground beneath her feet doesn't feel real; she still feels like she's falling. She listens in the darkness, expecting to hear a distant barking or the galloping of paws, but everything is silent.

Previously, she would've bet anything that Victor engaged a private security firm for his safety but ever since her visit to his villa, she knows better.

'I have paid a fortune to avoid having any annoying neighbours or snoopers staring into my garden. I want my peace and quiet and that's that. How would having a pair of brawny birdbrains patrolling my garden help me anyway? Birdbrains who are supposed to chase away other birdbrains? The dogs are enough for me,' he grumbled and then looked at his two Dobermans, Alistair and Dexter, who had settled at Liz's feet with Dexter on his back, letting Liz scratch his stomach.

She has to smile when she thinks of the two animals. Nevertheless, she won't delude herself – the two Dobermans are dangerous fighting machines, and there is no guarantee that they will be as docile in their master's absence.

Straining to see, she peers towards the lakeside. Between the tree trunks, she can make out a few lit windows at the villa in the distance. She slowly staggers towards the lights. Her boots leave deep prints in the wet ground. The building seems like it's moving behind the trees, as if it wanted to hide.

In daylight, the villa looks like a quaint Belgian country lodge, constructed out of light-brown fired brick in numerous patterns, its white windows and doors framed with a wide sandstone frieze, and the pitched roof lined with slate tiles. The floor plan, a massive square, had been laid out with a classic U-shape for the entry foyer. Arches project out from the middle of it, covered with a wide balcony that is supported by four round columns. Behind the columns is the entrance, a wide, double-sided oak door.

Now, at night, the villa is more like a gloomy fortress, whose massive silhouette rises out of the darkness.

As Liz climbs the imposing stone steps in front of the entrance, two spherical lamps turn on, one on either side of the steps. Undeterred, Liz squints and goes up the staircase between the columns. The crunch of gravel beneath her boots echoes under the porch. On the black-brown oak of each of the two doors is a shiny brass lion's head with a circular doorknocker in its mouth. To the right of the door is a brass bell with a polished nameplate beside it, but no name. According to the nameplate, Victor von Braunsfeld does not exist.

Liz reaches for the doorknocker, assuming that the bell is off, but the door swings open before she reaches it. Liz freezes mid-motion. She is staring down the barrel of a hunting rifle. The owner has his cheek resting on the butt of the rifle and glares at her over the notch-and-bead sights. His stance suggests he's well-practised in handling the weapon. His snow-white hair is tangled, his brow furrowed.

'Hello, Victor,' Liz says softly and takes a half step back. 'Are you alone?'

The old man squints – he's short-sighted. His bony right hand is pressing the trigger. A hoarse whimper makes Liz look down. The two Dobermans are standing in the doorway beside their master. Slowly, almost tenderly, she shows the animals her palms. 'Hello Al, hello Dex.'

The larger of the two black watch dogs comes closer, sniffing at her, nudges her finger with his brown snout and then starts to lick Liz's palm where it still smells like the dog bones.

The old man squints down at his guard dog and then looks up again at the woman in front of his gun.

'Dog bones,' she says, winking at him.

'Liz?' he asks incredulously. He slowly lowers the rifle. 'Have you gone mad? How did you get in here anyway?' His eyes run across her lean, scratched face. 'You look like a plucked chicken.'

Liz forces a smile.

'What are you doing just standing around like an idiot?' von Braunsfeld snorts. 'Come in! And then I want a full explanation of what this nonsense is all about.'

'Only if you're alone,' Liz says softly.

Von Braunsfeld furrows his brow. 'I'm always alone. You know that.'

Chapter 46

The door closes behind Liz and the sound is dark and regal as it echoes back through the marble entry hall. A massive nine-teenth-century gas lantern hangs in the middle of the stucco-framed ceiling, its light casting flickering shadows of her and Victor von Braunsfeld on the floor.

Von Braunsfeld pushes open the door to the living area and leans his rifle against the cloth-covered wall. Liz first sees the fireplace, where some logs are smouldering. The photos are still on the mantel.

'Sit down.' Von Braunsfeld gestures to the three sofas, which are grouped around a large glass table in the middle of the room.

Liz looks down at her muddy boots. Von Braunsfeld waves for her to come in. 'The floor can handle it; bog oak. At night, you can't see the dirt, and in the morning, someone will come and wipe it away.'

Liz nods. Her eyes wander across the paintings in the room, which include a Monet and two Renoir nudes lit with spotlights. She looks at the black-pronged chandelier, taupe curtains and modern beige sofas, remembering the extravagant furnishings from her first visit and the strange mixture of styles – modern, classical, art nouveau. At the time, when Liz had filmed the interview with von Braunsfeld in this room, she had been confused by the inconsistencies – as if von Braunsfeld lived between the worlds.

'You remember our agreement?' he had asked, as she sat down on the sofa back then. The small red light on the camera was already glowing. Liz nodded. She had no other choice.

'Of course. No questions about the family.'

She stares over at the fireplace now, the flames licking the charred wood.

'Cognac? Sherry?' Victor von Braunsfeld is over at the bar, swirling the contents of two different crystal decanters. 'You look like you could use some.'

Liz shakes her head. 'Water.'

Von Braunsfeld shrugs and pours an amber liquid into a cut-glass tumbler in front of him. Then he clumsily leans forward and removes a bottle of Perrier from an elegantly panelled fridge.

Liz walks up to the fireplace. Her eyes fly over the framed photos on the mantelpiece. She can feel the heat of the fire and the warmth makes her tremble lightly. After the torture of the last few weeks, it's as if the sun were hugging her. She pulls off her cap. Her red hair sticks out in all directions. She tries to smooth it flat out of habit. Her attention is mainly directed at the photos, particularly one, which draws her gaze. Despite the heat, she gets a chill.

'So,' von Braunsfeld growls.

Liz winces. Von Braunsfeld's eyes rest on her and she feels as transparent and fragile as a glass.

'Considering that you just strolled in here like this, you seem awfully nervous. You owe me an explanation. Why are you here in the middle of the night? What's this all about? And what's wrong with you? What have you done?'

Without a word, Liz picks up the second photo from the left, turns to von Braunsfeld and holds it out to him. Her fingers are trembling. The photo has a simple silver frame and shows a beautiful woman with long ebony hair, dark circles beneath her eyes and a stoic, patrician bearing. In front of her is a teenager; blond, with watery blue eyes, an exact copy of her own. She has her arm lovingly around his shoulder.

Von Braunsfeld furrows his brow.

'That's your son, isn't it?'

'Markus, yes. With my wife Jill.'

'Didn't your son have another, middle name?'

Von Braunsfeld hesitates a moment. 'Markus Valerius, yes, why?'

Valerius. Liz's blood runs cold. 'How long ago would you say your son disappeared?'

Von Braunsfeld narrows his eyes. 'You break into my house in the middle of my night to ask me this? Have you become some kind of gossip reporter? Or do you just need this for your celebrity scrapbook to be complete?'

'Neither,' Liz says softly and her eyes fixate on him. 'You want an explanation for why I'm here? This here,' she waves the photo around, 'is the explanation. How long has your son been missing?'

Von Braunsfeld takes a big sip from the crystal glass without letting Liz out of his sight. 'Since October 1979, a few days after his eighteenth birthday.'

October '79. Liz feels a tingling sensation all the way down to her fingertips.

'It was a long time ago, almost thirty years. I have since resigned myself to the fact that he is probably dead. In the photo,' he comes slowly towards Liz, takes the picture from her hand and puts it back in its place, 'he's fourteen. It's the last picture of them together. A few months later, Jill died.'

'So in 1979 . . . he was eighteen,' Liz says. 'And there was never any evidence of what could've happened to him? Not the slightest trace?'

Von Braunsfeld looks at her suspiciously. 'Why?'

'Because,' Liz says softly and tries to control the shaking in her voice, 'I have met him.'

'That's impossible,' von Braunsfeld says brusquely.

'He's different. *Very* different. Half of his face,' she draws a line through the middle of her own face, 'is covered in burn scars. But I'm sure it's him.'

Von Braunsfeld goes pale. 'You . . . you must be mistaken.'

'Why? Why must I be mistaken?'

'Because . . . because he . . .' von Braunsfeld goes silent.

'I am sure, Victor, *absolutely* sure. You know why? Because your son is a sadist, a psychopath. Because he kidnapped and tortured me and I'll never be able to forget it for my entire life. I will always be able to recognise his face. I can remember every wrinkle. I wish it were different, but his face is burned into my memory.'

Von Braunsfeld goes even paler. He looks as if he's seen the devil.

'Do you know where he took me? Where he held me prisoner? In a house in Switzerland, in Wassen. A house that belongs to *you*.'

'No,' von Braunsfeld whispers, horrified. 'No. No. No.'

'And the whole time,' Liz says, 'the *whole* time in my prison, I should've known. Sure, I recognised the face, I had seen it once before. I just didn't know where. It's only when I got away and found out that I was being held prisoner in your house that I knew it; suddenly, I remembered the photo on your fireplace.'

Von Braunsfeld's eyes glaze over. The glass with the amber liquid slips out of his hand and shatters on the wooden floor. His breathing is loud enough to be audible and he sways hopelessly.

Liz quickly takes two steps towards him and tries to support him. Victor von Braunsfeld collapses into Liz's arms, almost knocking her over. She struggles to gently lower him to the ground, while her lower back screams in pain.

'Oh god . . .' he groans, 'my blood pressure. I need . . . my drops . . .'

'Your drops? Where are they?'

'The stu– study, top drawer of my . . . de– desk,' von Braunsfeld stammers.

Liz spins around and pulls open the door of the entrance hall. 'F– first floor.'

As fast as she can, she hurries up the stairs, which lead into a long hall with walls covered in green cloth and several doorways on both sides. Without thinking, she opens one door after another. In the third room, there is a massive antique writing desk. She pushes the leather chair aside and pulls open the top drawer. A brown medicine vial with a white cap rolls across the drawer. 'Effortil' is written on the label.

Bingo.

She is about to go back through the door when she sees the chaise longue and freezes in place. A man in a grey trench coat is lying on the dark-grey fabric. He has a cut on his head, and his arms and legs are tied. He appears to be unconscious.

His eyes flutter lightly behind round-framed glasses. He is in his late fifties, balding, slim, with thin pale lips. An accountant, Liz thinks, he looks like an accountant. There's a grey hat on the floor.

Liz's thoughts run in rapid succession. She slowly backs away. Fear takes hold of her like an old enemy who knows her weak points and shakes her. She tries to find an explanation for why an unconscious man is tied up in Victor von Braunsfeld's study. But she can't and it only makes her more afraid.

Even though the man is defenceless and his eyes are closed, she hardly dares to walk by him, as if he could jump up and pounce on her at any moment. She slowly counts to ten in her mind.

Then she opens her eyes and focuses on her destination: the door to the hall.

On tiptoe, she sneaks past the unconscious stranger. She quietly closes the door behind her and hurries down into the living room with the blood-pressure drops firmly in her hand.

When she opens the living room door, she finds von Braunsfeld half lying, half sitting on the floor, leaning against one of the sofas. He feebly reaches his hand out for the medicine. He doesn't notice how much Liz's fingers are shaking. Von Braunsfeld unscrews the vial, leans his head back and lets the medicine drip into his mouth.

When he puts the bottle back down, he's looking down the barrel of the hunting rifle. Liz stares at him, her pupils dilated with fear.

Von Braunsfeld groans. Exhausted, he lets his head sink back again. 'Listen, Liz, I . . . I can't do anything about what my son did to you, that . . . I . . .'

'Who is the man upstairs?' Liz asks with a shaky voice. The only reason she doesn't collapse is the rifle in her hands – even if she has no idea how to handle it.

'The man . . . *where?*'

'The unconscious man tied up in your study. Who is he?'

'I . . . have no idea what you're talking about,' von Braunsfeld mutters, confused.

'Upstairs,' Liz says with painstaking self-control, 'there's a man lying on the chaise longue. Late fifties, glasses, a cut on his head, tied up like a parcel . . .'

Von Braunsfeld looks at her as if she's lost her mind. He presses his hand against the wooden floor for support and tries to sit up, but he still doesn't have quite enough strength. 'Liz, I have no idea what you mean. But please, for god's sake, put down the gun.'

Liz doesn't move.

'Liz, please.' His skin gradually regains its colour. 'My dogs might really like you, but they have a keen sense for threatening situations. I don't want them to tear you to pieces.'

'What about the man?' Liz insists.

'Al? Dex?' von Braunsfeld calls. 'Come!'

'Shut your mouth.'

'Al! Dex! *Come!*'

Nothing.

Liz holds her breath, listens and expects to hear the scratching of paws on the highly polished parquet at any second.

But nothing happens.

'Where are the dogs?' von Braunsfeld whispers. 'What have you done with my dogs?'

Liz blinks. '*Me?* Nothing. I didn't . . .' She goes silent and stares at von Braunsfeld. *The unconscious man, the dogs . . . oh, no.*

The old man's eyes suddenly widen. 'The man in the study is tied up, you say? And he's bleeding?'

Liz nods.

'He's here,' von Braunsfeld gasps. 'I'm sure of it, he's here.'

'Who's here?' Liz asks.

'Valerius.'

Liz lowers the rifle. Her neck hairs stand on end.

'The man, the dogs. It's *him*. It can only be him,' von Braunsfeld whispers.

A single muffled bang penetrates the silence, then another and another, more and more, until the individual sounds turn into a constant assault.

'What is that?' Liz looks around anxiously.

'Hail,' von Braunsfeld whispers. 'It's hail.'

The sound swells into a deafening roar, as if it were raining stones.

'We have to get out of here immediately,' von Braunsfeld says. 'If he is really here, if he's free, then he will kill me.'

'What do you mean by that? "If he's free?" And why the hell would he kill you?'

'Help me up. I'll explain later. Now we have to get out of here.'

Liz puts the gun aside, grabs him under the arms and heaves von Braunsfeld to his feet. 'Can you walk?'

'I can manage. The drops are already helping. Come on.' He clutches Liz's arm with his bony right hand, pulls her into the adjoining conservatory and opens the terrace door. The hail roars like an avalanche. 'Come on, come on.'

'Out there?'

'We've got to get to the greenhouse. It's the shortest way.'

Von Braunsfeld steps through the doorway out into the hail and pulls Liz behind him. On the staircase leading into the garden, pea-sized balls of ice jump around on the steps. Her head hurts as if it were being hit by a hammer.

With their shoulders hunched, they stumble through the garden. The lawn is covered in a thin layer of ice with individual green blades of grass poking out. A hard blow just above her forehead almost forces her to her knees. Lumps of ice, some of them as large as walnuts, rain down on her.

'Quick,' she roars against the noise and protectively holds her arms above her head. She suddenly realises that von Braunsfeld's rifle is still inside the villa. She curses quietly and hurries onward after him.

Glass suddenly shatters in the distance. Liz looks up.

The greenhouse! Some of the hailstones are now the size of eggs. Another windowpane bursts and the shards rain down into the greenhouse.

'We can't go in there,' Liz yells.

'Come on, we've almost made it.' Von Braunsfeld pulls on her arm, hurries over to the greenhouse and tries to open the glass door, but it doesn't budge. 'It's stuck. Help me.'

Liz pushes against the door's metal frame while von Braunsfeld presses his shoulder against the glass as hard as he can. All of a sudden, the door swings open. Von Braunsfeld stumbles into the greenhouse and falls to the ground.

He struggles to get back up and has a strange expression of surprise on his face.

Liz gasps.

Victor von Braunsfeld stands there like a statue and stares down at his stomach. There is a tear in his white shirt and a dark red stain is blossoming around it. In a trance, he pulls a long shard out of his stomach and drops the bloody piece of glass on the ground.

Paralysed with horror, Liz watches the bloodstain grow. The time between her heartbeats stretches into infinity and even the hail seems to be falling more slowly. Von Braunsfeld moves his lips, but nothing comes out; not a word, not a sound. A big lump of ice hits his head with a thud. Time starts moving again.

'We have to . . . to . . . get to the cellar,' von Braunsfeld stammers. 'We'll be safe down there.'

'Where?'

'Under the wooden planks.'

Liz pulls the old man behind her, further into the greenhouse. There is a deafening crash above them and then shards of glass come pouring down. The wooden planks are strewn with broken glass. She crouches down and tries to find an opening between the planks. There! A small square about two centimetres wide. She sticks her index and middle fingers into the opening. A sharp piece of glass cuts painfully into her hand as she hoists up the boards, revealing a grey concrete staircase beneath the floor that leads about three metres down and ends in front of a smooth door with no handle. A keypad is mounted into the wall on the right.

Von Braunsfeld pushes past her. 'Quick,' he says and hobbles down the stairs. His hands are shaking so much that he can hardly hit the numbers on the keypad. It's only on his third attempt that the door swings open. Liz's heart races as she follows him in. She closes the hatch above them and they step into the dark corridor behind the door. Above them, another glass pane shatters and they hear the muted patter of more glass shards landing on the wooden planks.

'Pull the door shut, hurry!' Liz gropes around in vain for a handle and then just grabs the edge of the door and pulls it inward. At the last moment, she pulls her hand out from between the door and the frame to keep her fingers from getting crushed. The door slams at full force against the frame and all sounds of the outside world are cut off. It's pitch black. The silence roars in her ears as if the hail were still reverberating. She hears von Braunsfeld's rattling breath beside her.

'Next to the door,' he gasps, 'there's a light switch.' Liz's fingers grope the bare wall like spider legs. She finds the switch and the lights finally go on. The corridor looks like it was cut into the concrete and leads back towards the villa.

'OK, let's keep going,' von Braunsfeld gasps.

Liz looks at his blood-soaked shirt. 'You need a doctor.'

'I have to rest. If you go in front of me and I can lean on you a bit, it'll be quicker.'

Liz goes past him and von Braunsfeld rests his hand on her shoulder. Then they go single file down the corridor, which soon bends to the left and leads gently downwards. After about twenty metres, the smooth concrete walls turn into old, carefully laid brick, with lamps affixed at regular intervals. A cool breeze blows towards them. After another fifteen metres, they are blocked by an old but intact wooden door.

When Liz opens the door, she gasps. There is an old crypt in front of her, an underground vault that's at least fifteen square metres. A dozen free-standing Romanesque columns support the heavy vaulted ceiling. In a semi-circular niche at the back is a block of stone with a relief around the outside: a sarcophagus.

Entering the columned hall, Liz is startled by a figure behind the stone coffin. It's only at second glance that she realises that she's seeing herself in a large, half-opaque mirror that's standing in the niche behind the sarcophagus. 'Incredible,' she whispers.

'Help me,' von Braunsfeld says and gestures to the right-hand wall. Positioned between the columns protruding from the sandstone are large red chaises longues. The wall hangings on the stone behind them depict bizarre scenes that look like paintings by Hieronymus Bosch.

Liz grabs von Braunsfeld under the arms and pulls him over to one of the sofas. With a pained groan, von Braunsfeld sits on one of the chaises longues.

'Is there a telephone here?' Liz asks. 'We have to call the police. And an ambulance.'

Von Braunsfeld shakes his head. He presses on his stomach with his left hand. Shiny red liquid oozes between his fingers.

'And a second exit?'

'None that we should use.'

'Where does the second exit lead?'

'Into the villa cellar,' von Braunsfeld whispers.

Liz raises her eyebrows. 'Why, for heaven's sake, didn't we go that way to get here?'

'I was afraid we'd run into him.'

'Your son?'

Von Braunsfeld nods. 'Markus, yes.'

'Are you sure he's in the house?'

'The man tied up in my study, the dogs and what he did to you . . . it's him!' Von Braunsfeld winces in pain.

'You're bleeding to death,' Liz says softy.

'I shouldn't have taken the drops, they're only making it worse.'

Liz looks at him, concerned, but says nothing in response. 'Before you said "if he's free". What did you mean by that?'

'Markus,' von Braunsfeld strains to speak through his teeth, 'is a . . . a . . .'

'Psychopath,' Liz finishes his sentence.

'He was even unpredictable as a child, impossible to control. Jill was no match for him. He was only ten when I found him on the beach with cigarettes and beer – the others were all sixteen or even older. They knew him already. Every night, he would climb out of the window in the attic when Jill was asleep or drunk. She didn't even notice when he needed to sneak past her with his stinking clothes in the mornings and give them to the housekeeper. I tried, I tightened the reins, really tried . . .' He groans and tries to lift his head to look at his wound, but realises that it takes too much strength. 'When Jill died, it was finally over. Like a planet without a sun. No more gravity. Bam and gone. Out of orbit. I had no alternative, he had . . . behavioural problems. I had to do something. It was no longer bearable. *He* was no longer bearable.'

'What do you mean "do something"?'

'I had him committed to a psychiatric clinic, so that things were calm and he could return to his senses.'

Liz stares at him. 'You institutionalised him? I thought he was missing.'

'In a manner of speaking. I didn't want it to be public. I took him to . . . a Swiss clinic.'

Liz's mouth hangs open in shock. 'You locked him away for *thirty* years in a Swiss clinic?'

Von Braunsfeld shrugs.

'Just because he was no longer "bearable"?'

'You really have no idea . . .'

'Now I understand why he wants to kill you.' Liz says, disgusted.

Von Braunsfeld avoids eye contact.

'But that's not all, is it?'

'What do you mean?'

'It's not the whole truth.'

'Truth.' Von Braunsfeld practically spits the word out. 'You reporters and your truth.' His eyes roll back in pain, eyelids twitching.

'What happened on the night of October 13th, 1979?'

Von Braunsfeld writhes in pain. 'I don't quite understand what you mean.'

'You understood me perfectly,' Liz whispered. 'Shortly after that he went "missing", as you put it. Right?'

Von Braunsfeld's mouth is a quivering line.

'Something happened that night. I don't know what, but that night is the key.'

'You're drawing crazy conclusions.'

'Me? *I'm* crazy? Your son wanted to kill me. And the most important thing for him was that it happened on October 13th because he wanted to take revenge on Gabriel, my boyfriend. Gabriel Naumann. Does that name mean anything to you?'

'No, nothing. But maybe you should ask your boyfriend. He probably knows what it's about.'

'But I'm asking *you*.'

Von Braunsfeld shakes his head.

'Goddamn it, Victor! What have you got left to lose?'

The old man closes his eyes. His head looks like a skull, his skin stretched like translucent parchment over the bone. When his eyes open again, there is a haze over his pupils. They seem to be looking inwards.

'*What*, Victor? What happened that night?'

Von Braunsfeld stares into space, all strength and defiance have left his eyes. 'Markus killed a woman.'

'He did . . . *what?*'

'That night,' von Braunsfeld muttered, 'he killed a woman. Quite a young thing, maybe twenty, down here in the crypt. He . . . he'd gone totally mad and he . . . had a knife. He cut her open while she was still alive. Starting between her legs and then moving up.'

'Good god,' Liz gasped. Her eyes wander up to the wall-hanging over the chaise longue. A man with a long white beard that might be god is being mobbed by monsters and hideous faces. A gnarled hand pulls on his snow-white hair, a reptile with a bird's beak pecks at his fingers and a giant eagle thrashes him with a stick. At the very edge is a large toad on its back, its legs spread. A stark-naked man, just as large as the toad, straddles it and is killing it with a club.

A grim realisation grows in her mind.

'He killed her down here? Why down here?' She asks softly. 'What is this?'

Von Braunsfeld follows her gaze and smiles weakly. 'Ah, yes. *The Temptation of Saint Anthony*. The Isenheim Altarpiece, 1512, a real masterpiece . . . Simply fantastic. I would have liked to have the original. But that was unfortunately impossible . . .' He points to the image and suddenly laughs; it sounds like hoarse barking. 'Can you see the painted note over in the corner?'

Liz looks down at the lower-right corner of the image. There's a piece of paper painted with letters.

'Latin,' von Braunsfeld mutters and giggles. 'Do you know what it says?'

Liz shakes her head. Nothing interests her less right now.

'*Where were you, good Jesus, where were you?*' von Braunsfeld translates. '*And why did you not come and dress my wounds?*' His chuckle turns into a cough. 'Fitting, don't you think?'

'Why did he kill her, Victor?' Liz asks. 'What happened here?'

Von Braunsfeld shakes his head and coughs blood out between his teeth. Tears well up in his eyes. 'I wouldn't have . . .' a violent tremor runs through his body. 'I wouldn't have allowed it. I couldn't . . . I couldn't do anything to him . . . he is, he's . . . my . . .'

Von Braunsfeld's eyes are glassy, his pupils flicker and search for some invisible spot behind the vaulted ceiling. A flat, rattling breath escapes from his throat. A last cloud, rising into nothingness.

Liz holds her breath and rubs her hand across her face. All at once, the pain has returned – in her abdomen, her back, her burning muscles, the broken glass in her hand.

She looks at von Braunsfeld's body. Suddenly, she realises that she's stuck down here. The passageway they entered is blocked by a door that has neither a knob nor a handle, but instead an electronic lock, protected by a numerical code she doesn't know.

And the second exit?

Victor von Braunsfeld made no mention of the exit's location and, even if she knew – the exit leads into the villa. To him.

Her eyes dart around between the columns until she suddenly realises that the same Latin inscription is carved into the stone around the top of each one: *CARPE NOCTEM* – Seize the Night.

A shudder runs down her spine. She remembers the phone call between Bug and von Braunsfeld that she'd overheard in the toilet at the Linus that night. *Carpe Noctem*, Bug had said.

Suddenly, the connection is clear and she can imagine what took place down here in the crypt.

Chapter 47

The cold water shoots onto Gabriel's head and streams down his neck. He leans his head back a little and feels the water change direction, running icily over his eyelids. He still doesn't manage to wash away his exhaustion.

When he woke up half an hour ago, he was lying on a sofa, the blanket pulled up to his chin. He heard David's restless but steady breathing and, for a fleeting moment, he felt like he was at home, under the slanted ceiling in their childhood room, covered with a blanket that looked exactly like David's. Luke and Luke. Double Skywalkers.

Until he realised that he was on a sofa in David's living room. And that David was lying on the other sofa, as if he had decided to take care of him. When Gabriel got up, David was startled awake. It took a minute for him to remember their situation and then he stood up and made coffee – black for Gabriel, and since there was no more milk, black for him, too.

'You're still wanted by the police, right?' David asked, while Gabriel leaned over the steaming mug.

Gabriel nodded and sipped slowly to keep from being scalded.

'For murder, taking a hostage and fleeing from custody, right?'

Gabriel nods again. 'But it's all bullshit,' he said.

'What's bullshit?'

'The murder.'

'And Dressler? Did you really send the old man naked through the city?'

Gabriel's mouth twists into a grin.

David also can't help but grin. 'The bastard deserved no less. Is there anything else I should know?' he asks, limping to the kitchen to pour himself a glass of grappa.

Gabriel shakes his head.

A bit later, he staggers into the shower, where he's now standing, shivering, his fingers slowly going numb in the cold water. He gropes around for the shower dial and turns it in the opposite direction. The water is immediately warmer.

The change in temperature stimulates Gabriel's circulation and it's as if a thousand needles are piercing him. Goosebumps form on his entire body and the pain in his shoulder and arm seem to melt away. If only he could do the same with his mind! Wash it all and be clean. The drain under his feet makes an ugly gurgling sound, as if it can't tolerate so much filth.

Gabriel turns the knob back without opening his eyes. He doesn't want to open his eyes. The world beyond his eyelids has kicked him more than once. He feels powerless, useless and stupid.

It's as if someone had drilled into his brain, into his memory, deeply and painfully, and he still hasn't got anywhere – Liz is still at Val's mercy. And Val has gone silent, for whatever reason, and simply isn't calling.

Gabriel turns the knob back to hot and suddenly the thousand needles return. At that moment, the phone rings.

Gabriel opens his eyes. *Val!* He quickly stumbles out of the shower and grabs his mobile, which is beside the washbasin. With dripping wet fingers, he presses the green button. 'Hello?' he says, out of breath.

'Liz?' a woman's voice asks. 'It's me. Sorry, I know it's early, but good that I caught you,' the woman cheerfully babbles on, 'listen, about those telephone numbers yesterday, I –'

'I don't know who you are,' Gabriel interrupts, 'but you can't reach Liz on this number any more.'

'But . . . then can you just give her a message for me, from Pierra, it's –'

'Forget it,' Gabriel interrupts. A puddle of water has formed at his feet. He wishes he could just throw the phone in the toilet.

'Crap. You have no idea how I can reach her? You know, Liz told me yesterday that she absolutely –'

'*Yesterday?*' Gabriel's heart skips a beat.

The only sound is the rushing water in the shower.

'Do you always interrupt people when they're talking,' the woman says angrily, 'or did you just get up on the wrong side of the bed this morning?'

'Have I understood you correctly?' Gabriel is suddenly wide awake. 'You spoke with Liz *yesterday?*'

'Yes, of course, I was happy that she'd finally got in touch again.'

Gabriel is dizzy. He sits on the toilet lid. 'Are you *sure* that it was Liz?'

'My god, *yes*. What is wrong with you? Are you her lover? Has she left you?'

'No, no, that's not it,' Gabriel is quick to respond. 'Listen, Liz is in terrible danger. Please believe me and tell me everything you discussed with her yesterday.'

Silence.

'Tell me what that whooshing noise is in the background.'

Gabriel rolls his eyes, stumbles to the shower and almost slides into his own puddle. 'That's the shower, hang on, I'll turn it off. He quickly turns off the tap. 'There.'

'How do I know,' the woman says distrustfully, 'that you aren't some mad stalker who stole Liz's mobile and is now following her?'

'Please!' Gabriel pleads. 'I'm her boyfriend. She's pregnant and she's in great danger. I can't be more specific –'

'She's *pregnant*? Liz? Oh my god.'

'Yes, she is. All the more important that you tell me what you know now. I have to find her by any means necessary.'

The woman on the line goes silent. Gabriel can practically hear her thinking.

'She called me. Yesterday,' she finally says. 'She didn't talk for long. She never does. And she sounded like she was under some sort of pressure.'

'Was someone with her? Did you get the impression she was being threatened?'

'No, actually, I don't think so.'

Thank god! Maybe she's free! 'What did she say?'

'She wanted some telephone numbers, I actually wondered about that, but apparently you have her mobile . . .'

'What telephone numbers?'

'For David Naumann. And for Victor von Braunsfeld. That's why I'm calling, actually. She said she absolutely had to talk to Victor von Braunsfeld. Typical Liz – once she gets something in her head, it has to happen immediately. She was a bit put out that I could only give her the number for his office. But early this morning I got the number for the landline in his villa . . .'

'Did she say why she wanted to talk to this von Braunsfeld?'

'Unfortunately not. She was being secretive again. If you ask me, she's found something huge, a big story, something to do with television.'

'Who is this von Braunsfeld guy?'

The woman stops short. 'You don't know von Braunsfeld? Are you serious?'

'Television is not my thing,' Gabriel says.

'You don't need to watch television to know who he is. Just Google him, then you'll know what I mean.'

'And what else did she say?'

'Nothing. That was it. Then she hung up. But if you ask me, I would bet that she showed up at von Braunsfeld's villa yesterday.'

'And can you remember anything else? Where she was calling from?' Gabriel asks. 'Any sounds during the phone call . . . ?'

'No, actually . . . yes, wait. There was a whooshing, it sounded like rain, almost like it did on the phone a minute ago before you turned off the water. I think she was outside, in a callbox or something.'

Outside! Callbox! 'You know what? You've helped me a lot! Thank you,' Gabriel says. His voice sounds raw and he can hardly contain himself. The feeling of hope is overwhelming.

He hangs up and stares at the mobile. Then he pulls a towel from the rack, wraps it around his waist and storms out of the bathroom, straight into the living room.

David is sitting on the sofa and has nodded off again with the fingers on his right hand still wrapped around the handle of the coffee mug. Gabriel shakes him roughly on the shoulder and hip.

'Ouch, damn it,' David exclaims and sits up, spilling coffee on the carpet. 'Can you be more careful, man? It hurts like hell. I was shot in the leg, in case you don't remember.' He puts the cup down next to a pile of painkillers on the coffee table and leans back again slowly.

'All right, all right,' Gabriel says in a hurry to get to his point. 'I just got a phone call.'

David is suddenly wide awake. 'From Val?'

'No,' Gabriel says hoarsely. 'But I think I now know where to find Liz.'

'Where?' David asks.

'What do you know about Victor von Braunsfeld?'

David stares at him, astonished. 'That all depends,' he says slowly. 'What story do you want to hear? The one where he sacks me from TV2 or one of the thousands of others?'

'I think it's best if we start with where he lives. You can tell me the rest on our way there.'

David turns as white as a sheet and swallows. 'I don't know what you have in mind, but I . . . I'm not like you, I can't do that – whatever it is you have in mind.'

'I just want to find Liz.'

David hesitates. 'And why would she be at von Braunsfeld's mansion?'

'I'll explain soon, but let's go.'

David nods slowly, slides a blister pack of dipyrone in his jeans and then sits up. 'By the way, you know what's strange?'

Gabriel shakes his head.

'It could just be a coincidence,' David says, thinking back, 'but the house you were telling me about, the one in Lichterfelde, didn't you say that the owner was named Ashton?'

'Yes, why?'

'Jill Ashton?'

'Yes, exactly. Jill Ashton. It was on the nameplate on the door.'

'David raises his eyebrows. Ashton is the maiden name of von Braunsfeld's wife. Jill Ashton. She died over thirty years ago in a car accident, shortly after moving out of von Braunsfeld's house. They wanted to get a divorce.'

Gabriel stares at him in disbelief.

'Like I said, it could all be a coincidence, but . . .'

'That's too much to be a coincidence,' Gabriel says. 'Do you have a car? Or is that gone, too?'

Chapter 48

Berlin – 28 September, 6.18 a.m.

Liz sat for several minutes on the cold stone floor beside von Braunsfeld's body with her back leaning against a column. The gruesome dark red bloodstain on the white shirt looked like it came from a horror film.

She thought about Markus – Valerius – and his two-sided demonic face. He was out there somewhere! She had somehow walked right into the lion's den and now she was stuck down in this crypt where Valerius had already killed a woman.

She felt her pulse speed up as fear finally took hold of her.

Do something! she thought. Distract yourself.

Liz stood up. Her legs ached from the strain, but pain was decidedly better than doing nothing. She pushed open the door to the corridor and ran back to the entrance under the greenhouse. When she stood in front of the electronic lock, she was overcome with anger and scolded herself for not watching more closely when von Braunsfeld entered the code. She pushed against the door, ran her fingers around the edges and looked for damaged sections. The brick walls were soaked through, even crumbling in places, but there was nothing she could do with just her bare hands.

So she went back and began examining the crypt, feeling the walls, looking for gaps, doors, openings or anything else that might indicate an exit. Even if there was no way she was going to escape through the second exit – because it led into the house and straight into his clutches – it still seemed important to know where he was.

But there was no second exit. At least none that she could find. She was overcome by deep fatigue. She sat down as far from Victor von Braunsfeld's body as possible on one of the other red chaises longues.

When she starts awake some time later, she is confused and has no sense of how long she slept. It could have been hours or just a few minutes.

Her fear returns, so she decides to examine the crypt again. Groaning, she sits up and looks between the columns to the sarcophagus. She goes to it slowly and her steps echo from the ceiling back into the crypt, as if they were in front of her at one moment and then again behind her.

The mirror in the niche behind the sarcophagus is about two metres high, set in dark cracked wood, the glass splotchy and clouded. The intricate relief that surrounds the sarcophagus plays with the light, casting countless shadows of intertwined human figures, which seem to grow out of the stone. Most of them wear helmets and thrust weapons at the others, some look like demons or gods of war, others like normal warriors and some like innocent farmers or women, caught up in a deadly battle.

Liz's fingers run across the carved stone. The majority of the heavy sarcophagus lid is smooth, almost flawless, but this front part is darker; trails run across the relief like tears. Liz shudders.

At that moment, the light goes out without warning, as if someone has cut the line. Within a split second, everything around her turns pitch black like the inside of a coffin deep beneath the earth. Liz lets out a strangled cry that echoes under the vaulted ceiling.

'Isn't it beautiful?' a voice whispers right beside her. Liz recognises the voice immediately. It's Val.

The shock makes her tremble.

This cannot be. Just a moment ago, she was alone . . . and now?

'Like an altar,' Valerius breathes in her ear.

She instinctively takes a swing in the direction of the voice. Her hand painfully slams against stone. She screams again.

'How does it feel to be here alone in the dark?'

Liz doesn't answer. Her lips tremble and she gropes for the stone next to her. It feels round and smooth. A column.

'You're strong,' Valerius whispers. His voice seems to be coming directly from the stone column. 'I knew it from the start. You nearly killed Yvette. But here, there is nothing and no one to save you.' All of a sudden, the voice seems to be several metres further away, as if Valerius has jumped.

He's not here. This is a hallucination.

'Do you know,' he whispers right beside her again, 'how angry I am?'

Liz tries to keep her breath calm and clenches her jaw.

'Do you know why I'm so angry?'

Silence.

A hand savagely grabs Liz by the throat and pushes her back against the column.

'Answer when I ask you something,' Valerius hisses. Spittle sprays her face. For the first time, he seems completely beside himself. '*Do you know why I'm so angry?*'

'No,' Liz says, choking.

Valerius lets go just as suddenly as he grabbed her and Liz struggles to stay on her feet.

'Do you know how hard I've worked? How long I waited for my chance? For my freedom, then and now?'

Now . . . now . . . now. The echo rolls softly along the vaulted ceiling.

'*Do you know how long?*' he roars.

'N– no,' Liz chokes out.

Silence again.

Long and agonising silence.

'Is he dead?' he asks abruptly and coldly. His voice sounds surprisingly far away.

'Yes,' Liz says and swallows.

'How long now?'

'A . . . a while . . .'

'Why did you have to interfere here?' The question floats through the room like a ghost, as if Valerius were here and there. 'I was entitled to his death. *It was mine, damn it.* It was my death! I wanted to see him die. His arrogant expression, his gentlemanly posturing, his fondness for all of these pictures here, all the big titles. *Temptation, hell, paradise* – nothing but a shitty facade, empty drivel. What do you know about temptation when your name is Victor von Braunsfeld, when money pours out of your arse like diarrhoea. When you can buy everything for your paradise. When you are too cowardly for any temptation that can't be bought with all the money in the world. Hell, Liz, it's only fascinating when seen from the outside. I would have pushed him in, taught him humility. He should have been looking into *my* eyes as he perished. And *you*, you just had to interfere, just like that, you get between me and my death.'

'I . . . I'm sorry,' Liz says, her voice shaking. 'I understand that –'

'You understand nothing. Nothing! It's all just pathetic drivel.'

'If my father had left me in a psychiatric clinic for thirty years –'

'Psychiatric clinic?' Val hisses. 'I wasn't in a clinic. Oh no.'

Liz is silent.

'He told you that, right?'

Liz nods automatically and then realises that he can't see her in the dark.

'I knew it,' Valerius whispers.

Apparently, he didn't need her answers at all. *Or he can see me*, shoots into her head.

'You let him make a fool of you, Liz, like all the others. He was always very big on that.'

'What . . . what do you mean?'

'With a psychiatric institute he would've had too much to explain. He would have had to say that I was his son. Would have had to sign documents with his own name. He would have had to stand by me,' Valerius whispers. His voice seems to be dripping down from the ceiling, right into Liz's ear. 'No, Liz. *He* built me a prison, a cell, just for me. He locked me up there alone for almost thirty years.'

'Oh god,' Liz breathes out the words.

Valerius laughs quietly. 'You know it first-hand. I made sure you got to spend some time there. A cellar, carved into the rocks in the middle of Switzerland.'

Liz's throat constricts. *The house near Wassen.* Von Braunsfeld held his son prisoner for thirty years in the cellar of his own Swiss chalet, built specifically for that purpose, without anyone knowing about it.

'He may as well have buried me alive. He would've done better to kill me, but he was too much of a coward for that. He just pretended I was dead. After he had built the house, he never set foot inside it again. Do you know what he did? He bought me a nurse with his fucking money. Her name was Bernadette, a frustrated old hag who brought me food and toilet paper. The greatest excitement was a few books, cheap novels or medical texts – if didn't matter. That was the only topic I could discuss with her: medicine. And why she never finished her studies. And then she just dropped dead one day. Boom. Over. And no one noticed. How could they? There was no one there. So, I went hungry. The only thing I had was running water. For forty-three days. Do you know what that's like? Then came Yvette. The next nurse, or maybe prison guard is the right description. She never opened the door, not a single goddamned time. And believe me, I would watch and linger every time someone knocked, *every time!*'

'How . . . how did you get out of there?' Liz stutters, shocked.

'I knew that Yvette was just as lonely as me. She was younger than Bernadette. That was his mistake – he should've got me another old hag. When you're young, you can't keep a man locked up in a prison for decades and also lead a carefree life. So, we talked; somehow, it was almost like a marriage, except that the bars were always there. And she never got too close to the bars. Never. Just this one time last year, in October, only very briefly. I grabbed her. The space between the bars was big enough for my arm. And the foolish woman was so careless, she had the key on her with all of the other keys to the house. When I stuck it in the lock, I nearly broke it. It would hardly turn.'

'And Yvette? What . . .'

'I could have killed her. The desire was almost overpowering. But it was . . . it couldn't happen. I locked her up in my place. And later I was glad. I could use her when you came, I had someone that could take care of you.'

Liz is dizzy. With both hands, she feels her way around the column just to get away from his voice. 'What do you want with me?' she whispers hoarsely.

'You already know,' Valerius quietly exclaims. 'I want you to die for me.'

The fear burns like acid on her skin. 'Why?' she asks.

'I've already told you.'

'Because of October 13th?'

'Yes, but now it will have to happen sooner. Your fault. This is all your fault.'

'What happened on October 13th?'

'He never told you about it, did he?'

'No.'

Silence.

Suddenly, the light in the crypt is glaringly bright and Liz has to close her eyes.

'Look at me,' Valerius demands.

Liz squints past the column and sees him and his split face.

'Your Gabriel is the reason I became this monster. And your Gabriel is the reason why my father locked me away. I was young, just learning to spread my wings. I was ready. Ready to enter his world. I would've flown higher than he ever had, much higher. I had only just begun. Until he came, your Gabriel. The name alone! I should have known. A fucking archangel.'

Chapter 49

Berlin – 28 September, 6.57 a.m.

'And this von Braunsfeld,' Gabriel asks, 'now what is that –'

'Stop, stop, in there!' David waves his arms around and points left.

Gabriel spins the steering wheel and makes a sharp turn from Kronprinzessinnenweg onto Wannseebadweg. The worn tyres of the Saab 900 skid across the wet asphalt.

'God, shit. Can you please not drive so fast? I have to give the car back in one piece.'

'Mhm. So, what's he like, this von Braunsfeld? Why did Liz interview him?' Gabriel presses on the accelerator.

David holds tightly on to the door handle and looks at the dashboard, where the speedometer needle is continuously climbing. 'He's on the German top ten list, the man is a billionaire.'

'And how did he make his billions?'

'It's hard to say specifically, but it started in the seventies and eighties in publishing, and then later in the private television market. He also has shares in DEW.'

'The energy company?'

'Exactly.'

Gabriel stops talking as he steers the Saab through a right turn and grazes the kerb. There's a crunching sound and the car jumps left. David holds his tongue.

'Didn't you say he fired you? So, he was also your boss?'

'I worked for TV2 like Liz. The station belongs to his media group, but Liz was always freelance, while I had a permanent job.'

'Great,' Gabriel mutters. 'And you know who still works for TV2?'

'Who?'

'Yuri Sarkov. Python handles all security systms for the station.'

David looks at him from the side. 'You mean that Sarkov and von Braunsfeld know each other? But how is that part of it?'

'I'm not sure, but somehow it all goes together. That house at Kadettenweg 107 that von Braunsfeld's ex-wife owned was empty for over thirty years. Yuri tried everything to keep me away from it. And then this whole thing with the film that I allegedly stole from the safe there . . . Why is Yuri after a tape that was in von Braunsfeld's ex-wife's safe? It must have been the same film that Val had been looking for in Dad's lab. What the hell is on there? And, most importantly: what does Liz want with von Braunsfeld, and why is she suddenly free?'

'I don't understand,' David says. 'And what I also don't understand is: if Liz was really kidnapped, why hasn't she called you now that she's free? That would be the first thing I'd do.'

Gabriel makes a face. 'Because I don't have my mobile any more. Instead, I've been dragging *hers* around with me everywhere, but there's no way for her to know that. Maybe she tried calling my old number at first. I know she also asked that Pierra woman for your number . . .'

'But what does she want from von Braunsfeld? Do you think that von Braunsfeld is Val? Maybe that's why Sarkov didn't want to give a name.'

Gabriel shakes his head. 'I don't think so. Von Braunsfeld is too old.'

The Saab nearly flies onto the bridge to Schwanenwerder and Gabriel takes his foot off the gas. 'Where to now?'

'Just keep going straight over the bridge. Then you'll end up right on Inselstrasse.'

The tyres tear through a puddle, throwing a metre-high wave out on either side of the car.

'What happened with von Braunsfeld's wife?' Gabriel asks.

'A tragic story,' David answers. 'Jill, his wife, is, or rather, was from Canada and a real beauty. The two were the perfect couple and the tabloids practically mobbed her. She played along and went to all the parties and galas and whatever came up. At some point, her public appearances got more and more infrequent and she essentially just went into hiding. The papers wrote about their separation and divorce in the seventies. When it first began to get ugly between the two of them, she swerved off the road in her Mercedes Cabriolet and flipped over several times. She was killed on the spot. Later, they determined that her blood-alcohol level was well over the limit. The whole thing was swept under the rug by the coroner. Apparently, she had long-term booze problems. And at the end of the seventies, their son disappeared, too.'

'They had children?'

'A son, yes. Hang on, what was his name?'

Gabriel slows down without thinking about it. He can picture the photo on the mantelpiece in the house on Kadettenweg – the black-haired and hauntingly beautiful woman with dark shadows under her eyes and the young blond man. 'The son is missing? How come?'

'No idea. The way people just disappear. It was right after his eighteenth birthday. Damn it, what was his name?' David furrows his brow. 'Well, whatever. In any case, he was probably celebrating and then went off somewhere and has been missing ever since. But they never found a body.'

Gabriel nods, deep in thought, and drives slowly along the narrow bridge. The metal grate in the asphalt at the end of the bridge rattles as the tyres drive over it.

'Bloody hell, I can't remember anything,' David complains. 'The boy's name ... hang on, something Roman, Mark ... *Markus*. That's it. Markus Valerius von Brauns—'

Gabriel slams on the brakes, stopping the car in the middle of the street. Thin, light-grey clouds billow out of the exhaust.

'*Valerius*?' Gabriel whispers. 'Oh god. Val! Of course.'

Gabriel pulls over and switches off the engine. 'What house number?' he asks hoarsely.

'I don't know, I think it's fourteen. A double-wing iron gate. The house is light brown brick.'

Gabriel throws open the door and storms down Inselstrasse.

'Hey! Hey, wait,' David calls. He gets out, closes his door and Gabriel's and then hobbles after him. 'Why aren't we taking the car?'

'You want to park in front of the house and honk?'

'You really want to go in there?'

Gabriel doesn't answer. He doesn't even turn around.

David stops. 'Gabriel, I don't know . . .'

'Then stay here and watch your Saab.'

'It's not *my* Saab,' David shouts and looks at Gabriel.

'Oh, shit,' David finally groans. Then he starts limping onward. Soon, Gabriel is standing in front of a gate that is opened a crack. On each of the stone gateposts is an oblong camera. Gabriel stares up at them and then pushes the gate. It swings open silently and David watches as Gabriel slips through.

Chapter 50

The sun breaks through the clouds in the south-east for a moment and shines down on the villa. The shadows of the surrounding trees stretch towards the brick building and leaves swirl down to the ground like confetti.

David hurries after Gabriel. He can feel the bandage pressing against the wound in his leg, but the medication numbs the pain. Giving it a wide berth, they run around the villa and approach from behind.

David feels the sweat on his palms, cold and slippery. *What the hell am I doing here?* He thinks about Sarkov and the last words he said to him that day. *Miserable coward.* The contempt in his voice had clung to him.

'You see that?' Gabriel whispers.

David flinches. 'What?'

'The door.' Gabriel points to the terrace door at the back of the villa.

David peers in that direction. 'It's open,' he mumbles, surprised.

'And what do you think?' Gabriel asks.

'I don't like it. Not at all. Either von Braunsfeld is sitting in there, happily clueless, eating breakfast and left the door open to get some air, or it's a trap. But either way,' David whispers, 'if we go in there, we're in trouble.'

Gabriel stares at the open door and nods, thinking.

David sighs with relief. Despite all of the madness, apparently Gabriel is still capable of learning and, unlike before, open to sensible considerations – even when they come from his little brother. *And now? What will you tell him now? To go to the police?*

'Does von Braunsfeld have any staff?' Gabriel asks in a muffled voice.

David shrugs. 'He probably couldn't live in such a big place without any help. But I have no idea when they'd show up. From what I know, the old man really values his privacy. But I wouldn't –'

'We'll risk it,' Gabriel mutters and hurries toward the villa, crouched down the whole way. The wet, freshly cut grass rustles beneath his feet. It must have rained a lot overnight.

'Hey! Wait –' David says, but Gabriel has already reached the villa. Under cover of the windowless basement, he stays close to the brick wall and sneaks over to the staircase.

'Fucking shit,' David hisses. He clenches his fists and limps up the stairs after Gabriel. Taupe curtains blow gently in the breeze. The swishing sound they make is eerie in the silence.

'The coast is clear,' Gabriel whispers and then enters the living room.

As David steps through the open doorway, it feels like he's crossing a line. There's no turning back now.

He continues following Gabriel through the living room and his eyes dart from one painting to the next. Monet, Renoir, an unmistakable Picasso over in the corner. Alarm bells go off in his head. No one with such valuable paintings would leave the door open like that! It's also just as cold inside as it is outside. Without a sound, Gabriel opens the door to hallway. A lively gas flame flickers in an antique lantern hanging from the ceiling of the marble hall. There is a wrought-iron railing along the matching marble staircase leading upstairs and then another, much smaller staircase leading down into the cellar. Gabriel freezes on the spot, seizes David hard by the arm and points down the cellar stairs.

At the foot of the stairs are two large animal carcasses, apparently dogs, in the middle of a large black puddle.

Gabriel's hand is like a clamp on David's forearm and it keeps him from running out of the house.

Without batting an eye, Gabriel holds his finger up to his lips, points to himself and then down to the cellar. Then he points to David and indicates that he should stay where he is.

David nods. It's hard for him to swallow. His throat is dry. He looks at Gabriel as he climbs over the dogs without making the slightest sound. As he disappears through the cellar door, his face is tense and pale. He's just as scared as me, David thinks. With a soft, echoing click, the cellar door closes and the silence takes hold of David.

Miserable coward, Sarkov whispers in his head.

He looks up; his eyes follow the railing to the first floor. He reluctantly starts moving and tries to control the ugly monster inside of him that's rebelling with all its might.

Each step is a shot aimed at the monster. Each step a bite out of the monster.

On the first-floor landing, David stops and looks around. The light is switched on, as if someone had just been there.

There is a hallway in front of him with eight doors, four on each side.

Everything inside of him screams: get out of here!

The open door, the dead dogs, the crushing silence. But he can't take his eyes off the doors. There is a shiny brass door handle on the left in front of him with a couple of dull spots, maybe a greasy handprint.

David cautiously turns the handle and the door swings open. The light is also on in this room, where a heavy antique writing desk sits in the middle of the space. David steps into the room as if drawn by a magnet and looks around – and then freezes.

On a grey chaise longue by the door he sees Yuri Sarkov, tied up like a parcel and lying there with his eyes wide open. And those eyes are looking at him.

Pull yourself together! He's tied up!

David suppresses his impulse to run and quietly shuts the door. His knees tremble as a feeling somewhere between triumph and uncertainty comes over him. He cautiously removes Sarkov's gag.

'Glad you're here, David,' Sarkov gasps.

'Really?' David asks.

'Listen, David, no matter how angry you are – you're really angry, aren't you? I can see it in your face. No matter what, we have to get out of here. Otherwise we won't make it.'

'To be honest, I couldn't care less if you make it.'

'Don't be a fool, David. Believe me, this is all too much for you. Is Gabriel here?'

David narrows his eyes. 'He's looking for Liz downstairs.'

'Untie me. We have a better chance of getting out of here in one piece if we're together. We have to warn him.'

'Warn him? Of what? What's going on?'

'Now don't be an idiot, damn it,' Sarkov swears. 'He'll have killed us all before I'm done explaining it to you.'

David freezes. 'Who? Valerius? Is he here?'

'So, you two figured it out on your own? Good, there you go.' Sarkov reaches his bound hands out to him. 'Come on.'

David turns to the door and looks back at Sarkov.

'It's about saving your arse, you idiot, we have to get out of here and you won't get very far without me. The cellar is a labyrinth and, if you want to find Gabriel, you'll need my help.'

'Well, then just the feet. No more,' David says and clumsily unties the tight knot at Sarkov's feet. When his feet are finally freed, Sarkov moves his numb ankles around and then gestures at his bound hands with his chin. 'Help me up, my legs are still a bit weak.'

David reluctantly bends down towards him. At that very moment, Sarkov's bound hands come crashing into David's jaw from the side, pushing him to the ground. The strong scent of the freshly polished wooden floors fills his nose. Everything is spinning around him. The baseboards form a horizon line, and even they are alarmingly unstable.

'Stupid idiot,' Sarkov growls, rolls to the side, gets up on his knees and holds his bound hands out to David. 'Open it,' he says and presses a knee against the gunshot wound in David's leg. The pain is overwhelming, like an electrical current that also mobilises all of his reserves at once. David's hands shoot up and dig into Sarkov's thin, wrinkled throat and squeeze with frantic force.

Surprised, Sarkov gasps and loses control momentarily. Driven by a bottomless rage, David rears up, throws Sarkov off of him and pounds the back of his head into the floor. He clumsily swings his right fist against Sarkov's cheek, making his glasses slide across the wooden boards. David maniacally jumps up, grabs the first object on the desk that seems useful – a glass letter opener – and presses the tip against Sarkov's throat. 'Don't make me kill you,' he gasps.

Sarkov stares at him, still dazed from the punch, and then a smug grin spreads across his face. 'With a letter opener?'

'You owe me answers,' David says. He is breathing heavily from the exertion.

Sarkov laughs. 'And how's a coward like you going to make me talk?'

David locks eyes with Sarkov. 'I want to know what's going on here. Why are you here? And what do you know about von Braunsfeld and his son?'

Sarkov glares at him. 'Find out for yourself. Or do you seriously think that I'm going to talk just because you've got a letter opener held up to my throat? Look at yourself! You're a fucking coward, clinging to your mother's skirt. You don't know how to take matters into your own hands. You've never done it and you never will. You're too scared. I can smell it, boy!'

David's hand trembles, the narrow glass handle of the knife wet and slippery. 'Could be,' David says with a shaky voice. 'Could very well be. But what if you make me so furious with your blathering that I stab you in the leg with this thing here, just like you shot me in the leg? Maybe I'll also lose control, who knows? Then I'll stab you again and again in both legs.

And then, what if, because I'm such a coward, I get *really* scared? Scared of you, Yuri, that you could wind up following me for the rest of my life, hoping to get your revenge. Out of fear of you, I might just end up killing you. The fear would just have to be strong enough. Fear – as you must know – is the main cause of murder. It's not from being cold-blooded, but from fear. So what do you think? How scared am I now?'

Sarkov stares at David silently. The smug grin fades from his face.

'Can I have my answers now?'

Sarkov's pale lips open so slowly they almost seem stuck together. 'None of that is relevant,' he says. Suddenly, his voice sounds weak. 'Someone like me has more to lose than you can imagine. Let me go, and I promise you, I'll leave you alone. But don't expect me to give you your answers, which would be far more dangerous to me than your letter opener.'

'Who are you afraid of? Of Valerius? Or his father?'

Sarkov presses his lips together and remains silent.

'What about *Treasure Castle*? Weren't you going to get me the licence? What do you know about that? Or were you just bluffing?'

'If I answer *that* question, then will you let me go?'

David suspiciously looks for any sign that in his eyes he's lying, but Sarkov gives nothing away and there's little more than a vague sparkle. 'Fine,' he says. 'Yes.'

Sarkov smiles, pleased with himself. 'You should look into the owners of the company that lost you your licence.'

'I know who the owners are. It's on the companies register. Is that all?'

'I'm not talking about the companies register. Haven't you learned to look behind the curtain?'

'Behind the curtain? So the owners are just a front?'

'The owners are the owners. But if you look at their accounts, you'll find another consulting firm collecting vast sums. It's just a question of why. And do you know who owns this consulting firm?'

'Who?' David asks.

'He's been right in front of your nose this whole time,' Sarkov replies. 'It's Bug. The firm belongs to Dr Robert Bug.'

David stares at Sarkov with his mouth agape and drops the letter opener. He grows dizzy and his cheeks are fiery red with anger and shame at the same time. 'Bug,' he gasps hoarsely. 'That shithead.'

'Now you know,' Sarkov says. His lips curl into another smug grin. 'Let me go.'

David considers Sarkov for a moment. 'One more,' he says and presses the letter opener up to Sarkov's throat again. 'I have another question.'

Sarkov presses his lips together.

'Before, you said that the cellar was a labyrinth. What's waiting for me if I go down there?'

Sarkov narrows his eyes and looks at David as if he's misjudged the slender blond man kneeling over him. 'I can't tell you much,' he begins.

David's hand trembles as Sarkov speaks. When he's finished, David nods distractedly.

'And now,' Sarkov demands, 'get that damned thing away from me and let me go.'

David sits on Sarkov and doesn't move. If he gets up, what will Sarkov do then? Just leave? Beat him to death?

'Let's go, now, damn it.'

David shakes his head. 'I can't trust you.'

'You're an idiot. We have to get out of here, don't you understand that?'

David still doesn't move.

'Oh god,' Sarkov says, horrified. His eyes dart over to the door behind David.

David instinctively turns around, but there's nothing there.

At that moment, Sarkov pushes David's hand aside. The letter opener clatters onto the floor and Sarkov rams his fist against the gunshot wound in David's leg.

David screams and then sees Sarkov reaching for the letter opener. The pain in his leg makes him furious. With both hands, he grabs Sarkov's head and slams him against the wooden floor again. *Once*. Sarkov's eyes widen with surprise. *Twice*. David closes his eyes. He only hears the dull pounding and Sarkov's groaning. He imagines it's actually Bug that's between his hands. *Three times*. A thump against the floor, but no groan. He has to tighten his grip, since the head is slipping out of his hands. *Four times!* A burning pain sears the fingers on his left hand, which are sandwiched between Sarkov's skull and the hard wooden floor, but the pain is good, almost better, because he can finally feel his own rage for once. Otherwise, he couldn't believe what he was doing right now.

When David opens his eyes, he's startled at the sight of Sarkov's face. His eyelids flutter over the whites of his eyes. His focus floats off in the distance until it's lost entirely and

Sarkov's whole body succumbs. David immediately hopes it's just a deep state of unconsciousness, but then he realises it is more.

He slowly gets up and doubles over almost right away. The bullet wound hurts like hell. He can't believe what he's just done or how little he feels.

Chapter 51

Nothing. Gabriel has reached the end of the cellar and is now hurrying back to the door to the stairs. *Not a goddamned trace in the whole cellar.* The hallway crushes him like a tunnel that's too narrow, the brick walls, the doors, the concrete floor – everything seems to be getting narrower. The adrenalin feels endless and his body just keeps pumping more and more stress hormones into his overworked system.

Liz! Where are you? he would like to shout, but he knows how dangerous that is. At least he doesn't feel the pain any more; that's disappeared in the frenzy.

At the foot of the stairs, he nearly stumbles over the dogs' bodies. The two Dobermans lie across each other like freshly butchered pigs. With a wide step, he jumps onto the stairs and runs up into the marble hall.

Where the hell is David?

The gas lamp flicker in its glass cage. Everything in his head starts to spin around. Not David, too!

Then he remembers that David was downright terrified. He hurries through the living room out onto the terrace. His eyes scour the garden from right to left.

Here, too: nothing.

Goddamned idiot! Where are you?

Maybe he's gone back over the fence.

Didn't I tell you, Luke? He is a coward.

Gabriel cringes.

Surprised?

Rather . . . well . . . I thought you were . . .

What? Gone? Never. I would never let you down.

Let me down?

You're upset. You should calm down, Luke. Look at your hands, they're shaking.

Gabriel looks at his hands and decides to ignore the trembling.

His eyes scan the garden again. Suddenly, he stops and squints to see better. Way over to the left is a broken glass structure.

Gabriel's heart speeds up again.

Wait, Luke! Think about it!

Gabriel doesn't even think for a second before he runs off. A greenhouse, he thinks as he approaches, a shattered greenhouse.

His skin is covered in goosebumps as he stops in front of the metal frame and stares at the glass shards, the plants, flower-beds and wooden floors. A few rays of sunlight make their way through the surrounding foliage, making the dirty glass fragments sparkle. He looks at the middle of the wooden floor: there's a clearly cut rectangular surface of about two square metres with almost no glass on it.

A door in the ground. And recently used!

His heart races as he pulls up the hatch and looks down the stairs.

In a feverish haze, he climbs down them and feels around the edges of the door at the foot of the stairs. No handle, nowhere to pry it open. The keypad for the lock is flush with the plaster. When he knocks against it, the wall sounds hollow.

He rushes back up the stairs and his eyes dart between the broken glass and the flowerpots. Then he finds what he's looking for: a small metal trowel.

The trowel digs into the area around the keypad like a pickaxe. Chunk by chunk he removes the cement that's been weakened by years of water damage. When the hole is large enough, Gabriel simply prises the plate out of the wall. The rest is easy, thanks to his years at Python.

When he shorts out the wire, the door opens with a soft click.

Gabriel opens the door.

A door to a secret cellar, he thinks.

He blocks the lock from snapping in place and peers into the semi-darkness. The cut concrete walls disappear back into the darkness. The corridor seems to lead back in the direction of the villa. Something deep in the pit of his stomach pulls him onwards. *Fear*, he thinks, stunned. Not his fear for Liz. Not his fear of a Rottweiler snapping at his throat or someone trying to choke him. The tugging in his stomach is a deep-seated fear, more primal. He stares into the pitch-black centre of the corridor. An immense force pulls him in that direction, and he begins to move.

After progressing about ten metres, he reaches the point where the walls dissolve into the darkness. Now his eyes have adjusted to the darkness, he sees the concrete walls have been replaced by bare brickwork. A strong breeze runs across his neck, making the hairs stand on end as if he were a puppy.

He glances back. Radiant morning light makes its way in through the door and a stream of fresh air blows across his face. Suddenly the beam of light narrows to a thin crack – and then the door falls closed. The sound it makes as it clicks into place is amazingly soft, but to Gabriel it sounds like two freight trains crashing.

He is enveloped in an unnatural silence. Dead silence.

The only thing that he can hear is his breath.

He can feel the tugging in his stomach again. He recognises the feeling; he experienced it a lot as a child.

His hands touch the raw, slightly damp bricks and he feels his way further down the corridor, as if it were his bare feet leading him down the stairs. Keep going. Just keep going into the centre.

Control yourself, Luke, control yourself. Someone like you should be fearless!

I'm not Luke! I'm Gabriel.

So, the voice whispers maliciously, *you think you can make it without me?*

'I don't know what I think,' Gabriel whispers back.

Then kindly stop being so thick. This is bigger than you. You shouldn't refuse a bit of help. It's not what Luke would've done!

The pull in his stomach takes control, his body seems to shrink. 'I'm not Luke. I'm Gabriel!' he blurts out. His words echo like multiple voices whispering down the corridor and then fade away. His tentative steps gently scrape across the slightly downward-sloping floor.

It's more an instinct that makes him stretch his right hand out in front of him than because he doesn't want to crash into the end of the corridor when it comes.

When his fingertips feel a wooden door, he stops abruptly. He sweeps his hand across the door and finds the cool metal of a handle.

His heart is pounding. Much too quickly, much too loudly. Just like when he stood in front of his father's lab.

He knows that he needs to open the door. That he needs to know what's behind it. But he also knows that he will never be able to close this door again. And now the pull seems to be tearing his stomach apart.

Then he turns the handle. He opens the door.

The light blinds him, even though the vaulted ceiling isn't particularly brightly lit. Further back, straight between the columns, one spot is bathed in intense light.

Gabriel stops breathing.

A pitch-black figure is standing there with its back to him. Behind it, there is a grey stone altar. There is someone lying on the altar – a woman, half blocked by the broad back of the black figure. The woman is chained down by her arms and legs, lying on her back in a white, hauntingly beautiful, but somehow strange dress, like a bride's.

Liz!

For a short moment, like a balloon bursting, Gabriel only has this one thought:

Liz!

His eyes land on the old oversized mirror positioned behind the stone altar. In the lower part of the mirror, he can see a reflection of Liz in her white dress. Over her rounded stomach, there's a slit down the middle of the dress, as if someone had intended to do a caesarean section. The mirror shows her bare legs sticking out at an awkward angle, like she's seated in a gynaecologist's chair. The black figure stands between her thighs.

Gabriel is staring at the mirror in sheer terror when he realises he's looking right into the face of the dark figure.

It's a face like he's never seen before. The face of a demon, a grotesque face from a horror film, a face split in two – one half a gruesome, acid-burned devil mask and the other beautiful, sophisticated, almost pristine and somewhat arrogant. Gabriel is paralysed by the contrast of beauty and monstrosity. In slow motion, the face turns to Gabriel and stares at him in the mirror like Zeus and Hades. The undamaged eye has a red glow, like the eye of a monster that's just emerged from hell.

That one look and the burning red glow, like the red light by the peephole in his father's lab that had drawn him in for so long, clears the way for him to remember again. Like a supernova that bathes everything in a devastating light, that look evaporates every wall, every limit, every hard and deep cut in Gabriel's memory. Like hot liquid metal, everything in Gabriel's head pours back into place, into a large, whole, painful remembering, feeling and reliving.

The door is open. And now it can never be closed again.

In just a few seconds, he is hit at full force by a night that never should have been. The night he wished had never happened. In front of him is the man he'd banished from his memory. The man he later thought he'd killed. The man who was burned in his father's lab.

In front of him is the policeman.

Chapter 52

Flashback

Eleven. Eleven years old. No one had prepared him. No one had told him that there were doors that were better left shut – like the door of the lab.

Dad's lab.

As if of its own accord, Gabriel's index finger had approached the buttons of the VCR and pushed one. He had jumped when there was a loud click inside the device. Twice, three times, then the hum of a motor. A cassette! There was a cassette in the recorder! His cheeks burned. He feverishly pushed another button. The JVC responded with a rattle. Interference lines flashed across the monitor beside the VCR. The image wobbled for a moment, and then it was there. Diffuse with flickering colour, unreal, like a window to another world.

He had leaned forward unconsciously – and now he jerked back. His mouth went totally dry. The same image as in the photo! He wanted to look away, but it was impossible. He sucked the stifling air in through his gaping mouth, and then held his breath without realising it.

The men, the women . . . and the person very close behind the camera . . . He had seen his mother naked, but other women or girls . . . He wanted to look away, but it was impossible. His breath blew through his parted lips. A very, very young woman was lying on her back with her head very close to the camera on some sort of stony table or altar. She was wearing a black dress that had been cut open from top to bottom. Around her, it looked like she was in some kind of underground church with all the columns and arches. The men and women looked like crows with baroque, crooked-beaked masks, dark cloaks and hats. Bare skin was shining everywhere.

There was a man standing between the thighs of the young woman on the altar, right in front of her dark vagina. The hairy triangle pointed at him, or rather, at his penis, which peeked out between the fabric edges of the cloak like a limp sausage.

The woman – or was it a girl? – laughed and arched her back, so that her hand touched the man's penis. The man's mouth twitched below the mask, which only covered half of his face. There was something he didn't like. He hit the woman's hand away and then, very quickly, he slapped her twice across the face, left and right. It was a gesture Gabriel recognised, as he'd already received several from his father, just not like that.

The man seemed to like it more.

He tore the woman's mask from her face. Grinned. His left hand grabbed her by the throat and the other slapped her breasts with all his strength.

It hurt her, he saw that immediately. It all hurt her. And then she couldn't breathe any more. The colour on the video flickered and faded, but her face still seemed to turn red, then she began to cry, and then turn blue. She flailed her arms around. The man's penis was no longer in her hand, but it was now long and hard and he pushed it into her, in and out, in . . .

Suddenly, the girl reared up. Her arms flailed, she reached for his face and tore off his mask.

The man looked like a pop star. Or an actor. Young, very young, and beautiful like in a magazine. And the man grinned tauntingly, breathless, like the stars on the red carpet or on stage.

Gabriel saw this face for just one or two seconds and then one of the other masked figures grabbed the man and pulled him aside like a mischievous dog.

The boy fought back with all his might and tore the masks off of a few of the others. The men were strangely panicked, holding their hands in front of their faces or hiding behind their cloaks. They looked like a group of vulnerable children. Their naked bodies shone grotesquely, their limp members swinging frantically back and forth.

The boy wasn't strong enough. One of the men kicked him in the testicles and he doubled over in pain. Two others grabbed him and held him down. He gave up, apparently exhausted.

All movement in the room had stopped and then suddenly, the boy broke free and reached for a table full of plates, dishes and food. Like a snake, he whipped through the room to the girl and rammed something shiny between her legs.

He had never seen a face like the girl's in that moment. And never an expression like the young man's. He was sure that he would never forget those two faces. Just as he wouldn't forget the cut.

The boy pulled the shiny thing that he had rammed into her black triangle upwards through her abdomen and all the way up to the valley between her breasts, the knife moving unevenly through her like a plough in overgrown land.

The images hammered away at him like a disturbing strobe light and he couldn't help but watch, breathless.

He could practically feel the cut in his own guts. Everything was spinning. The four large televisions stared at him viciously. Trembling, he had still managed to find the button. Off. Away.

The image collapsed with a dull thud, as if there were a black hole inside the monitor, just like in outer space. The noise was awful, but reassuring at the same time. He stared at the dark screen, at the reflection of his own face. A ghost stared back, eyes wide with fear.

Don't think about it! Just don't think about it . . . He stared at the photos, at the whole mess, anything but the monitor.

What you can't see isn't there!

But it was there. Somewhere in the black hole. The video recorder made a soft grinding noise. He had wanted to squeeze his eyes shut and wake up somewhere else. Anywhere. Anywhere but here. He was still crouched in front of his ghostly reflection in the monitors.

Suddenly, he had been overcome by the desperate need to see something nice, maybe even *Star Wars*. As if it had a will of its own, his finger drifted towards the other monitors.

Thud. Thud. The two upper monitors flashed on. Two washed-out images crystallised, casting their steel-blue glimmer into the red light of the lab. One image showed the hall and the open cellar door; the stairs were swallowed by darkness. The second image showed the kitchen. The kitchen and – his parents. Voices came out of the speakers.

'You make me sick,' his mother stammers.

'Shit, don't put on a show like that! You're acting as if I did it myself.'

'No. You're . . . even worse,' she whispers. 'You watch and do nothing. Through your fucking camera, as if it's got nothing to do with you. But it does. It has got something to do with you. You film what you want. How is that possible? Did you rejoice when that young thing died? Job done? Money already on the way?'

'Oh god! Please. You don't know what it is. I . . . I can't get out of it. I'm as much a victim as . . .'

'Oh, no! Don't you say that. Just don't say it.' Mum's voice was hysterical. 'You're disgusting. A monster. I won't stay here a second longer. Me or the kids. I'm packing our bags and in the morning I'll go to the police.'

'You can't do that, you have no idea.'

'Like hell I can't. Don't try to stop me. I –'

'I can't let you. I would rather kill you.'

Dead silence.

Gabriel dug his fingernails into his palms. *I would rather kill you.* The sentence lingered in the air like a gunshot.

His mother stared at his father in disbelief.

'You have no idea,' Dad repeats. 'What kind of people do you think these are? They would rather kill all of us than allow something like that to happen.'

'They can't . . . do that . . .' she stammered, and then: 'You're scared that they'll kill *you*. That's it.'

'They don't have to do it themselves. They have people for that. They have so much money they can always find someone. And if it has to be, then they'll kill all of us. First you three – that's what I'm afraid of – and then me. Can't you understand that, damn it?'

'You're mad.'

'You're the mad one here. Why are you just so fucking naive?'

'Naive? You call that naive? I've had enough. I'm leaving now.'

She wanted to go past him, but he pulled her back, threw open a kitchen drawer and suddenly had a long carving knife in his hand.

'You – stay – here.'

'You . . . you wouldn't dare.'

Up until that moment, he had thought that the horrific film was the worst thing he would ever see. Now he was sitting before the monitors and couldn't believe what he heard. His eyes were wide open. He pressed his hands to his mouth to keep from screaming, stared at the image of his mother and father and wished that he were blind! Deaf and blind.

Tears welled up in his eyes. Everything blurred into a red haze. The chemical smell mixed with the vomit outside the door made him gag.

He had tried to think, but his head was ready to burst. He wished someone would come and hug him and talk it all away.

But no one would come. He was alone.

The realisation had hit him like a crushing blow. He was chilled to the core. He got up and pressed his feet against the cold floor. He had to do something. He was the only one that could do anything now.

Only, what?

What would Luke do?

Quietly, he crept up the cellar stairs, his bare feet no longer able to feel the cold floor. The red room behind him glowed like hell.

If only he had a lightsabre!

And then he thought of the telephone. The telephone in the hallway. He had to call the police. And that's exactly what he did, he had called the police. When he hung up, he closed his eyes and prayed that they would come in time. In time to keep anything from happening to her.

Just don't let anything happen to Mum. Just don't let Dad do anything to her! He looked like a monster. Would the police shoot? Surely they would if it were an emergency.

Quietly, he had stepped outside into the garden and crouched beside the front door with the key in his hand. The ground was cold, but he felt nothing.

When there was a rustling and he heard footsteps, his heart had skipped a beat. A jump for joy.

'Well, who are you?' The voice was surprisingly young, but the man looked strong. Just, why wasn't he wearing a uniform?

'I'm Gabriel . . . I . . . I called you. Are you from the police?' he sobbed.

The man's eyes narrowed. The light from the street in front of the house made him look like a hero, one of those special policeman in plain clothes. 'Don't worry, boy. I'm here now.'

'Do you have a gun?' Gabriel asked, both suspicious and hopeful.

The man smiled again and pulled a shiny black gun from his jacket.

Gabriel was weak with happiness. *Finally*. 'Hurry. You have to help my mum. My dad is in there and he wants to kill her because of something about . . . about a video.'

The man squinted again, and his grin suddenly fell flat.

Determined. He is angry and determined, Gabriel had thought. Like the police officers in the film.

He unlocked the door as quietly as he could and went into the hallway with the police officer. It was strangely quiet. 'They . . . they are in the kitchen,' he whispered hoarsely. 'Please make them . . .' but he couldn't continue.

Like an animal, his father pounced out of the kitchen onto the policeman. The force of impact made them both tumble into the adjoining living room. They crashed to the ground and the policeman's gun flew out of his hand, spun around and landed on the ground in front of Gabriel's feet.

He stared at his father, or rather, the monster that had once been his father and was now straddling the policeman. He stared at his father's hands, choking the policeman, banging his head against the floor. He stared at his father's mouth, which was moving, yelling something his ears couldn't process.

'Noooooo,' Gabriel bellowed. 'Stop!'

His father continued choking the man. Where was mum? Why hadn't she come out?

She's scared, Gabriel thought. Maybe it was better if she stayed in the kitchen.

Dad was still choking him. The police officer's face was turning blue. Did that mean he was dying?

He couldn't die. Not the policeman.

His eyes landed on the gun at his feet. It was huge. Bigger than in a film. Maybe it was because he was so small?

His trembling fingers wrapped around the rough grip. It was also heavier than it looked in films. Much heavier. He could smell the metal, the oil. It smelled like the machinery in a camera. Gun oil, he thought. Dad always oiled his cameras with gun oil.

He raised the gun. Not the policeman! he thought. Just don't hit the policeman. The gun wavered in front of him. Look through the sight, he knew that much. But where was it?

The police officer's head was being pounded against the floor. He was hardly fighting back. Aim over the barrel. Look over the barrel! His right index finger was barely long enough to reach over the trigger. So, he used both index fingers. Tears ran down his cheeks when he saw his father at the end of the barrel of the gun. He had already shot one once at the funfair. The owner of the shooting gallery had given him a gun, ancient and worn, and he aimed at tin cans while Dad stood behind him and watched. This was something else.

The water in his eyes made everything hazy and the weapon shook in his hands. His father seemed to tremble over the barrel of the gun, as he strangled the policeman with both hands.

Not Mum! Not the policeman! Not Mum! Not the policeman! had pounded in his head.

His index fingers bent in a joint effort. He closed his eyes. Tightly. Desperately.

And fired.

The shot had thrown him.

He let go and the weapon clattered to the ground. He heard something like a sack falling to the ground. Don't open your eyes. Don't!

He had opened his eyes.

The policeman gasped and panted. Then he smiled at him, out of breath. He stood up. Stroked him across the cheek.

Gabriel had winced. He hated being touched on the cheek. Dad had never understood it.

The officer bent down for the gun and smiled again.

Like a shadow, the policeman towered over his father, who was lying on the ground, groaning and clutching his stomach.

Still smiling, the policeman shot Dad straight in the heart. Gabriel's mouth hung open, he stared at the policeman, his hero. No, not hero. He looked more like a pop star or an actor. As beautiful as someone *in a magazine* . . .

His heart stopped.

That . . . that's the man from the film!

Everything began to spin around him, he had trouble breathing. His mind couldn't grasp what had happened there.

With shaky steps, his mother had come out of the kitchen, looked at his father and then at him, stunned.

No, everything inside of him screamed out. *Oh god. No!*

Then the policeman had shot his mother. Twice. Two hits. One shot went right through her eye.

'And now, my boy,' said the man from the film, pointing the gun at him, 'show me where your father has been keeping that damned video you were talking about.'

Chapter 53

Berlin – 28 September, 7.59 a.m.

Gabriel stares into the mirror and Valerius's glowing red eye, which is still focused on him. Little more than two or three seconds have passed since he opened the door to the crypt, but in those few seconds lie an entire night – no, an entire life – that's been derailed.

'Welcome,' Valerius hisses. The vaulted ceiling throws his voice back and forth. The face in the mirror looks like a hideous mask of triumph: wild fury and restlessness.

'Valerius,' Gabriel says hoarsely. It's only now that he's said the name aloud that he knows he's actually there in reality and this isn't one of his nightmares. He is still trembling and feels like he's being ripped between the bodies of his forty-year-old and eleven-year-old self.

'I should have known,' Valerius says. 'I should have known that you would come early. But this early? You're breaking every fucking rule!' His voice shakes with anger. '*The thirteenth!*' he suddenly shouts. '*I wanted you to be here on the thirteenth!*'

The echo booms in Gabriel's ears.

'Couldn't you wait for the invitation?' Valerius hisses, now whispering again. 'Apparently, it's not enough for you to step in shit. You always have to dig in and play with it, too.'

Gabriel's knuckles crack as he clenches his hands into fists. His gaze lands on Liz, who is trying to look over at him. Her eyes are red around the rims and the fear in them pierces right through Gabriel's heart. She opens her dry lips. 'Help me, Gabr–'

'And *you*!' Valerius snaps at her. 'Shut up, you hear? Don't move!'

Gabriel can feel his blood pressure rising. Hatred flares up inside of him and sets him in motion towards the dark figure.

Valerius sees the hatred in Gabriel's eyes.

'Stay where you are,' he roars. His gaze flits down, focusing at a point between Liz's legs.

Gabriel follows his gaze and freezes.

The force of déjà vu nearly knocks him to the ground. He is eleven again, standing in the lab in the cellar and wants to cry, scream, run away. Something that's bigger than him pulls him out of his childhood.

Forty again, big again, but still lost like a child, Gabriel stares at Valerius, at his fist, which is wrapped around a knife. A knife that is uncommonly thin, like a scalpel, only larger. The shiny metal blade is pointed between Liz's legs.

'Don't you dare,' Gabriel threatens.

'Just a little bit further . . . if I stick the blade in just a tiny bit further,' Valerius whispers, 'then her blood will pour out onto the stone. And then . . . just a bit more, just a tiny bit more, then I'll be scratching at your little son, Gabriel. Or is it a daughter?'

Gabriel bites his tongue until he tastes blood. The warm, sticky liquid in his mouth and the taste of iron slow down his thoughts. He is paralysed with fear. He can't take his eyes off the blade between Liz's legs and from her round stomach, which is sticking out of the slit in the white dress. He can practically see the line that the knife will make if Valerius cuts upwards, as he did in the crypt almost thirty years ago and then again with Jonas's mother.

'Well, well, well,' Valerius says under his breath. His eyes are fixed on Gabriel's. 'You can remember again, can't you? I can see it in your expression . . .' A vicious smile forms across his disfigured, two-sided face. 'Are you scared? You should be. You've seen what I'm capable of, right?'

Gabriel releases his teeth from his tongue and swallows the blood. The metallic taste fills his mouth. In his mind, he measures the distance to Valerius in steps. Eight metres, no more. *Give me a moment, just one!* His heart is pounding. He goes over every step, every possible blow, breaks all of Valerius's bones, snaps his neck, stabs him, but no matter how many times he goes over it, he always gets there too late.

Valerius stares at him in the mirror and it's as if he can read his thoughts. Then he turns to Gabriel and his eyes leave the mirror, losing sight of him for an instant. Gabriel moves a tiny bit closer and, when their eyes meet again, it's as if he hasn't moved. Valerius is now standing to the side. The hand with the knife is still between Liz's legs, while his head is turned to Gabriel and he's looking directly at him. The glowing red point in his eye has disappeared; instead, the beam is still shining on the mirror and is illuminating the back of Valerius's head like a third eye.

It's behind the mirror, Gabriel thinks in shock. *The red light is behind the mirror.*

Valerius's face glows; his mouth is an ugly slit. The eye in the disfigured half stares at Gabriel, strangely emotionless.

'Take the knife away,' Gabriel growls.

Valerius begins to laugh, loudly and uncontrollably, and then turns back to Liz. Gabriel quickly takes another step forward.

'Why should I?' Valerius says and looks down at Liz, who is not moving, even though her chains leave her a bit of slack.

'I'll kill you if anything happens to her.'

'*Kill* me . . . ?' It echoes between the walls of the crypt. 'Do you think that I'm afraid of that? We've gone through it all already, haven't we? First you shoot your father and save my life. Then you push me into the fire and make me a cripple. Have you ever considered that death could also be a form of salvation for me?'

'Believe me,' Gabriel says, 'when it's come this far, there is no salvation. All that's left is to be scared shitless.'

Valerius narrows his eyes. 'Is that so? Someone like you is afraid?' He tilts his head then laughs again, cold and soulless. 'No, Gabriel. After the fear *always* comes the salvation. I know it. But most people have so much fear for so long that it's too late. And then the salvation is always too brief. But believe me, it's still there. You can see it in their eyes at the very end. It was the same with all of them. The little cunt here in the crypt and then the others, and Kristen, that model, and – what was her name, the fat one? Jonas's mother?

'But us, Gabriel, we've already eaten too much shit and been too afraid already. For people like you and me, there's hardly any fear left. Death might not be pretty, but death doesn't matter. For *us*, there is only *salvation*.'

'What do you want from me? To kill me?'

'I wouldn't do you the favour! Don't expect me to be the person to bring you salvation . . .'

'Fuck your salvation,' Gabriel says, and the words float through the crypt.

Gabriel's eyes dart around the room in search of something, anything, that could help him distract Valerius, something that could get him a couple of crucial seconds.

David! Where the hell is David? For the first time in his life, he desperately needs his brother's help. It's completely different from when he was in the clinic and held a knife to David's throat and just relied on him to keep quiet.

Now everything is different.

Do something, little brother. Please!

Suddenly, his eyes rest on the wall of the crypt. There's a man lying on a chaise longue. His white shirt is soaked through with blood and his vacant eyes are staring at the bottom of a picture filled with grotesque figures that could only exist in a nightmare. His eyes are fixed on some foreign words in the artwork, which Gabriel understands to mean:

Where were you, good Jesus, where were you?

Chapter 54

Berlin – 28 September, 8.09 a.m.

David hobbles as quickly as he can down the marble stairs, Yuri Sarkov's voice still ringing in his ears. His hands are shaking with a kind of nervous energy. He looks nervously at the time. Ten past eight. Not much longer before von Braunsfeld's staff will arrive, if they haven't already. But where the hell is Gabriel? And where is Valerius?

David glances through the open double doors into the living room. Nothing. Just the open door to the terrace.

He hurries to the basement stairs and struggles down them, hesitating when he reaches the bodies of the two dead Dobermans at their foot. The dogs stare out into nothingness with their cold eyes. The door is opened a crack. *It's somewhere behind there.*

David tries to climb over the dog carcasses in one step, but his left foot lands in the puddle of blood and nearly slides out from under him.

Quietly cursing to himself, he pushes open the cellar door and can see a dark hallway with many doors in front of him. He tries to get his bearings. Sarkov described the way to him, but it's suddenly all so unreal that for a brief moment David wonders if he tricked him.

David's breathing is too loud and sounds like a bellows. He tries to hold it and listen. But there is nothing. He stares into the cellar.

The nervous energy he felt before has now been replaced by a dull, throbbing fear, and he hopes that Sarkov told him the truth. He forces himself to enter the hall and limps forward metre by metre.

His left shoe leaves dark red prints on the floor behind him.

Chapter 55

Berlin – 28 September, 8.09 a.m.

Gabriel stares at the corpse below the picture. The old man must have only died recently, since the crypt doesn't have that cloying smell of death.

Valerius's glances feel like pinpricks. Gabriel looks away from the body and back into the mirror, where Valerius's mismatched eyes are fixed on him. The red point is now shining on the mangled part of his forehead.

'Who is that?' Gabriel asks and gestures to the dead man. Valerius closes his disfigured eye, as the other blinks a few times and then looks back at him. *He's blind in one eye*, Gabriel thinks. *That means he has poor depth perception.*

'Allow me to introduce my esteemed father. Another bastard in love with his secrets, just like your father,' Valerius says. He looks down at Liz.

Now! Gabriel steps forward. The soles of his shoes slide over the stone.

Valerius looks back up immediately. 'Stay where you are,' he shouts. His good hand pushes the knife a little bit further into Liz. 'For every step you take closer, I will push it deeper into her.'

Liz groans miserably.

Gabriel clenches his teeth. His fists shake from rage and powerlessness. Distract him! Talk to him, Gabriel thinks. 'In love with his secrets? Just like my father? What is that supposed to mean?'

Valerius snorts with disdain. 'When did you discover your father's dirty little secret? When you were eleven? Or even earlier? I was ten. God! Shit! He was *so* careful. It was always late at night. The limousines never parked in front of the house, on the property, but always far enough away from the house. And then down into the crypt to fuck. And I would always crouch back there,' he gestured to the side with his head, 'behind the picture. I scratched a hole in the mortar and then crouched back on the other side of the wall. At ten, I'd seen more fucking, arses and cocks than others have in their entire lives.'

'What a shitty excuse.'

'*Excuse?*' Valerius cries.

Gabriel takes advantage of the outburst to move his feet a few centimetres forward.

This is going too slowly, runs through his head. *Much too slowly!*

'I wasn't suffering,' Valerius snarls. 'I *wanted* to be there! More than anything else. Didn't *you* want to be there, too? In the cellar with your father? What would you have done for it? Did you ask? Beg? I did. And him? He said I was lying and locked me up in my room. Imprisoned. He was always good at that. But then he wasn't so careful, so I could always get out without him noticing . . .'

Centimetre by centimetre, Gabriel makes his way forward.

Where the hell is David?

'Until my mother found out about it. The mothers always find out. Always. Imagine, your mother finds out that her perfect husband disappears every month into a cellar, puts on a mask and properly fucks some young thing with a few other high-ranking men, while you watch. Sounds like a bad film, right? And it really is. What do you think your mother would've done?'

Gabriel's throat constricts and he can't answer.

Valerius snorts scornfully. 'Of course! What could a mother do? She screams and shouts in a shrill voice: "You perverted bastard" and "the boy is only fourteen", as if that mattered! And then she will leave him and she will move out and take you with her. And what do you think, how would you feel then? Tell me, Gabriel. How would you feel then?'

'Relieved,' Gabriel says softly.

'*Relieved?* You've spent four years standing in front of the open door, peeking through with your heart beating into your throat. You've already taken coke, but that was crap by comparison. Nothing felt the way that felt! Your mouth was dry and your trousers had a full-on bulge. And you've imagined it a thousand times – standing there in the crypt instead of your fucking father! And *you* would be *relieved?*'

Gabriel says nothing. He stares at Valerius, trying to watch his eyes, so he can work his way forward bit by bit, centimetre by centimetre.

'Do you know what my father always said?' Valerius whispers. 'The truth is that "*every impulse that we strive to strangle broods in the mind, and poisons us.*" That was his favourite quote. Oscar Wilde, *The Picture of Dorian Gray*. Poison, you understand? That's how you would have felt! Poisoned.'

An icy shiver runs down Gabriel's back.

The truth is that every impulse that we strive to strangle broods in the mind, and poisons us.

Suddenly he is overcome with a terrible suspicion. 'You didn't want to stay with your mother, you wanted to go back,' he whispers. 'What did you do?'

Valerius's eyes light up like gas flames. 'I didn't have to do much. I would have never suspected that it was so easy. A snap of the fingers, nothing more. Just cut the brakes in her car and bam! She was dead. That very evening, I stood on my father's doormat and said: "I'm back." Then he knew it. He could tell by looking at me.'

'Didn't they say she had been drinking?'

Valerius shook his head. 'No, no. Even better – he said she had been drinking, but that it had been swept under the rug . . . that was his doing! And, of course, Sarkov's . . .'

Sarkov's . . .

Sarkov's . . .

Sarkov's . . . the name echoes in the silence.

'Sarkov? Yuri Sarkov?' Gabriel asks.

Valerius grins bitterly. 'A man like Victor von Braunsfeld doesn't get his hands dirty. Sexually, maybe, but not otherwise. That's why he had Sarkov. Sarkov shovelled the dirt and my father gave him jobs.

Yuri. For Gabriel, it's as if the curtain has dropped and he still cannot grasp everything that has suddenly appeared in front of him. 'My god,' he mutters.

'God?' Valerius chuckles. 'No! My father.' His expression changes to deadly serious. 'My father was god and god punished me. Instead of being happy that she was gone, he punished me. She had scolded and despised him. She had left him and taken his son away. And he still loved her, at least in his own way. For four years, he locked me in my room. I was allowed to go to school, but that was all, and even that was only with a chaperone. If anyone asked why, then he said that he was scared of kidnappers. After school, I had to go back to my room, always with one of Sarkov's men in front of the door.'

'What happened on the thirteenth?' Gabriel asks.

'You want to know what happened on the thirteenth? I'd had enough. More than enough. I had turned eighteen and there was a guard at my door every fucking day. For four years, I never went down into my cellar, into *his* crypt. I could hear the limousines when they pulled up once a month and I knew I couldn't be there. Four years of deprivation poisoning the body and mind. So, I summoned all of my courage and threatened him: "either I get to be part of it from now on, or you'll read about it in the morning paper. And so will your friends."' Valerius's eyes sparkle. He's talked himself into a frenzy and his whole body is shaking. 'And that was it! It was unbelievable! He gave in.'

Gabriel looks at Liz, her lips squeezed together, the tears in her eyes, staring down at Valerius's arm as the knife moves in rhythm with his words. Gabriel slowly moves forward.

'I had hit the target, you understand? Can you imagine my excitement? October 13th was *my* night. Have you seen it? The video?'

Gabriel nods.

'Everything? Did you see *everything*?'

'I have,' Gabriel says.

'I knew it. I should have killed you then and there. There shouldn't have been any witnesses. None!' Valerius goes silent a moment. 'And the other films?' he then asks. 'Did you see them, too?'

'Other films?'

Valerius stares at him almost amused. 'Do you really think,' he whispers derisively, 'that was the only film your father made here?'

The sentence echoes under the vaulted ceiling and shocks Gabriel to the core, casting him back to the lab, surrounded by photos, rolls of film, videocassettes and cameras. *Of course!* How could he be so stupid!

Valerius's laughter painfully roars in his ears. 'My father was ultra-careful about that. Once someone had proved their skill with dirty work, he would never let them go. Not even your father. Wolf Naumann! How do you think your father paid for your little suburban house? Your father was only there to immortalise my father's insatiability on a few celluloid and magnetic strips. How many times do you think he stood there?' Valerius gestures to the large mirror behind Liz with his chin. 'And how often do you think he filmed through the glass?'

Gabriel stares into Valerius's mutilated face in the mirror and sees himself – the way he peeks out over Valerius's shoulder, so small, so infinitely far away and so pale, with an expression that he's never seen on himself before.

'There were dozens of films that my father watched over and over again. And no one knew about them. No one! Not even me. I only found out about them when it was too late. Not even his high-class friends knew that they were being filmed. Had they known, then they probably would have been scared shitless – the lawyers, judges and politicians! *After all, they did . . .*' He twists his mouth into a terrifying smile and looks down at Liz, at the blade between her legs.

Gabriel's heart is racing. Cold sweat covers his body. He tries with all his strength to suppress the horrific images that are rising up.

'"*The average gives the world its substance,*" Valerius mutters, "*the exceptional its value!*" Another one from Oscar Wilde. My father loved that shit. He just didn't live it. I lived it! Me!' he roars. The vaulted ceiling echoes.

'When I rammed that knife into that girl's cunt, that was it, you know? Her eyes, as I pulled it up and she could look inside of herself, it was extraordinary! More extraordinary than anything he'd ever done, my holy father . . .'

The last word faded away in the crypt. Then the soft clinking of the chains pierces through the silence.

Gabriel didn't dare look at Liz. He wanted to close his eyes and wish himself into another place, as he had back then, when he was eleven and had wished himself out of the lab. At the same time, he knows that he can't so much as blink, because the image of the dying girl will be there in the dark behind his closed eyelids.

'I imagine your father,' Valerius says. 'How he stood behind the mirror with his camera and shit himself like all the others did in here. None of those miserable cowards was good for anything. And you know what happened when they were all gone? I watched him in front of me, my father, as he ran around and around the body and heard him say the same thing over and over again, as if he were praying:

'"You're taking care of this," he says.'

'"What am I taking care of?" I ask and think: What's the point of that? She's dead. There's nothing else to take care of.

'And he says: "The film. I need the fucking film."

'"What film?" I ask him. "What are you talking about?"

'And he stares at the mirror there and tells me about your father and his fucking camera and that he always filmed everything, including the whole thing with the girl. And that we are all on the film. Without masks. Then I knew what he meant!

'Have you ever heard your heart beating loud, loud and fast, and then been very still because of it? And then it gets slower, your heart, you can hear it from beat to beat as it calms down.

'It was a moment like that. The moment before you do something you know will have a meaning for your entire life. I knew it was *my* moment!

'So, I went to take care of everything. To take care of the film and your father. It was supposed to be *my* night. Mine! And then it became yours.'

Gabriel stares at Valerius, his mouth agape. *My night?* he thinks. My parents are dead, my house burnt down and that was *my* night? He is so overcome with anger that he thinks he will be devoured by it.

'You thought I was dead, didn't you? Burnt. Charred. That probably would have been better,' Valerius says and looks down at Liz, lost in thought. The red light rests on the reflection of his forehead. Then he looks up. 'I know, I know. I should be thankful that I actually made it out of there . . .

'Did you know there was another small room in the back of the lab with a toilet? I soaked towels in the toilet bowl, splashed water over myself and the door, flushed and splashed again. I even peed on the door to keep it wet and breathed through the ventilation. . .'

Gabriel's eyes are fixed on Valerius's face, as he moves his feet forward by the centimetre every moment that Valerius isn't paying attention.

'When I crawled out, the house was in ruins. It was still night and there were fire engines and police everywhere. I was lucky and ran off through the garden without anyone seeing me. And then I came back here, home, with all of this.' Valerius points to his face and prosthetic arm. 'My father calmed me like a little kitten, gave me a sleeping pill, for the pain and whatever else I needed. One of his friends was there, a doctor. He bandaged me, which just felt so right at that moment. God, I was naive. I was so grateful to him. When I woke up, I was down here. Locked in and chained up.

'And then he stands in front of me and says: "Where is the film? Do you have the film?"

'I was still not able to answer him, but I thought: look at me, look at me, can't you see how I'm suffering? My face, my skin . . . and you are asking about the fucking film?

'And he roared again: "Where is the film?" Always just: "Where is the film?"

'Then I knew he was like all the others. He was scared, just scared. Not for me, just for himself.

'And now you have it. I finally gave him what he wanted all that time. You know what I said to him? I said: "Fuck the film, I won't give it to you. I have it. I hid it at Mother's house on Kadettenweg." Of course, I hadn't. The goddamned cassette melted in the heat, like everything else in the lab. But I told him I hid it and that's what he believed.

'It made him insane. Completely insane. Even when I told him that everyone but you was dead. "How old is the boy?" he asked. "What has he seen?"

'But for him, the worst part was the idea that the film was lying around somewhere and someone might recognise him on it. It drove him mad. When he realised that he was getting nothing out of me, he ransacked the entire house looking for it. But he found nothing. There wasn't anything to find,' Valerius laughs bitterly. His hand with the knife shakes. Liz bites her lips and tries frantically to adjust her hips to the blade.

'At some point, he gave up. He probably just locked the door, gave Sarkov the key and left the house to rot. Maybe he even thought I would tell him eventually if he just waited long enough. And then he took me to Switzerland, or rather, Sarkov took me to Switzerland, and buried me alive. More than twenty-eight years under a goddamned Swiss chalet in a cellar hole cut into the rocks especially for me.'

Gabriel gasps. For a brief moment, like the beam of a torch in a dark tunnel, he has a sense of how horribly lost Valerius must have felt.

'It took me twenty-eight years to free myself.' He looks down at Liz. 'And the little witch here managed it after just a few weeks. But you didn't get very far, did you?'

Liz's answer is a soft groan.

Now, Gabriel thinks. *Just a bit further!*

'Stay there, where you are,' Valerius roars, pushing the blade in further. Liz cries out in pain and starts hyperventilating. Her knees shake violently on either side of Valerius's hand.

The blood in Gabriel's guts freezes.

How much further? Six metres? Six and a half?

Even if Valerius has poor depth perception and seems not to have realised that Gabriel is now quite a bit closer, he is still at an advantage.

Six metres is too much!

'What the hell,' Gabriel asks, 'are you planning? What do you want from me?'

Valerius sneers at him. 'From you? I just want you to watch. Like your father. You understand? I want something from your little Lizzy here.'

'What do you want?'

'I want her to die. *Over and over again.*'

Gabriel's heart skips a beat. 'Over and over again?'

'That was the plan on October 13th,' Valerius says. 'I wanted to give you some time. And I wanted you to guess what it was all about. That's why I left the dress and the photo of the model in the house on Kadettenweg. I wanted you to remember and be afraid. Oh well. The plan is different now. It's good this way too. In the end, it makes no difference.'

'Over and over again? What is that supposed to mean?' Gabriel asks hoarsely.

'Are you holding out on me? Or have you really not guessed?'

Gabriel is silent.

'Ashes to ashes, dust to dust. You know what that means, Gabriel? The beginning and the end are always the same. Always. And for us, it all started with a film. With a film in which a girl dies.' Valerius's gaze flickers. The burnt half of his face looks like a piece of raw meat. He gestures at the mirror with his prosthetic arm. 'You see the red dot there? That's been lit up this whole time? That's a camera. It's behind the mirror, just like back then. You can see through from the other side. The red dot shows that it's been recording the whole time, every useless minute of our conversation.

'Every useless step you take to get closer. The longer we speak, the longer and more agonising it is for you – your film.

'Since this film is *my* gift to you, Gabriel. I don't want to kill you. I won't do you the favour. I want to give you something: a film of a girl dying. Your girl. And your child.

'You'll see yourself in it again later. You will wonder what you did wrong. Or whether it would've been better if you'd said different things. Or if you hadn't come any closer. Or if it would've been better if you'd apologised to me or begged on your hands and knees or if you should've pounced on me immediately. *Over and over again.*'

Again . . . again . . . again . . . it echoes back from the ceiling. Time holds its breath.

Gabriel opens his mouth, stops, can't find the right words. Even the most desperate hope dissolves, the inevitable solidifies before his eyes in the mirror, in the fucking red spot.

Valerius grins. 'And what shall we talk about next?'

'You're a disgusting, evil, sick monster.'

'God, how moral! I'm not evil. I'm just intelligent. And I only do what I have to do.'

'Call it what you want.'

'Were *you* evil,' Valerius hisses, 'when you held your knife up to your brother David's throat to get out of the psychiatric clinic?'

Gabriel grimaces as if he's been punched.

'And when you pushed me into the flames? When you shot your father? Was that *evil*?'

'How do you know about the time with David?'

'Were you *evil* when you worked for Python? For Yuri, that shithead? Be honest, what did he really ask of you? Probably a bit more than just to check up on an alarm system here or there. And what about when you killed Jonas?' Valerius's eyes are glowing. His chest pumps up and down, his breathing is heavy.

Gabriel stares at the red light in the mirror. It's only now that that he understands how carefully Valerius must have planned all of this from the first moment. 'The alarm on Kadettenweg, that was you?'

'Of course. I knew that you were on duty. And I knew you would drive out. I caught your little girlfriend at the very moment you were probably holding the dress between your fingers. Only, those morons had to come along and get in the way . . .'

'Pit and Jonas.'

'I should have been more systematic then. It would've been best if I'd killed them both right away, or maybe actually I only had to shoo them away, and then Liz wouldn't have been able to call . . .' The corners of his mouth twitch. 'The irony of fate. Also, since you didn't find the photo and you couldn't remember anything any more . . . I couldn't believe that. Or rather, I just couldn't imagine. That must be something, I thought. I remember it well. You know, I found out a lot about you, I just couldn't look inside your head. But, as I said, it makes no difference in the end. Things fell together of their own accord.'

Gabriel feels like the ground is falling out from under him. *Time!* he thinks desperately. *I need to buy some time.* He stares at the knife between Liz's legs, sees her pleading expression.

'The film keeps getting longer,' Valerius says.

'How do you know so much about me? How did you find me?'

The corners of Valerius's mouth bend upwards again. 'You want to buy time, don't you? You must already suspect how I found you. But OK, I'll tell you.

'For decades, I've been forging my revenge from inside my tomb. When I freed myself around twelve months ago, you were gone. Swallowed up by the earth. So, I looked for Sarkov and watched my father. And then I saw you with Sarkov. Can you imagine how

I felt? My heart beating faster and then slower, like after a long run, when you're waiting for your breath to calm down.

'A while later, I found out about Conradshöhe and got hold of your file. The fact that Sarkov became your legal guardian is typical of my old man. He always needed to have everything under control.'

Gabriel swallows bitterly and looks past Valerius to Liz. Tears are running out of the corners of her eyes. Her pale lips are open and he can hear her shallow breathing.

Valerius laughs triumphantly. 'And now we are here and you are getting your film, your very own film.'

Six goddamned metres runs through Gabriel's head. One moment, just look away for one moment . . .

'Forget it,' Valerius says, 'if you so much as move in my direction, I'll have stabbed her four or five times and slashed her open.'

'I'll kill you,' Gabriel whispers hoarsely. 'One way or another.'

'Release me, if you can. Go ahead! But you'll have to see all of this for the rest of your life. You will always see how you dived at me and came too late. Can you live with that? Having your parents on your conscience and now your girlfriend and child too?'

Gabriel clenches his fists. 'What's the difference?' He grits his teeth. 'If you're going to kill her anyway, then I can kill you now.'

'But isn't it interesting that you're not doing it? Valerius says, raising his eyebrows. On the contrary – you'll wait, hoping for a miracle, trying to buy time. Every second counts for you, for her! And you know what? I'm happy to do you that favour. You and her. I like talking. I love to talk! For almost thirty years, I only spoke to myself. I was alone with my hatred. Now I can finally unload it on you. And how delicious that you are practically begging for it . . .' A razor-sharp smile comes across his lips. 'But now, to be honest, I have to put an end to this chatter.'

Panic rises in Gabriel and suffocates him. At the same time, his muscles are burning with rage.

Dive at him!

No, wait!

Make up your mind and do it already!

'It's time, Gabriel,' Valerius whispers. 'We've reached the climax, the climax of your very own horror film.'

The small red recording light practically drills a hole in the mirror. Gabriel stares at it helplessly. For a moment, he's eleven again, he has the gun in his hand and he has to decide if he's going to pull the trigger.

Do it, damn it.

But you'll kill her if you do it.

If you don't do it, then you'll kill her.

Gabriel's heart races. The red point dances in front of his eyes, and then – very suddenly – it goes out.

Gabriel stares at the spot where the red light was just glowing.

Valerius's eyes are fixed on Gabriel's face and he tries to figure out why his expression has changed, but can't.

'The camera,' Gabriel whispers.

Valerius furrows his brow. He scans the mirror and then is clearly shocked.

Frantically and clumsily he feels around the stone table beside Liz with his prosthetic arm and hand, the knife tip twitching back and forth in Liz's vagina from the movement. Liz bites her lip and groans.

'Stay where you are,' Valerius threatens. He lifts up the prosthetic arm and Gabriel sees a remote the size of a matchbox between the artificial finger joints of Valerius's prosthesis. He wildly presses the buttons again and again, but to no avail.

The red light doesn't turn on.

Cursing, he tries to change hands to use the remote with his good hand. The rigid fingers of the prosthetic hand reach for the knife, miss and the knife falls to the stone altar with a clatter.

'Now!' Liz cries.

Gabriel lunges like an unleashed predator.

Liz thrusts her hips forward as far as her chained joints will allow, throwing her entire backside on top of the knife.

Valerius freezes, one finger on the remote control, his eyes directed at the point where the knife should be. Then he abruptly turns around, throws his prosthetic arm up and thrusts it into Gabriel's quickly approaching chin.

Gabriel stumbles. His legs give way and he falls on Valerius, who's straining to keep from being knocked over.

Liz desperately tugs at her chains and tries to bring the knife further back with her hips to take hold of it.

Gabriel is still in a daze from the blow to the chin as Valerius pushes him away with one hand so that he bangs against one of the stone pillars. With a cry of fury, Valerius charges at Gabriel, raising his prosthetic arm like a sledgehammer.

'Look out!' Liz cries.

Gabriel sees the blow coming. He is paralysed. His muscles simply don't react. As the prosthesis plummets towards his head from above Gabriel instinctively moves to one side, so it cracks down on his shoulder instead – the same shoulder that was already injured. The pain almost finishes him off. It's as if an iron spike as thick as a finger has been driven into his flesh and he falls to the floor.

Valerius's heavy breathing rattles. 'It won't help. You'll lose her,' he hisses ferociously and moves towards Liz.

'Gabriel! Get up!' Panicked, Liz presses her body against the cold stone slab and on top of the knife. Valerius's grin is an expression of hot rage. The burnt half of his face glows fiery red in the mirror. He steps in front of Liz, who is tugging at her chains, and slowly raises his arm as if to enjoy every second of her pain. He looks at Liz, but she is staring past him.

He immediately turns around, just in time to step out of the way as Gabriel charges at him and then falls.

When Gabriel rams into the stone slab, it knocks the wind out of him and he doubles over. Valerius takes advantage of the moment and wraps his prosthetic arm around the throat of his attacker.

Headlock! pops into Gabriel's head. It seems ridiculous for it to end this way. The prosthesis presses on his windpipe like a car crusher. The lack of oxygen weakens him and he moves like a helpless eleven-year-old, flailing, twisting around and trembling. He hears the chains around Liz's wrists and ankles clinking in the background – and hears her calling him over and over again. He's dizzy. His field of vision is shrinking, getting smaller and blacker around the edges as if he were falling into a well.

He knows that he only has a few seconds before he loses consciousness. With a final, almost superhuman, effort, he throws himself forward against the stone sarcophagus and levers Valerius's supporting leg out from under him.

Valerius staggers, topples over, falls face down onto Liz and pulls Gabriel down with him.

At the same moment, Gabriel feels the pressure suddenly release from around his throat, the grip of the prosthetic hand loosens and Valerius twitches uncontrollably. Gabriel pulls his head out of his clutches and collapses to the ground, gasping for air.

Above him, Valerius releases a long, drawn-out groan, as if he'd had a terrible dream.

Gabriel tries to push himself up with his arms. His brain feels like it's filled with water and he's seeing double. Valerius stands up with a deep throaty cry. He grabs Liz's hand that he landed on and twists it around. Liz screams in pain. Long, thick red drops fall to the ground from Valerius's stomach. It's only now that Gabriel sees the object that Valerius wants to pry from Liz's hand – it's the knife, which Liz was somehow holding in her hand when Valerius fell on it, stomach first.

The chains clatter softly as Liz drops the knife beside her in pain. 'The knife, Gabriel!' she screams.

Gabriel shakily stands, sees that Valerius is reaching for the knife, sees how his fingers close around the handle and how his arm rises to plunge the knife into Liz.

With both hands, Gabriel wrenches Valerius's arm back. Valerius screams with rage, flails around wildly, tries to free his arm and thrusts the knife in all directions. With a horrible sound, the blade scrapes the stone beside Liz and then cuts through the air. Gabriel reaches into Valerius's hair to grab his head with one hand, while the other hand is still trying to hold the arm with the knife. Gabriel desperately tries to find his footing, but steps into a dark puddle and slips. In the fall, he feels a dull thud and hears a bone-dry crunch like a walnut being crushed as Valerius's neck meets the edge of the stone sarcophagus.

All of the tension leaves Valerius's body, which goes slack as he falls to the floor. The knife hits the old tiles with a clink. Valerius's intestines spill out of his stomach and a pool of blood rapidly forms.

'Oh god!' Liz gasps. 'Is . . . is he dead?'

Gabriel heaves himself up on the stone sarcophagus. His breath rattles. He looks at her and only now realises for the first time that her eyes are the same colour as his mother's.

'Yes, I think so.'

Liz sighs. She tries to take a deep breath, but chokes and coughs. The chains clink around her limbs. Then she begins to sob uncontrollably.

Gabriel can't get a word out. He gently places his right hand on her stomach, as if he can feel whether everything is all right under the surface. He quickly loosens the metal bands around her wrists and ankles and then he bends over her and hugs her. He feels her breath against his skin, her trembling chest rising and sinking, her sobbing tearing at his eardrums and her scent surrounds him like a bewitching perfume, more beautiful than anything he has ever smelled.

I've found you, everything inside him rejoices. His chest and his soul want to burst. *I've found you!* That is all he can think. Like a mantra, over and over again.

Chapter 56

28 September, 8.29 a.m.

David can't move in the narrow chamber and is fighting to keep his composure. He can see Liz and his brother hugging right in front of him. *Gabriel in the arms of a woman!*

And now he can see how much she must love Gabriel and he feels an uncomfortable twinge in his chest. The idea that his brother can actually love someone is deeply comforting – and at the same time alienating.

He hears himself breathing in the tight space. The camera in front of him is still on; it's just not recording any longer.

No red light any more.

On the small colour display panel folded out of the camera, Gabriel and Liz are lying in each other's arms, Liz in her extravagant white dress. The disturbing cut down the middle is hidden from view. It seems almost surreal, sentimental, like the last scene of a film. Only, Valerius's body beside them with his stomach cut open and innards bulging out is all too real, ugly and much too close. The puddle of blood has stopped growing and now forms a large, sticky black film over the floor.

David looks at his hands. They're shaking.

He takes a deep breath and listens as his heart rate slows to a normal speed. Then he tries to push the heavy mirror aside, first gently and then with all his strength. But the mirror doesn't budge.

He reaches for the only solid object in the room: the camera. He pushes together the cumbersome legs of its tripod and swings it into the mirror like a golf club. The crash of the old silver glass pane is deafening. The large sharp shards rain down on the stone floor of the crypt.

Liz and Gabriel jump with fright.

Gabriel quickly sits up and stares in shock at the small chamber revealed behind the broken mirror. 'My god, *you*?'

David nods silently. His chest rises and falls. His face is ashen and he's holding the black aluminium tripod with the camera at the end.

'Where have you been? And how in the world did you get in there?' Gabriel asks.

'Sarkov,' David says. 'After you were gone, I walked through the villa . . . I found him upstairs in the study. Valerius had knocked him out.'

'Yuri is *here*?'

David nods. 'I'll tell you later,' he says flatly. 'I . . . I knew there was a chamber behind the mirror because . . .'

'How . . . how long were you in there?'

'I don't know. I think I got here just after you arrived.'

'Did you see everything? The whole time?' Gabriel gasps.

'Everything. The whole nightmare. I didn't know what to do. I thought that if I broke through the mirror, then . . . then he would cut her . . .' He stops, looks over from Gabriel to Liz.

'I saw where the knife . . . I mean, it would have been enough just to startle him . . .'

Gabriel looks at him and then suddenly realises. 'The camera!' he says. 'That was you. *You* turned off the camera.'

A crooked grin comes across David's face.

Liz looks at him with infinite gratitude.

'I should have done it much sooner,' David says. 'But I had no idea that you could see the red light. It was only when he pointed to the mirror and asked if you could see it that I had the idea to turn the thing off. I thought it was the only thing that could throw him off and give you a chance.'

Gabriel stares at David in disbelief. 'That . . . that was . . .' he stammers and then hugs his brother so abruptly and so hard that David can barely breathe.

'. . . Thank you.'

Gabriel can feel David's face, wet with tears, and his own eyes well up. He lifts his head, and thinks about a blue sky beyond the crypt.

Light blue.

Without clouds, like on the sloped ceiling of our old room.

He knows all too well that the sky today is cloudy. But it doesn't matter now.

He looks at Liz, her round stomach and her eyes, and he wishes for the first time that he will have a future.

Chapter 57

Berlin – 28 September, 8.47 a.m.

The motor starts with a low growl, then the wooden hull speeds forward out of the open boathouse and onto the Wannsee. Icy rain shoots horizontally into Gabriel's face. David is at the helm of the motorboat and steers it in a ninety-degree angle away from Schwanenwerder Island. The bow hits hard against the choppy water.

Gabriel sits on the floor of the boat and squeezes up next to Liz, who is wrapped in a blanket, crouching beside the helm. Her teeth chatter and her lips are turning blue. She is still wearing the dress.

No one says a word.

Once Valerius and his father lay dead in the crypt, there wasn't much time left for them to decide their next move.

'I want to get out of here,' Liz had stammered. 'Please!'

'What about the police?' David asked, uncertain.

'Police?' Gabriel looked at Liz.

'Just get me out of here, OK?' Liz repeated. 'As quickly as possible.'

David nodded. Without a word, he got up and took the tape out of the video camera. 'We can't go through the house. Unless we get lucky, the first members of the staff will already be there and wonder where von Braunsfeld is. It's just a matter of time before they find the dogs and think to call the police.'

'Down by the lake there's a boathouse with a private dock,' Liz said. Her voice was shaky, but still sounded strong. 'Von Braunsfeld showed it to me back when we were filming. But the door to the greenhouse is closed.'

'It's broken. I jammed the lock before I came in,' Gabriel said.

In the tunnel on the way to the greenhouse, Liz's legs gave out. Gabriel picked her up and carried her the rest of the way, walking sideways through the narrow hallway. Outside, large raindrops landed on them. After about a hundred and fifty metres, they reached the boathouse. Gabriel broke open the door, hotwired the ignition and within seconds they were out on the open water, which was now splashing against the hull.

The roaring diesel engine speeds them down the canal to Pichelsee, through the small harbour and they continue on down the Spree River, which winds through the city. David slows down and the rain suddenly starts falling.

Beneath the metro bridge near the riverbank at Helgoländer, they get into a taxi in front of the train station, which takes them to David's flat. No one has said a word the whole time. It's all unreal, so strangely peaceful, so calm, like something was bound to happen at any moment.

But nothing happens.

The day passes without event and that night, they sleep like the dead.

Chapter 58

The next day starts like the last one ended: with constant rain, eerie calm and the worry that the police will be knocking at David's door at any moment. No one turns on the television. Or the radio. The telephone is unplugged and the flat looks like it's been hit by a tornado.

Just before nine, Gabriel went to the bakery around the corner to get sandwiches and croissants and caught a glimpse of the newspaper headlines: *Victor von Braunsfeld Dead. Mysterious Drama in Billionaire's Villa.*

While Gabriel waited for the sandwiches, he skimmed the article. Apparently, Yuri had been found by the cleaning staff in von Braunsfeld's study and was now lying in a hospital bed. The dead dogs, the crypt and the bodies of von Braunsfeld and his son next to a stone sarcophagus with iron chains caused great speculation. When Gabriel was handed his food, he put down the paper; he didn't want to bring the story into the house.

Liz sits on one of the grey sofas, wrapped in a blanket and staring at the wall with the missing painting.

'You should go to the doctor,' David says.

She shakes her head, pulls the blanket tighter around her legs and warms her hands around a mug of tea. But it doesn't do much for the coldness she feels inside.

Gabriel moves to sit next to her. There is a copy of his file from the clinic on the table; nightmares written up as protocol.

Liz takes a sip of tea and clears her throat. 'How come you never told me you were in a psychiatric clinic?'

Gabriel shrugs. 'Probably for the same reason that I forgot what happened that night.'

'Suppressed,' David says softly, 'not forgot.'

Gabriel looks at the floor.

'Hey – sure, you shot him, but you didn't kill him. That was Valerius. You were eleven. And you were in a fucked-up situation.'

'I might just as well have killed him. The fact that I only hit Dad in the side was just chance,' Gabriel replies.

'With what happened to you, there is no right or wrong. Not in that moment,' Liz says. 'It doesn't make it better, but maybe easier.'

Gabriel nods, even though he doesn't believe it could ever feel easier.

For a moment, a heavy silence falls over them.

'Why did Sarkov actually get you out of the clinic? I thought he and von Braunsfeld were in cahoots,' David finally asks, 'and as long as you were in the locked ward, there was no real danger from you any more.'

'What kind of danger could there have been anyway?' Liz asks.

'I was the only witness to all of this madness. Von Braunsfeld knew from his son that I had seen how Valerius shot my parents. And he must have been afraid that I had seen the film. Von Braunsfeld probably found out very quickly that I couldn't remember anything, but he couldn't have been completely sure that I wouldn't turn into a problem in the future.'

David shakes his head. 'What would you have done? Gone to the police? The story is so outrageous that no one would've believed you anyway. And there was no more evidence.'

'To be honest, I had plenty of other reasons not to go to the police,' Gabriel said, 'but that probably wasn't enough for von Braunsfeld.'

Liz shakes her head. 'Well, from what I've come to know about von Braunsfeld, he was more of a strategist and liked to hedge his bets. He had a lot to lose. And as a mega celebrity, when something like that really gets going, then the press is suddenly on your doorstep and the whole thing takes on a dynamic that's impossible to control. And that would've been it for him.'

'There's some truth to that,' David says, nodding. 'But then Sarkov taking Gabriel out of Conradshöhe makes much less sense. Why did he do it?'

'Probably because of Dressler,' Gabriel says. 'There's a note in my file from shortly before my release. It says that Dr Wagner was my new attending psychiatrist. From then on, all of the reports are co-signed by Wagner. I still remember Dressler getting into trouble because of his treatment methods.'

'You mean the electroshock?' David says.

Liz's eyes widen. 'Shit, they gave you electroshock?'

Gabriel nods. He gets up, walks over to the window and looks out at the iconic television tower, magnificent in the rain. 'At the end of the eighties, it was leaked. There was suddenly a huge scandal and Dressler was sacked.'

'And what did all of this have to do with Sarkov and von Braunsfeld?'

'I looked at the file again,' Gabriel says. 'Dr Wagner took a different direction with his treatment. It looks as if I started to remember with him.'

'You mean von Braunsfeld sent Sarkov to prevent Dr Wagner from successfully treating your trauma?' David asks.

'He could well have,' Liz says. 'Von Braunsfeld probably had Dressler in his pocket. But then when Dressler was sacked and Wagner began to dig into your memories, it was all too precarious for von Braunsfeld.'

'Ultimately, it was brilliant,' Gabriel says bitterly. 'From the moment I was out of Conradshöhe, Yuri was my guardian for a while. So they had me perfectly under control. At the time, I would've done anything for Yuri, if for the sole reason that he got me out of that hell. And Yuri kept me so busy that I never really questioned it all that much.'

'I wonder what they would've done if you'd suddenly started asking questions and thinking about your past,' Liz says.

'Well,' Gabriel replies, 'that's essentially what happened. Only, it was after almost thirty years of nothing happening, and they had probably already considered the topic closed for a long time. That's why Yuri reacted so strangely.'

'What do you mean?'

'It started with Valerius triggering the alarm at the house on Kadettenweg. Yuri had no clue as to why it happened, but the way he wanted to keep me away from the house seemed odd. And later, when I asked Yuri about my file, he blew a fuse. The fact that he kicked me out that day was probably more of a rash decision.'

'It must have been,' David mutters. 'A little while later, he was at my doorstep and wanted to find you at all costs.'

'Why?' Liz asks.

'Because he wanted the film,' Gabriel explains. 'I guess von Braunsfeld put pressure on him. The house on Kadettenweg had been broken into and when he found out about the hidden safe in the fireplace, then he remembered the film. Valerius had threatened him with it, saying that he'd hidden it in a secure location. And von Braunsfeld and Yuri immediately thought that I'd found it and taken it with me.'

'But why,' David asks, 'didn't anyone think that Valerius was connected to all of this? The two must have found out that he escaped.'

'Not at all,' Liz says and pulls on the blanket. 'Valerius was just as much of a clever bastard as his father. He locked up his prison guard, Yvette, and made her obey him. Yvette was terrified of him. And the few times when von Braunsfeld called, Yvette pretended that everything was in tip-top shape. And apart from that, Braunsfeld avoided the chalet like the plague.'

'What happened with those women he mentioned? The ones he killed?' David asks.

'One of them was probably a model. Yvette told me that there were others locked in the cell before me. Valerius had already been free for a year – so he just picked up where he left off.'

'A model?' David asks and stares at Liz. 'Not that model Kristen? The one who disappeared without a trace along with a sack of haute couture dresses?'

Liz goes pale. 'Oh god, the dresses. Of course.' She groans. 'Ciara Kristen. I should've thought of that.'

'Maybe we should go to the police,' David suggests.

'Forget it,' Gabriel refuses. 'They won't believe a single word I say. They'll just send me right back to the clinic.'

'Well, this time you have a couple of witnesses,' David says and smiles. 'And then there's also the film.'

Gabriel stops. 'Of course. You're right. That should be enough – there isn't a better confession.'

A crooked grin forms across David's face and, for a brief moment, Gabriel recognises himself in it. 'That's the real irony,' David says. 'Valerius had the camera running just to take revenge on you. And now the film is going to save your skin.'

Gabriel looks out of the window again. 'Hmm. Yes and no. After all, I took a hostage and broke out of a police station. And I doubt Dr Dressler will look past the fact that I made him walk stark naked with his hands taped together in public.'

Liz snorts and some tea runs down her chin. 'You did *what*?' She looks at Gabriel in disbelief. When she starts to laugh for the first time in weeks, it's an immense relief. 'That's great!' she chuckles. 'A belated thanks for the electroshock.'

David's smile grows wider. 'It gets better. My dear brother also taped a gun into the psychiatrist's hands. It was on the news. The police approached with their sirens wailing, and the special commando unit, too, and apprehended the naked assassin. It took them a while before they realised that they didn't have a runaway madman in custody, but instead a runaway mad doctor,' he says, smirking.

Gabriel laughs too, and even if it isn't totally liberating, it feels good. 'Well, in any case, it won't be easy if we go to the police.' He quickly becomes serious again. 'Tell me, though,' he says, turning to David, 'what really happened with Yuri?'

'I . . . had a little disagreement with him,' David says hesitantly.

'You? A fight with Yuri? And you survived?'

'To be honest, I wasn't sure he'd survived until recently,' David says awkwardly. 'I pounded his head against the floor. Many times.'

Gabriel looks at his brother, stunned.

'I was really furious,' David adds.

Gabriel nods and looks at him for a long time.

'What are you looking at? He's in the hospital, you said it yourself.'

Gabriel smiles. 'I'm just seeing a new side to my brother.'

'Oh,' David says.

'And what about that . . . that girl?'

'Shona?' David asks. 'That girl is over thirty.'

Gabriel rolls his eyes.

'Well, all right. I'll call her and try to meet up,' David says. 'But only if you,' he points at Gabriel, 'aren't anywhere nearby! I'm going to have to anyway, so I can explain a few things and also talk to her about Bug.'

'I don't understand a thing,' Liz mutters. 'What does Bug have to do with the whole mess?'

'Don't worry about it. That's my deal. I'll settle it on my own.'

'"My deal!" Good for you. I know that sort of answer well. You can tell that you're brothers.' Liz yawns and leans her head back. Then she looks at Gabriel. 'Please just think about it,' she says softly and rubs her stomach.

'What?' Gabriel asks.

'The whole matter of whether we call the police. I don't want you to be on the wanted list for the next few years. And she,' she points to her stomach, 'certainly doesn't either.'

'*She*?' Gabriel asks.

Liz smiles. 'I have a feeling.'

'And if it's a he?'

She shrugs and an exhausted smile flits across her lips.

David gets up, goes over to the wardrobe and rummages through his jacket pockets. When he comes back, he has a dark videocassette in his hand that's about the size of a matchbox. He hands it to Gabriel. 'Your decision,' he says.

Gabriel looks at the breakable, nondescript plastic tape in his hand. It weighs no more than a pack of cigarettes. And the film was so close to becoming his lift to hell.

Thanks

This book would never have existed without the many people who helped me with inspiration, criticism, praise, uncomfortable questions, honesty and patience.

For that, I thank my wife Mieke, my toughest critic and my emotional backbone. I would also like to thank my boys Rasmus and Janosch for their patience with me, as I was often 'away' with my mind between the pages.

Thanks to Norik for his praise, which was always given when it counted – and never when it didn't. Thank you Annette for the parallel reading as I wrote, so I always knew where I stood. Thanks to all of my friends and acquaintances who read this book in its different stages; it always gave me the opportunity to improve it.

Special thanks to Sabine Schiffner, as her recommendation on the right location took off. Additional thanks to Ms Eichorn from Agentur Graf for her quick, unerring mediation.

A big thank you to the book professionals at Ullstein Verlag, especially Katrin Fieber, for the house-wide positive energy and for standing behind this book as I'd always hoped a publisher would.

And finally, thank you to each and every reader who made it up to this point – and therefore knows: I did not do it alone.

Marc Raabe

About the Author

Marc Raabe owns and runs a television production company and lives with his family in Cologne. *Cut* is his first thriller and was a German bestseller.

Turn the page for a sneak preview of the next thrilling read published by Manilla . . .

HANNA WINTER
SACRIFICE

MANILLA

1

Berlin, Sunday evening, 8th May

The rain ran down her face, her quick, springy footsteps bounced on the wet tarmac and her sweaty T-shirt clung to her back like a second skin. Dusk had already fallen when Lena Peters got back from her run and reached her front door in Boxhagener Street. Out of breath, she dropped to her knees for a brief rest. With her thoughts already on her meeting the next morning, Lena pulled her front door key out of the pocket of her tracksuit bottoms, then jogged through the inner court-yard lit only by the windows of the surrounding flats. Just a few metres from her ground-floor flat, she suddenly stopped in her tracks. A man in an anorak was standing by her bedroom window.

What the hell . . . ? Lena's pulse began to race. Gingerly she stepped closer and watched as the man peered into the lit-up room. He stepped over the terracotta planter into the small, bare plot behind the flat, which according to the estate agents was supposed to constitute a garden, despite its lack of plants. The man went over to the patio. Lena briefly considered calling the police, but then decided to deal with the situation herself. Just as she had always done.

Carefully, she picked up the small trowel that was leaning against the wall near the sandpit, and crept up behind him. The man seemed not to notice her, even though she was now close. He was about to slip his hand into the gap in the slightly ajar patio door when Lena struck him with the flat side of the trowel, square in the face.

'Get out of here or I'm calling the police!'

The man staggered back, groaning with pain and clutching his face as he fell backwards to the ground.

'Jesus, are you out of your mind?!' he snapped angrily at Lena, holding his bleeding nose. 'I *am* the police!'

Lena realised that she knew him.

'Herr Drescher? Volker Drescher?'

Horrified, Lena dropped the trowel and stepped closer. Shielded by the hood of his anorak was a slender man, in his mid-forties, with a gaunt look and a pointed chin. When he got to his feet, he was barely a head taller than Lena.

'For goodness sake, how was I supposed to know you'd—'

Drescher leaned against the wall, groaning as he set his glasses straight. He stared at Lena. 'For a woman of your build, you pack quite a punch!'

His response was no surprise; Lena knew people didn't expect much strength from her.

'Can I ask what you're doing here in my garden?'

'I rang the bell, but there was no answer. And when I saw that the light was on—'

'I never turn the light off when I go out.'

Drescher looked at her, surprised, but said nothing.

'Your nose – is it broken?' asked Lena, genuinely concerned.

He touched the bridge of his nose. 'No.'

Lena held her hand out to him, but Drescher ignored it. She watched as he composed himself and brushed the dirt from his anorak.

'Come on, I'll get you a plaster,' she said quickly. She turned to open the front door.

Shit! Shit! Shit! Did I really need to floor my new boss?!

'And perhaps a whisky, if you'd like – to help with the pain,' she added, waiting for Drescher to follow her.

Lena had chosen her small apartment primarily for the affordable rent. It was in an old building, but the flat hadn't been renovated and needed a lick of paint. The kitchen was right by the front door. Then there was the small dining room, which connected to the sitting room. At the end of the long corridor were Lena's bedroom, the bathroom and a tiny study. Apart from a few pieces of furniture, there was nothing to indicate what sort of person lived here. No family photos, postcards or holiday souvenirs. Not a single clue about her past.

Lena slipped off her damp trainers in the hallway, piled high with mostly unpacked boxes. Still a little dazed, she greeted her tabby tomcat, Napoleon, who wriggled between her ankles impatiently, meowing. Lena picked him up and gave him a little stroke.

'A nice place you've got here,' said Drescher. He pulled his hood back to reveal his light brown hair.

'Everything's a bit makeshift. I still haven't quite got round to unpacking.'

She put the cat down and led Drescher into the bathroom. In truth she couldn't imagine spending the next few weeks or months between these four walls. Although she had moved often, more or less of her own volition, she still found it hard to get used to new surroundings. But in the next few weeks she would probably only be coming home to sleep; the investigation into the ongoing series of murders – to which Drescher would be welcoming her tomorrow as the new criminal profiler, and which would keep them on their toes around the clock – was already keeping her pretty busy. Lena had been swotting up on the case; for days she'd barely had anything else on her mind.

'Where on earth were you, anyway?' Drescher asked, as Lena reached for a bottle of iodine, cotton wool and a plaster from the mirrored cabinet above the sink.

'I went for a run.'

'Damn it, Peters – I've been trying to call you. Didn't you have your mobile on you?'

Drescher was now standing right behind her. Lena, who was long accustomed to the curt tone taken by the police, turned around.

'No,' she said and dabbed his bloody nose with cotton wool doused in iodine, trying not to show that she was feeling nauseous and short of breath.

It always happened. Even just a few drops of blood evoked the memory of that day. Of the burning wreck of the car where she and her twin sister Tamara had been crushed in the back seat.

Blood.

Blood everywhere.

And smoke.

And shards of glass from the shattered windows.

Her mother lying unconscious on the passenger seat beside her father. And all the time the firefighters were trying to free Lena and Tamara from the wreckage, Lena clung to her mother's bloodied hand. She refused to let it go. Not even as the flames burst up around her mother. No sooner had the firemen dragged Lena from the debris, than the car exploded.

Help had come too late for her parents. The accident was around twenty years ago and yet, even after all this time, Lena still saw the blood on her hands.

'Why not?' asked Drescher, staring at her over his small glasses.

The question brought her abruptly back into the here and now. 'We agreed that I would come to HQ tomorrow morning and—'

'Tomorrow, tomorrow! Tell that to our killer!' He flinched suddenly. 'That stuff burns!'

Lena stopped dabbing and looked him straight in the eye. 'Another victim?'

Drescher's sigh spoke for itself.

'Tonight?' she asked.

'What, do you think this maniac only kills during office hours?' Drescher shoved his glasses up onto his hair, took the cool flannel that Lena handed to him and pressed it against his red, swollen nose.

'No, of course not . . .' she said calmly.

She couldn't afford to slip up again, if she wanted to preserve her last scrap of authority in Drescher's eyes. She suspected that Volker Drescher was the sort of policeman who had had to be persuaded to bring a profiler in on a case – because doing so proved that the investigation had reached a dead end. In most cases, Lena was only hired if the lead investigator had utterly failed to get anywhere, when the team's nerves were frayed and bringing in someone new was an act of desperation. She was quite used to being received with a mixture of suspicion and curiosity. This time, too, she knew she would be facing her new colleagues' glares boring into her neck as they tracked her every move, a critical eye on how she went about her work. But she'd developed a thick skin and enough confidence in her ability to shrug it off. At least that's what she told herself.

'Give me five minutes. I'll have a quick shower and be right back.' She handed Volker Drescher the plaster.

Drescher held up three fingers. 'Three minutes,' she heard from under the flannel. 'And if your offer still stands, I'd be glad of that whisky now.'

Lena stood smiling in the doorway. 'Help yourself. The bottle's on the kitchen table. There should be a glass somewhere.'

With that, she closed the bathroom door as Drescher headed towards the kitchen.

Moments later, Drescher placed two generously filled whisky glasses on the coffee table in the living room and sat down on the brightly coloured sofa, noticing as he did that it still had the crinkly protective covering on it. Drescher looked at his watch as the patter of the shower came from the bathroom. Eventually he picked up his glass and got up to look around. Bare walls, naked light bulbs, more removal company boxes. He peered into the open rooms as he walked past. A futon bed, an oversized desk with a laptop on it. The bookshelf was lined with hefty tomes about sex crimes and analysis of historical cases and court proceedings. He allowed himself a patronising grin when he spotted his latest book. *Let's see if she's got what it takes . . .*

Lena kept her eyes closed as she felt the warm water relax her neck. *Yet another victim. The intervals between the killer's attacks are getting shorter and shorter,* she thought as she turned off the water.

First there was a new victim every few weeks, then weekly, and now it's been barely three days since he last struck. With today's victim, that makes twelve women cruelly mutilated. She stepped out of the shower and dried herself quickly. *What is he trying to tell us?* She slipped on some clean knickers and a T-shirt, then pulled on her jeans. *Is he just flexing his muscles? Or is he getting carried away?*

Lena looked at the confused-looking woman in the mirror and quickly combed back her wet hair. She picked up her mobile, which she had left on the edge of the sink, and was just about to head back to the living room when she glanced at the screen. Confused, Lena stared at her phone for a moment before walking to the living room with the phone in her hand.

'You said you'd tried to ring me?' she said. 'That's weird, because there are no missed calls.'

'It was just a test,' said Drescher, his expression unchanged. 'I wanted to see how you'd react.'

A test? Lena wondered what was coming next.

Drescher cleared his throat. 'We're dealing with a brutal case, the likes of which we've never seen. And exceptional cases require exceptional measures, and exceptional qualifications, if you see what I mean . . .'

'What's your point?' Lena asked sceptically, as she sank into the leather chair opposite him.

'There are certain people who think this series of murders might be too much for you to handle.'

Lena felt her temples throb. 'But apparently you disagree, otherwise you wouldn't have brought me in.'

She noticed his glance down at her bare feet, then her flat chest and skinny shoulders. He then looked down at the glass of whisky and touched the plaster on his nose.

'You have an impressive academic background, Peters. And I don't just mean your outstanding marks in psychology and criminology, but above all your excellent research into criminal profiling.'

'Thanks.' A smile came to Lena's lips, and then quickly vanished. 'But you'd still rather your profiler was six foot – and built like a boxer,' she added, looking at his battered nose.

'Your words, not mine.' Drescher cleared his throat and pushed his glasses up with his middle finger.

Lena picked up her whisky from the coffee table and held herself back from emptying it in one swig. 'You yourself stated in an academic journal that good people are rare, and that it's as difficult to tell the competence of a team member from looking at them as it is to detect the motivation of a criminal.' The throbbing in her temples grew stronger as she felt a surge of rage come over her and she felt angry with herself for letting him get to her. To calm herself down more than anything, she stroked the soft fur of her cat, who had just jumped up beside her and was making himself comfortable.

Drescher cracked his knuckles and looked up from his glass. 'This is Berlin, after all – not Fischbach or whatever suburb it is you're from.'

How incredibly astute. 'If I may remind you, the red-light district murders, the dead children at the port and the poisoner were not in Fischbach either.'

'But this is completely different terrain,' he replied with a vehement shake of the head.

Lena held his piercing stare and wondered how she was supposed to convince him that she was right for the case. But did she even have to? After all, he was the one who had asked her to join the team, not the other way around. Lena washed away her irritation that he seemed to doubt her before she had even started work with a decent swig of whisky. Unexpectedly, she found herself smiling.

He wants to put me to the test? Fine, let him.

Lena gave the glass a shake and waited until she had his full attention. Then she closed her eyes and said, 'You're wearing a light blue cotton Ralph Lauren shirt with cuffed sleeves. It has six buttons, not including the one missing in the middle. In your right breast pocket is a charcoal grey Lamy pen, engraved with your name. It is slightly chewed at the end, perhaps because you're under pressure. You're not married. At least you haven't worn a wedding ring recently – there isn't the slight indentation you get over the years. Your Hugo Boss glasses have a small scratch at the front of the left arm, perhaps because you dropped them. You use Vetiver by Guerlain. Although this morning you only sprayed it behind one ear, most likely because you were in a hurry.' Lena kept her eyes closed. 'You value punctuality and you're clearly always punctual yourself, because,' she said, tapping her wrist, 'your watch is two minutes fast. You wear classic leather shoes, with heels a good four centimetres, which suggests that—'

'OK, Peters – that's enough,' Drescher interrupted. 'OK, you've won.'

When she opened her eyes again, she saw his astonished expression.

'I just wanted you to be warned, that's all,' said Drescher.

She stifled a grin and, for a moment, an oppressive silence hung like a deep abyss between them.

'I thought you lived alone?' Drescher asked abruptly, his eyes turned to a game of chess, which was set out on a plain white chest of drawers. 'Who's your opponent?'

Lena forced a smile. She didn't like to talk about herself. Besides, she didn't have the slightest desire to be interrogated by Drescher about her private life. She brushed his question aside with a shrug.

The abyss grew deeper.

She saw that Drescher was holding back a comment. He pulled a photograph out from the breast pocket of his shirt and placed it on the coffee table. Lena looked at the print and saw a young woman with a warm smile. She was wearing a short dress and high-heeled, strappy sandals. The picture was obviously taken at a party, and it looked like she was having a good time.

'The victim?' Lena asked.

Drescher took a deep breath. 'Her name is Yvonne Novak; twenty years old.' He bit his lower lip and shook his head. 'Barely more than a child.'

'Where was she found?'

'She hasn't been found,' he said, frowning. 'She's doing maths at Humboldt University and she disappeared without a trace after her lecture yesterday.'

Lena gulped, but for the time being she wanted to remain optimistic. 'That doesn't necessarily mean ... She might have just left town. She could be anywhere.'

Drescher shook his head again and had a sip of his whisky. 'My instinct tells me it's related. Besides, yesterday she was supposed to pick up her brand-new car, a present from her parents for doing well in her studies. A red Beetle with all the frills . . . She chose it herself and according to her roommate she's been looking forward to it for weeks. It's not the sort of thing you just forget about, is it?'

'No, maybe not . . .'

'Ms Novak lives in a shared flat in Kreuzberg. Eyewitnesses have on several occasions seen the same windowless black van parked near the entrance door. A similar one was seen in the area before the other victims disappeared.'

Lena put her glass down, annoyed. 'Why didn't you say so?'

'Good God, there isn't a single day when this accursed case isn't dominating the headlines. We've already spent far too long treading water in this investigation and we cannot allow there to be any more victims. The press and the police chief are really piling on the pressure.'

Lena pressed her lips together. 'Nevertheless, we still don't necessarily need to assume the worst for Yvonne Novak.'

'No,' said Drescher. 'We don't.'

But Lena had the feeling there was something else was he wasn't saying. That there was a crucial piece of information that Drescher was holding back.

CONTENTS

09. ALL ALONE   3

10. IMPACT   75

11. A GIRL IN THE SNOW   139

3

ALL ALONE

'09.

Farewell, My Dear Cramer